On the Third Day

Also by Rhys Thomas

The Suicide Club

On the Third Day

Rhys Thomas

Doubleday

LONDON • TORONTO • SYDNEY • AUCKLAND • JOHANNESBURG

TRANSWORLD PUBLISHERS
61–63 Uxbridge Road, London W5 5SA
A Random House Group Company
www.rbooks.co.uk

First published in Great Britain
in 2010 by Doubleday
an imprint of Transworld Publishers

A CIP catalogue record for this book
is available from the British Library.

ISBN 9780385614733

Addresses for Random House Group Ltd companies outside the UK
can be found at: www.randomhouse.co.uk
The Random House Group Ltd Reg. No. 954009

The Random House Group Limited supports the Forest Stewardship
Council (FSC), the leading international forest-certification organization. All our
titles that are printed on Greenpeace-approved FSC-certified paper carry the FSC logo.
Our paper procurement policy can be found at www.rbooks.co.uk/environment

Typeset in 12/14.25pt Bembo by
Falcon Oast Graphic Art Ltd.
Printed and bound in Great Britain by
Clays Ltd, Bungay, Suffolk

2 4 6 8 10 9 7 5 3 1

To Chris, Rhid, Anna and Rachael

PART ONE

THE SADNESS

'I need to get away from here.'

He lay on his side and looked at his wife. The bedroom window had been left open all night and the air was cold. The curtain fluttered and beyond it the sound of passing cars came in and out.

'From here?' she said.

She leaned in to kiss him, but he did not respond and so she leaned in further and brushed her lips against his forehead.

'Not from here.' He dropped his hand softly on to the bed. 'I mean from London.'

Miriam looked at him. He was lying on his side and his hands were underneath his face, clutching the pillow like two talons. They gripped so hard that his knuckles had lost their colour and she saw the blue lines of tiny veins running between them. He was looking at her but it was through eyes she did not recognize and then she was awake, fully, and something heavy and dangerous stirred inside her. There was something missing from him. Something intrinsic and vital was gone.

She sat up, the blanket fell away from her leg and a current of cold air crept along her skin.

'What's wrong, Henry?'

Henry lay still and blinked slowly and said nothing.

He looked at her as if he didn't know who she was, then released the grip on his pillow and rolled away from her.

Miriam squinted in the morning's brightness. She tilted her head to one side. This was not like him. Henry was always happy; that was his way. The thin, wintry fingers of the silver birch in the garden clicked against the window.

She felt sands shifting beneath her. As she looked into Henry's face she could see the change. It was almost imperceptible, but perceptible enough to know that she should be frightened. Her heart rate quickened with the automatic sense of danger.

'Henry?' she said. 'What's wrong?'

|||

It took her two days to get him to the doctor's waiting room in which they were now sitting. For most of those days he had lain still and silent in bed. Sometimes he would sit up and go over to the window to look down on to the street and when he did this she would try to speak to him. But Henry would say nothing in reply. He would just stare out of the window with his head pressed against the glass. She would have brought him to the doctor earlier but it was too hard to admit that something was wrong. The news reports seemed so out of range; what they described could not possibly be happening to her family.

Now she sat next to Henry and held his hand. The waiting room was full. The staff told them they would have to wait longer, just because. Because of what was happening. There were more people like Henry in the room. Some of them were even sitting like him: head leaning forwards, feet tapping the ground. Some of them were sobbing. There was something heavy about them, as if their mass had swelled. She hooked her arm under Henry's and rested her head on his shoulder.

Everybody in the room looked scared. A man on the street outside had told them it was the end of the world and they had hurried past him as if he was saying something that was impossible.

Henry leaned forward. He pulled his arm away from Miriam. She looked at him and then she looked along the line of people.

'Mr Asher,' a voice said from the loudspeaker on the wall. 'Dr Eberly will see you now. Room Five.'

|||

The doctor's eyes glanced across to Miriam as she lowered Henry into the seat and she saw the nervousness in them right away. He looked so young. An emotion crossed his face as wind across water.

'How long has he been like this?'

Miriam shifted in her chair. 'Two days, since Wednesday morning.'

The doctor turned to Henry. 'How do you feel, Henry?'

Henry's head slumped towards his knees. He ran his hands through his hair and stared at the floor.

'I don't know,' he said.

His voice had altered since the change had befallen him. Its modulation was flatter, it was slower, the song in the timbre had gone.

The doctor looked at Miriam. 'We just don't know what it is,' he said, openly.

'Isn't there anything you can do?'

'It's just come out of nowhere.'

His nervousness disturbed her.

'Aren't there pills, antidepressants – would they help?'

The doctor tapped a finger on his notepad and fidgeted in his seat. 'They tried that. It's just—' he stopped. 'They don't know what it is.'

Claustrophobia shrank the room. Henry sat up in his chair and looked at the doctor calmly. There was the quiet of his breath through his nose.

'I feel like I am numb. Like everything has gone cold.' As he spoke his body seemed to grow, as if being inflated by a new clarity. 'I woke up and all of the lies I have accumulated over my life, the lies I have drawn down like a veil in front of me to make the world liveable, have been stripped away and I am gazing at a truth.' Henry's eyes had sunk into two red depressions. 'I never realized . . .' He trailed off and the room quietened.

'Does he have any history of depression, or of mental illness?'

'No,' Miriam answered.

The doctor lifted his pen in his hand but did not write anything down on the blank pad of paper in front of him. 'Do you work?' he said to her husband.

Henry nodded. 'I work in advertising,' he said, slowly.

'A good job?'

Henry nodded again but this time said nothing.

Miriam listened in silence. Henry had hardly spoken from the time he fell ill until now. An image crossed her mind: of Henry rowing a boat in Regent's Park. Their baby son, Edward, was in her arms. She remembered how Henry's face had lit up like a new star when she told him she was pregnant with Mary. But now a silent and creeping dread was settling into her, like a cold fog coming in off the sea.

'Can you tell me anything about this . . . truth, that you mentioned?'

Henry shrugged. His eyes fell to the thin, grey carpet and he spoke. 'Life has no meaning, I have no meaning. We are just animals scratching blindly in the dirt.'

Miriam was afraid now. Henry should not be saying things like this. The man sitting in the chair next to her was not her husband. It was some automaton taking his place.

'Doctor, please,' she said. She controlled her breath. She closed her eyes tight and put the knuckle of her middle finger to her forehead. 'Surely there must be something,' she said through a dry throat.

Henry's thick black hair was flecked with grey. The delicate features that made him look so much younger than he was were drooping.

The doctor rose from his seat and went to the door. Miriam could see into the waiting room. She saw the lines of patients, all of them, sitting in their chairs, hunched over, heads in their hands, like lines of bats hanging upside down in an inverted cave.

||||

'We need to get away from here.'

Through the radio they had been warned to boil tap water before drinking it. If possible, they said, use bottled water.

Miriam looked up from her book that she hadn't been reading. She had been staring at the words, at the incomprehensible black shapes against the grainy, dusty white, and trying not to cry. The children were sitting contentedly at the breakfast bar, drawing pictures with their crayons.

'Henry?'

His face was drawn. 'Pack some bags. We'll go to my father's.'

'Henry,' laughed Miriam, nervously. 'Don't be silly. We can't go to Cornwall. I promised my mother I'd take the kids to her tomorrow.'

Henry shook his head. 'We can't stay in London. There are too many people here. It's dangerous.'

The children looked up from their drawings. Miriam closed her book and stood up.

'Can I speak to you in the living room, please?' They left the kitchen and Miriam closed the door. 'You're scaring the children.'

He did not reply.

'Henry, what's the matter? Can't you tell me?'

'I can't . . .' Suddenly Henry was leaning against the wall, unable to stand without it. 'I just . . . can't. You wouldn't understand.' He clamped all the fingertips of his right hand together and tapped them to his chest, indicating something on his insides. Breath was coming out of him too fast and he broke into tears.

'I'm sorry,' he cried. 'I'm so sorry.'

They had been together for fifteen years and married for eleven and not once had she seen him like this. She could not stop thinking about the television reports, and dread pierced her body. This was happening all over the world. They had already given it a name.

'Please,' he said. 'Let's go to Cornwall.'

Sadness, she thought, and the word turned over in her head, as if it was gloating.

III

They drove out of the city. The motorway was quiet for a Friday evening. The sky stretched out in front of them, a huge blueness of void studded with a few grey clouds. Miriam loved the sky when it was big like this. It breathed free. The sky was always so tiny in the city.

Henry sat in the back with the children. He stared out at the fields that waved gently up, gently down, brown here, green there. Miriam glanced at him occasionally in the rear-view mirror.

She switched on the radio and listened half-heartedly to the news that the Chancellor of the Exchequer had left the government. Something had happened over in the Olympic development but they didn't know what. They thought it might be riots but the story was sketchy.

She called ahead to Henry's father and told him they would be visiting. He seemed pleased. Miriam could only guess at how lonely he must be without his wife and in that house so far away from other people. The sun was dropping over the horizon, a last line of electric orange the only demarcation between the haze of sky and land. The beauty of it struck her hard in her chest and she gripped the wheel tight, stifling her tears.

They arrived at the house a little after ten. Henry's father rushed out to greet them. He crouched and threw his arms around the grandchildren and as their heads disappeared into his shoulders he looked at Miriam as she led Henry from the car to the house. His long face was older in the dim light and Miriam watched his features slump when he saw his son.

Miriam put the children to bed and went into the garden. It was dark and the sky was clear. The moon reflected off the ocean. The low garden wall was just a hundred feet from the cliff edge. She could hear the surf crashing against the rocks below as pockets of sound exploding in claps. Down the hill to the west was the dark beach and there, on the point beyond it, the disused lighthouse. The stars twinkled so brightly, even on the horizon, that she could see the shape of the tower like a dark paper cut-out.

To the east was nothing but undulating fields. She felt herself a little like the house, cut off and remote, as if whatever it was that was happening to the world was outside of her little sphere, and Henry wasn't really suffering from the same thing as all the other people. He was too unique to become one of the horrible statistics that just kept getting larger and larger with every bulletin. Tomorrow they would walk down to the beach and he would remember who he was and everything would be fine. The hope drizzled happily through her but it was a lie because Henry died that night.

Henry's father, unused to being woken, found it difficult to orientate himself. The bedroom door sounded again. He blinked the sleep from his eyes and reached for his spectacles. He cleared his throat.

'Yes?' he called.

Miriam was crying, a thin silhouette in the doorframe.

'James,' she said. 'It's Henry.'

Awake now, he rushed to the guest bedroom. His son's body lay as a lump in the duvet. The old man crossed the room and pulled the blanket down. Henry's face was white. His father placed the back of his fingers against his cheek but it was cold.

His son's eyes were half closed and the moonlight put a small white glow in them. Henry's father looked frail in his pyjamas, his back was crooked and his legs were bowed, and as he stood over his son's body his skeleton seemed to deflate. He turned to Miriam and opened his mouth to say something but nothing came out. He closed his mouth and blinked, then went to speak again. He looked scared.

'What happened?' he said.

Leaning against the doorframe, unable to enter the room, she put her arms across her chest and shook her head. The tears on her cheeks made her face cold.

'I don't know.'

Henry's father turned back to his son and Miriam felt as if she wasn't there. There was a nakedness to Henry's father as he hunched over the bed and gently shook his son's body.

'Henry,' he said, delicately, his voice thin with fear. He shook him again, harder this time, more desperate. 'Henry.'

An ambulance came out of the blackness and took Henry away. The sound of it woke the children and Miriam took them into the conservatory at the back of the house. She sat them down and looked at them. She felt as if something had been amputated from her body, a sense of disruption to her balance.

'Kids,' she said.

Her voice was shaking. She didn't know how to do this.

The children shivered in the cold air of the conservatory. Miriam found a shawl that had belonged to her mother-in-law and covered them.

'Your father,' she said, and stopped. 'Umm.' She rolled her eyes up to the ceiling and bit her bottom lip. She made her mouth into a small hoop and breathed out the boiling air in her throat. 'Dad's . . .' She stopped again. She used her little finger to scoop out the small tear that had formed in the corner of her eye. 'Your dad . . .'

'Mum? What's wrong?' said Edward. 'Where's Dad?'

She looked at Edward but he was a blur.

'He's gone with the angels,' she said.

The children didn't say anything at first as the fact crossed to them and then into them, settling slowly, like rain on hard soil. Then she noticed Edward move a tiny bit closer to his younger sister, their mass underneath the shawl shrinking. He lifted his arm and put it around the little girl.

III

Henry's father sat at the window in his favourite chair and looked out into the solitary darkness. An image of Henry running along the beach as a boy, the sand spitting about his feet, the shrill song of his laughter, played in his head.

Just before the dawn came, he picked up the telephone from the little table next to him and called Henry's brother. The connection bloomed open and there was no turning back from the realness now. It swelled all around him.

'Joseph, it's Dad.'

'Dad . . . it's the middle . . . what's wrong?'

Henry's father closed his eyes for a moment. 'Joseph, it's your brother.'

A delicate silence grew up along the phone line.

'Is he dead?' Joseph said, his voice rising at the end of the sentence.

'Joseph . . .' He didn't know how to proceed. 'Yes. Henry died last night.'

Joseph was Henry's older brother by eight years and his father had always known how, as a child, he had prided himself on protecting his little brother.

'Where is he?'

'He's here. He's in Cornwall.'

'What happened? Why is he in Cornwall?'

'He . . .' he paused. 'It's this thing they've been talking about.'

'I'm coming down. I'll leave now.'

Henry's father knew there was no way to dissuade Joseph.

'Take care on the roads, son.'

III

At seven o'clock the next morning, Miriam pulled on the overcoat and boots that she kept in the house for the coastal walks she and her family had always taken, and pulled the front door closed behind her. It was cold and she lifted the collar of her overcoat.

The road in front of the house gave on to a wide patch of short grass. A solitary sheep chewed lazily. Miriam made her way to the tip of the headland that extended out into the ocean like a knife blade and looked out to sea. Her bones rattled in the wind that stormed in as a great mass, a solid block moving in on the coast. The sun was barely up. The distended, painful tide rose up at the cliffs, its waves drawn into sharp mountains by the angry breath of blasting wind.

She stepped towards the edge of the cliff. They should have put a fence here. The land fell away so fast. Making her way along the path to the right, away from the house, she stifled her tears.

She halted and looked down at a gull. Its grey feathers assumed a dirty shine as it glided inland between her and the water. There was not a soul in sight. It was the absence of human audio that struck her more than any other sense. The howling silence was disconcerting. It explained how tiny she was, and how massive nature is. If she were the last soul alive she would let its size cover her, smother her and pull her apart.

For a moment she wondered if the headland on which she was standing might crack away and fall into the sea. Maybe it would cleave off along an invisible fault in the rock and sink, slowly, toppling by degrees, away.

There was a bench further along, past the entrance to the cliff path that led to the beach. Henry had proposed to her on that bench. She wanted to see it again. The dawn light began to grow and as Miriam found her way along the line of the cliff, heading back inland, she caught a glimpse of the bay down below. The sand was orange in the morning light. A gap opened in the low, foggy clouds and a cylinder of sunlight hovered delicately over the beach. A wrecked ship lay in the sand, a ribcage hull the only survivor of the years of salt and water and wind. Soon it wouldn't be there at all. Time came and went and nobody knew about it. Perhaps it is all hidden away in the folds of the dimensions, she thought, and one day scientists will unlock the fabric and all of time will dazzle outwards in a yawning lurch of history. Then Henry would come back to her.

She passed the entrance to the cliff path and clambered over the rising hummock and down the other side to where the bench was. A man was sitting on it, watching the sunrise. Cautiously, Miriam approached. He wore a hat and a scarf but he did not have a coat. He must be freezing. She went closer, but the man didn't move.

III

He looked around the same age as her: late thirties.

'Hello?' she said. 'Are you OK?'

He didn't answer. She stood for a moment, just looking at him. The only things moving were his clothes, the scarf blowing around his head in the wind, his T-shirt fluttering against his arms. She waited for a quarter of a minute, maybe longer, and then started back towards the house. She walked quickly and then started to run. Tears burst out of her and blurred the landscape. She ran as fast as she could, painful oxygen burning her insides.

'Oh God,' she whispered, over and over.

Possibilities tumbled through her mind. The enormous spectre of death rose up from behind the cliff as a giant black shadow. As she ran across the desolate grass, her chestnut hair swirling around her, an abyss to one side, the dawn light suddenly penetrated the clouds and the sky became viscous with an eerie red-orange vapour and it really did feel, then, like the end of the world.

III

She came to the house and found herself slamming the front door shut behind her and turning the key in the lock. Taking several deep breaths, in through the nose, out through the mouth, she tried to stop crying. Levels of horror swelled around her in pulsating shockwaves. She went into the kitchen.

A stranger was standing at the kettle, his back to her. Miriam gasped with shock and stepped backwards.

'Henry?' Her voice trembled. The man at the kettle turned slowly. A sad smile softened his face. The wheels of her mind began to turn correctly again. 'Joseph?'

'I came down last night,' he said.

Although Henry was eight years younger than Joseph they had the same mouth, the same large teeth, the same nose and eyes. They stared at one another for a moment, each unsure as to the correct protocol for offering or receiving condolence.

The kettle hissed and steam rose from its spout.

'Tea?' Joseph offered.

Miriam shook her head. She couldn't understand why he should feel the need to come to Cornwall. Henry was dead and there was nothing he could do about it. Why would he come now?

She sensed a new presence, behind her.

'Joseph,' said Henry's father.

He walked past Miriam directly to his son and embraced him. Joseph's body relaxed as his father held him, and his head rested down into the old man's shoulder. She pictured Joseph fifteen years younger when she had first met him and remembered that that was how he was then: emotional, giving. It was as if she was looking into an echo of him from the past. The two men came out of the embrace and Henry's father turned to Miriam.

'What's the matter?' he said, immediately picking up on her feelings.

She stood there and it was all she could do to stop herself crying again.

'I found something,' she said. 'Up on the cliff.'

|||

As they left the garden, Joseph closing the green, wooden gate behind him, Henry and Miriam's eleven-year-old son, Edward, watched them from the window of the spare bedroom. Dressed only in his cotton pyjamas he could feel the intense cold trying to push past the wooden frame and single sheet of glass.

'They're going somewhere,' he said, and looked back into the room towards his little sister.

Mary threw the covers off the double bed and jumped down to the carpet. She joined her brother at the window and gazed out through tired, sleep-laden eyes. Together they watched the adults cross the road in front of the house, move out in single file over the grass and head towards the cliff edge. Beyond them lay the vast openness of the choppy grey sea.

Edward felt his sister fidget on the carpet, the wooden floorboards of the old house groaning underneath her bare feet in spite of her slightness. He knew she was about to start crying again.

'Come on,' he said awkwardly, trying to sound cheerful, 'let's go downstairs and watch TV.'

She wasn't listening. She spun around and threw herself face down on the bed. Her small frame underneath her white nightdress made him feel sorry for her because she was so small and he knew that small people need more help than big people.

'Come on, Mary,' he said, sitting down beside her. He placed an open palm on the centre of her back. He thought of his father: what would he do? 'Don't be sad,' he said.

|||

Joseph held the man's wrist in his right hand. It was a futile gesture because he was clearly dead.

Henry's father and Miriam watched Joseph turn towards them and shake his head. The morning light was brighter now but the cold remained entrenched in the air.

'We'd better call an ambulance,' he called over the wind.

Henry's father stood between Miriam and the sea. He acted as a shield. He looked confused, as if too much information was hitting him too fast.

'James,' she said, 'what's going on?'

|||

The television burned to life. They listened as they were told to take precautions, to watch for signs, not to panic, to call the emergency services only if absolutely necessary, that this was the first wave, that doctors did not know what it was. The deaths had started in the middle of the night.

Miriam heard shuffling behind her. The children came into the room and stared at the television. Henry's father reached for the remote and quickly turned it off. Miriam stood. There was a sense of growing nausea in her. She went into the hallway and called her mother but the phone didn't connect. She checked that she had keyed correctly and as she did this a voice came down the line. Quickly, Miriam brought the phone back up to her ear and said, 'Mum?' but stopped when she realized that it was not her mother. A cold, recorded voice told her the network was currently busy and that she should try again later.

She went into the kitchen and tried the house phone. This time the line connected. She waited for her mother to answer but it just kept ringing.

'Jesus.' She replaced the phone and tried again but still nothing.

Then she was aware that her mobile was ringing. The sound of it ballooned in her head and she pulled it from her pocket.

'Mum?'

'Miri?'

Miriam looked at the screen. It wasn't her mother. 'Sophia?'

Her friend was afraid. She was breathing hard and spoke quickly. 'Miri, thank God. I've been trying to call you but the network – Miri, it's Daniel. He's got it. I know he has.'

Her friend was sobbing.

The dull weight that had been sitting in Miriam's gut since Henry had fallen ill intensified and the weight crept into her bones. It was as if the world had inverted itself.

'Where are you?'

'At home. Oh God, he's just sitting in the chair. He won't even talk to me. He's going to die, I know it.'

She was becoming hysterical, her own words scaring her.

'Sophia, stop. Just wait. I'm going to drive to you, OK? But I'll be a while. I'm in Cornwall. I'll be as quick as I can. Just stay where you are, OK?'

There was no answer.

'Sophia, are you there?'

'Yes.'

'Just stay in the house, OK?'

'OK. Wait.' There was a pause on the line. 'He's getting up. I'd better go.'

The line went dead.

|||

She went upstairs to the children's room. Their clothes were strewn all over the floor so she bundled them up into a ball on the bed and found their bags. Her head swirled. An image of the still, dead man on the cliff top flashed into her mind. The ends of his scarf had flapped violently in the wind.

There was a knock at the door and the crack of sound startled her.

'What are you doing?'

Joseph came into the room.

She sniffed and didn't look at him as she stuffed the clothes into a bag. 'We're going back to London.'

'Have you seen the news?' he said.

Miriam nodded and tried to act cool. She didn't want him to see her upset.

'Maybe you should stay here.'

'I need to check on my mother. I can't get through to her.'

Joseph closed the door and stepped further into the room. Miriam stopped what she was doing and her head fell forwards. There was a wooden chair in front of the dressing table. Joseph sat down. His face had aged. There were thin lines at the corners of his eyes, scored deeper than she remembered. He put his head in his hands. The action frightened Miriam. There was a tender injury in him.

'This is insane,' he said.

Neither of them said anything. There was more grey in his hair than before. He seemed somehow less intense, deflated. He didn't seem like the man she remembered. His old self-assurance had waned.

'Miri.' He paused with uncertainty. 'What was Henry like? Before he died.'

She closed the zip of the bag and sat down on the bed.

'He was . . .' Forming the words felt odd. 'He was just . . . quiet. I don't know.' She thought of Henry sitting in the back seat of the car, looking out of the window with no expression on his face. 'Like they said on the news.'

Joseph's silence resounded in her chest. She could feel his thoughts, hear the ticking of his mind, sense his confusion. He turned towards her and she caught the smell of coffee on his breath.

'Miri, don't worry, OK? We'll deal with everything. I promise. Everything is going to be fine.'

She thought how stupid that sounded.

'I'm going back to London as well,' he said. 'I need to get back to Pele.' Pele was his black Labrador. 'We can go together. Where does your mother live?'

'North London. Enfield.'

'Will you come with me?'

Miriam shook her head. She didn't want this. Joseph wasn't part of her life. 'No.'

'Miri, think about it. We'll go back together and the kids can stay here.'

'What? No. I need to check on my friend as well. We have to go back.'

'I'll take you to your friend's.'

'We're going back, me and the kids together. London's our *home*, Joseph.'

The chair creaked as he shifted in it. 'I know that, Miri. But something's happening and I don't think it's safe to be in the city at the moment.'

She snorted. He was so dramatic all the time.

'We'll hole up here until everything blows over. The kids like it here, I know that.' How did he know that, she thought. He didn't care about the kids. He never came to see them. 'They can stay here while we go back. We won't be gone long.'

'No,' she said, sternly.

Joseph paused. 'Miri, you have to be rational.'

'Please, Joseph, don't tell me to be rational. Not now.'

'Look,' he said. 'What if you and I go back and then, if it's safe, we'll call Dad and he can bring the kids?'

She couldn't understand why he was pretending to be so concerned about the kids or why, for the matter, he seemed so concerned for her.

'I'm not leaving the kids. Jesus, Joseph, how can you even ask me to do that?'

The bleating ambulance sirens grew from the window and Joseph stood up.

'Because it's the right thing to do, and you know it is. Just think about it, OK?'

|||

From the window of the bedroom Edward could see all the way along the coastline, from the point to the west with the tall, white lighthouse sticking up out of the land, all the way along the cliffs, past the fields and barns and patches of trees to the church steeple in the village, a few miles to the east.

Miriam lay on the bed with Mary. Edward placed his fingers on the glass and when he took them away he could see his finger-prints on it. He went and joined them on the bed. He and Mary both rested their heads on Miriam's chest. She held bunches of their hair in either hand and wondered if she really was thinking about leaving them.

'I have to go away for a few days,' she said.

Edward raised his head. She could see fear flicker in his deep brown eyes.

'No,' he said.

'I have to go and see Grandma in London.'

'Please don't,' said the little boy.

Miriam sat up against the headboard. Both children looked at her now. She was going to start crying again.

'I have to go to check that she's OK,' she said with naked honesty. 'It'll only be for a day or two.'

'We'll come with you.'

Miriam shook her head. She wished she could just pull the covers over them all and stay in the bed for ever. She hated the fact that Joseph was right.

'No,' she said.

Desperation ran all through.

Edward had always been a bubbly child, but since she had told him about his father he had withdrawn – his whirling inner mechanisms had slowed. He hadn't cried, or stamped and screamed. Instead he had become still.

'You stay here and look after Granddad for me. Uncle Joseph and I will go back, and Granddad will bring you home later in the week.'

'No.'

Mary's lower lip wobbled, the sure precursor to a crying fit.

'It's only for a few days, that's all.'

She pulled Mary close to her and kissed the top of her head.

'I want you to be good for Granddad.'

|||

They left for London after dinner. The weather had closed in and needles of rain rattled against the windows of Joseph's car. It was a rusting old Peugeot but he had insisted on driving. The wind buffeted them as they drove in silence. Miriam watched the raindrops on the passenger window. They clung to it intensely, vibrating back and forth, wrestling to keep their position before being peeled away and scattered to the wind.

Time, even in short hours, had a calming effect on Miriam. Whatever this thing was, it couldn't be as bad as the television said. Things like this never lasted. The world was too stable now; the systems and laws and technologies too rigid.

'Won't be long before we reach Swindon,' Joseph said.

In the road ahead, visible only for a second at a time in the now heavy rain, the traffic began to build. The car slowed.

'What's going on?' he said quietly, to himself.

The vehicles in the fast lane veered quickly across to the middle, the brake lights tiny blotches of red in the gloom. Other cars sounded their horns angrily.

As they approached they saw that a car had gone into the back of a second and the fast lane was blocked. They filed past the accident and Miriam looked out of the window. A woman and a young couple were standing on the central reservation, talking animatedly and pointing at the wreck.

'You shouldn't stare,' said Joseph. 'It's voyeuristic.'

Miriam sighed and looked ahead. There was a third car stationary in the fast lane, fifty yards further up the road. The driver-side door was open.

Joseph had almost stopped by now. The wipers squeaked across the windscreen.

'Look at that,' said Miriam, pointing at the third car.

In front of them, a green Ford pulled over. Miriam sensed something grow inside her. She didn't know what it was but she could feel it very strongly. It wasn't a vague tingling; this sense was strong and definite, fact-like. It was warning her. She looked across to Joseph and wondered if he could feel it too but his eyes stared steadily ahead. She said nothing to him.

The line of traffic moved slowly on. Miriam noticed a flash of colour in the road. A man had run from the green Ford out into the road, through a gap in the traffic. He was wearing a bright red rain jacket and he held his hands aloft: let me get past.

At last Joseph had to stop. The man in the red jacket ran to the stationary car in the fast lane and looked inside. Then he stood up and looked around, as if searching for someone. He pulled the hood of his jacket over his head to shield himself from the driving rain and ran further along the road, into the headlights of the stationary car.

Joseph pulled forward a few more yards, keeping as close to the vehicle in front as he could. As they crawled forward Miriam saw what it was that the man was running towards. There in the road, sitting Buddha-like on the asphalt, was a person. The rain was so thick that Miriam couldn't tell if it was a man or a woman.

'Oh my God,' she said.

She wound down the window and leaned her head out.

'What the hell are you doing?' Joseph yelled. 'Wind the window up.'

Miriam's body clammed. She turned her head to him.

'Wind it up,' he said again, angrily.

Old memories tumbled out and she was looking at the Joseph she remembered. She wanted to argue with him but knew what it would bring. Her reluctant hand, trembling, reached for the window handle and rolled it up and she said nothing.

The person sitting in the road was a woman. She had long hair and it was slicked to her head. Rainwater dribbled off her nose like a waterfall. The man in the red coat knelt at her side and put his arm on her back but when she felt his touch, the woman fell to her side and rolled away into the central reservation.

'We can't take any risks,' said Joseph, trying to modulate his voice.

'I just wanted to see if she was OK.'

Miriam could feel her whole chest beginning to shake, her nerves gossamer thin. She felt in some way linked, through Henry, to the woman in the road. The woman gathered around her the same dense gravity, a funnel of spinning space that collected atmosphere into her. She was looking at Henry and Joseph would not let her help.

'We should stop.' The rattling of the engine and the rain against the steelwork of the car filled the silence. 'Joseph?'

'And do what? Are you a doctor? No. So what are you going to do?' The pitch of his voice changed. 'Say a prayer?'

Her anger grew quickly, like a flame, fanned by the years of memory that had opened up and snapped away. Her body tautened.

'Why do you always have to bring it up?'

She looked out of the window at the rain. Why couldn't he just leave her alone?

His fingers moved off the wheel and stretched, then curled back around.

'Look, Miri,' he sighed, 'I want to help you, I want to make sure you're safe. But you have to listen to me, OK? I'm sure whatever this thing is will go away, but until then you have to understand that we just need to get through it. We can't take stupid risks, or waste time stopping on motorways for strangers. That woman in the road wouldn't have stopped for you.'

'You don't know that.'

'Yes, I do. People aren't all like you. They don't help each other. Not when it comes down to it.'

'The other man stopped.'

Joseph slammed his hand on the steering wheel.

'Well, I'm not the other man,' he snapped, his voice frayed. 'I will *never* be the other man. This is serious, Miriam. Whatever it is, it killed Henry and it's killing lots of other people too. It isn't a game. We have to look after ourselves. That's what everyone else is going to do. We can't just go helping people out, all right?'

She knew better than to argue with him when he became intense like this. She looked in the wing mirror at the man in the red coat and the woman lying in the central reservation. She pictured Henry in bed that morning, the life gone out of his eyes. She pictured the man she had found on the bench at the cliff top. Her eyes started to sting again. She did not want to cry in front of Joseph.

The sound of a phone sang out into the car. Miriam felt a tear roll over her cheek. She clicked to answer.

'Sophia?' At the other end of the line she thought she could hear something that sounded like a hiss. 'Hello?' she said again.

She wiped her nose.

And then there was a voice speaking into the mouthpiece, but it did not belong to her friend. She didn't recognize the voice.

'There were seven colours before,' it said. 'That was the promise.'

'Daniel?' she said, her skin prickling.

She turned to Joseph, who stared unerringly ahead.

'No colours any more though,' said the voice. 'The mercy took them, and turned them to white.'

|||

Henry's father opened the door to the airing cupboard. He pulled on the light switch he had rigged up when the kids were young, and squinted at the shelves. On the top shelf were the games he had played with his boys. He reached up and felt his skeleton expand and creak. Surely the shelf hadn't been this high before. He took down an old box and blew the thick covering of dust away. Extinguishing the light he sensed a great wave of loss for his son. He paused for a moment and steadied himself. Dizziness swirled into his head and he reached out his hand for the doorframe. The wood was warm to the touch. He remembered the day he had put up the shelves. Henry hadn't even been born then. He was still four years away. Joseph had helped hold the tools and the perspex box in which their grandfather kept his nails, screws and tacks.

Regaining himself, he walked along the narrow landing to the top of the stairs and went down, slowly, to the kitchen. The children were waiting for him at the table.

'OK,' he said, cheerfully, 'who knows how to play Snakes and Ladders?'

They looked at him blankly.

'Then all will be revealed,' he proclaimed.

The children sat up warily and leaned forward, Mary bringing her legs up under her body to kneel on her chair. Henry's father noticed the delight on her face when she laid her eyes on the colourful, smiling snakes.

'What's your favourite colour, Mary?'

'Uum,' she said, drawing the word out, 'purple!'

Henry's father peered into the box. 'Oh,' he said. 'Look at this.' He withdrew a purple counter and held it up between his thumb and forefinger. 'You're purple.

'And what about you, Edward?'

Edward didn't answer.

'Edward?'

'Red,' he answered, with reluctance.

'Red it is.' He fished for the red counter.

'Granddad,' said Edward. 'Is Dad really dead?'

Henry's father stopped.

'Yes,' he said.

'Has he gone to heaven?' asked Mary.

'Yes. Good people go to heaven, don't they?'

Mary nodded slowly. Her whole upper body moved when she nodded.

'Is he going to come back?' she said.

Henry's father sat down in a chair on the opposite side of the table.

'He's not going to come back.' The children stared at him. 'I know you won't understand this, but you should not be frightened of dying. Everybody dies, but that's not such a bad thing. All you're doing is returning a favour, really. The world does you a pretty big favour when it lets you be born and become a person. Just imagine: you could be born a termite and get gobbled up by a big old anteater, but you're not. So if you're going to be born, then you have to die at the end. That's the deal.' He smiled. 'And it's a pretty good deal. Dying is just the same as being born, but the other way around. You come in and then you collect up all of these wonderful memories and have fun times, and then you go out again.'

He smiled to his grandchildren, though he did not know if he was trying to console them for the loss of their father, or prepare them for what seemed to be a likely future.

'I'm not scared,' he said. 'So you shouldn't be either. It's a natural thing. It's no different from leaves falling off trees in the autumn. Do you understand?'

Mary shook her head without hesitation. 'No,' she said categorically.

III

London was different. The buildings were taller, greyer. The city with all its walls and height assumed a new, stark menace. Anything could be around the corner. The newly realized fear of the unknown made the place cold and ominous.

The rain had stopped. The orange from the street lamps reflected in the wet roads. There were few people on the streets. The grand townhouses in this part of London were set back from the road.

Joseph pulled the Peugeot to a stop and Miriam unclipped her seatbelt.

'Are you coming?'

'I'll wait here.'

She pushed open the heavy iron gate and walked towards the house. The gravel on the path crackled beneath her. The porch was dark. There were no lights on, either upstairs or down. Six low concrete steps led up to the porch and as Miriam reached the first, she saw the front door hanging ajar. With caution, she went into the darkness.

'Hello?'

The hall was bathed in an eerie orange light from outside. As quietly as she could, Miriam moved down the stretch of woodblock floor to the doorway on the left, which led to the living room. Her shadow stretched before her, grey and indistinct. The door was shut. The metal of the handle was cold on her skin.

She flicked the light switch and her eyes were instinctively drawn to the office chair in front of the far window, out of place in the elegant décor of the living room. Sophia's husband was sitting in the chair, facing away from her, staring out of the window.

'Daniel?'

He didn't move. Her instant reaction was that he was dead.

A messy red line in the cream-coloured carpet led from Daniel's chair to the centre of the room, out of sight behind the sofa. Despite her fear she crossed the room quickly. The red line led to Sophia's body. She was covered in blood; an android outline, toes pointed at the ceiling, the idea of a human.

Miriam screamed and covered her mouth, her whole body shaking. She ran to her friend and fell to her knees. The blood was still warm, Sophia's long, black hair slick with it. It was coming from her chest. There were so many rips in her shirt where she had been stabbed.

'No, no, no.'

The image of Sophia's face hung frozen in a shining red mask. Miriam's hands trembled as she tried to wipe the blood clear but whenever the pink of flesh appeared it was quickly enveloped again in the red sheen. Three stab marks, two in the right cheek, one in the left, were like underground springs recycling blood on to Sophia's face.

She dropped the body in an instant slam of horror. Scrabbling backwards, she gagged for breath and brought her hands to her mouth. The taste of Sophia's blood was acrid and she spat on to the floor.

Out of the corner of her eye she saw a movement. Rigid with metallic shock she moved her head round. Daniel was looking at her. His face had appeared from behind the office chair. For a moment they stared at each other. His eyes were dead. There was no expression on his face. He regarded Miriam for a long time and then, slowly, turned back and his head disappeared behind the chair once more.

Miriam snatched for air. There was a loud bang from the hallway and then a pair of legs appeared in front of her. A set of arms pulled her to her feet. She closed her eyes.

'Come on,' said Joseph's voice. 'We have to go.'

|||

He bundled Miriam into the car and sat alongside her. She was trembling violently. Her shaking hands clutched her face. He started the engine and pulled out into the street. The car raced down the quiet road and out into the dark streets of London. A mist had started to settle over the city. The street lamps were visible now only as indistinct orbs of orange. Joseph threw the fog-lights switch.

They travelled along the edge of the river. There was more traffic here. It was reassuring to Joseph to see this version of normality. London was still alive. They crossed the water. A single riverboat sailed towards them, its lights shining through the dark space and the fog. He checked his phone. No calls, no messages. There was a quiet patch of road and he pulled over. Across the river the Houses of Parliament hummed ochre, their reflection just a golden shimmer on the water. Joseph called the police and passed on Sophia's address. He climbed out of his car, not wanting Miriam to hear him speaking, and the freezing air made him shiver.

'Is there anything I need to know? Do you know what's happening?'

'I'm sorry, sir,' said the woman at the other end. 'Just follow the instructions on the television and online. That's all you can do.'

He looked down the street and took a deep breath. He couldn't see far in either direction.

When he reached his apartment building the brightness of the halogen lights in the underground car park gave the world a new, eerie, luminescence. He felt afraid suddenly. Moving quietly around to the other side of the car, he checked that nobody else was in there with him. He thought he could feel eyes on him.

'Miri,' he said, opening her door.

Her eyes were closed. Her forehead was resting on the dashboard and she was not moving. Joseph stepped away from her instinctively. Tiny sparks shot up his arms and laterally across his chest. He waited for a moment. He turned away and took a breath of air from behind him.

'Miriam?' he said again.

She opened her eyes and looked at him.

'OK,' she said, and climbed out of the car. 'I'm OK.'

III

He put Miriam to bed and went into the living room. Pele was curled up in his basket in front of the French windows. The flat was small: a porch area, a bedroom, a bathroom and the living room. The kitchenette was just an L-shaped line of cabinets with a stove in the back corner. He switched on the radio and made up the sofa bed.

The news reported an event taking place in Russia. The entire country had gone silent, all lines of communication cut. No messages had been received, no messages had been sent. The whole country had closed. Joseph smiled. This was ridiculous.

He collected up the mess that had accumulated in the little room. He took the dishes to the sink and washed them. He cleared all the rubbish into the bin and took it to the refuse collection area at the back of the building, still ensuring that he separated out the paper for the recycle bin. He took some sheets from the laundry cupboard and laid them over the sofa bed. Papers from work were everywhere. He bundled them together and took them over to the table in the corner of the room.

Over by the doorway to the porch was a small display shelf. On it was a framed photograph of him and Henry. He lifted it up and looked at it. It was from a fishing trip they had taken years ago. They both looked like young men and there was a great expanse of blue sky behind them. Joseph wished he had spoken to Henry again, just one last time. The weight of everything that had been left unsaid, the stuff he had promised he would say one day when he got the chance, sat heavily on his body.

He remembered the day well. They had bought some crab lines and dangled them into the still, oily waters of the harbour and collected the crabs in a bucket. At sunset they had climbed down the steps to the water's edge and dropped them in and watched their red bodies glimmer, fade and disappear into the darkness.

He placed the photograph back on the shelf and tried to stifle the immensity of regret. He wondered how it was possible for so strong a relationship to have become what it did.

He looked around the flat again, went over to the French windows and drew the curtains across. Pele wheezed in his sleep.

Next, Joseph went to the store cupboard in the porch. There were piles of blankets and clothes. He found the pair of old running shoes he was looking for and took them into the living room. They had belonged to one of his old girlfriends and he thought that Miriam should have them because her own shoes were woefully impractical for what he thought might just be the end of the world. He placed the shoes down over by the French windows and climbed into bed where he cursed himself for shouting at Miriam the way he had and then fell asleep, listening to the radio, listening to the news that the government had released an official statement saying that the Chancellor of the Exchequer had passed away quietly in his sleep.

IIII

Miriam lifted open her eyes and stared at a ceiling she did not recognize. The sound that had taken her from sleep came back, a low rumble somewhere on the horizon, unsettling and sustained. Soon it split in two, a taut, tense high end peeling away and clashing discordantly against the low rumble; twin sounds raking over the city. The noise was growing and assuming a machine-like form.

She went through to the living room where Joseph lay asleep. A set of French windows led out on to a small metal balcony. Miriam opened the door and a freezing wind swept into the room. With it came the sound, louder now, furious on the wind. Quickly, she slid through the door and closed it gently behind her.

A black ribbon of canal ran behind Joseph's apartment block, hardly visible through the fog. The noise filled the whole sky. It was everywhere now. Miriam opened her eyes. She was afraid but determined to remain where she was. A wall of resolve was building within her.

'I'm not moving,' she said to the sound.

It screamed at her, a fury without source.

And then two white lights appeared in the fog. They moved

together across the sky, towards her. She imagined to what machine they might belong. Was an aircraft really about to crash into London? The sound filled her head: a dreadful, raging turbulence.

She lowered her head and felt her palms press together.

'Please help us,' she said.

When she looked up again an invisible force streaked through her. A second, unnatural wind caught her hair; the wind from the machine. The two white lights were separated by a wider distance than she realized. The thing was huge. It would obliterate her. Its dissonance thumped into her as waves. The fog from the canal was being drawn unnaturally into the sky in vast, curling torrents.

Black forms appeared in the fog and Miriam felt a rush of adrenalin fire along her veins. Two enormous military helicopters tore out of the night. She covered her eyes and turned away as the white searchlights picked her out on the balcony. Her pupils re-adjusted and she stared directly up as the two machines thundered over the building, their massive underbellies so close she thought she would be able to reach up and touch them. And then they were gone and the sound retreated with them.

She remained on the balcony. Her head was clear. The chemicals in her blood equalized her senses and brought them to peaks of hyper-awareness. She could smell the canal below. She could feel the vapour of the fog on her face. She could hear the distant chopping of the helicopters.

|||

The waves were gentle against the man's legs. The tide marched to the beach in foamy white scimitars. The man moved strongly through the water, pulling his rowing boat over his shoulder, clutching the tethered rope, taking one step at a time, like a robot.

The dawn was beautiful. A low bank of cloud sat aloft the horizon, far in the distance, its underbelly glowing pink from the rising sun. At the top of the sky, high up in the atmosphere, the furrowed lines of stratus roofed the dome of the world. The sun-rise was different. At last there was spring in it.

Deep enough now, the man pulled his rowing boat to him and released the rope. He climbed smoothly into it and sat on the low bench at its centre. He took the oars in his hands and struck out for the horizon. Gulls flew all around him. A shoal of fish must have come inshore, guided by the currents, and the birds circled around and dived for their food. The man did not stop to watch them. He simply kept rowing, his arms beating a circular action, his muscles adjusting and settling into the repetitive motion.

James watched from his open bedroom window. He considered going down to the beach to call the man in, but he also saw freedom in the little rowing boat. If you could choose somewhere to die, there were far worse places than out at sea.

The boat grew smaller. It lurched endearingly over each cylinder of tide that rolled so massively underneath it. Up and down, further and further.

The old man could smell the salt on the air. He loved it when that happened. Years of living in the house had accustomed his ears to the sound of the ocean but today he made a point of appreciating it. He looked down at his hands, at the knuckles that stood out sharper than they had when he was a young man, and pulled the window to.

He could hear the murmur of the television set downstairs. His grandchildren were watching their cartoons. He would have to ready them soon. They needed to go to the village and pick up a few things. Joseph had called and asked him to buy seeds at the garden centre, but that could wait. He looked out of the window again to see if the man in the rowing boat had turned back and was heading into shore. But there was nothing there. The sea was just its plain old self.

He crossed the room and sat at his wife's dressing table, which he used as a writing desk. He still kept a picture of her in a silver frame. For the first time in eleven years he was glad she was dead. He would not have wanted her to experience this, the death of a child. He knew things were going to become bad. He had never before sensed the lingering panic that hung in the air now. It was everywhere. He was scared for the future.

His stationery was in one of the drawers underneath the

tabletop. He pulled it open and gathered up his pen and a sheaf of papers. Placing the pen to his lips he wondered what he should write.

III

The room came into slow focus. She was cold and the place was silent. Slowly, she rose from the bed. Her knees stung as they stretched and a sudden fear opened inside her. She went into the living room but it was empty.

'Joseph?'

There was no answer. He wasn't in the bathroom and he wasn't in the hallway. Pele was in his basket, looking out at her through solemn eyes. There was a note taped to the fridge door and as she read it needles of anger pricked in her throat.

He had left her. The note said he had gone to the university to pick up some things, and that he had found her some running shoes she should use. She could hear herself breathing. It was so like him. He knew she needed to see her mother but he didn't care. He just did whatever he wanted. He didn't care about her, or the kids. She was nothing more than a tendril between Joseph and his brother, a rope for him to hold on to.

Isolated and angry she crossed to the French windows. Pele stirred in his basket. A thick plume of black smoke rose on the horizon. It crept slowly upwards, perfectly defined, its edges crisp against the pearlescent vista of the late winter morning.

She had to get to her mother. It didn't matter how she got there, she had to see her. She scribbled a note, and went to the door.

A picture frame stood on a shelf in the porch, of Joseph and Henry standing on a pier, holding fishing rods. There was a wide smile on Joseph's face and he was lifting his thumb to the sky. Miriam found it difficult picturing Joseph as the carefree person she was looking at. That part of him was so far gone that it was difficult to believe it could ever have been there at all. Life had chewed him up and spat him out.

The air was freezing outside. It blasted her face and hair and she pulled the collar up around her neck. Old deserted shops were separated by modern, ugly, red-brick structures like Joseph's apartment building. She hurried to the busier road around the corner.

As she turned on to it she was struck by the sense of normality. She didn't know exactly what she had been expecting, but this was not it. After the horrors she had seen she assumed London would have fallen apart, but that was not the case. People were walking up and down the road, clutching shopping bags, holding cardboard cups filled with coffee. None of them seemed panicked. The world just kept going.

The bus she needed was a quarter of a mile away. She walked quickly up the street and tried to empty her mind. Further up the road a man was standing on a wooden crate. He was holding a banner and shouting. As she approached his words started to clear in her head. His banner was daubed in black paint. It read '333'. It was mounted on two wooden poles that he held above his head.

'It will come for three hundred and thirty-three days,' he called.

Miriam kept walking. She wanted to keep her head down but it was difficult to ignore him. His voice was so clear. She looked over to him and their eyes locked. He lifted the banner even higher.

'I have seen it,' he shouted, directly to her. 'I walked the desert and I saw the number. The earth will swell for three hundred and thirty-three days. You are not safe. Are you listening? You, the woman across the road.'

Miriam's heart quickened with her pace.

'You should listen to me,' he called after her. 'I came to an oasis and I saw a pool of water in the sand. It was as blue and clear as sapphires and the sand underneath rippled like lines of ribs. Fourteen fish swam in the waters, two for each colour of the rainbow.'

Miriam slowed.

'I watched the fish swim in silence for three days. And then I turned and saw a woman on her knees beside a bright green stem that was topped with two leaves. One pointed at the North Star, the other at the Lion.'

His voice echoed off the buildings so that it was coming at her from all directions. Two men were standing at the corner of a junction, watching and listening. The younger man was holding a baby wrapped in a blanket. There was no traffic on the road now and the ambient sound of the city had diminished to little more than a few dead leaves bristling in the gutter. A young woman had stopped directly opposite the prophet. She sat down against the front wall of a building and pulled a packet of cigarettes from her jacket.

The man on the wooden crate looked like any other man. He was wearing a pair of jeans and a red T-shirt, despite the freezing weather, like the man she had seen on the bench.

'The woman was weeping,' he called. 'I went to her and looked into her eyes. Past the tears I could see colours swimming inside her. The fish. She had taken them for herself and put them in her eyes. And so the Earth had taken her. Do you not see this? Do you not understand the theft of the fourteen fish? There are ancient rivers in us, between us, and now they run again. I sat with her for seven days and on the morning of the eighth day three sand dunes grew out of the desert and I felt them saying to me that this was the duration for which they would come. The Earth will swell around us and take our souls for three hundred and thirty-three days.'

|||

Miriam moved along. She crossed the road and turned right at the junction that would take her to the bus. A pub was on the corner and several people were sitting on the benches outside, smoking, happily enjoying their drinks.

The road led round a bend and when it straightened Miriam stopped. There was a church up ahead. A large crowd of people had gathered outside and were spilling out into the road. Even from her distance she could hear the sounds of people crying. She regarded the scene for a moment. The road was quiet and there was a gentle melancholy hanging over the people outside the church. She went slowly forwards.

There was a patch of wasteland on her left. Thick grass shot up in clumps between the hard, ice-bound mud. Discarded lengths of rusting metal sat at awkward angles on the ground. Large laurel bushes grew between the piles of rubble and there, amongst it all, a man was standing upright, arms limp at his side, very still. And he was staring at her.

Tears formed in her eyes when she saw him and an upwelling of grief curdled inside. Whatever it was that had taken her husband had taken that man out there in the dry, ochre wastes. Something vital had gone from him and she could sense its absence keenly. She wondered if the man was going to die; whether there was any coming back from it.

She was running now. Her hair caught in the wind and her face pricked with cold. Her vision blurred. Something very dangerous and very evil was in the world and it had not been there before. It had descended into the places between places, the forgotten edges of the world that only come back to us when they are disturbed; those cracks and alcoves that invisibly order themselves into a construct over which reality drapes itself and becomes solid.

The people gathered round the church looked up when they saw her running towards them. Most of them were black. The tears wobbled on the surface of Miriam's eyes and fell away.

The priest, who was female, saw her and stepped to the front of the crowd.

'Please,' said Miriam, no longer aware of why she was crying, for whom she was crying. 'Please help.'

She stopped and the priest smiled at her. Miriam took a deep breath and wiped her eyes.

'It's OK,' said the woman, with a rich Caribbean accent.

'There's a man,' said Miriam, out of breath.

Her lungs were stinging. Her mind was reeling, falling over itself, tripping on outcrops of sharp images. She just wanted to see her mother, to get her kids back, for things to be the opposite of what they were. Her chest heaved. 'Back there. He needs help.'

The priest tried to calm her.

'OK, OK, honey. It's going to be fine.' She turned to the crowd. 'Anton,' she called, and gestured for one of the men to come over.

Miriam's eyes went past the priest and fell on the scene outside the church. There were so many of them. The pores of her skin clammed shut and she felt blue ice in her flesh. They were just lying there, those stricken down by it. Twenty or thirty of them.

Miriam tried to breathe too fast and coughed. Her eyes swept over the faces, all of them expressionless, looking at nothing. Families sat around the victims, crying in disbelief. Bunches of bright flowers were lined up against the wall of the red-brick church.

One of the victims was a little boy. He was dressed in a grey school uniform and he lay on his side, half on the pavement, half off. His mother and grandmother were huddled over him, each holding one of his hands. The boy stared out across the road, his lips slightly parted, his eyelids a quarter down. Miriam took a step backwards.

'It's OK,' said the priest. She lowered her head and looked up into Miriam's eyes. 'What's your name?'

Miriam steadied herself. She thought she might be about to throw up.

'Miri. Miriam.'

'My name is Grace.' The priest turned back to the crowd. She was tall and slim, with a long neck and short-cropped hair. 'Anton, I said come over here, please.' The priest turned back to Miriam and smiled.

A large black man who had been leaning against the closed and heavy-looking wooden doors of the church stood up.

'What about the doors?'

A large, metal padlock held them shut. Several thick metal pipes were leaning against them and a group of big men were standing in front.

'Just come over here, OK?'

Anton picked up one of the metal pipes and approached them.

'What's locked in the church?' said Miriam, quietly.

Grace hooked her arm under Miriam's and turned her round. As she did so there was a loud bang from inside the church, of something heavy being slammed into the door. Miriam jumped and went to turn but Grace pulled her back.

'Don't you worry yourself about that,' she said, patting Miriam's arm. 'Come on, let's go and find your man. Just keep walking.'

|||

'They're calling it the Sadness,' said Grace. They walked down the road towards the wasteland. 'Nobody knows what it is, or where it's come from.'

Miriam stared straight ahead. She remembered that she was supposed to be going to her mother, that she was losing time, but the thought was indistinct, nebulous.

'Has anybody you know been affected?'

'My husband,' Miriam answered quickly, surprised by the speed of her response. There was adrenalin in her blood and her body felt light.

Anton walked a few feet before them, clutching his metal pipe. He was taller than six foot, with broad shoulders and a long straight back.

'Why has he got that pipe?'

She noticed the tiny hesitation in Grace before she answered.

'Not everyone reacts to it in the same way,' she said, unwilling to add anything more than that.

The sound of people crying outside the church receded. A gentle but cold breeze drifted over their faces as they reached the wasteland. The metal fence that had once separated the land from the pavement lay flat on the rocky soil. Anton lifted his pipe over his shoulder and stepped over it.

'Watch your footing, ladies,' he said, in a voice rich and deep. He climbed on to a block of concrete and looked around, his metal pipe swinging lazily at his side. 'I can't see anybody.'

Then there was the clashing of metal against rock as Anton dropped his pipe and stumbled backwards. Something had struck him. Blood was coming from the side of his head.

A scream broke out from the direction of the church and Miriam swung her head round. There was too much happening, too many stimuli. Anton fell from the concrete altar and when his feet hit the ground his legs buckled beneath him. Dark red blood flowed freely down the side of his face, visible as a glistening stream against his skin.

There was movement from the wasteland. A man scorched out of one of the low laurel bushes, dust spitting up around his feet as his shoes pounded into the dirt. It was the same man Miriam had seen, but now he was wholly changed. He was running in a straight line towards Anton. It did not seem real. He was moving too fast, as if it was some trick of the light, an illusion.

'Anton!' called Grace, dashing out across the open space.

Miriam felt helpless. She couldn't move. She just watched as Anton tried to lift his bleeding head. She willed her brain to get into gear and then, quickly, she ran after Grace.

The man sprinting across the wasteland did not stop. He hurdled the larger rocks, his ankles buckling on the rough terrain, but he kept coming.

'Get away from me,' he screamed. His voice tore viscerally across the air. His words were contradictory to his actions, as if his body was ruling his mind. 'Get away – I don't want to do this.'

The man was going to reach Anton before Grace. He was running so fast. His legs seemed to take strength from the ground itself. When his feet hit the dirt it was as if the earth fired them back up. He was not running across the ground, he was skimming along it like a cat. He reached the concrete block, lifted Anton's metal pipe off the ground and stood over the limp mass of human at his feet, ready to strike.

'No,' screamed Grace. 'Get away from him. Get away from my brother.'

Miriam saw the man's face saturate with pity.

'I can't,' he cried. His chest heaved with exertion. 'It won't let me.'

He lifted the pipe above his head and pushed his shoulders down to swing but Anton threw dirt up into his face. The man jerked his head sideways. He coughed, stopped and then went to swing again. The brief pause was enough to allow Anton to lift his forearm. The force with which the metal pipe swung through the air was shocking and violent. It whirred, made a low whistling sound and crashed into the bone of Anton's arm with a deep, metallic clang. Anton grunted, his face contorted in pain as his arm depressed in on itself.

Grace threw herself bodily at the infected man. He stumbled sideways under her weight but realigned his balance almost immediately. He prised Grace from his back and pushed her down. She went sprawling across the rocks, too far for a normal human, as if being dragged backwards across the ground.

Ignoring her, the man swung at Anton. He seemed able to draw every ounce of energy from his body, to tap into some ancient reservoir that had been long since forgotten in humans. He moved like an animal. The pipe came down into the side of Anton's head with an unnatural power and his body went instantly loose. Miriam stopped. Anton fell between her and the infected man and when his body hit the floor, the man was looking at her, his mouth open, baring his teeth.

'Run,' he snarled.

Miriam turned. Her legs circled beneath her. The ground was uneven and she almost tripped. Only the sheer will to survive kept her upright. Behind her, Grace started to scream. She daren't turn back. She needed to get help. Everything was out of control. The footfalls of the man chasing grew louder as he gained on her. She just kept running.

She reached the street and screamed towards the church.

'Help us! Somebody help us!'

The men guarding the church door looked up and when they saw Miriam, waving her hands wildly in the air, picked up their metal pipes and ran for her. That they had heard her, that they were coming to help, brought a great breath of relief. It moved through her and fogged her mind. She had to stop. Exhausted, she put her hands on her knees and tried to breathe. She looked down at the trainers that Joseph had insisted she wear; the trainers that had borne her safely over the wasteland.

The sudden sound of feet coming too fast cut her breath clean off. The man who had been chasing her. A jarring, physical blow sent her sprawling across the floor. Her knees skidded painfully across the tarmac of the road, the material of her jeans ripping open and exposing her skin and then flesh to the concrete. She felt her centre of gravity roll up her body and spill forwards as the sky turned upside down.

She jumped up and spun around blindly. Screaming pealed from the church. The doors were open and the crowd started to spread out and away from the building.

Men spilled out of the doors and chased the fleeing crowd. They moved like the man on the wasteland; too fast, not like humans. One of them leaped on to the back of an old woman, who fell to the floor under his weight. Miriam watched, half in horror, half in utter disbelief, as he grabbed the old woman mercilessly by the back of her hair and smashed her face into the road.

There was a scream now, much closer: her own voice. With unknowable ferocity the man lifted the old woman's head again and brought it down once more into the concrete.

Everything now, all of the violence, the death, the unknown, had congealed into a pulsing conglomeration in her chest. It smothered her and cut off the links to rational thought. She ran as fast she could in the opposite direction.

She passed the wasteland. Grace was lying over Anton's body. His eyes were open and lifeless. Miriam hooked her arms under the priest's, her mind swinging recklessly between primal and rational.

'Grace,' she whispered into her ear. 'We need to go. It's too dangerous.'

There was surprisingly little resistance from the priest. Her body was light as Miriam lifted her to her feet. Anton's mouth was stained red and his skull looked an odd shape. The skin was no longer tight along the forehead.

Grace herself was injured. She held her arm and there was a cut somewhere beneath her hair that leaked blood down her face. She was crying.

'Grace, please,' Miriam said softly.

'I can't leave him. He's my brother.'

Miriam pulled her back towards the road. Grace's feet dragged in the dry, dusty dirt and carved out small, wafting clouds of yellow sand. Miriam stumbled back over the collapsed fencing and looked down towards the church, at the mass of people running and screaming.

They stumbled along the road arm in arm. Those who were not hurt overtook them. Nobody stopped to help.

|||

Joseph's apartment had changed. Slabs of canned food were stacked in the centre of the living room. A plastic box full of paper lay on top. Next to the food were three large water containers, all full. Next to those was a large metal toolbox. The French windows across the room were open and a song was playing on the radio.

Now that she was still, Miriam felt the pain in her knees return. The muscles tensed around the cartilage and seized the joint. She looked down. Her trousers were torn open and hanging from her knees in untidy triangular flaps.

'Where are we?' said Grace.

Her voice was groggy, her eyes half closed. The cut on her head was worse than Miriam had thought.

Movement came from the bedroom and the black form of Pele lumbered slowly across the room.

'Where have you been?' Joseph came from the bedroom. He looked tired. His eyes passed from Miriam to the female priest she had brought into his home, and back to Miriam. 'What are you doing?'

His voice was tense and the anger she had felt that morning came back quick and strong.

'Give me a hand, Joseph.'

He paused. She felt like screaming at him.

'Through here,' he said, at last.

He led them into the bedroom and found a towel from his wardrobe, laid it over the pillows and rested Grace down on the bed.

'We need to have a word,' he said to Miriam.

|||

'Why did you leave the flat?' said Joseph, sternly.

'Don't you dare,' she started, and then stopped. She couldn't believe he was going to try and turn this around to put the blame on her. 'Why the hell did you leave me?'

'I know what I'm doing.'

'What's that supposed to mean?' Her voice betrayed her rising emotion. He always thought he knew best, that he was the proprietor of some great insight that other, lesser people did not share. It was hard to believe he was Henry's brother.

How could such similar boxes have such differing contents?

'I had to go to the university, I told you that. And I had to collect all this stuff.'

He gestured at the stacks of food in the centre of the room.

'You knew I wanted to see my mother.'

He shook his head, as if he was talking to a child, as if he had done nothing wrong and she just couldn't understand that.

'Where have you been?'

'Where do you think I've been? I've been trying to get to my mother's.'

'Fuck,' he said shortly, closing his eyes. Miriam gasped. 'You mustn't go out without me. Can't you see what's happening?'

'I can see just fine.'

'How can we get to your mother if you're dragging strangers in off the street?'

Miriam said nothing to that.

'You have no idea about people, Miriam. You have no idea what they'll do when forced into a corner. You just don't understand how dangerous it is out there.'

Miriam went to say something but had to stop. Her voice was about to break. She looked at her feet and sensed Joseph's eyes on her.

'What have you done to your knees?' he asked.

'They're fine.'

He went to the cupboard underneath the sink. Through the open windows droned the sound of a passing aeroplane.

'I'm sorry,' he said, with his back to her. 'It's just that I feel responsible for you.'

'You're not responsible for me.'

'Well, I feel like I am.' He filled a bowl with water. 'You're a better person than me, Miri, there's no doubt about it. But you have to be more careful. You can't help everyone. It's craziness.'

'She's hurt.'

Joseph lowered his voice.

'I know, but we can't help everybody who's hurt. It's just not possible. I know you want to help but we can't. We have to concentrate on being safe. What would have happened to your kids if you'd been killed?'

Miriam stopped.

'We can't be ideological now. This is reality. Fifteen thousand people are dead, Miri. In London alone. Something bad is going on and I don't get why you can't see that.' He shook his head incredulously. 'Please, Miri, no more stupid risks until the government tell us what's happening.' He knelt down before her and placed the bowl of water at his side. In his other hand he was holding a green first-aid box, which he unclipped. He paused. 'You're going to have to take off your trousers for me to deal with this.'

They looked at one another. He had said it quickly and offhand but still Miriam flushed.

'Go and help Grace first.'

'No. You're first.'

Joseph picked a band of wadding from the first-aid box.

'Her head is—'

'I'm not going to help her until I've helped you first. That's the way it is. Think of it as a rule.' Miriam knew it was useless to argue. 'Look, have you got a dress or something? You can go and put that on if that's what you're worried about.'

'It's not that,' she lied.

'I won't be offended.'

He looked so much like Henry from certain angles. The sound of the outside world came in through the French doors, but it was diluted and separate from the room. She made her decision, unfastened the buttons of her jeans and pulled them down over her hips. She felt exposed in her underwear. She sat back, her knees two inches apart. Joseph took her left knee in his hand and when he did a complicated tingling ran up her thighs. He placed a cloth into the bowl of water and washed away the blood. The water was cool on her flesh.

'What happened?' he said, softly dabbing her wounds.

'There was an accident,' she said slowly.

'An accident?'

A breath of wind caught the curtains.

'I don't know what it was.'

Joseph leaned his head to the right to inspect his work. He took from the first-aid kit a small bottle of disinfectant and placed the wadding over its neck.

'What's that box of papers?'

'I printed them off at the university, from the internet. It's the government's plans for emergency.' He looked at her and saw she was smiling. 'You're mocking me,' he said.

Miriam laughed, suddenly aware of how ludicrous this all was.

'I'm sorry, Joseph,' she said.

Joseph lowered his head and dabbed her knees. The pain burned up her legs and she winced. She eased open her eyes and looked towards the windows at the blank white sky and the tops of tall buildings that made their clutching grasps at it.

III

Miriam was sitting on the bed next to Grace with Pele at her feet. She stroked his head and the dog panted contentedly. This was the first time things had been still.

Joseph had bandaged Grace's head and she had fallen asleep. When she woke she covered her face with her hands, the memories coming back with consciousness.

'We left him there,' she sobbed.

'We had to,' Miriam said quietly. 'He was gone.'

'No.' Grace brought her knees up into her. 'We left him. He was my brother and we left him.'

Outside the window, behind the clouds, the sun was beginning to set. Soon it would be night again.

'Here,' she said, offering the priest a glass of water.

Grace took it in a shaky hand. 'I have to get back.'

'You can stay here.'

'No, I need to make sure that everyone is OK.' Suddenly Grace looked away and her mouth widened. She covered it with her hand. Her eyes narrowed and her body started to shake. 'What's happening?' she cried. 'Why is this happening?'

Miriam shook her head. 'I don't know.'

'Miri.' Joseph was standing in the doorway, his face in darkness, his hand leaning against the frame. 'The Prime Minister is about to speak,' he said.

III

'Last Wednesday the first cases of a previously unknown disease were reported. The emergent illness has caused a great deal of fear, not only here in the United Kingdom, but across the globe. The World Health Organization has confirmed cases in one hundred and twenty-seven countries thus far. In the United Kingdom, every area has been affected, the large population centres and the remote areas alike.

'Because of the speed and seemingly instantaneous surge of this phenomenon, details are still unclear.

'Before I begin I would like to assure the British public that its government is doing all it can in these extremely difficult times. Cross-departmental programmes for dealing with such an event have been formulated meticulously over many years and, as we speak, agencies across the country are rolling out their contingency plans in accordance with government policy and thinking.

'The phenomenon has claimed many lives, this is the truth, and we expect it to claim many more. Despite our best efforts, there will be many deaths. We need to be prepared for this difficult truth. I should also say at this point that the death rates being announced in the media are not accurate. There have been a total of four thousand deaths related to the illness in the UK up to this point, not the two hundred thousand that have been reported in the press. Such rumours only help to stoke the fear that could prove extremely damaging for the country. The figures may seem frightening, but you should be aware that winter flu alone claims between twelve and twenty thousand lives every year.

'I want to state categorically that our plans are strong and will certainly save lives. Together as a nation we can conquer this. It has been my long-held belief that the ability to face adversity head on is the people of Britain's greatest strength. It is in times of crisis that we excel, and this is a time of crisis. We must excel.

'And now I will outline information that we have as hard fact. More details will be available from various sources. My speech will be followed by the Chief Medical Officer and he will give website addresses and phone lines that the public can use free of charge. You may want to get a pen and paper so that you are ready to take down necessary details. Further to this, leaflets with pertinent information will soon be available from hospitals, doctors' waiting rooms, walk-in centres, post offices, banks, libraries and many shops. There will be no postal scheme for the distribution of literature and information at this stage. This literature will be distributed in due course as and when we have more understanding of the illness.

'Scientists across the world are striving night and day to gain insight into the nature of the illness. Results so far have proved inconclusive and further testing is being conducted. The life cycle of the disease stands at the moment at between two and a half and three and a half days. The victim shows no physiological decline in health over this period but the illness has so far resulted in fatalities through causes that are at the moment unknown. We will not speculate about the cause of death – we will only report facts to you.

'The symptoms of the illness are not uniform but do seem to follow a distinct pattern in the early stages. The visible symptoms usually begin upon waking, though this is not always the case. The patient will appear withdrawn, or uncommunicative. They may become silent or speak of a depression that has descended on them.

'Many people have been worried about the effects the illness has on its victims in the later stages. Early estimates suggest that four per cent of infected patients undergo radical personality changes after approximately one and a half days. These may manifest themselves in a number of different ways, the most worrying of which is a tendency towards violence, although many others have been noted.

'Many of you, I know, are worried about the current reports of disturbance. It is true that there has been a rise in incidents since the emergence of the illness, and the public should be alert. If somebody is stricken with the illness take them to your nearest hospital or GP surgery as soon as you can. Be vigilant. If they do show aggressive tendencies, call the police or try to get help from neighbours and friends. Restrain the victims as best as you can.

'As Prime Minister, it is my duty to report to you the facts. In this situation I have made the decision not to cloak any of the information that I have. As it stands, everybody who has contracted the illness has died. Neither we nor the World Health Organization have found any cases of the illness receding in its victims. This is not to say that we won't see people becoming resistant to it, it is just that it has not happened yet. This type of mortality rate is unprecedented in viruses and presents a challenge to our scientists, but they are confident that the human body will be able, in time, to adjust to this phenomenon.

'New information will be reported to you as soon as we get it. I'd like now to tell you what is going to happen in terms of the nation's infrastructure. And that is very little. People will still go to work. Without work the economy will crumble – food deliveries will not be made, foreign imports will slow, civil amenities will slide. The wheels of industry must be kept turning. I urge all of the public to put aside their fear and be cohesive, as a society. Everybody has a role to play. The schools will not close, public transport, including the London Underground, will continue to operate as normal. Cutting people off from one another to curtail the spread of a disease has been proven not to work when the illness becomes widespread across the population, as it already has. Closing transport links at this stage will only make things worse. The emergency services will still be available and will double their efforts to help the Great British public.

'There will be frightening times ahead but we must not bow to pressure. Only together can we succeed. Do not listen to rumour, do not pass up the opportunity to help your neighbour. We are one nation and as one nation we can and will go forward. God bless you.'

|||

The nearest village was two miles away. With the children safely loaded into the back of the car they wound their way along the narrow coastal road. Henry's father parked up in the small car park at the side of the shop and opened the back door for the children.

They clambered out, their puffy winter coats restricting their movements.

The sound of cars moving was noticeably absent. The village was small; the main high street was just a few houses, a shop, a pub, the church with its tall steeple, which he could see from his house, and a post office. Behind the high street were two small housing estates. Henry's father had half expected the place to have become a ghost town, and felt a lift in his heart when he discovered there was at least some activity. A couple were walking a dog and one man was sweeping his front garden path.

They headed for the shop. The shopkeeper was sitting behind the counter, reading a newspaper.

'Hello, Mr Asher,' he said.

Henry's father stared at the lines of near empty shelves.

'Not much left, I'm afraid.'

'So I see.'

He scanned the few dented tins of fruit and some broken boxes.

'Our deliveries haven't turned up today.'

'Don't you have anything else?'

The shopkeeper straightened his tie and shook his head regretfully. 'What you see is what I have. If they haven't turned up by lunchtime I'm going to go down the wholesaler's.'

'But . . . don't you have any stock?'

'It's all gone.'

'But we were told not to panic.'

The shopkeeper shrugged. 'You know how people are,' he said. 'Most of them didn't listen. I opened up this morning and everything went. Even the stuff in the back.'

Henry's father felt his face grow hot. He didn't have much food in the house.

'Why on earth would they buy everything?'

'It's the illness, isn't it? People are scared.'

'But it will all blow over.'

The shopkeeper looked past Henry's father to his two grandchildren, then back again. He wanted to tell him something.

'Children,' said the old man. He gave his car keys to Edward.

'Why don't you go and wait in the car? I won't be long. I just need to have a chat with Mr Chancery.'

Edward and Mary did as they were told. Henry's father approached the counter. 'What is it, Tom?'

'My wife is dead.'

The old man thought about this fact for a moment. His legs felt weak. He leaned against the counter. 'My son is dead,' he said.

'Which . . .'

'The youngest one. Henry.'

'James, I . . .'

The old man was staring at the confectionery stand. There were a few packets of sweets left. He picked them up and placed them on the counter. 'I'll take these. For the kids.'

The men made eye contact.

'Sure,' said the shopkeeper. 'Take them.'

'How much are they?'

'James, please. Just take them. Here.' The shopkeeper reached under his counter and produced a loaf of white bread. 'Take this as well.'

The old man smiled. 'Thank you, Tom.'

'Go to the supermarket. They've still got stock. Suppliers don't dare not turn up to them,' he said with a cynical smile.

'OK. Thank you.'

'Did you watch the Prime Minister on the telly?' The shopkeeper blew air between his lips and shook his head. 'Something's not right with all this. I don't know what it is, but something's not right. Four thousand people, he said. My niece works in a hospital and she said that they've had thousands of deaths in her hospital alone. And another thing – people started dying on Friday. Why does it take his lordship till now to appear?' He leaned forward. 'They're not telling us something. Remember that news about Russia? Nobody's heard anything from them in days. What's that all about? How can you not hear from a whole country?'

'I don't know.'

'I remember the Cuban missile crisis. Do you remember that?'

'I do.'

'Can you remember the fear?'

The old man did remember.

'Christ. It's all coming back to me. All of that. Every time a plane went over, wasn't it?'

James laughed. 'It really was. I went to a church to pray, you know. And the damned thing was locked. Can you believe it?'

Tom smiled. 'So,' he said.

'So.'

'Take care, James.'

And then he did something strange. He extended his open hand. James took it in his own and the two men shook hands.

|||

They left as soon as the Prime Minister's speech was finished. It was almost dark. Miriam had said nothing to Joseph of what she had witnessed outside the church. She packaged it away, along with the memory of Sophia's body. But she did not do the same with the memory of Henry. That, she kept close. When she had lain awake last night, thinking of her children in Cornwall, the children she was increasingly feeling she had abandoned, Henry's ghost sitting on the edge of her bed had given her some solace. Her grief was bringing her an inverted sense of comfort. She was not ready to package him away just yet.

The streets of London would never look the same again. Having the veil of familiarity lifted gave everything a new and dangerous edge. It was becoming clear that normality was beginning to fade from the world. Strange sights greeted them at nearly every corner: burned-out cars, people lying in the street – at one point a sycamore tree had been chopped down and was lying lengthways on the pavement.

'What are we going to do about the kids?' she said aloud.

'It's completely your decision.' Joseph's answer was quick. He had clearly anticipated the question, which only heightened Miriam's guilt.

'Do you think they should come to London?'

Joseph kept his eyes on the road ahead. 'Maybe.'

'I don't think we can just go to Cornwall and uproot our lives.

The kids are supposed to be in school. That's what they said on the radio.'

'It's your decision.'

'But what do you think?'

'I think it's up to you.'

They came to a line of traffic. Miriam sat back in her seat and glanced out of the window. The houses here were tall and thin, leaning over the road as if in a fairy tale. A man emerged from one of them. In his arms he carried a body that he laid gently down on the wide pavement. Miriam shifted round and placed the palm of her hand on the inside of the window. The man stood up, reached into his pocket and took out a box of matches. The strength went out of his neck for a moment and his head sagged over his chest. She knew instantly that he had been stricken by the illness. That new, alerting sense that she felt was tingling once again, as fact-like as pain. There was that inexplicable gravity around him.

The man lifted his head up again and slowly pushed out the matchbox. He took a match, cracked it to life and threw it towards the open door of his house. Its tiny flame extinguished immediately and the match fell dead on to the steps. He lit another and threw it. Again the flame faltered and died. Joseph eased the car forward. The man threw another lit match at the house.

'What's he doing?' she whispered.

'Trying to burn his house down by the looks of things, the poor fucker.'

'Jesus, Joseph, what is this thing?'

The man throwing the matches removed his sweater and placed it delicately on the pavement. Crouching down, he struck another match and dropped it on to the cloth. It kindled and smoked until small flames began to dance over its surface. He lifted the sweater and walked up the steps into the house.

'Oh my God,' said Miriam.

The man reappeared at the large bay windows at the front of the house. Through the glass they saw him hold his torch against the curtains and slide the large window upwards to let in air. The curtains became orange lines of moving light and the man disappeared.

He came out of the front door again, the sweater gone. He went down the steps, removed his shirt, set fire to it and threw it into the open doorway. After that he sat down on the pavement and crossed his legs. He was sitting next to the dead body he had brought out. He turned his head towards it, looked at it, and became still as the smoke billowed out of the window and he was lost beneath it.

III

Her mother's house was on a quiet street in north London. Joseph parked and Miriam ran up the garden path to the front door. Only the very last embers of light remained in the day. There was no answer at the door. She peered through the living-room window. The room was empty. She pressed her forehead against the glass, and scenarios of where her mother might be ran through her head unchecked and ferocious.

A faint noise came from the side of the house, like an animal mewing. Cautiously Miriam peered round the corner. The space between her house and next door was dark but there, sitting against the wall, in the murk, was the shape of a woman. Her legs were tucked up under her chin.

Miriam gestured for Joseph to come over. The woman sitting in the shadows was too large to be her mother. Her mother was tall and thin, this woman was dumpy.

'Are you all right?'

Miriam tried to make her voice sound confident. The woman did not answer. She did not even acknowledge that she had heard Miriam. Instead she just sat there, making the strange mewing sound again.

'What's there?'

Joseph was behind her.

'It's a woman. I think it's my mother's neighbour.'

Miriam took a step towards her. Joseph grabbed her arm.

'She might be violent,' he whispered.

'I know her.'

'She's fucked. Leave her.'

Anger swelled up inside her fast and hard. She spun

round and pushed Joseph back to the front of the house. 'What's the matter with you? How can you be so heartless?'

Joseph's face changed. His cheeks reddened and his mouth hinged open.

'That woman helped bring me up. You're not in charge of me, Joseph.' She felt herself shaking. 'You're Henry's brother, not mine.' As she spoke she felt a deep and slimy tension ooze out of her in slicks. It had been welling behind an invisible wall for days, for years.

'So that's what you think?' His face was hurt and confused. 'That I'm trying to, what, *own* you?'

Miriam wanted to stop but couldn't.

'Look at you. Why do you think Henry didn't want to bother with you? You're bitter and angry and you only care about yourself.'

Her fists were clenched. She could feel her voice wavering.

The two of them looked at one another for a long time. Slowly the redness drained from Joseph's face. His eyes deadened and his expression became impassive again. He opened his mouth, thought about what he was going to say, and continued: 'I've always resented you,' he said calmly and conclusively. 'I don't know why I bothered trying to help.'

He turned and walked away across the lawn of the front garden. Miriam watched, determined not to call after him. She watched as Joseph climbed into his car and drove away. Chemicals in her blood made her feel faint.

'It's all falling apart,' said a slow voice.

Miriam spun round. Her foot slipped on the raised edge of the path and she stumbled on to the front lawn.

The woman who had been sitting against the side of the house was now standing at the corner, half in shadow, half in light, her arms limp at either side, her shoulders hunched over like an ape's, her small, chubby fingers extended to the ground.

'Dorothy,' said Miriam. 'You scared me.'

The woman was nearing eighty. She was not wearing any makeup and her round face, which had always been so happy, was haggard. Her jowls drooped either side of her double chin.

'How are you?' She felt pathetic. It sounded so banal.

Dorothy considered the question. 'I'm going to die soon.' Her voice didn't sound her own. It was her voice, but not. It was slower and deeper, more thoughtful. Every syllable was clear and measured.

'You're not going to die.'

'Yes I am.' She was wearing the same apron she had worn when Miriam was a child. 'I know it's going to happen. I don't mind. I don't care. I don't have anything in my life worth living for anyway.'

'You're not going to die,' she said again.

'Yes I am, Miri.'

'They'll find a cure.'

Dorothy shook her head slowly. 'There's no cure for this.' She touched her chest, indicating her heart. 'You don't know what I'm talking about. You can't possibly know.'

Miriam looked at her and powerful forces of sympathy and affection collided inside her. The old woman's face was vacant as it stared wide-eyed at something invisible in the middle distance.

'I never really did anything with my life,' she said.

'Dorothy, please.' Miriam put an arm around her.

'I always said I would. Not to anybody else, but to myself. I promised I would fall in love and get married one day.'

'But you did get married.'

'I didn't love him. We both just settled for each other. I had to marry him because he was my last chance. It's funny, isn't it? The things people do so they are not alone.'

There was a low garden wall behind them. Miriam took Dorothy to it and they sat down.

'You have not wasted your life. Don't you know how much everyone loves you?' She looked at Dorothy's face in profile. Her left eye was milky with a cataract and Miriam felt an enormous pang of sorrow.

'I used to get so worried when I was lying in bed just thinking about it, but it's gone now. It's strange but I feel like all my wishes have just vanished. But I don't feel sad. It's odd but now they're not there, I don't feel as bad as I used to. You'd think it would be the other way round, wouldn't you? But it's not. My wishes were making me sad. I understand that now. They were never going to come true and yet I clung to them like they were precious diamonds when really they were nothing but blocks of dust stuck together, weighing me down.'

Miriam felt Dorothy's warmth next to her. The old woman was sad, but not in the same way as Henry. Whatever this was, it was different for everyone. She imagined a great monster in a deep, dark cave somewhere, collecting trophies of humanity and storing them greedily in its nest.

'I know what death is going to be like,' said the old woman. 'It's going to be like I'm looking through a large circle that will get smaller and smaller and then it will be gone. I'll fall back inside my mind and then I'll die.'

Dorothy fell quiet and all Miriam could do was stay by her side. They sat there in silence. The night came in and the distant sounds of sirens never stopped. And then Miriam let go of Dorothy. She was on her feet and sprinting across the lawn. Tears flooded from her eyes uncontrollably. Her throat was heavy with moisture.

'Mum,' she cried.

Her mother saw her only daughter coming towards her and opened her arms. Miriam pressed her mouth against her mother's shoulder and cried.

'Shush, shush, shush,' her mother said. She stroked Miriam's hair.

The scent of her mother's perfume wafted into her nostrils and its old familiarity made her cry harder. 'Mum,' she said again. Just saying the word made her feel safer. 'I'm so scared,' she whispered. 'I don't know what to do.'

|||

'I should never have left them.'

Steam rose in a swirl from her cup of coffee. Her hands were cupped round the ceramic, the warmth sinking into them. The house was quiet with Dorothy asleep in the bedroom upstairs. They were sitting at the small table beneath the only window.

'You did the right thing.' Her mother smiled at her. She

looked smaller and frailer every time Miriam saw her.

'I wasn't thinking straight. I just . . . Joseph said . . .'

She stopped and looked down at her cup. It wasn't Joseph's fault. She had gone along with it. She had left them. Guilt leaked into her chest. She pictured Edward after she had broken the news to him about Henry and how his body had slowed down. An image of him walking through a park at night in pitch blackness came into her head. Phantoms surrounded him, crossing behind him as silvery streaks of light. And there was nobody to protect him.

'I've got to get them back.'

Her mother said nothing.

'Do you think it's safe?'

'It's safe.' The old woman reached across the table and clasped her fingers over Miriam's hand. 'Feeling guilty won't do anybody any good.'

Miriam felt so hollow. She rose from her seat and went to the kitchen cabinets. 'Have you got any aspirin?'

Her mother didn't reply immediately, and then her voice came, soft and gentle.

'Henry wouldn't want you to be afraid.'

Miriam paused, her hand stopped on the round, wooden handle of one of the cabinets and the latticework that kept her body rigid sagged and slumped. She closed her eyes.

'He just . . . died.'

'He's not really dead, Miri,' she heard her mother say behind her.

Miriam tucked her top lip into the bottom one and swallowed. She did believe that, she really did, but as her mind showed her once again the image of Henry lying dead in the darkness of the pre-dawn there remained a gaping and unexplained hole.

Her mother had moved towards her. Miriam felt her presence at her shoulder. She turned.

'Come here,' her mother said, and took her into her arms. 'It's OK.'

Miriam cried again, more deeply this time. 'It all happened so fast,' she sobbed. 'There was no warning. I didn't know.' The tips of her mother's fingers pressed into her back. 'It's not fair,' whispered Miriam. 'It's not fair.'

III

Henry's father replaced the telephone receiver and took a deep breath. He was unsure whether he should take his grandchildren into such a dangerous situation. He did not want to be complicit in anything that could lead them into harm. And yet they were not his children. The choice was made. They would go to London.

'Granddad.' Mary was holding her second finger up to him and turning it back and forth. 'My finger hurts.'

He looked at his granddaughter. There was so much life in her. It was bursting out of every pore.

'Let me have a look,' he said.

Mary climbed on to his lap and brought her finger right up to his eyes. He had to lean his head back to see the injury clearly.

'There's nothing wrong with it.'

Mary pouted. 'But it hurts.'

He took the finger between his own. 'Perhaps I should bite it off,' he said.

Mary's eyes widened and she smiled. 'No!' She laughed.

He opened his mouth and pulled the finger towards it. She squealed with delight as he made a chomping sound and pretended to devour the offending appendage.

Edward lumbered into the room. Henry's father saw him from the corner of his eye and stopped playing with Mary. His grandson's dishevelled hair fell almost to his eyes and he collapsed on to the sofa. He lay there for a moment, his eyes vacant.

The old man's body stiffened.

'Edward?' he said, nervously.

The boy turned his body over to face away. Mary jumped down from her grandfather's lap and skipped across to her brother. She clutched his shirt with both hands and gently shook him.

'Edward?' she sang cheerily.

The old man forced himself to rise. The fear mushroomed

inside him, creeping along his veins from his centre in great sweeps. He knelt on the carpet, his muscles tightening with the effort.

'Edward, what's the matter?'

Edward did not respond. Instead he wriggled further into the sofa as if trying to disappear inside it.

'Edward.'

This time his voice was stern and loud.

The boy jolted and he fell on to his back. There was a look of shock on his face. An emotion. He had never heard his grandfather's voice so terse.

'What?' he said.

The light in his eyes was still there. He was still alive. Henry's father said, 'Oh,' and grabbed Edward and hugged him. 'Oh, my boy,' he whispered. He thought he might squeeze the life out of him. 'You mustn't behave like that.'

'Like what?'

'Like –' he thought about what he was about to say – 'like you're sad.'

The boy's face was confused. 'But I am sad.'

'I know you are.' He thought for a moment. 'OK, we're going to invent a code.'

The children's ears pricked up.

The old man swallowed, his heart still beating fast.

'If I say, "Robin Red Breast One" – that's you, Edward – or "Robin Red Breast Two" – that's you, Mary – and then, erm, I say, "Robin Red Breast One, where are you?" you have to say, "In the clouds. Everything is sun."' He paused. 'OK?'

'What's the code for?' Mary asked.

'It's just a code. A secret code to let me know that you're all right. Shall we try it?'

The children nodded.

'All right.' He looked at Edward. 'Robin Red Breast One, where are you?'

Edward sat up and his eyes centred on his grandfather. His feet didn't reach the carpet. Mary watched in silence.

'In the clouds,' the boy said, seriously and slowly, in concentration. 'Everything is sun.'

|||

That night a smoke fell on London. Miriam watched it from the living-room window. It was heavier and more still than the fog of last night. It was threatening.

She checked on Dorothy. Her sleeping mass lay huddled beneath the blankets. Miriam waited to watch her chest rise so she knew she was still alive, and closed the door behind her. For a moment she considered calling Joseph but it was late. She went to her bedroom and removed her running shoes. The cool air on her feet felt good. She climbed into the bed and lay on her side.

There was a large mirror mounted on the wall that glimmered orange from the street lamp outside the window. Somebody had once told her that mirrors were tunnels through space, like wormholes, and if you knew how, you could climb through them and come out through another mirror somewhere else in the world altogether. She had always liked that idea. She looked at the mirror on the wall and wished she could climb through and come out from the one hanging above the fireplace in the living room of the house in Cornwall. Then she could see her kids again. The guilt of having left them grew with every passing minute.

They would be reunited soon enough, though. Henry's father would bring them to the house by tomorrow evening. Less than twenty-four hours, she thought, less than twenty-four hours. One thing she knew for certain now was that she would never, ever leave them like this again.

|||

Edward woke to the sound of crying. There was a faint line of moonlight marking the wall opposite the window. He could feel his sister writhing next to him. She was in the middle of a nightmare. He jolted her awake. His eyes were becoming accustomed to the gloom. He could see his sister's eyes open, blinking awake.

'What?' she said sleepily.

'I think you were having a nightmare.'

His sister took a few moments to order her thoughts. Her eyes flicked around the room. She paused for a moment and rolled over.

'Were you dreaming about Dad?'

She was too tired to answer and was already falling back to sleep. Edward looked at the back of her head. He was beginning to realize that he was the man who would have to look after her now. He was four years older than his sister. He had received four more years of Dad than she had.

'Are you awake?' he whispered into her ear.

A damp patch of sweaty hair had fallen across her face. Delicately, Edward lifted it from her skin and placed it behind her ear.

'I promise I won't let anything happen to you,' he whispered to her, and also to himself, because when he made the promise a new resolve stiffened in him that ensured that what he had just said was the truth.

III

Miriam's mother had been volunteering at the hospital. The children wouldn't get to London until the evening and Miriam didn't want to stay in the house on her own. They walked the half-mile to the hospital.

The main building was old and made of small, red bricks. A wide clock tower in the centre of its front wall loomed above the trees. They reached the main drag and the hospital looked as if a giant spider had spun a thick web over it. White nets had been erected over some sections of the front wall, tethered to the building by long, thick ropes attached to a framework of scaffolding. A large white tent stood in front of the main entrance just beneath the clock tower, and smaller tents were dotted around the grounds.

To her right there stood a large pagoda-type structure. It had no walls, just a pointed roof covered with shiny, white tarpaulin, held up by thick steel frames. It was circular, maybe fifty yards in diameter. Two men were standing at one of the giant poles, looking up towards the hospital. They were dressed in army fatigues. They both wore gas masks. It was the first time Miriam had seen soldiers out in public since the spread of the illness began.

They had watched the television that morning for news of the fire that had caused the smoke they had seen the previous night but there were no reports. Internationally, many countries were in even more desperate times than Great Britain. In Japan, it was reported, an incident had occurred in a nuclear power plant but details were still hazy. Miriam had absorbed the news calmly. Just another thing to go wrong. In America ten per cent of Congress were dead, they said. There was still no connection with Russia and an envoy from the United Nations was flying into Moscow. The news circled around Miriam but she paid it little attention.

The only way to deal with the situation was to live each day as it happened, just ensuring survival, praying that the illness would not come for any more members of her family. She would help all she could but she would not be able to help everybody. This fact had revealed itself in the early hours of the morning when Dorothy's dead body had been taken away.

As they approached the building, Miriam was told to put on the white mask her mother had given her.

'I thought you said it wasn't contagious,' she said.

'People are happier to be around you if you have it on.'

There was a yellow circular vent on the front of the mask. It was the same type that Miriam had seen the paramedics wearing when they had come to collect Henry. That seemed like more than just a few days ago. Time was slowing down. Every moment was a struggle. There were eight hours before Henry's father would be able to bring the children to her and those hours would concertina out into interminable units of for ever.

|||

The smell was the first thing she noticed: strong and chemical, more pungent than the usual disinfectant used in hospitals. Her face felt warm. The mask made her breathing claustrophobic, as if she was in an incubation chamber.

The main reception area was filled with people. Doctors in white coats rushed between them. Nurses carried boxes. Cleaners tried to manoeuvre through the crowds with their equipment. Some of the staff wore white suits with hoods over their uniforms. Most did not.

'This way,' said Miriam's mother.

A dark, narrow corridor led off reception with a handwritten sign taped above its entrance: 'Volunteers this way'. They came to a wooden door. Miriam's mother knocked once and entered. The room was quiet.

'I don't think many people are volunteering at the moment,' her mother said. 'They have enough to worry about already, I'd imagine.'

Miriam looked around her. There was not a single person in the room. Her mother completed a form on the desk and gave Miriam a volunteer badge to pin to her clothes. They went back into reception.

The hospital seemed to have no order.

'I thought they would have things under control.'

'Lots of the nurses aren't able to come to work if their families are sick.'

'But the Prime Minister said we should keep working.'

'Are you going to work tomorrow?'

Miriam didn't need to answer. The idea of serving tea, cake and coffee in the café as if nothing was wrong was ridiculous.

'Come on, we'll go where I was yesterday.'

The ward was split into separate rooms. She had half expected to see mosquito-net defences and people walking around in space-suits but that was not the case. The ward receptionist, a young Japanese girl, called over from behind her desk.

'They've switched things around,' she said, recognizing Miriam's mother. 'They've had a breakthrough.'

Miriam's heart skipped. She felt her breathing quicken in her mask.

'We had people come in last night.' She spoke conspiratorially, in a strong Japanese accent. 'I don't know who they were. They talked to the families and moved some patients out and some patients in. They think they know what makes them violent.'

She paused dramatically, waiting for a reaction.

'What is it?'

The receptionist shrugged. 'They don't tell me. But they say this ward is safe.'

Miriam looked into the rooms again, at the patients lying still in their beds. Her heart was thumping. She sensed something in her, a stirring of hope. It had been gone only days but its absence, now that it had returned, became suddenly obvious.

'Didn't they give you some idea of what it might have been?'

'Not to me, I'm just a secretary. But it's good news, no?' She smiled expectantly.

Miriam's mother nodded quickly.

They took some white tunics and put them on. A nurse appeared from one of the wards. She looked up and down the central corridor and when she saw Miriam and her mother her eyes drifted down to the volunteer badges they were wearing.

'We've got a woman in here that needs changing,' she said. 'Will you be able to deal with it?'

'Of course.'

'Bed six.'

And the nurse walked quickly into another dorm.

'Changing?' Miriam asked.

Miriam's mother opened the door to the store cupboard opposite, reached confidently up to a shelf and handed Miriam some paper underwear. She then took out two pairs of plastic gloves, some plastic bags, two pairs of perspex goggles and some toilet paper.

Bed six was in the far corner, underneath a large window. A woman of Miriam's age lay facing them, in the foetal position. A man, probably her husband, was sitting in the armchair at her side. When he saw Miriam and her mother approach he looked away.

'Hello,' said Miriam's mother, cheerily.

Her voice sounded strange, filtered through the mask.

The man smiled, embarrassed. 'I'm sorry about this,' he said. 'I just don't think I can . . .'

Miriam's mother shook her head. 'It's fine. Don't worry.'

Miriam drew the curtain around the bed. She looked at the man in the armchair.

'If you don't want to stay, you can go and get some fresh air.'

'Thank you.'

He stood up and left.

With the curtain drawn the smell of faeces was cloying. Her mother drew back the sheets.

'All right, dear, can you roll over for me?'

The woman did not move.

Miriam's mother took her arm and pulled her on to her back. There was no resistance. Miriam straightened her legs. Patches of brown stained the sheets. Her mother lifted the woman's nightdress and Miriam winced. Stains ran down the inside of both thighs.

'Are you OK, Miri?'

Miriam glanced at the woman's face. She had turned away, looking out of the window. Her neck was long and slender and she was attractive. The humiliation of what she had done did not seem to register.

'I forgot the water,' her mother said. 'Can you go and get it from the store cupboard? It's in spray flasks, like you have for watering plants.'

Miriam went out into the corridor and opened the first door on her left. But it was not the store cupboard. It was a small, rectangular room with a window in the far wall. The blinds had been pulled down and it was gloomy and silent. A dozen blank faces turned in unison towards her. The people were sitting on benches that lined each wall. They said nothing. Their skin looked white in the low light, peering out of the darkness. As she went to close the door a young woman put her hand into the air, as if Miriam was a school teacher and they were in a classroom.

'Yes?' she said, feeling foolish.

'I don't believe in ghosts any more.'

Miriam hurriedly pulled the door shut, and then she heard the voice again, whispering out between the crack of the door and its frame. 'There is no such thing as hope.'

The words made Miriam stop. The door handle was in her hand and something compelled her to go back into the room. She went to turn when another voice spoke to her.

'Are they all right?'

It was a nurse. Miriam smiled and closed the door. 'What are they doing in there?'

The nurse shrugged. 'Their families have gone and we needed the beds. They're all in their third day. It won't be long.'

'So they're just being left?'

The nurse stopped. 'What else can we do? We can check on them, but that's all.'

Miriam waited for the nurse to disappear and then turned back towards the door. She pushed it open slowly. Again the dozen faces turned towards her. They looked like robots. There was nothing left in them. They were proxy, not there; deep down in the ancient sense that had been awakened by Henry's death, she knew the creatures she was looking at were no longer human beings at all.

III

When the doctors came to the ward they wheeled before them a drugs trolley. The taller man had large, puffy bags under his eyes. He lifted the first box and placed it gently on the reception desk. From it he brought a tray of small vials, each filled with fluid. A nurse was working on another trolley. On top was one large box that contained hypodermic needles.

Miriam watched them in silence from the corner of the ward.

When the doctors had unloaded all the vials from the first box, one said to the nurse, 'How many do we need?'

'We have twelve staff, two volunteers, and you two.' She looked at the doctors.

'How many patients?' he asked, with a hint of reproach.

The nurse reddened. 'Fifty-two. Eighteen are in Day Three.'

The two doctors conferred.

'OK. All the staff and volunteers get one. Give one to each of the patients. But not the Day Three ones. It won't help them anyway.'

Miriam watched the medical staff go about their calculations. They worked smoothly, counting out the vials and needles. She turned to her mother.

'Mum,' she called. The old woman looked up from the bed. 'They've got something. In Reception.' She turned back to the doctors. 'It looks like medicine.'

There was a sudden burst of shouting from the corridor outside the ward, the sound of fast footsteps clicking on the hard floor. A group of men appeared at the reception desk. When the doctors saw them, they instinctively placed themselves between the men and the trolley of medicine.

The man at the front of the gang stepped threateningly forwards.

'Give them to us.'

He pointed at the vials. There must have been fifteen of them, maybe more. The doctor's voice was muffled by his mask.

'We can't. We need them.'

'So do we. Now give them here before we hurt you. I'm not going to ask again.'

The doctors took a step backwards.

'Please, there are procedures for this,' said the smaller doctor. 'The staff need them. Don't you see that?'

The leader raised his voice menacingly.

'If you don't give me that fucking stuff, I'll—'

One of the nurses took hold of the drugs trolley and wheeled it back into the room behind them.

'Stop,' the leader shouted. The room was becoming a shock of disturbed air. He went to side-step the doctors. The taller doctor moved to block him. The leader pushed him hard in the chest and rushed for the trolley. Miriam saw another member of the gang lifting the two cardboard boxes from the receptionist's desk. The men didn't look like thugs: their faces were fearful and confused but they did nothing to stop their leader. They wanted the medicine.

'Stop!' Miriam's mother ran up the corridor.

The crowd turned their heads towards her. The leader did not stop. He wrestled the drugs trolley from the nurse. Some of the vials rolled on to their sides and over the lip. They smashed on the floor, spilling their contents in viscous pools.

'What are you doing?' the shorter doctor yelled.

There was more shouting. The situation was on the brink of chaos. The balance of the room was swirling. A solitary security guard barged past the gang and into the ward.

'Get away from that trolley,' he shouted to the leader.

The man stopped. He seemed to be thinking about something.

'You can't just take them,' Miriam's mother said.

The leader looked at her for a moment, lowered his head as if in submission, and then lifted his shirt. From his belt he pulled a gun. Miriam screamed. The nurses, doctors and gang backed away, leaving the leader in his own large circle of space.

'I am taking them. You can't hoard them for yourselves. We all pay our taxes. They're as much ours as they are yours.'

The doctors raised their hands to the air.

'Please,' said the smaller one. 'Take them. But leave some for us.'

'If you had just given them to us we wouldn't have had to do this.'

The shorter doctor tilted his head. 'Please, leave the trolley. Take the boxes and needles, but leave the trolley. We have sick people here.'

'Yeah, leave the trolley, mate,' said one of the members of the gang, 'we've got enough here.'

The leader of the gang was holding his gun up but not pointing it in any one direction. There were several seconds of silence.

'All right,' he said at last. 'Let's go.'

The gang backed slowly out of the ward and when the doorway was clear the leader left with them. At the door he turned back into the ward, looked at the two doctors, at the trolley of medicine he had left behind, and walked away.

Miriam ran up the corridor to her mother. She was shaking with anger. How dare those men come in and take the medicine? The only way to survive was to hold strong together. Everybody. How could they not see that?

She hugged her mother. 'Don't do things like that,' she said.

'I had to say something.'

Her mother was trembling. Her body felt small in the embrace.

'We have to be careful,' said Miriam. As she spoke the words she knew that they were the same words used by Joseph, and which she had ignored.

She lifted one of the vials. The contents were milky.

'What is it?'

'Just antivirals,' said the doctor. He pulled his mask down off his face. It left a red imprint. 'These masks are pointless.' He lifted the elastic strap over his head and threw the mask on to the desk. 'They probably thought it was some miracle cure.' He shook his head, visibly shaken. He lifted up a vial, plunged a needle into it, unrolled his shirt sleeve and injected himself quickly. The speed of movement seemed reckless. 'These things aren't going to do anything anyway.' He threw the empty needle down on to the trolley and took a deep breath.

'Are you OK?' said the nurse.

He breathed in and out. 'I'm fine.'

'We'll be OK.'

He laughed. 'Will we?' He wiped some sweat from his forehead with the crook of his wrist. 'Miracle cure. We don't even know what it is. How can we cure something that doesn't even exist?'

The other doctor stepped towards the trolley. 'That's enough, John.' He looked at Miriam and her mother. 'We'd better give you your jabs. In case they come back.'

The doctor lifted a needle and vial from the trolley and Miriam rolled up the sleeve of her shirt.

'These are a new type of antiviral,' he said.

'Why did you move the patients around last night?' she said. 'How do you know what makes them violent?'

The taller doctor snorted. 'We moved out the pricks and kept the nice people,' he said. 'It's as simple as that.'

|||

Darkness fell as they left the hospital. Floodlights had been erected outside and bathed the main drag in front of the building in white light. The sound of rushing traffic filled their ears. The ever present sound of sirens wailed somewhere in the city. Everywhere now, a great tide was being fought, the defences stretching to breaking point.

Miriam checked her watch. The kids wouldn't be far away by now. She tried to call but there was no network again. She stared at the useless luminous screen of her phone. A yellow smiley face grinned back at her.

There was activity at the pagoda-like army marquee on the left. There had been only two soldiers there that morning but now they numbered fifty at least. They wore gas masks and held rifles casually at their sides. Six trucks were parked up on the lawn next to the marquee. The guy ropes holding it in place glowed silver in the light. An entrance awning had been erected and ropes had been slung around the perimeter. People dressed in normal clothes were being held inside its confines. The noise of many people speaking at once drifted across the lawn.

It was clear what was happening. They had been rounded up. The difference between those affected by the illness and those unaffected was obvious: those unaffected were talking and gesturing loudly at the troops. The ill ones were standing still and mostly looking at the grass around their feet.

There was a metallic sound as the back doors of one of the trucks opened. An army officer stood on top of a box, brought a megaphone to his lips and pulled his gas mask on to the top of his head.

'Bring them in.'

The troops stationed at the entrance awning beckoned to the people nearest them. They were reluctant to move. Some of them eased backwards.

'It's all right,' came the amplified voice. 'We are here to help you.' The voice was emotionless. It did little to placate the crowd. 'Two family members may travel with the sick to the new hospital. We are moving out of the city. You will be safe.'

Inside the marquee the first few rows of the crowd started to move tentatively towards the truck.

'There seem to be an awful lot of them,' said Miriam's mother. 'I thought it was only supposed to be a small number that became violent,' she said.

'They don't look very violent to me,' said Miriam.

The army did not look right set against the backdrop of a normal city. Their uniforms and their machines and their artillery were like rips in the blanket of society.

Miriam noticed that all the infected people were men. They watched for ten minutes until one man being passed into the truck stopped. His family, which consisted of two women, said something to one of the armed guards. The guard gestured and pointed to the side of the truck. The family moved to one side and the stream of people continued to flow. Soon the first truck was full. The doors were closed and bolted shut with ominous slams. The truck rumbled over the lawn and down the road.

A second vehicle was brought. The family who had refused to board were still waiting. An officer came over. He was not wearing the fatigues of his subordinates. The armed guard spoke to him and the officer looked at the family. He went over to them and started talking. He pointed at the second truck and shrugged. He looked at the ground and placed his hands on his hips. One of the women spoke to him. Her neck leaned forward and her palms were outstretched. She was trying to persuade him of something. The officer shook his head. He swung his arm around in a sweep behind him and brought it to a rest, pointing at the armed guards. The woman who had been speaking slumped her shoulders. The family remained where they were for a moment until the officer stepped towards them in a friendly manner and placed his arm around the infected man. He ushered him over to the truck and he climbed aboard. The two women were pointing angrily at the officer and he held his hands up: it's not my fault.

|||

The children had been quiet in the back seat for the last half-hour and in that time many things began to settle. Driving relaxed him, and the streets were clear. He was able to focus. A huge void had opened in his heart but he could see it clearly now. It was something he would have to find a way to accept, though he knew it was important to keep the void as it was, to give the wound space to breathe, to oxygenate it before any cauterization, so that it would never fully heal over.

He pulled into the side of a road and switched on the little overhead light to check the map. He was almost there. As he made a mental plan of the final few streets he saw a garage across the road. There were cars there, but no queues. Not like the other garages, which had been either crammed or closed. They must have just had a delivery. He checked the gauge, started the car and it bumped on its suspension springs as it climbed into the bright lights of the forecourt. The children stirred and looked out of the window.

He filled up the tank and as he did so he looked around him. The garage was silent. Apart from the man filling up at the next pump there was nobody in sight. They nodded to each other and smiled. Through the window a cashier leaned over his desk reading a magazine as if it was just another ordinary day.

With the petrol tank full, Henry's father took the children into the shop to pay. The light was so bright it made his eyes feel swollen. The shelves were half empty but he picked up some sweets and the last two loaves of bread. From an unseen speaker somewhere in the shop a saxophone and piano played a bland, inoffensive melody. He went to the checkout and the assistant seemed aggrieved to be pulled away from his reading. Reluctantly, he tapped some keys and the receipt roll chugged and the price appeared as green digits on the little black display panel above the till.

The wind touched the back of the old man's neck and he felt one of the children pull at the hem of his sweater. The cashier's face stared past Henry's father and fell blank, and then Henry's father felt afraid as he turned round. His whole body surged and jarred with chemical shock under the force of the bang. His eyes snapped shut and behind him he heard the cashier shout something, something like 'Please don't hurt us,' but his mind couldn't process the words. There was a smash somewhere in the shop. He grabbed the children and looked at the naked man who had stepped in through the doorway. Oh God, he thought. We were so close.

|||

They found their way along the busy road that led to the hospital and were soon passing down quiet residential streets. The sight of people sitting on the walls gazing balefully at the cracks in the pavement was becoming normal now.

Up ahead the silhouette of a woman cut a dark space in the amber light. She was holding what looked like a stick. She ambled slowly down the pavement.

Miriam and her mother moved closer together. As they neared her they saw that the object the woman was carrying was leaking something. The end was bulbous, with tendrils of material dangling from it. The leaking fluid pattered into the concrete. They passed the woman and only at the last minute did they understand that the object she was carrying was a human arm. The arm was naked and blood dripped from the shoulder blade, which was somehow still connected to the humerus bone, like a giant chicken wing.

She was small, with short, straggly blonde hair; perhaps only twenty years of age. She wasn't even a woman really; more like a girl. In the street lights they saw specks of blood on her face. She did not stop walking and she did not look their way. When she was behind them, her voice called out.

'I only found this,' she said.

Miriam and her mother stopped and turned. The girl held up the arm. She was speaking slowly, in the way that all the infected people at the hospital had spoken, how Dorothy had spoken, how Henry had spoken.

'I didn't take it.'

They smiled, turned back and started walking again.

'It belonged to my father. I don't have the Sadness. I'm not ill. Honestly.'

Miriam whispered to her mother. 'Shall we stop?'

'The kids will be home soon.'

She looked at her watch. 'We have time.'

'Are you sure you want to stop?'

Miriam thought about this. 'Yes.'

They turned. When they stepped towards the girl she took a step away from them. They took another step forward and then she sat down in the street, holding the arm in her lap.

'I'm not ill. I don't have it,' she said, as she stared vacantly into the road.

Miriam and her mother glanced at one another.

'How long have you felt like this?'

The girl's face fell blank. It was boyish and pale, her eyes two black holes. Her lips started to tremble and she brought a blood-smeared hand to her mouth. Tears fell from her eyes.

'I'm so scared,' the girl cried.

Miriam's mother sat down on the pavement next to her and placed a hand on her shoulder. The girl took shallow breaths before each sentence.

'I'm going to die.' Her hand clutched the wrist of the severed arm tightly.

Miriam had not seen this before. The girl was infected but she refused to accept it. She was still a human being. In the others the illness had swept everything away and left no sense of awareness.

'I'm only nineteen and this is it,' she said, staring down at her feet.

'Come on,' said Miriam's mother. She exchanged glances with her daughter. They had to do this. They couldn't just leave her. 'We'll take you home with us.'

|||

The girl's name was Dora. They had managed to get that much information from her before she refused to speak any more. They cleaned her face and arms and found an old T-shirt of Miriam's to put her in. They checked her clothes for a wallet or a purse or something that might tell them where she lived but she had nothing on her at all. Her pockets were empty.

They changed the sheets in Dorothy's bed and tried to persuade Dora to go to sleep but she refused. She wouldn't get into the bed so they took her downstairs to the living room at the front of the house. She sat in the old armchair in the corner behind the door and rested her arms in her lap.

'Let's just leave her there,' her mother said. 'We'll need the spare bed anyway.' She picked up her daughter's worry as if it was nothing. 'Just relax, Miri. They'll be here soon.'

Miriam tried calling Henry's father but the signal had dropped yet again. He was late.

|||

'Please,' said Henry's father. 'Just let us go.'

Outside, the bright neon lights that illuminated the petrol pumps made everything hyper-real.

'I am evil,' said the naked man. He stroked the barrel of his pistol and smiled. 'I am the very thing you never imagined you would see in this world. But here I am.'

A streak of blood that had spat cartoon-like from the cashier's head, like the juice from a squashed fruit, stained the naked man's chest.

'I always knew I would be like this in the end,' he said.

'Please just let us go.'

The man screamed to silence Henry's father. It rang around the forecourt.

'You don't understand. You can't see it.'

Henry's father thought he could see regret in the naked man's eyes, as if there was a second person inside the body, trying to get out. He just had to keep his attention.

There was a second man, an uninfected man, creeping along behind the row of shelves, out of sight of the naked man with the gun. He had told Henry's father not to give away his position by raising his finger to his lips, and shown him the baseball bat he had taken from the shelves.

'I feel like I'm . . .' The naked man trailed off, scrunched his eyes tight, shook his head violently as if trying to get the demons out, and then he held up his gun decisively and pointed it at Mary, and fired.

'No!'

Edward threw himself in front of his sister. There was a mass of movement. The man behind the shelves ran out from his position and clubbed the gunman on the back of the head. Edward and Mary fell to the ground as one. The gunman fired off another shot.

It pinged into the shelves behind the counter. Henry's father rushed across to the gunman and kicked the gun from his hand. It spun across the tiles and collided with the drinks stand.

'Edward,' said his grandfather, scooping him up, his body firing with panic. Edward's head fell limply back over his arm. 'Tell me where it hurts, Edward. Tell me where it hurts.'

The boy was sweating.

Mary was crying hysterically.

'Get him out of here,' called the man who had attacked the gunman. He was lying on top of the naked man, trying to pin him down. But the naked man was struggling. His body was pulsing with movement, his flesh slapping against the hard tiles. 'I don't know how much longer I can hold him for.'

The old man looked at the gun lying on the ground. He hoisted Edward up and hurried past the two men. Mary ran out after him.

'Thank you,' said Henry's father. 'Thank you so much.'

They ran out on to the garage forecourt.

'Mary, sit in the front seat, darling, there's a good girl.'

He opened the back door and laid Edward along the back seat. He unbuttoned his winter coat. A patch of blood was seeping through his sweatshirt at his side.

'Oh God.'

He laid the overcoat over Edward and ran round to the front of the car. The sound of Mary's crying rang in his ears. He got into the car and started the engine.

Mary was still on the forecourt. He lowered the electric window.

'Mary, honey, get in.'

The little girl was crying uncontrollably.

Another gunshot exploded from the garage shop. The naked man was running for the door, gun lifted towards the car. He fired. The glass door shattered but the bullet sang past them uninterrupted. Henry's father leaned across and pushed open the door.

'Mary, get in!'

At last she did as she was told. The naked man was in the open now. Henry's father pushed his foot against the pedal and swung the car towards the exit. The naked man ran out in front of him and raised the gun again. Henry's father ducked. The frame of the car above the windscreen thudded as the bullet slammed into it. He kept his foot on the accelerator. The bonnet struck the naked man across his hipbone and the car jolted. The man fell back into the path of the car. The tyres lifted up over his body. Henry's father changed gear and accelerated again. The car engine roared and they sped off.

The old man's hands clutched the wheel tightly. His heart thumped in his chest. How could this have happened? he thought. They were so close. He looked back at his grandson lying prostrate across the back seat.

'Hold on, Edward,' he begged. 'Just hold on.'

|||

A car horn sounded outside the house. Miriam's whole body lifted weightlessly with anticipation and she looked out of the window. She could see Henry's father waving to her from the car. She waved back, smiled and ran to the front door.

'It's them,' she shouted.

Miriam swung the heavy door open as if it was made of balsawood and stepped into the cold night air. Henry's father was already out of the car, standing directly beneath the street lamp.

'Quickly,' he called.

The fresh draught that had blown so easily through her faded. Something was wrong. She ran along the garden path and nearly fell down the steps near the gate.

'It's Edward,' said Henry's father.

The upper layer of her skin bristled. She could see him lying supine on the back seat of the car. The monster had come for him. She pushed past Henry's father and looked at her son. His eyes were closed and sweat glistened orange on his face. In the gap between the two front seats, Mary watched her brother with a confused expression. Miriam's eyes met Mary's and time slowed.

'What's happened?' she said.

Her voice sounded as if it was coming from somewhere outside her body.

'He's been shot,' said Henry's father.

Miriam stopped. Tiny white stars flickered to life across her field of vision and her head felt light.

'Come on. We need to go to the hospital. Get in the car,' said Henry's father.

'Wait.' Miriam looked at Edward lying beneath his warm winter coat, his hair slick with sweat. 'I don't understand.'

Her mother came out to join them. 'What's going on?' she said.

'Take Mary inside,' he said. 'And let's go.'

Miriam started to tremble.

'What's going on?' her mother asked again.

Miriam ran round to the other side of the car and opened the door. Edward was lying in deep shadow.

'Eddie?'

Mary crawled up from her seat and put her arms round Miriam's neck. Miriam hugged her tight and kissed her cheek. The little girl started crying instantly, as if Miriam was squeezing the tears out of her. She took Mary to her mother. She didn't want to let go and Miriam had to prise her clear. Her little arms stretched out to her.

'I want to come,' she cried.

Miriam pulled the door closed, confused, her mind swirling, and they rushed towards the hospital. She looked into the back seat and reached out her hand. Edward's skin was cold. His eyes were half open but he didn't respond to his mother.

'What happened?'

Henry's father gripped the steering wheel, his knuckles popping out of his hands like mountains as he threw constant glances at the mirror.

'I don't know,' he said. His voice was watery, indistinct. 'We were getting petrol at the garage round the corner.' He shook his head to clear his thoughts. 'A man just walked in and . . .' He looked at Miriam. His face betrayed his fear. 'He killed the boy working there, just shot him. And then . . . it just happened so fast, Miri.'

He swallowed.

She wished she could have said, 'It's OK, James, take your time,' but she couldn't. She couldn't speak.

'There was no warning. It was just so barbaric. He turned his gun on Mary and it went off, and then Edward was lying on the floor.'

They overtook a car and the engine roared.

'He jumped in the way of the bullet, Miri.' The old man's voice faltered.

Miriam placed the fingers of her right hand to her forehead and closed her eyes. She turned back to her son. His head shifted a little and his eyes flickered gently open.

'He did what?' she said.

'He saved Mary.'

'He—' She cut herself off, unable to speak. She looked at Edward again. 'Edward?'

The boy couldn't fully open his eyes. 'Mum?' he said, groggily.

'We're almost there,' she said. 'You're going to be fine.'

They arrived at the hospital. Henry's father pulled across the road and into the main sweep. Two army trucks blocked the entrance. A powerful white floodlight threw the trucks into vivid colour. Several other cars were queuing, trying to get into the hospital grounds. A few troops were gathered in front of the road block, waving the cars back. Miriam jumped out and ran up to the guards.

'What's going on?'

One of the guards removed his gas mask.

'Hospital's full. We're not admitting any more.'

'But my son's been shot.'

It didn't even register.

'I'm sorry, but there's nobody allow—'

'He's eleven years old, for God's sake.'

The guard's face changed. He looked at his colleague, an enormous man, much taller than both Miriam and the first soldier. He pulled off his mask.

'We're not supposed to let anybody in.'

'He's not ill,' she said, quickly. 'He's been shot. Please.' She felt warm tears trickle over the edge of her cheeks. 'We can save him. Please.'

The two soldiers looked at one another again and, after a few seconds of silence, nodded their assent to each other.

'OK, where is he?' said the big soldier.

'Over here,' she said, running back to the car.

She turned to the soldiers. They were both younger than her. Their faces did not look confident; they looked as lost and as scared as she was.

'Thank you,' she said.

The little soldier pulled open the back door as the other one leaned into the darkness and lifted Edward out easily. Quickly, he stumbled past the road block. The people in the other cars wound down their windows and shouted their disgust at the two guards. Miriam and her father-in-law followed them to a roofless army truck on the other side of the barriers.

Around the side of the main building they were met by a doctor and nurse, who bundled Edward on to a gurney and rolled him inside, into the bright white lights. In here there didn't seem to be any infected people. There were hundreds of people injured and bleeding. All of the chairs were occupied and many people were lying on the floor, others prostrate on beds that had been wheeled out into the corridors. Medical staff ran around frantically between patients. There was a kinetic energy in the room.

The doctor stopped the gurney in the centre of the waiting room.

'We'll have to work here,' he said.

He was tall and thin, with sure, confident movements. He cut Edward out of his clothes. There was blood everywhere. The nurse brought wipes and cleaned it away in professional silence.

'Will he be all right?' asked Henry's father.

The lights brought his face into sharp focus. The lines of age scored his cheeks.

'We'll see,' was all the doctor replied.

He leaned over Edward and concentrated fully on the task at hand. The bullet had entered Edward's body above the left hip. Whenever the doctor lifted the wadding from it a deep, purple ooze dribbled out of the wound. A chunk of flesh flapped free as the nurse tried to clean it.

Miriam stood back from the gurney. Everything was happening at terrifying speed. The doctor peered at the hole in Edward's side, his face inches from his belly. He placed his hands under the boy's back and his brow furrowed. He said something very quietly to the nurse that Miriam didn't catch. He looked at Edward's face and prised open his eyes between his thumb and forefinger, first the left eye, then the right. Returning to the wound he rolled Edward gently over and peered beneath his body. And then, dramatically, the doctor stood up straight.

'This is going to be OK,' he announced. 'It went straight through.'

Miriam's knees lost their rigidity and she grasped the metal bar on the gurney. The doctor's shoulders slumped, giving away his true exhaustion.

'You're a very lucky boy,' he said. He turned to the nurse. 'Stitch him up and he'll be fine. Give him some morphine. One mil'll be fine.'

He looked down and spotted the white volunteer badge on Miriam's chest. The tense bonds of his muscles relaxed.

'Oh,' he smiled, nodding to the badge, 'well done.'

And he walked away.

The noise of the hospital came back to them: the sound of quick talking, of machines whirring, of feet squeaking on the tiles.

'Is that it?' said Miriam.

They looked about them but they were just two islands in the stream of people that flowed by.

They took Edward back into the night and wheeled him to the car. The number of people trying to get into the hospital had grown to such an extent that the roads leading into the main drag from either side were blocked with traffic. Miriam looked out of the window for the guards who had let them in but all she saw were anonymous androids in gas masks.

As she did this Henry's father leaned into his grandson and took hold of his hand.

'Robin Red Breast Number One, where are you?'

The boy opened his eyes a fraction. He regarded his grandfather through tiny cracks.

'I'm in the clouds,' he whispered back.

His lips were dry but he managed to stretch them into the faintest of smiles. The buzz of the world washed all around them but for that moment it was just the two of them, boy and grandfather, held in a tiny space away from everything else.

'Everything is sun.'

III

It started to rain heavily the next day. The rubbish had not been collected and there was a faint odour of decay in the air. The illness had first appeared nearly a week ago. Nearly one week had passed since Henry had woken that morning and told his wife he wanted to leave London. The relative stability of the city was starting to unravel as it became clear that the onslaught being delivered by the illness was showing no signs of abating.

The government told its people that the number infected was still low but it did not seem that way. The bulletins did not come from the Prime Minister now: members of government organizations were delivering the messages. That morning the latest news was that members of the families of those infected should not go to work. If a large number of those infected had worked in the same building then you should remain at home. Quarantine was voluntary, they said. The government did not have the power to quarantine members of the public involuntarily, nor did they have the desire to enforce such measures, they said. Schools were closed. They still had no idea what was causing the illness. Miriam turned off the small television set in the kitchen.

It was six o'clock in the morning and it was still dark outside. Everybody else was in bed. Her own night's sleep had been fractured. Pangs of absolute terror were sated by pockets of gratitude that came to her – gratitude that Edward was still alive, that he was lucky, that they were all back together again.

The small kitchen window had been left open and the smell from outside had seeped into the house. She closed it and cold droplets of rain fell on to her hand.

She went to check on Dora, the girl they had brought home,

who had refused to move from her armchair downstairs. Miriam flicked the light switch and her eyes were drawn to the centre of the carpet. The television was on the floor, though really it was no longer a television set at all. Its screen and its large plastic backing shell were standing side by side. The innards had been dismantled and laid out in front of the screen.

Miriam looked at Dora. She was staring at the carpet. Two dots of light were in her dark eyes.

'What have you been doing?'

Miriam knelt in front of Dora's handiwork. A screwdriver the girl had found was lying at a perfect right angle to the television screen. The components had been arranged into neat piles: screws, washers, bolts, clips, wires flattened straight in all the differing colours. The old cathode ray tube was on the far right-hand side of the little piles. Miriam turned back to Dora.

'How did you do this?'

Dora did not look at Miriam when she answered: 'I wanted to take it apart.'

Her hair looked even more lank than it had last night.

'Are you ready to tell us where you live?'

'I had a vision last night, as I slept.' Her eyes did not flicker as she spoke.

'You had a dream?'

The girl blinked. 'I won't dream again. Not between now and the time I die; it won't let me dream. I had a vision. I was in some woods. It was night time and I was in my nightdress. The woods were lit by a strong moon. The trees were bare and I could see deep into the forest. There were others there, people like me. They were all dressed in their nightclothes as well. They moved between the trees aimlessly. They looked down at their feet and they were so sad.'

As she spoke tears formed in her eyes and cut wet lines down her face towards the edges of her lips. Miriam made no attempt to approach her. She did not want to break Dora's thread. The girl put her palms to her face and flattened the skin of her cheeks.

'I walked into the woods. The wind made my nightdress flutter against my thighs and my arms. I didn't try to approach any of the other people, and they did not try to approach me. We were separate but the same. Then I saw an old woman. She wore a black shawl thrown over her shoulders. In my vision she walked towards a man. The man brought his eyes up from the forest floor and looked into the old woman's face. As soon as he did it he disappeared from the woods. The woman had collected him. She changed direction and walked away from me but I followed. She found a little boy. He looked into her face and when he did he disappeared. The woman passed between the trees. As people looked at her face they vanished into nothing. And then the old woman turned my way. Her head was bowed and she stopped in front of me. My bare feet were standing on a bed of pine needles and their scent was strong in the air. The moonlight dimmed as she came close. She lifted up her head and I felt her gaze on me. She was pale and wrinkled and as I looked into her eyes I saw colours. Her eyes were black, but in the blackness were wriggling colours. And then I was gone. I had disappeared. The woods had been rushed away. I closed my eyes and when I opened them again I was standing on a rocky plain. There were three moons and the sky was vermilion. The wind blew dust over rocks. I could see the curve of the planet. And the people were there, the ones in the woods the woman had looked at. We had been transported to that rocky, forlorn place. Everyone like me had been taken.'

Dora stopped and brought her bottom lip into her mouth. It came back moist. She looked at Miriam.

'Take me with you, Miriam. Don't leave me.'

The girl looked at her and then Miriam could see him, Henry, in her eyes. Her eyes were exactly the same as his had been. They were the same. Dora was Henry, just as he was her.

The first light of dawn took the shadows back from the room.

'I won't leave you,' she said.

A blazing, spinning ball of memory and emotion combined and turned in her body. She hadn't known. Her skin became hot and she felt like her body was turning to dust. For the three days that Henry was ill she hadn't known what would happen to him. She had not been able to grieve in the same way as everybody else. She looked up at Dora again, but the girl had turned her face away and was gazing out of the window at the new day.

'I need . . .' said Miriam, and then couldn't say any more. She stood and left Dora in her chair.

The room in which the children slept was dark. They were both asleep. Edward had stopped sweating and was breathing softly. Miriam sat on the edge of the bed, put her hands together and thanked God for saving her son.

As she did it she remembered a party she had been to, just weeks before. It was the first time in a long time that she had been asked about it, but the discomfort she felt when answering was still the same as it had always been. She told them the same thing as she always did, that she didn't know why she believed, but that was never enough for people. They always wanted more.

She went to the window and drew back the curtains. The back garden was as neatly kept as ever. The street light in the alley behind the garden shone on to the lawn but its circle of light was drawing in as the dawn rose. There was a pile of leaves in the corner that her mother had raked. Beyond the back garden fence was the parking area she had played on as a child. It didn't look much different, even now.

Behind her, a little voice yawned from the bed. Mary stretched her arms into the air and could barely open her eyes. Miriam went over to them. This was her family now: just the three of them. She picked a piece of fluff from the blankets and dropped it to the carpet. Edward and Mary looked at her through sleepy eyes.

'I'm sorry I came to London without you. I shouldn't have left you.'

Edward pushed his sheets forward and clambered over his sister towards his mother. He winced as his side stretched. He held out his arms and she took him to her. He rested his head on her shoulder and closed his eyes. Miriam took a bunch of hair from the back of his head between her fingers.

'I won't do it again. From now on, we stick together.'

'I want to go back to Granddad's,' Edward whispered.

'I know,' said Miriam, stroking his hair. 'So do I.'

|||

Stay inside, lock your doors, boil your water. Surely they must have better advice than that by now. She turned the car radio off. The streets were busier than she had seen them. The number of people stricken with the illness was visibly increasing. They had come out on to the streets to sit or lie down and wait for death.

'Why is everybody sitting down?' said Mary.

'They're very ill,' said Miriam.

'What's wrong with them?'

'I don't know.'

She tried to keep a steady mind. Just go to the house, get what you need and get out of there, she told herself. It was a simple plan.

They looped past Trafalgar Square and headed south. They had to queue at Battersea Bridge. To her right sprang six tall towers, stark and bare against the wintering sky. The clouds swirled overhead, spitting rain sideways across the windscreen. This was London as she now knew it – dangerous and massive. The river was swollen, its dark grey mass flooding past. It gushed underneath the bridge. There were no boats.

The crossing of the bridge was a return to an old life. It was the life she had to leave behind. South was where Henry had to remain. She had crossed this bridge hundreds of times but it had never appeared as it did now: small, narrow, decrepit. Flimsy legs plunged into the water, fastened to the bedrock by rusting, ancient bolts. It seemed so superficial.

They came to their street but it had changed. All the old things were still there: the large sycamores, the corner shop, the red post box. Those markers were in place, anchoring the memory of the old world. But some of the windows of the houses were smashed, there was litter blowing along the kerb, somebody had spray-painted a garden wall and there was a notable absence of cars. Miriam pulled into the side of the road right in front of her house and her heart sank.

The house was split into two separate living quarters. Downstairs and the basement were given over to one flat whilst Miriam's family lived on the upper two floors. There were two front doors: one at the left belonging to downstairs, one at the right that belonged to the family. Both were wide open.

III

The patch of carpet in the hallway was wet with rain. A few unopened letters had been blown along the hall to the stairs where they rested, some face down, some standing up against the base of the first step. The hallway was dark. Fear heightened her senses.

The door had been smashed in. Splinters of wood had snapped outwards where the lock had been beaten. There was a large, concave dent in the door. Miriam eased up the steps. She knew that the sixth one creaked and stepped over it.

She went into the flat. This was where Henry had hugged her and cried last week. She remembered his face again, and how it had been so like the faces she had seen in the dark room at the hospital – empty and inhuman. She brought the balls of her thumbs to her eyes and blinked the tears clear.

The place was empty. She passed from room to room. Every one had been ransacked. They had found and sacked her jewellery box. They had taken some of their electrical appliances and in the kitchen were unwashed plates and cutlery.

They had come into her house and taken their possessions. They had even eaten their food. She checked each room to make absolutely certain nobody was there. She tried to clear up some of the mess and went back to the car where she opened the doors and let the children out.

They were confused by the sight of the mess. Miriam packed clothes into two suitcases. The third she kept for personal effects. She took their wedding album and the family photo albums. She had always kept the journals she had written as a teenager and a young adult, before she had the children. There were various trinkets that held sentimental value – she saved as many of these as she could.

The children were told to pack a bag of their favourite things, which they did. Miriam remembered what an old friend who had once worked for a moving company had said to her. Often his job involved clearing the house of an elderly dead parent. He told her about how he had found the most wonderful things that the families never seemed to want. The life that had been lived was to be forgotten. Many times he would throw away boxes of black and white photographs, books filled with handwriting and old tickets, old musical instruments. She knew what he meant now. She was trying to collect the lifeblood of her old existence. The rest – the bones, the organs, the skin, the detail – would all be left behind.

|||

The traffic around Trafalgar Square was even busier by the time they re-crossed the river. Miriam stopped the car two hundred yards back. The top of Nelson's Column was just visible, and as she looked up at his black silhouette against the white sky her body began to tell her that something was wrong up ahead. She looked around. The cars were lined up behind her, ahead of her and to both sides. If something should go wrong they would be trapped. She breathed slowly and eased the car across to the outside lane. On the pavement next to them were several bodies.

'Don't look at them,' Miriam said, and checked again that the doors were locked.

The rain continued to beat down. She turned off her windscreen wipers, happy for the world outside to be blurred through the water. They were moving too slowly.

She turned on the radio. A man's voice. It sounded as if he was in a helicopter because there was a mechanical thumping in the background and his voice was grainy. He was shouting something about Red Square, about seeing dead bodies in the street, lying where they fell, all of them. She turned it off.

Her judgement was clouding. Her face was hot. She knew it wasn't just her that bad things were happening to but it didn't matter and she placed her forehead against the smooth skin of the steering wheel in a moment of self-pity. The traffic started to move again. Slowly they edged forward. There was tension in the air outside. She could sense it. She turned on the windscreen wipers again and lowered the windows a fraction so she could listen. The indistinct words of somebody preaching into a megaphone came through the rain.

There were other noises as well. Shouting.

An army truck came into view. It was parked up on the side of the road, to her left. People had gathered round it. Four soldiers had climbed on to its roof and were pointing their rifles at the crowd. The gas masks on their faces made them menacing.

The truck was swaying from side to side and as Miriam approached she heard a metallic banging. There were people inside trying to get out. And the crowd that had surrounded the truck were trying to free them. Miriam remembered seeing similar vehicles outside the hospital, loading people aboard. People whom the doctors thought— A corridor of common sense opened up in her mind. She turned to the children.

'Go into the bags and get some jumpers and put them over your heads.'

'Why? What's happening?' Edward leaned between the two front seats to get a better view out of the front window. He moved quickly, suddenly, like his old self.

'Get in the back seat and do as I say or I'll get *very* angry.'

'In a minute,' he said.

'Not in a minute,' Miriam snapped. She raised her voice in panic. 'Now.'

Reluctantly Edward obeyed. Mary handed him a sweater.

Everything happened quickly. The crowd at the rear of the truck stumbled back. Miriam saw the back doors swing open and a mass of people appear out of the darkness. The ones at the front were somehow not moving their limbs as they came forward; their bodies looked static, as if they were floating. Miriam gasped when she realized what she was looking at. They were already dead. Their bodies were thrown clear of the truck on to the crowd below, the people who had been trying to free them. After the dead bodies came the live. From the shadows. They were out. The rattle of gunfire consumed the soundscape. The soldiers on the roof fired indiscriminately into the crowd of people. They perched on one knee as they unloaded their clips. People fell to the ground. Screams cut across the air. The infected people streaked out between the cars.

The cars tried to pull away but there was nowhere to go. They collided with dull clangs. The crowd ran. The men and women who had been inside the truck leaped on whoever they could find. Miriam watched in horror as one sank his teeth into a woman's neck. The soldiers brought their guns round to the man and fired. Life fell out of his body instantly. The woman lay beneath his corpse, also dead. People were rushing towards Miriam. She closed her eyes and whispered, 'Please, let this be OK,' and revved the engine. She pulled up on to the wide pavement on the left. The car in front saw her and did the same. Miriam slammed on the brakes. The car in front jerked forward and Miriam followed in its wake. They passed alongside the army truck, between it and the front of a tall building, and one of the infected people from the truck – a woman – threw herself on to the bonnet of the car in front. A soldier saw her and fired, spraying his bullets in a wide arc up the pavement and along the car. The woman fell lifeless on to the bonnet and the bullets ripped into the roof of the vehicle. The head of the driver slumped to one side. The car stopped.

There was a slam to her left. A figure in the rain was punching the side window. Mary had hidden herself in the footwell and Edward had removed his sweater and was looking out at the attacker. On the third punch a fist appeared through the glass. Blood and rain ran over the knuckles. The fist was withdrawn and replaced by an eye. It peered inside at the occupants and then was gone. The hand came back in and searched for the lock. Miriam grabbed the heavy metal handbrake lock in the footwell and slammed it into the hand. It pulled back. The wrist to which it was attached was sliced by the jagged broken glass and blood streamed out of the wound. Still the hand searched. Miriam looked at the halted car in front and pushed the accelerator. She rear-ended it and shunted forwards. They moved slowly. A second hand grabbed at the glass and snapped it away furiously. The face reappeared.

'Hurry up and get away if you want to stay alive,' it said, as its hands clawed at the broken glass. The face came in close.

'I'm sorry,' said Miriam. Adrenalin burned through her. She took the blunt end of the handbrake lock and shoved it into the face, between the eyes. The hands fell away and their owner fell backwards. He came back, his face contorted out of shape in rage. The window was slick with blood.

They kept moving forward. More infected people had climbed up on to the roof of the army truck and were falling back to earth as the soldiers picked them off easily. Miriam forced the car past the truck and the road opened up before them.

The hands were clawing for the lock again. Edward was leaning over and struggling with the fingers, preventing them from opening the door.

'Hurry up, Mum,' he screamed.

Miriam pushed the car in front forwards another ten feet until there was enough room to pull back into the road. The car lurched with a violent swing as it dropped back down from the pavement to the road surface and Miriam accelerated away through a squeal of tyres. The hands that were trying to get in were drawn across the glass one final time and were gone.

Bodies were strewn along the road. Miriam manoeuvred the car between them as quickly as she could. She thought it might turn over. Some of the bodies reached up to her for help but she could not stop this time. In the rear-view mirror she could see the army truck, the soldiers still on the roof, still firing, this time off into Trafalgar Square itself. Screams merged with the gunfire. Her heart was thumping so fast she found it hard to breathe properly. The sounds receded as she sped away. The rain deepened and soon she could not see more than a few feet in front of her. That was all she could concentrate on – those few feet.

When they came to the house they ran up the steps and across the garden. The rain ran down her neck and along the line of her spine. Her fingers were shaking as she opened the door. The children ran ahead of her and she saw, in the dark hallway, the figure of a man looking at her. He stepped forwards and her heart started to beat with confusion. But it was not who she thought it was. It was Joseph. He had come back.

'We have to go,' she said.

In the kitchen she could see the portable television set glowing. Sitting in a chair in front of it was her old priest. She hadn't seen him in years. A trench of memory opened up beneath her and she knew now just how far away the old world was.

Joseph closed the kitchen door behind him and whispered, 'I know.'

III

'All I'm saying is we need to wait until the morning. It's just one night, Miri.'

Miriam shook her head. 'You don't understand.'

She couldn't explain properly what she had seen. He wasn't listening. The light of day was fading from the window and the corners of the bedroom were amassing a dark gloom.

'We can't drive in the dark, Miri. Surely you can see that. I need to get back to my flat and pick up my van. It's got all the stuff in it. It's too dangerous to go across town now. You've seen the news. You saw it for yourself.'

His eyes were red and he hadn't shaved. He looked tired, even more so than usual. He sat down next to her on the edge of the bed and they both stared at the carpet.

'The vicar from your mother's church is here,' he said, gently. 'Don't you want to have dinner with him? It might be the last chance you'll get for a while.'

'You should have seen them, Joseph. They just started firing. They didn't care.'

He put his hands together in his lap. 'Are you OK with staying for one night?'

Miriam nodded. She thought he might say something like, I told you so, but he didn't.

'We'll go to my place on the way tomorrow and get out of here, OK? It'll be fine.'

'OK.' She took a deep breath.

'Miri,' he started. 'I'm sorry for what I said.'

As she stared at the fibres in the carpet she felt a tiny shift in the air.

'I never resented you. Saying that just wasn't true.' He kneaded his knuckles with his fingertips awkwardly.

'You don't have to explain yourself, Joseph. I understand.'

'I do need to. You're a good person and I've just – I've never . . .'

'Joseph, please.' She looked at her brother-in-law. His face was flushed and he was embarrassed.

'Just let me finish. The way I've been with you, you know' – he still didn't look at her – 'since the start.'

She felt emotion rising in her own throat.

'I'm sorry. That's what I mean.' His head shifted slightly towards her. The air was thick. 'Since Henry died, I've just . . .' His voice shook under the weight.

With an old instinct she reached out her hand and touched his fingers.

'I had to come back. Not just for Dad, but for all of you. You know, I don't have anyone else now.'

She had never seen him this vulnerable. She patted his hands and then did something she never thought she would. She rested her head on his shoulder. His body seized for moment, then relaxed.

'Did you know that I always liked you?'

He didn't answer.

'I used to tell Henry I wanted you to show us around the university. You were all he used to talk about – the papers you used to write and the job you had. He was obsessed with you. But he always said you wouldn't be interested in showing us around, that you wouldn't want to be bothered.'

She surreptitiously wiped the tears out of her eyes. Joseph didn't say anything. It was almost dark outside now. They sat in silence as the beginning of night absorbed the ends of day.

'Will you tell me a story about Henry? From when you were kids?'

He thought for a moment. She thought she could hear his mind ticking.

'Did he ever tell you about the time when he won a tree-climbing competition but then couldn't get back down?'

Miriam half laughed and half cried when he said it. She could no longer hide the fact that she was nearly crying. She knew the story, Henry considered it one of the proudest moments of his life, but she shook her head anyway.

'Tell me it,' she said.

|||

'Miriam, how are you?'

He smiled a wide smile and opened his arms to her. He had changed little, impeccably groomed with his clothes well pressed and fitted, his hair thin at the crown. He still had an air of arrogance about him which she had always found more amusing than offensive. Out of courtesy she moved to him and he closed his arms around her. Father Moore's scent triggered a bloom of memory.

'I'm so sorry about Henry,' he whispered into her ear.

She looked over his shoulder at the television set, which showed a vision of Moscow, the Kremlin and the streets around it like a toy city. There were bodies lying in the roads and on the squares; hundreds of bodies, none moving. There were no cars, no cyclists, none of the little vibrations that brought a city to life. Everything was still.

The newscaster's voice was discordant and urgent.

'It is not known when the incident occurred, or how, or what the details are. The spread of the illness seems to stretch from far in the east of Russia all the way across the country as far west as the Ukraine.'

She noticed that everybody else was anchored intensely to the screen. She came out of the embrace.

'Fears are mounting now that Russia is not the only place to have suffered such a fate. Other areas that have lost contact are central China, the west of India and parts of Thailand. But with so many remote places on the planet, and international agencies already stretched to their limits, it is difficult to know where these pockets of death have struck.'

Henry's father stood up and turned off the television.

'We don't need to watch this,' he said. 'It will only frighten us.' He turned to his son. 'Come on, we'd better go.'

Miriam looked at Joseph. 'Where are you going?'

Joseph threw his coat across his back. 'Looking for food. We won't be long.'

'But it's dark outside.'

Henry's father joined his son at the kitchen door.

'Won't be long,' he said cheerily, and they left.

Miriam felt sick. The dense sensation in her gut that she had been feeling since Henry became ill began to petrify. She just wanted to get out of there, get to Cornwall, darkness or no. She felt trapped.

'I'll do those,' she said to her mother, indicating the peas on the kitchen table she had been shelling, trying to keep her voice even. 'You and Father Moore go into the living room.'

Her mother gave her a look that made Miriam feel like the scared child she had been after her father died. It was that same mixture of pity and knowing, a deep empathy that would flood through her and make her feel less alone.

'Dora's resting in the living room.'

'She can come in here with me.'

Miriam's mother smiled and when she did it set something off in Miriam's heart. It snagged on the inside of her throat; a jagged pocket of hopelessness.

||||

Miriam liked the surgical dissection of the pods; inserting the knife at the apex and splitting them delicately along their knaps took her mind away from her heart to her body. She worked deliberately slowly, stretching the process out for as long as possible.

Dora watched Miriam's hands work. The girl had been washed and Miriam's mother had given her some of her perfume, but her shoulders were still slumped, her eyes still vacant.

'Can't you remember where you live?'

Dora shook her head.

'Did you have any brothers or sisters?'

'I had a brother.'

'Wouldn't you like to see him again? If you tell us where you live we can take you home.'

Dora did not answer.

'Do you want something to drink?'

'No.'

'You should drink something.'

The girl turned her head to one side. Miriam could see the

bones in her long neck. The way she reminded her of Henry was eerie. It was like the souls of everybody who had been stricken by the illness had been lined up and when you saw them from a certain angle they merged into one thing.

'Have you always lived in London?'

Dora didn't answer.

'I've lived in London all my life,' said Miriam. 'Henry was from Cornwall but he acted more like somebody who had grown up in a city. You can always tell the difference with people who grew up outside cities, don't you think?'

Dora remained silent. Her hands rested on the table.

'He was my first real boyfriend. My first love.' She laughed at herself. 'It's funny, really, but I'm happy he was the only one. I know it's old-fashioned but if it feels right . . . that's what's important, isn't it?'

Dora didn't even look at her as she spoke.

'Do you have a boyfriend?'

The girl did not answer.

'How do you feel?'

'Slow,' she said.

Miriam stopped. 'Slow?'

'I feel as if everything has been finished inside me and there's nothing left to do. A week ago I remember being scared because my brother had caught it.' Her voice was extremely torpid now, as if the function in her brain that created speech was seizing up. 'I prayed he wouldn't die and then I was afraid it would come for me. But when it did come it wasn't what I thought.'

Miriam placed the knife on the table and dropped the peas she had been shelling into the pot.

'How did you know it had happened?'

Dora brought her hand slowly to her chest, placing her fist on her ribs in the exact same way as Henry had done.

'I felt it.' She looked at Miriam. 'In here, like a candle being blown out inside me.'

'Dora, can you tell me where you live?'

Two tears appeared like children's soap bubbles at her eyes.

'No. They were all killed.'

Miriam held her breath.

'It's funny how I had always wanted to do so much but I don't feel any of it any more. There is just a void where I used to keep my hopes. It's right there, in the middle of my heart, empty.' The tears broke. 'I'm just –' she looked at Miriam; her dark eyes were like planets drawing mass into them – 'all hollowed out.'

|||

Several candles were lit and as Father Moore recounted his own experiences of the illness, Miriam found her mind wandering to the girl in the next room. She knew Dora was there, just feet away from them on the other side of the wall, her life slowly ticking down against the counter. Tick, tick, tick. And as she slowly died, Miriam was eating dinner and drinking wine. An image of the girl came to her, of her walking through a summer garden. Down between the plants she glided, smaller and smaller, evanescent.

'There's no way of controlling it,' said Joseph. He dropped his spoon into his dessert bowl and finished off another glass of wine. 'There never was. If they don't know where it came from then they can't do anything about it. There are too many gates open now – airports, travel, trade routes. And what if birds are bringing it – how do you stop them? Maybe it's in the cats. Or the dogs. And now that the riots have started . . . it won't take long before everything falls apart.'

His voice was mildly slurred but not to the extent that the conviction in what he was saying was lost.

'I'm sure the army will get it under control,' said Father Moore. 'This "falling apart" that you talk about,' and he looked directly at Joseph, 'it can't happen in a society like ours.'

Miriam watched Joseph's face change. He wasn't accustomed to the priest's idiosyncrasies. Joseph stared at Father Moore as he dabbed his napkin delicately at the edges of his mouth.

'Do you want some more wine, Father?' Miriam said quickly.

She poured a glass. She had to close her left eye slightly to make sure it went in. She hadn't realized how drunk she was.

'I'll just go and check on the kids,' she said.

'You stay there.' Her mother stood up. 'I'll go. You relax.'

Miriam smiled, looked at the bottle of wine and agreed. She helped herself. As her mother passed her chair, Miriam leaned back.

'Don't forget to check on Dora.'

Her mother brushed Miriam's shoulder. Joseph's attention settled and he came back to his thoughts.

'The army can't control the riots. They're understaffed as it is. It said in the papers their troops are already down by twenty per cent. And it's going to get worse. There's no food, no medicine, and people are panicking. When people get desperate, well, that's when you'll really see what our "society" is.'

'And what is that?' said Father Moore.

'A thin veil we pull over ourselves to try and pretend we're something other than animals.'

His father leaned across the table and patted Joseph on the arm as he turned towards Father Moore.

'You'll have to forgive my son's verbosity. He's had a little too much to drink.'

Joseph shook his head. 'No, no. I'm fine. You'll see, when people really have their backs against the wall, when they're hungry and thirsty and there's nowhere else to turn, they'll turn on each other.'

Miriam smiled to herself.

Joseph looked at her through bleary eyes. 'You don't think so?'

'You know I don't. At some point people will rally round and things will get better, even if this Sadness, or whatever you want to call it, doesn't go away.'

'You're naive, that's all. Misinformed. There're precedents for it. We just can't imagine it because we've spent our lives wrapped up in our safe little cocoon. Look at all the great civilizations, right? The Mayans, the Romans, the Greeks. What happened to them? One thing they all have in common is that they never saw it coming. They thought their position was unassailable, that they could never go back to what they were in the olden days, but they always did. It's what happens. The world has a way of bringing things back. It doesn't matter how high you build, at the end of the day we're always going to be animals and we'll always have to obey the same rules of nature.'

'Everybody helped each other after the war,' said Henry's father. 'Things were tough back then.'

'That was different.'

His father smiled, humouring his son.

'It was.' Joseph took a large mouthful of wine. The low lighting cast black shadows across his face. 'Everybody had come out of a shared experience after the war and everybody knew who the bad guy was. Not this time though. People have already started hoarding food, including us. Look what happened to you,' he looked at Miriam, 'at the hospital, with the medicine. Those who don't manage to get any food will soon start taking it from people. Mark my words.'

'You're acting like it's the end of the world,' Father Moore said. A faint smirk crossed his face. Miriam knew that he was close to annoying Joseph. 'This thing won't last for ever. In a week's time it might be gone.'

'True. But if not, people won't help each other; that's all I'm saying. Look, we've become too separated. We'll do anything we can to avoid eye contact with a stranger, we buy all our things on the internet, we spend our weekends by ourselves or in small groups, shopping or finding quiet corners in restaurants. We've gone too far. Community is dead. We've spent so long getting away from other people that to be forced back together for the cause of some Greater Good won't work. We've done it to ourselves. The two things: our will to survive, and the death of community, will lead to very bad places.'

'I think you have too little faith in people, Joseph,' said Father Moore.

Joseph ran the palm of his hand along the stubble of his jaw line.

'You're bound to think that, though, aren't you? I mean, it's your job to think like that.'

'But I see kindness all around me. I don't have to search for it – it shows itself clearly. Look at this.'

He played his arm over the empty dishes in front of him.

'Yes, but Miri and her mum aren't exactly typical people, are they? I wish they were, I really do, but they're not.'

Miriam looked at Joseph. What he said made her chest lighten. She blinked to focus.

'You know your problem?' said Father Moore in a clear tone of reproach. 'It's not a great deduction, I know, but the truth is the truth, and you are too cynical.' The priest leaned back in his chair.

'You've spent too long thinking the world is a terrible place and it's only because you didn't get what you wanted from life. I've seen it a thousand times before. You're twisted up inside and it's skewed your perceptions.'

Joseph stared at the priest calmly. His face was ruddy and his eyes were two dark craters. Miriam sensed the delicate shift in atmosphere as Joseph placed his wine glass on the table with controlled calmness.

'OK,' he said. 'If the infection does just disappear and this is the extent of it, I concede that things will recover to what they were. What I'm talking about is what will happen if the disease carries on unchecked. And that's how it looks. It's not going to go away by some miracle.'

'Well, some might say that that is how it arrived,' said the priest, quickly.

Joseph went to say something but stopped. An unspoken message passed between them for a moment, like a flash, then it died back down again.

'You don't think it's going to disappear?' said Miriam.

'I think that assuming it's going to get worse before it gets better is prudent,' said Joseph. 'Don't you?'

'I don't know.'

Joseph took another swig of wine. 'You don't have to worry about it. I'll look after everything,' he said sarcastically. There was a down-swell of silence. 'Because I understand the full extent of what can happen, with people, so we won't get taken by surprise,' he said quietly.

Miriam's mother came back into the room.

'They're fine. They're asleep,' she said of the children, as she crossed the kitchen floor.

The soles of her shoes peeled away from the linoleum with faint sucking sounds. The room was hot and the wine was making Miriam feel drowsy.

'What about Dora?' she said.

'She's fine.'

Father Moore leaned forwards.

'Do you really have such little faith in people, Joseph? I mean, *really*?'

'Yes,' he said without hesitation, and with no further addition.

'You think we can become like animals? I don't mean through this illness, I mean hypothetically. Can a society as advanced as ours really fall that far back? That's what you're saying, but surely you can't mean it. You mentioned the Romans and the Mayans, but even you have to admit that our situation is simply not the same. We have better technology, have made medical advances, have more provisions . . .'

'People think our society is unbreakable but it isn't. Everything is being held together by the finest of strands but we refuse to believe it. We have this desperate will to fight against what we are but it's the animal part of us that makes everything so precarious, right? Things can get out of control very quickly if you're hungry. Civilization, even one as far advanced as our own, is like those weeds that grow on the surface of concrete. They look as if they've overrun whatever it is they're growing on, but pull at them gently and they come away easily, roots and all, as if they'd never been there.'

'Well I, for one, am not convinced. I like to think we're a little more civilized than that; that we *are* more than just animals.'

Joseph forced a smile. 'It's easy to say that. We're still rational at the moment. We don't know what it's like for our society to be anything other than it is. We have no reference point.'

'You seem to find this disaster all very exciting.' The atmosphere in the room deepened. 'You just want to see what happens because you think it might validate what you've always thought. That's all.'

Joseph regarded Father Moore with the detached intellectual gaze that Miriam had felt on her so many times in the past.

'So,' he said formally, 'has the Church been given any indication as to what the phenomenon might be?'

'Indication?' said the priest, guardedly. He squinted at Joseph through alcohol-hazed eyes. 'What do you mean?'

'I thought perhaps the government might have spoken to the Church about it.'

Father Moore laughed. 'The government doesn't speak to the Church about such things any longer. And even if they did,' he smiled to Miriam, 'they wouldn't come to me.'

'So what do *you* think it is?'

'I have no idea,' Father Moore snorted.

'Do you not have an opinion? I thought you said it was a miracle.'

Joseph's voice was becoming overly aggressive. The priest stopped smiling. His eyes flicked across uncertainly to Miriam.

'Well, whatever it is, it's beating the scientists.'

'You don't think the scientists will solve this?'

'What do you want me to say, Joseph?'

'I thought the Church would have an answer, that's all.' He leaned back in his seat and swirled the wine in his glass.

Father Moore made a decision. 'Would it be wrong if we did have an answer?'

'I don't know.'

'If you are not a man of faith then you must be a man of science. Or are you neither?'

Miriam watched Father Moore who, even though not as drunk as Joseph, was still heavily inebriated. The atmosphere in the room was distressed.

'So why would you be so against a non-scientific explanation, even if it's the most likely?' he said.

'And what explanation would that be?' coaxed Joseph.

'What do you want me to say to you, Joseph?'

'What you believe.'

'So that you can knock me down? Why should I give you the ammunition?'

'Because you believe it to be true.'

Father Moore sat up in his chair in a quick, sudden motion. 'Why should I not believe this thing to be divine?'

Miriam's attention spiked.

'Why should I turn my back on my beliefs? Especially now. I've given my life to my faith, Joseph. Do you think my dedication was insincere?'

'I think it was misguided.'

'And why are you so sure the illness can find its roots in science? Has science provided all the answers in the past? Hmm?'

Joseph lifted his hands in innocence. 'I was just asking what you thought it might be.'

Father Moore raised his voice for the first time. 'Forgive me for speaking frankly, but no you didn't. You want me to tell you that this is Judgement Day. Isn't that right?'

'Well isn't that what you think?'

'Son,' said his father. 'What's the matter with you?'

'Nothing.'

Joseph tapped his middle finger on the table nervously.

'You are so eager to believe in science that you forgot your basic principles,' said the priest. 'Evidence. How old is recorded science? A few hundred years? Maybe less. You think that what has been observed in the past few hundred years covers the entire cornucopia of the natural world? You can dig in the soil and look at the rocks and see back through time but it doesn't answer any questions about humanity. How can a layer of silt buried in the ocean bed tell us about what happened to our ancestors? Just because you've never known an illness like this, that cannot be explained, you assume it has never happened before. The earth is an ancient place, Joseph. Who knows what ill winds have blown across its surface in its past?'

'Hang on a second – so you think this is something that has happened before, a long time ago, is that what you're saying? Or are you saying it's something divine?'

'I don't know. Maybe both.' He stopped, thought about what he was about to say and continued confidently. 'But there are stories in the Bible that have no basis in science. How can you say for sure that they never happened?'

Joseph laughed. 'You think Moses parted the Red Sea?'

Father Moore took a moment to think about his answer. 'I do believe it, yes.'

Silence filled the room.

'Do you want to mock me now?'

'I don't want to mock you.' He regarded Father Moore coldly. 'But I do think you're wrong for believing it.'

'And I think you're wrong for not believing it.'

Joseph looked shocked. 'I'm sorry?'

'Am I not allowed to say that to you? But you are allowed to say it to me? I *do* believe you should have faith, and not only because I believe it, but because I want you to be saved. I won't do anything to change your mind, I would never dream of it, but I do believe in the redemptive power of faith. I'm a priest,' he said with a laugh. 'What do you expect me to say? There is something happening to the world, the likes of which our living memory has never known. Like the rivers of blood, or the Great Flood. Yes, I believe it is a biblical disaster. I do not believe it can be explained. I do not think it will be explained. These things happened during the ancient times and now they are happening again. If you have any evidence to the contrary I should dearly like to hear it.'

His words resonated around the table. Nobody said anything for a moment. Miriam wondered if everybody else was thinking the same as her. The hairs on her arms were standing on end.

It was Miriam's mother who finally cut the silence.

'What do you think it could be? The illness itself. What do you think it is doing to people?'

Father Moore put his hands on the edges of his dessert bowl and twisted it around slightly. 'I have no idea.'

'It's like people's hope has been blown out.'

They all turned towards Henry's father.

'Isn't that what it seems like?'

Miriam sniffed. Something changed on the surface of her skin. Thoughts and images ran through her head when he said that, like images on a strip of film spliced together. One image recurred: Henry in the rear-view mirror on the road to Cornwall. It flickered between scenes of the man on the bench wearing a T-shirt, the woman sitting on the motorway, those pallid faces in the hospital room, Dorothy sitting on the garden wall. The room was spinning.

All of a sudden she felt everyone's eyes on her.

'You OK, Miri?' said Joseph, across the table.

Miriam brought her wine glass to her lips. Her mouth was dry and the wine tasted good.

'I keep thinking of a river,' she whispered. She could hear how slurred her words sounded. 'I heard a man a few days ago saying that ancient rivers run through us, and it just stuck with me.' Her face felt warm but she wanted to say this. 'It runs through all of us and we dangle our feet in it.' She laughed. 'It's like a common bond between us. Like empathy.' She sensed the awkwardness in the people around the table and blushed. She looked at Henry's father. 'Like hope.'

'Of course, there's one other thing it might be,' Father Moore chirped, ignoring her.

Miriam cringed with embarrassment at what she had just said.

'And I'm sure I'm not the only person to have thought this, even if nobody says it,' Father Moore went on.

Joseph swung his head drunkenly towards the priest. 'And what's that?'

The priest looked at each of the people around the table, and when he looked at Miriam he smiled, but the smile was drunken and crooked.

'You said it before, Joseph. A retribution.' His lips curled up into an accidental snarl. The gap between his nose and his mouth fell into shadow.

Joseph lowered his shoulders, bringing his head down towards the table so that he was looking upwards into Father Moore's eyes.

'You,' he started, 'you're saying that my brother was being punished?'

The gravity of the sentence folded out like a giant bird unfurling its wings.

The priest stumbled. 'I didn't mean it like that.'

Joseph pointed aggressively. 'This illness has nothing to do with God, or your "Christian morals". You understand?'

But Father Moore was not prepared to concede. 'No.'

Joseph was losing control. His voice became tense and his body seized. There was something savage in the way he leaned forward, his forearm laid at right angles to his chest, his head and neck stretching over. His mind's machinations were clear on his face. Miriam hadn't seen until now how deeply Henry's death had affected him.

'Joseph,' said the priest, 'that's not what I meant.'

'That's what it sounded like to me,' Joseph slurred.

'That's enough, son.' His father sat up. 'You've had too much to drink.'

Joseph knocked back his glass. 'I'm just getting started,' he sneered.

Miriam's head swirled. 'I'd better go check on Dora,' she said, her voice thin and liquid.

'I've just checked on her,' she heard her mother's voice say.

Miriam couldn't look at them. 'Still.'

She stood and stumbled into the hallway. She didn't want to be a part of the cosy little dinner party any more. She didn't want to hear any more opinions.

She went into the dark living room and knelt at Dora's feet as she always did, as if Dora was a shrine to Henry and if she knelt before it her grief would fade away. The girl's eyes were open and staring. Her chest still rising was the only sign she was alive. Miriam looked up into her eyes. They were darker still in the amber glow of the night.

The words of Henry's father had affected her. She desperately didn't want to think of Henry living his last few days without the buoyancy of hope. She didn't want Dora to be missing it.

'How do you feel?'

Dora stared into Miriam, past her skin and flesh and into her centre. She could hear the girl's breathing.

'Are you holding on in there? Please try and hold on. I don't know if you can, but please try.'

Dora shook her head. 'No,' she said. 'I can't. It won't be long now.'

'You have to stay though. I promised I would take you with me.' The room spun with disturbed equilibrium and her body thrummed with the fusion of alcohol and emotion. 'We'll be going soon.'

|||

Screaming. Somewhere in the house. Miriam threw off her covers and ran to the door, through the darkness. She heaved it open and went into her children's room. Both were asleep. Downstairs. It was coming from downstairs. She rushed across the landing and felt her way along the banister. A dry panic crept up her body.

Flicking the light switch on in the living room, she closed her eyes from the brightness. The screaming hurt the high end of her audio. It pierced and frayed.

'Dora,' she said.

The girl was sitting on the back rest of the armchair. She had brought her knees up under her chin. Her face was turned to the side and her mouth was agape in scream.

'Dora, what's wrong?' she demanded.

The girl did not stop. She only paused to take air, which she gulped down furiously, her chest slumping down quickly and then rising slowly.

Miriam grabbed her wrists. They were damp with sweat.

'What is it?' she pleaded. 'What's happened?'

Still the girl screamed. Miriam pulled her arms apart and tried to hug her.

'Dora, you're scaring me,' she said.

The girl's pale face had turned red in exertion. The bones in her neck stuck out.

'They're dead,' she screamed.

'Who's dead?'

And then Dora started to cry. The screams died off and her body relaxed. She slunk down into the seat of the armchair and placed a fist to her lips.

'Oh God,' she cried. 'It came out of the night. From below them. And it lashed through them all. Oh God, oh no.'

'Dora, did you have another dream?'

The girl put her hands over her face and started to rub up and down against her cheeks.

'Dora, what's going on?'

She felt something behind her. A presence.

'What's happening? Why is she screaming?' said Joseph.

'She won't tell me.'

'She's going to wake up the whole street.'

Miriam ignored him. 'Dora, tell me what you dreamt.'

There was a secret inside this girl. Miriam knew it. She was still not dead and she said she had fallen ill four days ago and there had to be a reason. She was the pure thing that could not be taken by the monster. There was always something incorruptible somewhere. Dora held the light that would lead them all to safety.

The room started to rumble. Instinctively she looked at the ceiling, upwards.

'What's that?' she said.

Joseph went across to the window.

'It's a plane,' he said, holding the curtain in a bunch. 'It's low. Jesus.' He turned away. The roar crashed into the room, loud and painful. The windows shook as it passed over. 'What the hell are they doing?'

The roar faded and soon the dawn's silence had recovered the room. Dora sobbed heavily into her hands.

'Dora,' said Miriam, reaching up to the girl. As her hands touched her skin the girl jerked backwards.

'Leave her alone,' said Joseph.

Miriam felt her skin pimple. 'Jesus, Joseph.' She turned to face him. 'You just can't help yourself, can you? This girl has seen her whole family die and you still can't feel anything for her?'

'Everybody's seen their family die. That's what you seem unable to understand. Including you and me.' He paused. 'All you seem to care about is this girl you don't even know.'

'She's ill.'

'But you've got a family to care for.'

'That's none of your business.'

'I just don't see why—'

'Because she reminds me of Henry,' she screamed. Joseph froze. 'Because I want to look after her. Because,' she paused for breath, 'because when it came for Henry I didn't know what was happening.' She was almost crying now. 'I didn't get to live it,' she said, as a whisper. 'I didn't have the three days.'

Joseph's expression changed. His shoulders rounded from square. He understood. A common bond so bright and important cut through the murk. It was all that mattered. Nothing else carried the weight of shared loss which, in turn, grew in the relationship like a buttress. It entwined them and bound them together.

'It came,' said Dora, slowly. Miriam turned back to her quickly. 'It came and it took the colours from everyone, from all of them, from every one.'

|||

The old man woke at seven thirty. He had slept lightly and blinked in and out of sleep, but now it was time to leave his bed for another day in the new, hard world. He had taken a glass of water to bed and now brought it to his dry lips.

Before changing he went into his grandchildren's room and shook their little bodies awake. Together they exchanged their secret codes as they did each morning. He had never been overtly religious, but still, as he left the bedroom with the promise that they would get up, he put his hands together secretly and said thank you under his breath.

He showered and shaved. The razorblade made a crisp scratching sound against his hardened skin. The water was not warm enough really but he didn't want to waste the hot water in a house that did not belong to him. He returned to his bedroom and put on the same clothes he had worn the day before. Packing had never been his strong point.

He went downstairs and Miriam's mother made him a bowl of porridge. They switched on the small television set and watched the news. Overnight something had happened in the capital. He watched in silence, they all did, as they learned that the city had woken to find over two-thirds of its people stricken with the illness. The wave of it had washed up in a north-westerly sweep, cutting a swathe like a sword wound. They saw the map of London, the red shadow across it in a diagonal line. Those in that red area were dead, or would be within three days. Those were the rules now.

His son moved about quickly, rushing here and there, trying to use the telephone to no avail. The old man had always held out hope that Joseph would mellow as he got older, find a calm, but it had never come for him. The dog sat at his feet. He tore a piece from his granddaughter's toast and surreptitiously dropped it on to the floor.

His son needed to collect his van, he said. It was parked in the garage, beneath his apartment block, ready to go. The old man looked at the television screen. The red map of London appeared again. Joseph would have been dead, like Henry, were it not for the fact that he had come to this place to help.

Soon they would be leaving. They had to get to Cornwall. The time for delaying was spent. Joseph needed to get across town to the van first, to the food supplies that he had packed into it. They couldn't risk taking the kids there now. The old man looked again at the map of London that the television set showed over and over again. Little yellow banners with black capital letters ran along the bottom of the screen, each of them delivering more bad news about some unforeseen disaster in some far-off country. But it was the map of London he was looking at, and the red mark splashed across it in the shape of a fox's tail. Joseph's house was in the centre of it.

||||

'I'm not going with you,' she said, trying to keep her voice to a level the kids in the living room couldn't hear. They were standing in the gloomy light of the hallway.

'We have to get that van,' he said shortly. 'It has everything in it.'

'Jesus, Joseph, why didn't you bring it when we came here?'

'I thought we'd be able to pick it up on the way, didn't I?' he said. He scrunched his eyes closed and put the ball of his hand to his brow.

'Well, I can't go with you.'

'You have to.'

'I don't have to.' Her voice was gaining volume and she consciously made an effort to change pitch down again. 'I promised my kids I wouldn't leave them again.'

'Miri, listen to me.' He gripped the tops of her arms with his hands. 'We have to get that van. If we don't, we won't have anything to live off, OK? The shops are empty. There's no more food.'

She turned her head away from him.

'You have to do this, Miri. You're the only one who knows the way back if we get separated. We'll be in and out, quick as a flash. There won't be any trouble. All those people who are ill aren't dangerous. They were only infected a few hours ago. It takes at least a day before people turn violent, and that's if they turn at all. If we go now we'll be safe. If we wait any longer, we won't. We'll take your car, I'll get the van, and you can follow me back and we'll be away. We can get out of London and we'll be safe. We'll have food and we can sit this thing out, OK? We just need one final push.'

|||

Everything had changed outside. The level of control that had been in place, holding the seams of normality together, was gone. They could feel it in the air. Along the street several families were loading their cars in preparation for a coming exodus. Some were covering the windows of their houses with large wooden boards. London was evacuating itself.

Miriam, Joseph and his father climbed into Miriam's car, waved casually goodbye to the kids as if there was nothing to be worried about and pulled out into the street. They headed into the city but it didn't take long for the traffic to thicken.

It took them an hour to cover a mile. There was a steady increase in the number of cars abandoned at the side of the road. Army wagons had been parked up in lay-bys and soldiers watched the traffic, pretending they had some way of controlling the congestion.

Time passed slowly. Joseph refused to turn off the radio, insisting that the more they knew, the better. Violence had broken out again, they were told, although the reports were unclear as to whether it was being perpetrated by the victims of the illness or by rioters.

Infected people lined the pavements. Here it was now, made real, visible through her own eyes. They passed hundreds of them. They sat on the pavements, or against the walls of the houses and offices and shops, staring for the most part homogenously and blankly ahead at the train of traffic that crawled slowly past them. Some of them were lying down. Some of them were weeping gently into their hands. Others swayed back and forth as if trying to rock themselves to sleep.

'None of them try to kill themselves,' she said under her breath.

'Shit,' said Joseph, dragging her from her thoughts. 'Did you hear that?'

He switched off the radio. At first it was just the ticking over of the car engine, the sound of wind against the windows. But then there it was. A few stochastic blasts, sporadic, some in short bursts, others prolonged. When they went away the silence was intense.

'Is that gunfire?' said Henry's father.

Nobody spoke. Sometimes there would be nothing for a few minutes and it made Miriam believe it had gone. But then it would return, louder than before. Each time it came back she would feel the dense ball in her pulsate outwards. It was right at the bottom of her torso now, sitting on top of her hip bone, fusing into it. She could no longer tell if the density was separate from her, or a mere extension.

'What are we going to do?' she said.

'I don't know.'

There were buildings four or five storeys high to their left and right. It was like being funnelled along a vast concrete channel. Miriam envisaged a gang of violent infected people charging out from between the buildings.

'It sounds like it's getting closer,' said Henry's father.

Joseph kept his eyes on the road ahead.

From the back seat Miriam could see into the car behind. A man and his wife, about fifty years of age, as directionless as them, with the same quiet desperation on their faces.

'We'll get off at the next junction,' said Joseph in defeat. 'We'll have to think of a different way.'

His voice was flat. They all knew that everybody in the surrounding lines of traffic probably had the same idea and that, in truth, they were stuck. But there seemed little else they could do but hope and talk about a plan that might see them clear.

Every action was like an action for action's sake. Nobody really knew what they were doing or where they were going any more. There had been no government advice that morning because the area around Parliament was in the red zone.

'Something's happening,' said Joseph.

His father leaned towards the windscreen for a better view. 'Where?'

'Up there.'

The sound of more machine-gun fire clashed against the sky. This time it was much closer. Car horns rang out.

'Shit,' Joseph said under his breath. He unclipped his seatbelt and opened the door. 'Wait here. I'll just be a second.'

'Son, get back in the car.'

'It's OK, Dad,' he said. He ran over to the side of the road and climbed on to a green Electricity Board box. He looked for a moment into the direction they were travelling, and jumped down quickly. He ran back to the car, his head ducking down. Gunfire exploded around him and clattered into the car at his side. He jumped with shock and held his hands over his head as a shield. He reached them and pulled open the front and back doors. 'Come on. We're going.'

'What?' Miriam's heartbeat doubled.

Henry's father rose slowly from his seat. Joseph had to help him out of the car.

All of a sudden there was a new noise in the sky. The slapping of helicopter rotors.

'They're out of control,' said Joseph. 'Come on.'

Finally the gears of Miriam's brain clicked into place. She shuffled across the seat.

'What do you mean out of control? Are they ill? What?'

She clambered out of the door, keeping her head down. She looked down the road. There were people running towards her. Hundreds of people. They streamed between the lines of cars, coming up the carriageway like a wave.

The helicopter appeared from behind the buildings. The doors of the hold were open and Miriam could see two soldiers, one sitting at a gun station. Its massive frame drew round at right angles to the road and hovered lower. The downthrust caught some dust from the street and threw it into swirling vortices.

'Get away from this area. It is not safe. I repeat, it is not safe,' came an echoing voice. 'We are about to begin firing. We have to contain the area.'

Miriam's body felt light, her heart beating too hard, as if a piece of her being had come loose, unable to cope. She felt Joseph's hand around her arm. The helicopter was so low now that Miriam could see the bewilderment on the faces of the two soldiers.

They were looking at each other: are we really going to do this?

'We will begin firing in five seconds,' said the voice.

People were climbing out of their cars in panic and falling beneath the stampeding limbs of the crowds.

'Five.'

More machine-gun fire hammered out from the direction of the approaching crowds. And then the sound of massed screaming.

Joseph pulled her away. 'We need to get off the street,' he called loudly, above the roar of the helicopter.

Miriam looked at the tall buildings.

'We can hide in there,' he shouted.

They ran.

'Four.'

Henry's father led the way. He kept looking back to make sure his son and daughter-in-law were in tow.

'Three.'

'This is a fucking joke,' she heard Joseph say.

A boom shook the street and knocked them over. Rubble flew into the air. Something had exploded. Glass in the car windows cracked.

'Two,' came the voice through the debris.

'One.'

An enormous cacophony of sound tore the air to shreds. There was a high metallic end on top of the deep, throaty chugging of the gunfire. The sound attained its own substance in the particles of air that boomed through her skeleton. She could see hardly anything. Sound and dust was all there was. Screaming, firing, running.

Joseph and his father were two dark shapes in the smoke. She coughed and retched. Air was not air, it was sand. The first of the crowds collided with her and knocked her back to the concrete. She got to her feet and passed between the bodies, sideways, towards the buildings.

Another boom. Her ears rang and the ground was no longer beneath her. She reached for it but it was gone. She struck the concrete hard and rolled. Back to her feet. Running across unpopulated space, empty road. A whistle through the air, behind her, in front of her. Another explosion. This time further away. The ground shook. Her ears rang with a high-pitched shriek, like a banshee. There was blood in her mouth.

Concrete. Under her fingertips. Uneven. Pebbled. She felt her way along the building, searching for a corner, a way out. She blinked soot from her eyes, wiped them clean with her wrist.

'This can't be happening,' she whispered urgently.

'Miriam, go!'

It sounded like it came from underwater. The figures were pointing behind her. She looked. It was an alleyway. She could escape. The figures crouched behind a car.

She turned away and ran. There was gunfire everywhere, pinging into walls, into cars. It had no source. There was no explanation for it. Her eyesight refocused. She had reached the alley. She turned to look for Joseph and his father. They dashed from the cars towards the alleyway.

'James!'

Time slowed and the sky blazed white. She saw his eyes and went to reach for him but he was lifted into the sky by a tide of bullets that ran up his centre. She saw them as clouds of exploding cloth on his chest. He flew diagonally up and backwards and out of sight, behind the corner of the building. Joseph stopped.

'Oh God, Dad, no!' he cried. He turned, chased after him. 'Miriam, go!'

The words meant nothing. Her mind jarred. She stopped. She fell to the ground and lay still. She was in a courtyard. An apple tree grew in its centre. Its trunk and branches were gnarled and old and leafless. Its roots had pushed up and cracked the paving stones around its base. Her mind could not process. Her body was limp. She lay, eyes open, unblinking.

|||

She was there for maybe two minutes, that was all. Two minutes before she saw the courtyard glow electric blue, whiten, electric blue again. Two men approached her. They were wearing helmets. The lenses were hexagon-shaped. Their uniforms were yellow and made of a rubber material. Their boots and gloves were green and joined seamlessly to the uniforms at the wrist and knees. They looked like spacemen.

'Are you all right, my love?' said the first man. His voice was human despite his appearance. It came through a filter at the mouth that looked like a square showerhead.

Miriam did not answer.

The two men turned to each other.

'She looks gone.'

The second man nodded.

'Do you want to come with us?'

'We can help cure you,' added the other one, as if he was speaking to a deaf child.

Miriam still did not answer. Beyond the alleyway, on the main road, the noises persisted but they were not as they had been. The courtyard kept them out.

'Let's get her in the ambulance.'

They laid a stretcher at her side and lifted her on.

'Do you mind us taking you away like this? Are you happy with it?'

Both men, crouched on their hams, loomed over her. Miriam saw her reflection in their masks. Her lips were dark with blood. Her face looked pale but perhaps that was dust. Her hair was white and chalky. She watched herself impassively until her reflection moved away into the distance, smaller and smaller, until it was gone and she felt her body being lifted, her weight sagging gently into the cloth of the stretcher. She felt moving air on her face. It travelled up her neck, over her chin, over her lips. As it passed her mouth she drew some into her.

The two men loaded her into the ambulance. There were three other people in there. They all stared blankly ahead and said nothing. The rumble of the engine shook the frame of the vehicle and they pulled away.

|||

The doors opened again and a bright, white light spilled into the ambulance. Five men in white spacesuits appeared. A rectangle of black perspex, the visor on their mask, was the only darkness. The light was diffuse. It was as if it had not one source but was simply present in the air; a presence in its own right.

The first of the spacemen ascended the metal steps of the ambulance and stood in front of the woman opposite Miriam.

'Do you want to come with me?' he said.

The spaceman was tall and large. The woman said nothing. The spaceman was holding a light green strip of plastic.

'I'm going to put this on you.'

With gloved hands he strapped the plastic round her wrist and connected the two ends. His hand movements were deft despite the heavy gloves. He then put one arm beneath her legs and another round her back and lifted her up. Carefully he stepped down from the ambulance and carried the woman away into the light.

The second spaceman entered and stopped in front of Miriam.

'Are you ready to come with me?' said the detached voice of the faceless mask.

The man crouched before her and slid a light green wristband round her wrist. She looked at it. It was a thin plastic band that you would see in any hospital, but with a bulging around one section. Here, a metal sensor shone in the light. It was weightless. Next to the sensor was a number handwritten in red: 373.

Outside the ambulance she was in a plastic tube. It had been clipped to the back of the ambulance so the outside world could not get in. The walls were made of an opaque white material that let in the light. As they walked along, the walls shimmered in ripples before them. At the far end of the plastic tunnel was a room, large and square. Vinyl floor and whitewashed walls. She was carried through some double doors that opened automatically with a hermetic hiss. They were in an antechamber. To their left and right, along the walls, were lines of wooden chairs. The cushions were upholstered in a pink rubbery material cold to the touch. Several of the chairs were occupied. Miriam was carried to her own and placed into it.

An air-conditioning unit was set into the wall. A length of white cloth had been tied to the grille and flapped lazily in the current. Fastened to the ceiling was a black bowl of glass. A security camera.

Miriam looked at her green wristband again, at the red handwriting. Things came to her by degrees: the street, the lines of cars, the sounds of explosions. She was there again, watching Joseph disappear from view as he tried to help his father. A static current lifted the hairs on her body; an unpleasant, unnatural sensation. Her father-in-law had been killed. There were too many bullets in him. They had lifted him and thrown him down the street. He could not be alive.

The doors through which the spacemen had disappeared hissed open. A doctor entered.

'Thank you for coming,' he said, his voice high and quick. 'We need people like you. You can rest assured that if you want to stop at any time you just have to say so.'

Miriam looked about her at the other people sitting in the identical pink chairs. They were all infected. It was clear. And they were all wearing light green wristbands.

'This is a government facility, it is not a hospital. You're safe here. Nobody can get in. In this building we have the best medical technology available on the planet, and the best doctors and scientists to give us the best chance possible. This is where the fight back begins.'

Miriam caught his eye. She spoke. Her voice sounded odd, distant, as if she was listening to a recording of her voice on a stereo.

'Where are we?'

'You are in Colindale. In London.'

She could hear him but not clearly. She placed the tip of her little finger in her right ear. There was sand in it. Dust.

'We're grateful to you. The whole country is. We need more volunteers like you,' he said. 'The sooner we can find out what this thing is, the sooner we can kill it. And with people such as yourselves willing to help, we can do it.'

Miriam spooned as much dust from her ears as she could. It was crusty, already congealing with wax.

'We want to run some tests. It's nothing to worry about. Last night something terrible happened across much of London. We need to work quickly, and that is why you've been brought here in such a manner. I hope you can forgive us for that. But our facility was unaffected, and all of our staff were unharmed. It's a miracle.'

'Miracle,' Miriam whispered under her breath. She looked at the doctor. 'I think,' she said slowly, 'there's been a mistake.'

He paused and looked at her in surprise. 'I'm sorry?' he said.

'I'm not ill.'

The doctor came closer. He had taken three steps towards her when a man sitting in one of the chairs opposite said, 'No, I'm not ill either.'

The doctor stopped. Turned. The man was leaning forward and staring at the ground. He was holding the end of his wristband between his thumb and forefinger.

'I'm not going to be able to help you,' he said in a steady, slow drone.

'I am not ill,' said a third person, a woman, sitting in the chair furthermost along.

'I am not ill,' said a fourth.

Crystalline shards of panic grew up on Miriam's skeleton. Suddenly the room had become real to her. The colours were faded up. She did not know where she was. She had been taken away. Her mind started to race – it cranked around, its gears and pistons coming to life. Her head hurt. There was pain in her knees, at her hip, along the back of her forearms. She was trapped.

'I want to leave,' she said. 'Now.'

She wanted to stand but her legs felt weak. If she tried to stand she would fall.

'Fascinating,' said the doctor, quietly to himself. He looked about the room, at the dozen faces staring back at him. 'Just wait here for a moment,' he said. 'I won't be long.'

'I'm not ill,' called yet another person.

But the doctor had left.

Miriam could feel sweat forming under her skin.

'What are we doing here?'

None of them answered her at first. It was a man sitting three chairs down from her who finally spoke.

'They think they're going to cure us,' he said. His breath became heavy. 'They don't understand.'

The automatic doors opened and two large men entered. They

did not look like doctors. They wore navy blue boiler suits and heavy leather boots. They walked steadily towards the centre of the room. They said nothing but were looking in the direction of the man who had spoken. Their marching was purposeful. And then they broke into a run.

The man who had been talking jumped to his feet and burst across the floor in a flash of unnatural speed. He threw himself towards an elderly woman sitting opposite. It all happened in relative silence. There was no shouting, screaming, no human noise. The guards tackled him before he could reach the old woman. They tumbled into the far wall. The guards overpowered his writhing body. There were grunts and sighs, the slip of leather shoes on the vinyl floor. They carried him out by his arms and legs. He struggled but without making a noise.

As they passed her, they glanced at Miriam. She made eye contact. Panic swelled. They thought she was going to turn. They were going to come back for her next. They disappeared out of the antechamber. Miriam waited for the doors to seal shut before rising shakily to her feet. There was no energy in her legs.

'What are they going to do to us?' she said to unlistening ears.

They didn't care. They were not human any more. She went to the doors through which they had been brought in, one foot in front of the other. They were locked. She pressed her shoulder into them using her weight as a lever but there was no escape. The fear inside her was of a new kind, of the new world. This fear was unknowable.

She was in a government building. She was safe. The government did not harm its own people. And yet she was terrified. The new government was sinister. It glared at her through the inverted dome of black glass in the ceiling, through the tinted red light of an eye just visible through the murk.

She tried to get her fingers between the thin slit that cut the doors in two. There was no purchase. Her fingers fumbled. The men were coming for her. She could hear their dull footfalls on the soft floor but she could not bear to turn round and see them coming.

Their hands on her were heavy and intrusive. One of them pressed against her breast. A ball of anger welled in her throat.

'Get off me!' she screamed.

They locked their arms over and under her limbs. She kicked out but she was nothing more than a loose marionette of flailing bones. They hauled her out across the chamber and the doors shut tight.

|||

Down dark corridors they passed, the only illumination dull yellow emergency lights set along the ceiling too far apart to gain a sense of orientation.

'I'm not ill,' she protested. 'This is wrong.'

The guards did not answer. They turned left and right at gloomy internal crossroads. Soon she saw unidentifiable people walking around in white all-in-one lab suits, wearing their fried-egg masks.

The orderlies took Miriam into a smallish room, like a one-bed hospital ward. They laid her down and strapped her wrists and ankles to steel loops welded into the bed frame.

'You can't do this,' she said, arching her back uselessly. The orderly trussed the second ankle strap with a finality he clearly enjoyed. He looked at her, smiled emotionlessly and left with his colleague.

She pulled at her shackles. Her legs were open and she felt vulnerable and foolish.

The doctor came in, the same man who had been in the antechamber, the one with thinning hair and high voice.

'Please, I'm not ill. I'm really not. I have a family.' There was pleading in her voice. 'I have to get back home.'

'It's all right,' he said calmly. His eyes were red at the edges. 'You'll be well looked after here.'

'Why don't you believe me?'

He wasn't even looking at her. He was checking some papers on a clipboard.

'Believe you?' he said, dismissively.

'My name is Miriam Asher. I live in Waterloo. My husband worked for Hutchins and Leclerc. I have two children, Mary and Edward. I am staying with my mother in Enfield because my husband was killed by the illness. We're going to Cornwall to escape. Does it sound like I'm ill to you?' She spoke quickly. 'Would I be able to talk to you like this if I was ill?'

The doctor peered at her over the top of his clipboard.

'Please untie me.'

He cleared his throat. His expression had changed. 'When did you first feel it in you?'

'Feel what?'

'The illness. The Sadness you have in you.'

She shook her head. 'I don't feel it. I'm not ill.' She struggled with her ties. They dug into her skin. Small rivers of pain flowed laterally across her wrists.

The doctor looked worried. 'Something's gone wrong,' he said urgently. He glanced nervously through the square glass window in the door. His movements were jerky, with a new energy in them. 'I don't understand. How could—'

'Please. Just untie me.'

'Wait here. If anyone comes in, don't say anything.' He rushed from the room and closed the door tight.

The smell of disinfectant hung in the air. It was not strong, but strong enough to be unpleasant. The blood had dried on her lips, moulding them into place. She stretched her lower lip and felt the satisfying crack of blood splitting apart.

The doctor returned.

'I'm going to try and get you out of here.'

'Try?'

'Look, we're not really in charge now. In this building. The army are here and they have orders not to let people find out about what's going on.'

It was almost a confession.

Her stomach churned.

'Where am I?'

'You're in a Health Protection Agency building. We're a government agency.' He scratched his neck. 'We're the ones who are supposed to be helping.' He went to the door and looked once more through the window. As he spoke his eyes scanned the room outside. 'But we've hit some stumbling blocks and people are becoming afraid.' He turned back to Miriam. 'They're getting desperate. The army have been here for three days now.'

Miriam wondered who 'they' were. Surely this man standing before her was 'they'. The back of her consciousness told her 'they' was just something all humans needed, a faceless other to be held accountable.

'Can't you untie me?' she said.

The doctor was hesitant.

'We're doing tests and we're not exactly going through normal channels.' He noticed the fear in Miriam. 'It's nothing dangerous, we just need to cut through the red tape. Why do you think we're picking people up off the streets and not taking them from hospitals?' He shook his head.

'Why can't you untie me?'

'I'm trying to help,' he assured her.

'So untie me.'

'I can't, not yet.' He seemed just as scared as she was. He lowered his voice. 'If we hadn't tagged you I might have been able to get you out. But now you're logged. You're here. And they know you're here. When we bring people in we don't expect them to leave again. It's a self-containing cycle. Once you're ill, that's it.'

'But you made a mistake. I shouldn't be here. I shouldn't have to pay because you made a mistake. Let me go. I won't tell anybody.'

'It's not as simple as that – it's not the way they think.'

Little circles of sweat appeared at his high temples.

'I'm going to start screaming if you don't untie me.'

'That's not a good idea.'

Miriam pulled at her ropes again.

'Stop it. If they think you're violent they'll take you to a not very nice place.'

She was afraid now. Her hands and feet were cold with cloying sweat. 'What the hell is that supposed to mean?'

His eyes dropped. 'Nothing.'

'This is insane,' she said. 'How can you just stand there? What's the matter with you?'

'Oh come on,' he said, sharply. 'That's ridiculous. We're trying to help.'

'Are you helping me?'

'I don't think you understand just what is going on. This thing is all over the planet. It's eating the entire species. If we don't do everything we can, now, at this time, then who knows where it will stop? We just want to save people. Including us. We're all scared here too. You think we're not?' As he spoke his eyes flitted around the room, resting on anything but her. 'If you want me to tell the people in charge that you're in here and you're not ill, then I will. But it is your decision. I am not responsible for what they might do.'

'When you brought us in you said we could leave whenever we wanted.'

'I thought you were ill,' he said defensively.

'That's not an excuse.'

He tightened his hold on the clipboard. 'You have your choice. What do you want me to do?'

Her mind was back now. She could think. She had to make a decision based either on the laws of the old world, or of the new. In the old world she would have rights and would not have hesitated. In the old world common sense would have prevailed, society was in place to support her, she would be in no danger. She wanted to trust the doctor. He wanted to help, that much was certain. He was just scared.

'Can you get me out?' she said.

'I can try.'

She smiled, more for him than for herself. 'Thank you.'

'I'll come and help you later. I can't stay in here for too long.'

'What's your name?' she said.

He hesitated. 'It doesn't matter.' He took a deep breath. 'I have to go. If anybody comes in, just act ill.'

'How do I do that?'

'You know how they act.' He turned to leave. 'Everybody knows.'

||||

They came for her an hour later. A male and a female. They looked just like two ordinary people and spoke with gentle, modulated voices. The man had a mild American accent. An orderly stood by the door. Miriam was untied. The blood flowed freely through her wrists and feet and she felt the prick of pins and needles. She was transferred to a wheelchair. She did not say anything. Where was the doctor who had promised to help her?

Outside her room were several glass windows that led the eye into the centre of the building, past the partition walls by way of more large, square windows. She glimpsed computers, charts, people carrying white boxes, steel apparatus small and large, white sheets drawn along metal rails.

She remained still and tried to make her eyes blank, tried to slow her blood. It felt absurd to behave this way. She kept looking for the young doctor but he was nowhere to be seen. She started to worry that he would not be able to locate her now she was being moved. And all the while she was aware of being taken further into the centre of the building, further away from the exits.

The two doctors spoke casually to one another. They were discussing the illness, talking about some test results using scientific terms that Miriam did not understand.

'Here we are,' the woman said kindly.

Before them was a set of double doors made of flimsy plastic. The male doctor went ahead and held them open. Beyond was what looked like a hospital ward with twelve beds, six along each wall. The room was surgically clean. White veils, like mosquito nets, hung over each bed, rising to a pagoda-like point.

They wheeled Miriam into the ward. Behind the veils she could see the ghostly outlines of people sitting against their pillows.

They stopped at the third bed on the left.

'Here we go. Home sweet home.'

'I'll leave you to it,' said the male doctor.

The woman took a white shift from the cabinet beside the bed.

'Can you put this on?'

Miriam paused, unsure whether she should answer. She stood from her wheelchair and removed her sweater and trousers. She rolled off her socks and removed her shirt slowly. She left her underwear and looked to the doctor to indicate that she had finished. She did not want to be naked.

The doctor smiled.

'Thank you. Here.'

She handed Miriam the white shift and she slipped it over her head. Its texture was like waxy paper. It was cold on her skin. There were buttons on the chest that she began to fasten before the doctor told her to stop: the flaps of material were to be left open, leaving her chest exposed.

Several machines surrounded the bed; white plastic things on alloy trolleys. The doctor went to each one and flicked switches, tapped keys, turned dials, explained that the tests were very simple, standard and would not hurt. Miriam did not say anything.

A clip was attached to her thumb. It led to a red wire and into a screen. The doctor placed electrodes on her body and head to read the chemicals inside her. Blood was taken from her veins.

'We're all so grateful to you,' said the doctor. Her hair was sandy, shoulder length. She had pale green eyes, the edges of which folded into crow's feet when she smiled. She was probably around thirty years old. Younger than Miriam.

'We'll find an answer to all this.'

Miriam watched the lines on the monitor. Those lines were her insides, they were her life in function.

'What are you going to do to me?' She spoke slowly and felt idiotic in doing so.

The doctor turned her eyes from the monitors to Miriam.

'We're testing some new drugs. Some of them are fairly standard but haven't been used in this way before. Others not so. I won't lie to you. None of us will. They might make you sick.'

'Somebody said there is no cure because it comes from God.'

The doctor placed a plaster on Miriam's arm, across the puncture wound from the blood test.

'Well, that's not really my field, I'm afraid.'

||||

She awoke to the sound of shuffling. How much time had elapsed she did not know. She was exhausted. A blurred form moved across her vision.

'What time is it?' she said, without thinking.

'Ten o'clock.'

It was a high voice. The doctor. He had come back for her. She was instantly awake.

'How long was I asleep for?'

'You've missed a day. It's ten o'clock in the morning.'

She thought about this.

'Have you been able to do anything? About me getting out?' she said.

His head dropped a fraction. The movement scared her immediately. She went to sit up but couldn't. She had been strapped to the bed by two strips of material: one across her chest and one across her thighs. She could hardly move. There was an itch in her arm. She pulled it from beneath her bed sheets. There were pen marks all along it. Arrows, lines and figures. It looked like a map. Her mouth fell open and she looked back to the doctor. He was holding the marker pen in his hand.

'I'm sorry,' he said. 'It's too risky.'

Her mouth was dry.

'We're trying to do our best.'

'What is this?' She held out the underside of her painted forearm.

'We're just trying to make people better.'

Her breathing was fast. 'Oh my God, what have you done? I have children. I have to get back to them.'

He looked to his left and right and approached her bed. 'Sssh,' he said. He lowered his voice. He no longer looked to Miriam like the scared boy of yesterday – he now looked like a coward.

'It's not so bad. They don't think you will turn any more. I made sure of that. You won't get the bad stuff.'

She craned her neck forward to sit up but it was no good.

'I'm not ill,' she said loudly.

He held his hand up. 'Keep your voice down. Seriously. They'll change their minds if they think you're dangerous. They're looking for people like that. They're the ones they have to cure. Don't you realize what they'll do to you?'

'I don't care.' She was almost shouting.

He ran forward and put his hands over her mouth. His skin was salty and dry. White cracks ran like shattered glass where his thumb and forefinger met.

'I'm sorry,' he said. 'You have to be quiet. They only want to work on your arm. That's all. But if they think you're going to turn, that's it.' His eyes darted nervously. 'They'll cut your chest open.'

Her mind started to overload. She could hardly breathe. She thrashed her head from side to side until the doctor let go. She went to scream but stopped. The government could not do this to its people. But here she was, in the bed, surgical markers daubed all over her arm.

The doctor looked at his feet like a schoolboy.

'You don't understand,' he said, 'what happens when powerful men become desperate.'

He turned and walked away.

Miriam watched him disappear behind her white drapes. When his figure had been absorbed entirely she lay back on her bed. She released her balled fists and felt the cold clamminess of the rubber sheeting on the palms of her hands. They had almost made it. They had been so close. And she started to cry.

|||

Three hours passed. Outside the white nets she had heard voices and the sounds of somebody being taken from their bed but she did not call out for them. When her turn finally came she breathed in through her nose and out through her mouth. She looked at the two doctors who had come. One was the female who had tested her yesterday. Her hair looked lank and unwashed. With her was another doctor, a new one. He was old, thin and wore expensive-looking wire-framed spectacles.

'So,' he said.

They think you're ill, she told herself. She looked at the two lumps at the end of her bed that were her feet and could feel his eyes on her.

'When did you first feel it?' he asked.

Miriam paused. She hated the way that her survival instinct was so much stronger than her beliefs. She should not stand for this and yet she was.

'Yesterday,' she said slowly.

'What happened?'

There was a decisive, authoritative staccato to his voice that Miriam did not like.

'I don't know.'

'Did you notice any colour impairment in your vision?'

'I don't know,' she said.

'You don't know? Or you won't tell me?'

'I don't know.'

'Have you felt an increased level of anger inside of you? Or hatred?'

Her innards felt warm. Her throat was soggy.

'I was separated, from my family. I . . .' Her eyes misted. 'My husband died.'

The two doctors glanced at one another. The senior doctor removed his glasses.

'Can you tell me anything about murder?'

She could not answer that.

'What is the nature of murder? Or death – can you tell me that?'

Instinctively she looked at the doctor. Her eyes betrayed her immediately. His brow creased downwards at its centre. He cocked his head inquisitively. He knows, she thought.

'Kate,' he said to his colleague. He lifted Miriam's arm and turned it over to examine the markings. 'Can you go to my office and fetch my surgical kit please? I think I left it on my desk.'

Something reptilian slithered up her. He was looking at her arm as if it was a piece of food. She could hear the heart machine connected to her by the diodes on her chest bleeping faster. The bleeps were closing in on each other. They were giving her away.

The doctor looked at his colleague. 'Please,' he said.

She turned to leave.

Please don't leave me, Miriam thought. Not with this man. She looked at him and thought of Joseph. She thought about what Joseph had told her. People were flawed. The image of a sharp scalpel came into her head. In the distance the low-heeled shoes of the female doctor grew faint. And then they were gone. Miriam was alone with him.

'We don't have much time,' he said quickly. He threw off her sheets and untied the straps. She was free.

'Get dressed.'

Miriam froze.

He nodded and raised his eyebrows. 'Do you want to get out of here or not?'

She came to life. The doctor pulled the electrodes from her chest and they came away with little popping sounds. Her heart machine played a single note. The doctor rushed round to it and turned it off. Miriam threw off her white shift and quickly dressed.

'How the hell did you get in here?' he said.

He looked away as she changed into her clothes. She pulled on her sweater and brought her shirt collars into line.

'I don't know.'

'Jesus Christ, this is not good.'

He let out a loud and dramatic sigh. There was a kindness in his face that she had utterly failed to spot. He was going to help her.

'How could you tell?'

He held open the white mosquito net for her to pass beneath.

'It's easy to tell. Don't you think? That weird sense?'

Her heart fluttered. She knew.

'Thank you,' she said.

'There's no need. Really,' he said. They passed underneath the white netting and into the ward, his movements urgent. 'We're not monsters.'

||||

They moved quickly through the building; through doors, along corridors, past laboratories filled with people. The doctor told her to act naturally and they told each other their names. They stopped at a small, empty office where he made a phone call. He asked for a car.

'Where are we going?'

'I can get you out on the other side. It's a bit of a trek, I'm afraid. This place is like a maze.'

They entered a lift and ascended. On the next corridor was a laminated wooden door.

'This is my office,' he said. He poked his head inside. 'She's not in here.'

He went to his desk and took a security badge from it. He took some scissors from a desk tidy, cut off her wristband and pocketed it in his white lab coat.

'Do you really think you can find a cure?' she said, suddenly. There was a burning sensation in her face. She could feel it fizzling up. It was hope and it was radiating out and projecting into him.

'I hope so,' he said. 'With a bit of luck.' He smiled.

They left the office and descended once more through the building. Miriam could sense that they were underground when they re-emerged. All the light was artificial and it felt somehow trapped, as if it had been bouncing off the same walls for a long time.

'Where do you live?'

'Enfield.'

'Do you have somewhere to go, outside the city?'

'We're going to Cornwall. My father-in-law lives—' She cut herself short.

'That's a good idea. Get away from London. It will collapse soon.' He spoke with authority, sure of his words.

'Is it really true that nobody has any idea what it is?'

'That is true, yes.'

'So there were no plans for this?'

'There were plans, but not on this scale. Nothing like this. This is something nobody ever thought could happen.'

They were in a darkened corridor now. It intersected with another corridor at right angles. When they reached the intersection a human scream rang out along it. It was jagged and cutting, made by somebody in extreme pain. Miriam felt it jolt her bones.

The doctor looked left, to the source of the scream. He put his hand in the centre of Miriam's back and pushed her along.

'Ignore it.'

'What was it?'

'It was nothing.'

Everything was coming back to her all at once, as a great flood. Ahead was a solid steel door. It required the doctor to swipe his card along a magnetic reader. The internal mechanism of the door clicked and he pushed it open. They were in an underground parking bay. Two men dressed in army uniform were standing before them.

'Is my car here?'

'It's on its way,' answered one.

A car engine echoed through the hollow chamber. There was a screech of tyres and a door being held open.

'Good luck,' said the doctor.

She climbed in, confused, and he closed the door behind her. The seats were made of leather that crunched beneath her weight. She placed her hands on her knees and spread out her fingers. There was salt water in her throat. The car sped up a ramp. A thick tube of painted yellow and black steel rose in front of them and they ascended into bright daylight.

III

The roads were damp with rain. A frail sun waited just on the other side of the thin clouds, its disc visible as a ghostly rim.

There were bodies in the street. These were not the hopeless, desolate souls of the illness's victims; these were dead bodies. They lay prostrate and limp, their limbs set at strange angles. Small puddles of blood escaped from underneath their corpses like red shadows.

Miriam said nothing to the driver. There were official trucks – great white cubes of machinery – with men in full infection-control bodysuits. They were slowly gathering the dead like garbage men. The scale was fully apparent now. It towered and glared over the city. It had taken a week to reach this state. This was no instant disaster, a switch from one state to another. It had crept slowly up and in. Its power was in its sheer size.

The people looked so small against the buildings. They muddled helplessly along dangerous streets. She felt the hopelessness in them, reduced as they had been to mere fractions of what they once were. This thing sought out every corner of every person, every inch. It had come for everyone.

The car stopped outside her mother's house. She climbed out and closed the door. The smell in the air was putrid, acrid and warm, like rotting fruit. A small head stared from the window of the living room. It disappeared and a few seconds later the front door of the house was flung open and Edward was running fast down the garden path to her. His feet slapped on the compacted gravel. His hair bounced up and down on his scalp. He was calling her. She stepped forward. His movement was natural, his wound was healing already. He threw himself off the top of the three steps leading up to the garden and her body rocked backwards under his weight. In his mother's arms, he fell silent. His bare skin was against her neck. She could feel his breath on her chest.

'It's OK,' she said. 'It's OK now.'

Her mother was standing at the top of the steps, her face tired and confused.

'James?' said Miriam.

Her mother shook her head and looked away.

|||

Her head leaned against the plate glass. Dora was in her arms. Her head rested against her collarbone. Miriam stroked her hair. The girl's body was so small, so thin. It was light, like a bird's.

The car was silent. The road moved beneath them in heavy clicks. The fields darkened with the sky. The world was wild again.

And then Miriam felt it as it left the girl. It was nothing tangible. It left with a grace and quietness. It was delicate and fragile as it peeled off the girl. It fell from her and dropped away from the car and waited at the side of the road. It watched its old owner disappear into the horizon.

Miriam could not say anything. The body rattled more now. Every bump, every change of speed toppled its balance. She held the back of Dora's head with her hand and felt her own chest tighten. She wanted to keep the girl close to her for a little while longer. She did not want to say anything to her mother. She did not want to frighten the children.

She looked down on to the top of Dora's head. It bobbed with the car's momentum. She placed her lips to it and ran her fingertips along the curve of her ear. The skin was already cold. She was determined not to cry. She remembered that night when she had told Henry she was expecting Edward. His joy had been limitless and instant. There was no hesitation in it. More life was coming into his world. More life.

Darkness fell around the car and Joseph's van. They moved into the night, a tiny convoy under a giant sky. The fields were invisible now. They had turned to black. Dora's body grew heavy.

'Mum,' said Miriam, quietly. She had come to the end. 'We have to stop the car.'

PART TWO

JOSEPH

There were bulbs in her left hand. Joseph said it was worth the risk of planting now. Perhaps there would be a frost and they would die, but spring was coming and they needed the food. They had spare, anyway. With a trowel in her right hand she turned the soil, made a small hole and dropped in a bulb. Thin white noodles of matter grew out of its base with small, creamy nodules bubbling from them. It was trying to live. At her side was a bag filled with compost that Joseph had taken from the shed. Miriam had kept guard as he unlocked the door and went inside. She thought it was foolish. There was nobody around. But Joseph was insistent. 'It's the system,' he had said, again. 'We can't get into bad habits.'

She sprinkled the cool, loamy granules on to the bulb. They were soft in her hands. The rest of the hole was filled in with the loose earth. She thought about the life she was creating there, up against the stone wall that marked the end of the back garden. Know your onions! That was the phrase they used to use in Henry's work. She thought back to the day he had shown her a catalogue of fonts. He went through each page, pointing out the different typefaces he liked and what they meant: this one is powerful, this one means class, this one is cool. Miriam had laughed at his enthusiasm for things that seemed so trivial. 'Hey,' he had protested. 'You have to know your onions.'

She made another hole and into it she dropped another bulb. She layered in the compost and the earth and made another hole. Keeping busy was the only way of defending herself from the phantoms. Clean the house, prepare a meal, practise one of Joseph's 'Training Modules', as she had sardonically named them. By keeping busy, her emotional range could be narrowed. The deep waters could be closed off. It was easier being shallow. Any feelings now could not penetrate deeply into her. Instead they caused short, frenzied squalls, quick flashpoints of tears, but they soon passed.

Mary was playing in the garden behind her. She could hear her feet running up and down the path between the vegetable patches. She could smell the herbs from the pots near the house. Joseph had said that although things might become desperate, it was important to always have flavour. To lose it would be to lose their humanity, he announced one day. And so they grew herbs. At first they grew them in the kitchen. It was too cold, too near the sea for them to grow outside from seed, but now they were alive. She had been surprised on that day when the green lines sprouted from the soil in the pots. Bringing these things into the world from nothing had given her a deep sense of satisfaction.

She dropped the final onion into its hole and buried it. She brushed her hands together and got to her feet, looking out east, past the house. It looked so desolate. Deep, dark shadows cut long, thin triangles from the land. There was no sound. The rabbits were small grey circles on the grass, some sitting up on their hind legs looking out over the sea.

She looked the other way, out towards the point. The sun was setting again as a giant orange ball and the sky had turned red. She could see all the way down the hill to the deserted car park at the far end of the beach that people had used in the summer. Beyond that, the road led up to the pristine white tower of the lighthouse. As she watched the scene before her she knew it was time to go inside. Somebody was walking along the road towards the house.

III

She called to Joseph and told him somebody was coming. Edward and his grandmother came into the hallway with them and they all went down into the cellar. Joseph opened the gun locker and took out one of the three shotguns. He loaded two cartridges and clicked it shut before locking the cabinet again. He gave Miriam the keyring with all the keys and went upstairs. Miriam went with him and locked the door when he left.

It seemed strange that a man might come from the direction of the lighthouse. The road didn't lead anywhere and so he must have found his way through the forests on the other side.

Miriam went back down the steps. They had moved lots of things into the cellar since they arrived at the house. She went to the freezer and took out a tub of ice cream. She made two bowls and took them to her children. They didn't like it when they were locked in the cellar but the ice cream always helped. And anyway, they were getting used to it now.

III

The first five weeks had passed without any new horror. They buried Dora in the field behind the house and held a joint service for her, Henry and Henry's father. It had been nothing much, just a silent prayer. Joseph had said nothing. They marked the grave with a large pebble from the beach.

They had turned the back garden into a vegetable patch. Joseph had done most of the work on it. He had turned the soil for hours and hours, in silence, like a machine, as if expending his grief. He stopped to eat and sleep. For the rest of the time he worked. Miriam had watched him from the back bedroom window. He had removed his shirt on one of the warmer days. His body was longer and more lithe than Henry's had been.

On one day he drove away and returned with three rolls of barbed wire. The three of them unfurled it together – Joseph, Miriam and her mother – and ran it around the garden walls twice so that nobody could get in. Or out. Miriam did not like the barbed wire. It was ugly and dangerous. She thought it would attract unwanted attention more than deflect it. But Joseph had insisted.

They still had plenty of food. There were three freezers now in the cellar. Joseph said he was going to build a coal-burning oven. The television still worked.

|||

Thirty minutes passed before Joseph knocked at the cellar door. They had a secret knock. Like children. Miriam went up the stairs. She refused to carry a gun. She opened the door and looked at him expectantly.

'He's gone. It was OK.'

The children had to remain in the cellar. Miriam had agreed to this. They had bartered over the time and come to an agreement of thirty minutes. Just in case people came back after being turned away.

She looked at the table to the right of the front door. There was an empty plate on it. At least Joseph had given him the food this time. That was another thing they had argued over.

|||

It was a Tuesday night so they all went to their bedrooms, turned off the lights and waited. Joseph knocked on the door. Miriam and Edward rose from the bed.

'OK, honey?' she said.

He didn't answer but she heard him climb down on to the carpet. They went silently to the door and out on to the landing. Mary and her mother were already there. Joseph led the way.

It was a clear night and there was the small mercy of moonlight on the carpet. It was just bright enough for orientation. Up was up. The carpet on the landing was cold and thin. The banister was their guide, the grain of the wood coarse on her fleshy palms and fingertips. It forced her hand up and down unevenly, like a gentle ocean tide. Sometimes Miriam would drop her hand from the rail and run it along the wooden balusters underneath. She liked the dull jolt that came with each new collision. They reached the newel post at the end of the banister. They had passed Joseph's bedroom. Directly ahead was the bathroom and to the left of that was the room in which Mary and Miriam's mother slept. They turned back on themselves to descend the stairs. They were well versed in the process by now. They felt their way along the hallway.

Ahead, Miriam heard the click of the cellar door opening. The door was underneath the stairs, on the right. They went down. Miriam pulled the door closed behind her and slid across the lock Joseph had installed. They sat in darkness in the chairs of the makeshift living space, the children and Miriam's mother always on the sofa, and waited.

Miriam had bristled when Joseph had first suggested this. It was ludicrous and childish. It seemed as if it was all just a game to him and it was only slowly that she realized he was right. They did need to be able to do this sort of thing. And besides, there was no harm in it. Scrambling around the house in the dark took up some time at least.

'OK,' said Joseph at last. 'That's fine. Let's go to bed.'

III

Joseph would take Edward fishing. The boy enjoyed it. He liked the idea of providing food for his family. If they returned home with a fish Edward had caught, he would appear in the kitchen doorway with a great swelling of pride, the fish held aloft in triumphant glee.

They fished from the beach. For the most part it was mackerel they caught. Sometimes whiting. On one occasion Edward caught a bass. It was too big for him to pull in by himself and Joseph had helped. His mother had been delighted. They cooked it and garnished it with spring onions.

Edward liked the feeling of pulling the line hard and fast when a fish was on the end of it. He thought he could feel the hook digging into the mouth and that meant the fish could not escape. Sometimes he would tug harder and more often than was needed. He wanted to wound the fish so it would struggle less but the tactic never worked. They would flop around every time, slapping the surface of the water manically as they were wrenched from the sea.

Sometimes, like today, Mary would go with them. She grew

bored easily and would run up and down the beach, but not too far because if she ventured further than a few tens of yards she would be scolded by Joseph.

'How deep is the sea, Uncle Joseph?' she asked.

'It depends where you are.'

'Oh.'

III

Joseph woke up early, as always. He looked out of the window. There was nobody coming. He went downstairs and commenced his daily ritual of checking the doors and making sure that nobody had arrived surreptitiously in the night. He carried an air rifle at all times when making his checks because Miriam would not allow him to carry a shotgun around the house. That was how life had become between them: small agreements struck here and there; she would agree to one thing if he agreed *not* to do another thing, was the way it usually worked.

On the fridge door was a calendar. He ticked off another day. He liked to know what the date was, even if it didn't hold any relevance to his life. Time meant little now. It was hard to believe it was only April. Everything was happening so slowly. His brother and father's deaths seemed so long ago. The image of his father's face flashed across his mind as it so often did, just a fraction of time before it was gone again. He ignored it. Thinking about it was pointless, it served no purpose.

He went into the front room and stopped. Miriam was sitting in his father's old chair, at the window. She was never up before him.

'Hi,' he said.

Miriam said nothing. She kept looking out of the window. It was overcast and only half light outside. The near side of her face was in shadow. Joseph crossed the room in a second, his heart beating fast.

'Miri?' he said.

He squatted beside her.

Her eyes were blank, her face expressionless. Joseph did not know what to do. It had been so long since he had seen somebody like this. He had tricked himself into believing that people were no longer dying. He put his hand on her shoulder and shook her gently.

'Miriam,' he said.

He could hear the panic in his voice.

Her mouth changed. It moved. It curled upwards at the sides and she looked at him. She was smiling. Her eyes had regained their life.

'April fool,' she said.

III

In the evenings, if it wasn't raining, Miriam would walk with her mother to the cliffs at the front of the house. It was a short walk but had become something to look forward to in the long days. The occasional tanker still crossed the horizon but today the sea was empty.

'Do you think this will ever pass?' She pulled the hood of her jacket down.

'It has to. Everything passes eventually.'

'Aren't you frightened?'

'We seem to be safe where we are.'

'So you just don't think about it?'

The sea wind blew her mother's hair. 'I guess you could put it that way, yes.' She nestled some of her hair behind her ear. 'We've been here for nearly eight weeks and nothing bad has happened.'

'Not here. But people are still getting ill. Bad things are happening in lots of other places. Don't you think that it could come here?'

Her mother shook her head.

'I just try not to think about it.'

They didn't often speak about the outside world any more. Thinking about what was happening gave it power. Not speaking made it separate – it was not a part of their lives. It had already taken enough from them.

III

Joseph tucked his gunny sack between his belt and the waistband of his jeans, took his air rifle and a box of pellets and left the house. Edward had wanted to go with him but Miriam had said no.

Joseph usually chose the wide expanse of grassland between the house and the ocean. He crossed the road and lay down on a patch of thick grass. Up until a few weeks ago he had not hunted for rabbits since childhood. His father had never been interested in hunting but had finally succumbed to his son's insistence to learn on his thirteenth birthday, when he had bought him his first air rifle. The three of them had often gone out to the cliffs to shoot for rabbits, or to take pot shots at cans: Joseph, Henry and their father. For the most part Joseph had needed to persuade them to come with him. They didn't want to go but Joseph had not wanted to go on his own. He liked the idea of father and son on a hunting trip, even if it was just shooting for rabbits at the front of the house.

He was the only one left now. He saw his father's body in the street again, streaked with blood, shaking, mumbling, dying. There had been dust all over his face, in his mouth.

There was no warmth in the sun and Joseph felt cold. He set the rifle in the grass before him and propped himself up on his elbows. He liked lying hidden in the grass, watching the rabbits in the crosshairs of his sight. He felt like a lion watching a herd of unsuspecting gazelles.

He cocked the gun, placed a pellet in the barrel and clicked it shut. He had bought it in a hurry and wished now he had chosen something that did not need constant reloading. Bringing his weight on to his left elbow, he placed his right index finger slowly on the trigger. The telescopic sight was accurate – far more so than the sight on his old rifle. He looked down its length into the deep green haze and adjusted the focus, bringing the grass into sharp, flat clarity. The sight moved slowly over the grass, coming to rest on the first of the rabbits. It was a good size. Its brown pelt was tinged with grey specks. Joseph held his breath for one second and fired. The rabbit flopped on to its side. Joseph sniffed and reloaded. Two more would be enough. It was too cold to stay out here for long. He found another rabbit. This one had reared up on to its hind legs. Behind it, two smaller rabbits grazed silently. Joseph aimed for its head so he would not need to find the shot in the carcass when it came to skinning it. He fired. The rabbit fell backwards violently, rolling head over feet before coming to a stop. The two rabbits behind bolted across the fields, the white undersides of their tails sparkling in the cold sun.

That morning he had been rummaging through the boxes in the cellar and found his mother's old mincer, the one she had used to grind the rabbit meat he brought home. The meat was sinewy and tough but she added some herbs and pork mince to make it more malleable. Then she would mould it into patties and make burgers.

He had forgotten all about it but as he had taken it from its box the memory of those days came back to him. They sparked something inside. Something caught. His head felt light and his chest less tight. He lived in that memory, just for a few seconds, basked in it: the way the sunlight slanted into the house, the warmth in the walls at summer, sitting in the back garden drinking lemonade and eating the food he had caught. It had been a long time since he had had a feeling like that. He had leaned against the metal shelving in the cellar and closed his eyes.

He wanted to make some rabbit burgers for Miriam and the kids. They didn't have any pork mince but he thought that maybe he could add some mashed potato. He was sure she would like them. He killed another rabbit, a small one, and collected all three up into his sack. He didn't like skinning them. It was boring. Perhaps he could teach Edward how to do it. Edward should do it anyway. He had to teach them everything he knew because the day might come when he would no longer be there to help them. He had been thinking about that for a long time.

|||

Time was something that changed quickly. They still kept the clocks running and Joseph marked off the days on his calendar, but without having any need to be at any particular place at any particular time it became redundant. Day and night – that was all that really mattered. Time became fluid, punctuated only by light and dark, and the passing of events: somebody coming to the house, taking a trip into the village, a meal, watching vegetables appear tentatively one day from the soil. The structure on which so many things had run had now disintegrated. And yet he did not feel any different. There was no great mourning for it. If anything it made him feel a sense of liberation; just another control gone.

III

Miriam kept her mobile phone charged and on, but had not been able to get a signal for weeks. The people on the television said that mobile phones still worked, but mainly in the cities. She could not understand why that should be the case. Surely they were run by satellites up in space. She wondered what would happen to those satellites. Would they circle infinitely, for ever? Or would they one day come down, screaming into the land? And what about her bills? Would she still be charged? It was a trivial matter but one that she could not stop thinking about. She did not know how much money was in her bank. Perhaps payments would still be taken automatically, but then, would the bills of the already dead need to be paid?

The phone lines were still open, but nobody was running them. The electricity plants were still churning energy but for how long could they continue? Surely there must be accidents, fires, people unavailable to keep them safe. The rumours on the television said that a quarter of the world was dead. One in four. But surely there was no way of knowing something like that.

There was no familiarity in the faces of the people who appeared on the evening news any longer. There were no more reassuring speeches from the Prime Minister because he was dead. Army officials had replaced politicians. Suits became uniforms. Communications grew fewer and farther between.

There was no more internet for the time being, was what they said. For the time being. It implied a return to normality, a re-alignment of the systems, the re-ignition of money, time, work, services. Life would go back to the way it was and everything would be fine again. But when this return would come nobody knew, just as nobody knew if society was even under any form of control any more, whether or not 'they' were still out there somewhere, finding a cure, keeping a handle on things. Perhaps society was controlling itself only through a system of ever-diminishing shadow memories, routines. And as more people died, the more hopelessness pervaded the air.

|||

It was always in the morning that spirits were highest. The freshness from sleep, the bright light through the house, the promise of something new all funnelled together into lightness.

Joseph looked from his bedroom window. Nothing there. He went out to the landing and checked the east-facing window set into the wall above the staircase. You could look through it from the landing. Nothing coming that way either. He went downstairs and checked the front of the house, and then the back. He had to make sure that nobody had arrived during the night. The process was the same every day. Miriam called it overkill, but Joseph was unwilling to take the risk. Miriam was too trusting. She was naive. Joseph knew this, just as he knew that one day she herself would come to learn that. Even if the illness went away, too many people were dead. Society was on the edge. The cities were chaotic masses of disease and violence and soon there would be a final exodus.

Other countries had reverted to chaos within weeks but Britain had managed to hold itself together, tentatively. Those who had family in the country had already left the cities, but the people with nowhere to go – the immigrants, the lonely, the broken and the isolated – were still there. They would have to leave eventually, and what then? Where would they go?

He walked around the low wall surrounding the house. Nobody there. He checked the bolts he had punched into the stone to keep the barbed wire in place. He crouched on his knees and pressed his fists into the ground. There was no sign of frost. The plants were still safe.

He paused at Dora's grave. Already the tough grass of the coast was closing in on the naked earth. Ugly, patchy weeds were growing up like an old man's beard. Miriam had wanted to plant flowers on the grave but it wasn't the right time of year. He pulled some of the larger weeds away. The roots gave some resistance and came from the ground with a satisfying tear. He threw them to one side.

Bringing himself upright he stretched his back. The tendons and muscles expanded and released. He closed his eyes and thought, as he did so often, about what would happen if he became ill; what he would become, and what he would do to the family he was supposed to be protecting. He looked at the house through the jagged frames of the barbed wire and pictured them all in there: sleeping, safe.

|||

Joseph wished that Miriam's mother wouldn't use as much butter as she did. When he went back into the house there she was, starting breakfast, leaning over the butter and shovelling it from its tray as always. It wouldn't last for ever and supplies in the supermarkets, the only stores that remained open following the first great purge, were diminishing with every visit. Why couldn't she understand that?

'Morning, Joseph,' she said, with that chirpy jocularity of hers.

'Morning.' He went to leave the kitchen.

'How are you today?'

He stopped. 'I'm fine.'

'Come and sit down. I'll make you a nice cup of tea.'

Joseph turned reluctantly back into the room and sat at the table. Crescents of dirt lined his fingernails. He curled his fingertips into his palms.

'Is it cold outside?'

'Yes.'

'Spring will be here soon.'

'Maybe.'

She brought Joseph his tea and a piece of toast, this one unbuttered.

'The planets haven't stopped turning,' she said. 'It'll get warmer soon.'

He sipped his tea. The heat scalded the surface of his tongue and he winced. He had never liked tea without milk but there wasn't enough of the powdered stuff to go round.

The old woman sat opposite him. He looked into his cup, feeling her eyes on him.

'So this is the house you grew up in?'

He nodded. He didn't want this conversation. He knew what she was angling for – her interrogation techniques were not subtle. Soon she would ask again how he was, but with more force, as if the question had a deeper meaning. Joseph didn't want to dredge up old memories. Or at least, he didn't want to talk about them.

'I was amazed how clean the place was when we got here. Your father kept the house well after your mother died.'

'He liked to keep things tidy.'

'Not like my husband. Always so messy, he was.'

Joseph smiled wanly.

'How are you, Joseph?'

'I'm fine.'

He couldn't understand why she kept pushing him like this.

'We're worried about you.'

He took a bite from his toast and sank down into his seat. 'Why?' he said, his mouth deliberately full.

She paused. She and Miriam both did this. They left pauses where there should be words, waiting awkwardly for them to be filled.

'What do you want me to say?'

'Don't you want to talk about your father?'

'No.'

'It might make you feel better.'

'It won't. The way I feel has nothing to do with my father. He died. He's the lucky one.'

He could sense the shock in her. He wished that people wouldn't be so shocked by the things he said. They were always nothing more than true.

'Do you really mean that?'

'I don't know.' He dropped the toast on to his plate. 'All I want to focus on is getting things set up here and making you all safe.'

'And we appreciate it; we do. But you've got to take time for yourself as well. Miri told me not to say anything to you but I think it's important.'

He didn't like the fact they had been talking about him when he wasn't there.

'I just don't feel the need to talk about things. I'm not like you and Miriam, you understand? Talking about things doesn't help me. It might work for you, but not me.'

'If you bottle it up—'

'Look. Talking about it is only going to slow things down.' He sighed. 'We don't know what is going to happen up here. We don't know for how long we'll have to wait for the disease to go away. Maybe it won't ever go away. Maybe it'll come here.'

Miriam's mother blanched at the suggestion.

'Maybe I won't be here to help you. If I get ill . . .'

'You mustn't talk like that.'

Her eyes turned into triangles, creased heavily at the edges. Joseph wished he could hold his tongue, say things less harshly. He didn't mean to scare the old woman.

'This is a race against time,' he said. 'That's how I see it. I know you and Miri don't agree and you think I'm being too cautious but it's safer this way. So thinking about my father is not going to help.'

'But it's affecting you.'

'Please. How do you know what I'm feeling?'

Miriam's mother lowered her voice. 'What about his bedroom?'

'What about it?'

'We can't keep the sleeping arrangements as they are for ever. You know we need more space.'

'It might not be for ever.' He smiled at her cynically.

'Joseph. You know, it might make you feel bet—'

'We'll leave the sleeping arrangements as they are. Can you give me that much? Just for now?'

He was getting fed up with her persistence.

She regained herself.

'Of course.' She smiled, but with sadness. 'You take as much time as you need.'

|||

It rained for three days. It came down in great, gusting swarms. It shook the windows in their frames. It sluiced down from the guttering like waterfalls in a rain forest.

Joseph went into the cellar and took out two large recycling bins made of thick, black plastic. In the rain he sank them into the soil of the back garden until they were half buried. They would work as fresh water collectors. Miriam had smiled, as usual, because she still didn't understand, and for a moment Joseph was glad of it. Something was coming back to her, a lightness of energy that she had had when he first met her. She was laughing more and making jokes. The shadow of her grief was loosening. Things were going well. There were still dark moments, but she was getting better.

On the third night the rain stopped and the clouds drew up into the ether. The moon and the stars dazzled and what water had fallen was collected into a few bottles, the whole family working as a team, together.

|||

When they woke up the morning after the rainstorm the ground was coated in the dull silver of a thick frost. Joseph and Miriam stood over the soil. Thin spikes of crystalline ice criss-crossed the ground; the green shoots that had sprouted from the soil were encased in it. The ground crunched beneath their feet. Joseph held his palm an inch above the garden and felt the cold radiating upwards into his skin.

'Do you think they're dead?' she said.

Steam rose from their mouths as they breathed. The air was freezing and glacier fresh.

'I don't know. Probably. The young ones can't survive this.' He stood and looked at Miriam. Her body had deflated. 'Not that I know much about gardening,' he said.

Miriam's head and shoulders slumped.

'Are you OK?'

She nodded but was upset. 'It's not fair, is it? What's the point? Why kill our plants?'

He considered opening his arms and hugging her. It would not have been inappropriate. He wanted to do it, but he stayed where he was. He maintained the yard of space that separated them.

'Don't worry,' he said. 'We'll replant. We'll start again, OK?'

Miriam folded her arms and brought her thumb to her mouth.

'It'll be OK, Miri.'

She said nothing and stared at the ruined garden.

'I'll leave you to it,' he said. He felt pathetic. 'I'm going to go back inside.'

He walked past her and when he did it felt like an act of abandonment. He wished he had done something more, something to show that he knew.

He reached the back door to the house that led into the conservatory, then turned back to the garden. Miriam was standing at the far wall, looking out over the fields. Joseph felt the distance between them. She did so many things he didn't understand. He stared at her back. She was leaning on the wall in the same way she always did – her arms folded in front of her and resting on the top of the stone, her head placed carefully between two curls of barbed wire. She was looking at Dora's grave again.

||||

The children were usually in bed by ten. That was one thing that time still held power over. The women would go to bed soon after the children, leaving Joseph alone to lock the doors.

He wanted to make shutters to cover the windows but had not had time. There were just so many things to do. He had some sheets of metal he could use but he needed frames and sturdy hinges to fit them on to. Metal was best because nobody could set fire to them. There was a large hardware store a few miles away that had remained open that he wanted to visit.

When he reached the top of the stairs that night he went past his bedroom door and further along the landing. The door to his father's bedroom had been closed since the day they arrived. On that day Joseph went in there to make sure that it was tidy, had stared from the window out over the sea, and had closed the door behind him.

It was still his father's bedroom. Allowing people to sleep in his bed was something Joseph was not ready for. He would allow it, soon, but not yet.

He closed his hand around the cold metal of the handle and pushed his head inside. The lower edge of the door was too low and dragged on the carpet. A square of moonbeams lay on the floor, shining in from the side window that looked out towards the village in the east. The room was so quiet and so still. The same recurrent memory flashed through his mind again, still fresh, still emotive, still connected to him: his father lying with dust all over his face, blood at his lips, like a clown. Small raindrops clicked against the window and Joseph watched them gather, one by one, lines against the night.

III

Mary was fond of the rabbit burgers Joseph had made, and demanded more. She reminded Joseph of Henry. She had the same manner as him. She was clumsy and unintentionally funny, and had that same dreamy quality, as if she was never quite there, always away to some better, happier place. Edward had withdrawn and become quiet but Mary was the same as she had always been.

He went to Miriam's bedroom and knocked at her door. She was standing at the foot of the bed in a white bathrobe, drying her hair with a towel.

'Oh,' she said when she saw Joseph. She pulled the gown self-consciously closer around her chest.

Joseph pretended not to notice, that it was nothing, meant nothing.

'Can I speak to you?'

'Of course.' She sat down on the bed and covered her knees by throwing her towel casually across them. The action drew Joseph's eyes. Her knees were still dark underneath the skin, but the scabs were all but healed. 'What is it?'

She looked pretty with wet hair. It made her look younger. Her ears poked out between two clumped deltas. Joseph felt his heart deepen in its beat.

'I want to teach Edward how to use the air rifles.'

'I don't think that's a good idea.'

'They're harmless, Miriam. They can't hurt people. I just want to show him how to shoot rabbits.'

He was frustrated by her reluctance towards guns. It was unreasonable.

'I just don't want him using guns.'

Joseph sighed.

'What?'

'What if I get ill? What then?'

'Don't be silly. We're safe up here.'

'No we're not,' he said, quickly. 'People come up here all the time. You mustn't think we're safe. Not ever.'

'But we haven't seen anybody who's been ill for weeks. We can't catch it all the way up here.'

Joseph shook his head. 'Miriam, please, let me teach him.'

'Why can't you teach me instead?'

'Yeah, right.'

They looked at one another for an uncertain moment.

'I'm serious,' she said.

'Really?'

'If you really want to do it, then you can teach me.'

A few drops of rain tapped against the window. Their heads turned quickly towards the noise, to the droplets running down the pane.

'Why don't I teach both of you?'

'Joseph, I'm not comfortable with that,' she said quickly.

It was only an air rifle. If he had his way he would teach Edward how to fire the shotguns.

'Fine,' he said. It could wait. As long as somebody else could use the gun he was happy. He doubted that Miriam would actually pull the trigger to kill an animal, but if she knew what to do, how to load, fire, reload, then when the time came she would be forced to act. He breathed in deeply. 'There's something else I want to ask you.'

Bulbs of water were forming at the ends of her hair and dropping on to her bathrobe.

'You won't agree immediately but I want you to follow my wishes,' he said slowly.

Her forehead creased. 'Joseph, what are you talking about?'

He crouched down so that he was looking up into her eyes. 'If it does happen, if I get . . . it . . . I want you to put me in the car and drive me away.'

She laughed nervously. 'Come on.'

'I'm being serious. Miri, you know what they're saying about the sort of people who become violent when they're infected.'

She shook her head.

'If I get ill I'm dead anyway. You don't have to worry about me. It's what I want you to do.'

'You know I can't do that.'

'I'm afraid of what I might become,' he said plainly. 'Promise me you'll think about it.'

Miriam did not react. She stared at the wall, past Joseph's shoulder.

'Miriam.'

Their eyes met.

'Promise me you'll think about it.'

'I won't do it, Joseph. Never.'

'I know it's hard, especially for you, but you have to be practical.'

'Practical?'

'You know what I mean.'

'Why are you so sure you'll become violent?'

'Do you not agree with me?'

'No. I don't. Jesus, why are always so down on yourself?'

He thought for a moment she might have been telling the truth. Maybe she really did see something in him that he could not see himself. She seemed so categorical. It was even moving, despite the fact that she was wrong. But that was just who she was, the way she saw things.

'You can't take the risk.'

'You're a good man.'

'No I'm not, Miri,' he said, surprising himself with his forthrightness. He recomposed himself. 'What I mean is, there's no such thing as good and bad with this. There's only truth and non-truth. These people who turn, they don't do it through choice – they just are what they are. Don't you see that?'

'You are good, Joseph. You're protecting us. But you mustn't ask me to do this again. It's not fair.'

'If I'm protecting you then this is part of that protection.'

She wasn't listening to him. He needed to get through to her that he would never, ever harm her as he was but that if he was changed then he could not make such an assurance. He had seen the violence it provoked in people and he felt it in him, buried deep inside. She had to understand.

'Henry was right to lose contact with me,' he said.

She shifted uncomfortably. 'That was a completely different thing, and you know it. Henry didn't think you were evil – Christ. It was you that lost contact with him, not the other way round.'

'It wasn't. He saw me, Miri.' He prodded his hand to his chest.

'Stop talking like this. It's making me uncomfortable.'

'So promise me you'll think about it.'

'No.'

Why wouldn't she listen? 'You're impossible.'

Miriam stood up from the bed and went over to the dressing table. She picked up a hair brush and swept it through her wet hair. Their eyes met in the mirror.

'I'll tell you what,' she said. 'I'll drive you away and abandon you if you promise to do the same for me.'

Joseph laughed. 'Don't be so ridiculous.'

She raised her eyebrows and moved her body between Joseph and the mirror so that he could no longer see her face.

'Then this conversation is over.'

|||

The rain started again and the sky darkened. The clouds sank towards the sea like a jagged, bloated underbelly. In some places it fell in black funnels towards the water; in other places patches of light caught the cloud, illuminating from within, telling of texture dense and thick, wild and massive.

Miriam was sitting in Henry's father's favourite chair. It was a comfortable old thing, out of keeping with the rest of the room, but a piece of furniture the old man had refused to discard as the various redecoration projects of his wife came and went.

'Maybe we shouldn't have replanted so soon,' she said, looking at the rain.

Joseph was tired. He nursed his tea in his hands.

They watched the evening news alone; they did not allow the children to watch it any more because it frightened them, Edward particularly, as he was more aware than Mary.

There was a new presenter today, an unfamiliar face. She seemed too young. The first report carried pictures of New York, but not the New York Joseph remembered. There was a lot of litter in the streets, and few people. Many of the buildings were charred or sooty. There were cars and familiar yellow taxi cabs destroyed by arson. But at least the satellites were working – how else could they have broadcast the pictures? thought Joseph. At least there was still some level of connection between the continents. It was reassuring.

American cities had not been able to cope with the disaster – that was what this news report was about. Many had been deserted. Only scavengers and the very rich remained. The scavengers and looters moved from house to house, building to building, taking what had been left behind. The military were still in the cities but they were useless with no people to shepherd.

A po-faced reporter stood in front of a railing behind which was a large, open park. He said that only the most secure buildings were still occupied, those with twenty-four-hour security. The very rich stayed where they were. Vans would bring cargoes of food. The screen showed an electronic gate roll back to allow a truck access. The reporter clutched his microphone as he spoke about a death toll of seventy million and about a superpower falling into ruins; he called it a labouring relic.

'You'd think they'd try and make the news a little more light-hearted,' said Miriam, chirpily.

She had tied her hair back and Joseph looked at her long neck.

'The media have become too strong. They'll only tell the truth.' He paused. 'It's better this way. At least we know what's happening. At least the government can't tell us lies to try and make us feel better.'

'So you think it's more important to tell the truth than to keep people's hopes up.'

'Yes,' he said firmly, without hesitation, as if this thought had occurred to him often and he had arrived at a final conclusion long ago. 'Always. Truth first.'

III

The rain broke and Joseph wanted to go to the hardware store. The roads were soaked. They had to drive along several narrow lanes. High hedgerows towered either side leaving only a thin strip of sky. Run-off from the rain gushed in fast rivulets at the sides of the patchwork concrete.

'I wonder how quickly these hedges will overgrow if nobody cuts them,' said Miriam.

Her mood had lightened incrementally as each week passed. The horrors of London, it seemed to him, had been all but crushed by her positive nature. He was surprised at how light-hearted she could be. It was not that she didn't consider wide-reaching ideas like the end of the world and how society would re-order itself were this disaster ever to relent; it was more that she didn't seem to care as much as him. She preferred to concentrate on smaller, more personal things like making sure her kids were having fun, or stroking Pele's belly, or just poking fun at his seriousness.

She was one of those people he had always resented, accidentally selfish and unthinking, but he was beginning to realize that if everybody was like her then he wouldn't have to worry half as much as he did about how the future would be.

There were a few cars in the car park when they arrived.

'I can't believe this place is still open.'

She turned the key and the engine stopped. She looked at him and smiled casually, and realized he was looking at her strangely.

'What?'

Joseph shook his head. 'Nothing.'

|||

Some shops were still open – the larger chains. The army had helped keep them open. It was easier to control a small space than a whole city. Supplies still got through, under armed guard, and spending was limited. That was the system they had devised: buy as much bread as you want, as long as you stay beneath your spending quota.

But there were no army vehicles outside the hardware store. It had stayed alive on its own. Joseph climbed out of the car and went inside and Miriam watched from behind the steering wheel. She adjusted her mirrors and found herself checking that nobody was creeping along the side of the car.

A car pulled up in the space directly adjacent to hers. A man. He was messing with something in the passenger seat. He pushed his door open and climbed out of his car. He was holding something inside a large, polythene carrier bag. It looked heavy. It stretched the base of the bag, pushed out at the edges. She watched him go inside and then started the car engine. She eased slowly forward. The density in her body had returned. The seatbelt over her shoulder cut into her chest. She rolled the car up to the main entrance. She could see inside the store. It was startling in its ordinariness. She pictured it from above, people moving slowly along the aisles, unseen.

There was nobody in sight. In front of her were the lines of trolleys, all stacked neatly, one leading into the next. More than anything she wanted to sound the horn, to get Joseph out of there. She could tell that something was going to go wrong. She could feel it. The new sense was firing.

|||

Joseph could feel the human presence behind him. He kept walking until he reached the end of the aisle, passing lines of screwdrivers hanging on rails. Turning the corner he quickened his step. He pushed his trolley past two aisles and ducked left, out of sight. He slowed and listened.

The aisle was filled with pots of paint, the cylindrical tins gleaming under the artificial lights. He stopped. He was the only person on the aisle. His mind registered the colours at its edges: *magnolia, orchid, calico.* He waited for thirty seconds but nobody came. He turned to continue and when he looked up he saw two large men walking towards him.

Slowly, he turned his trolley round and headed back the way he had come.

The store was so empty. The absence of other humans made the place cavernous and alien. He looked about him for something he could use as a weapon. If the two men came too close he wanted to be ready. He had seen some hammers a few aisles over. He brought his trolley round, painfully conscious of his shoes clicking loudly on the cheap, tiled floor. He found the hammers. He stopped his trolley and then saw him, ahead. Another man. He was carrying something inside a carrier bag. Their eyes met and the stare was held.

Joseph could sense the other men now, coming up behind him. He lowered his head and listened. They were close. Slowly, he lifted his arm. His fingers closed around the thin handle of one of the hammers on the wall. Its head was small but one of its tines tapered away to a dull, dense point.

He turned and looked at the two men coming his way. They did not seem ill, but being ill was not the only thing that caused violence. Not in this new world. Not even in the old. When they saw him looking at them they stopped. Everybody was stationary; four men, all standing still, all aware of the danger in the strangers around them. Joseph readied himself.

Back and forth he brought his head, watching the two men on one side and the man carrying the bag on the other. The store was silent, a faint hum of lights but nothing more. The scent of paint hung in the air.

And then, on both sides, movement. Joseph kept his head low, his ears pricked. He brought his head up, looked up and down at them from the tops of his eyes. They were moving backwards, slowly, cautiously. He realized something. They were backing off from him, easing away. They were scared of him. He felt the weight of the hammer in his hands, his grip tight. The men receded from his peripheral vision, slowly. He watched them go until, at last, he was standing alone in the aisle, his chest heaving. His fingers loosened their grip and he closed his eyes. He was the one to be feared. He thought of the woman in the car outside, waiting for him. He was the one to be feared.

|||

She kept checking the rear-view mirror. He could sense the same tension in her that was in him. The sound of the road rolling beneath the wheels was loud.

'It's OK,' he said at last. 'I don't think the people back there were dangerous.'

'I'm sorry.' She gripped the steering wheel. 'I can't believe how untrusting I've become. I don't mean to be. It's just hard, you know?'

They drove between the tall hedgerows. The car came to a bend. It arrived too quickly and Miriam was driving too fast. The wheels lost traction, the balance of the car toppled and the tyres skidded on to the narrow grass embankment. Joseph held his breath. Miriam brought the wheel hard round and slammed on the brakes. The vehicle righted itself and they rejoined the rough road.

'Shit.'

Her voice wavered. She hit the wheel with the palm of her hand.

'Hey, it's OK,' he said.

She breathed heavily, trying to get herself under control.

'I'm sorry.' Her voice faltered. 'You think everything's going OK, and then . . . it's just small things. Christ, I'm a wreck.' She laughed.

Joseph said nothing. He glanced across to her and wondered

how often the thought of Henry passed through her head. Perhaps he was always there, in the back of her mind, like a dead weight.

The hedgerows gave outwards and the road widened. It was straight here. Forest grew on either side. Tall sycamores, the first vivid green shoots of spring flicking from their branches, towered over them and receded into the distance. Joseph looked into the trees. Maybe he could come here one day. It might be a good place to hide. He had played in these trees as a kid, ridden his bike out there in the woods and spent the days exploring.

It was still bright outside when they got back to the house. The days were getting longer. Edward and Mary were playing on the grassland, throwing a tennis ball over Pele.

Joseph looked at them, and looked at Miriam. A complex set of thoughts channelled themselves into the front of his mind. She was beginning to trust him. He could sense it, in the same way that he could see her coming out of her grief. She was never going to let him go.

Edward threw the ball in a high arc. Mary flailed her arms hopelessly in the air as the ball curled over her head and bounced gently on the soft grass. Joseph felt a steady stream of warmth grow up in his stomach. He knew what it was. It was happiness. His body felt relaxed as Mary ran to fetch the ball, her little legs circling fast and silent beneath her.

IIII

The world was breathing colours back into the trees and plants. It was nearly June and the sky was lighter, the afternoons warmer and the days longer. Today the sun caught the sea and turned it glaring white. Joseph and Miriam lay side by side on the cliff top, the sun warm on their backs. Joseph felt peaceful.

'So this is what you do,' he said. He lifted the gun off the towel he had used to keep the dust from getting to it. 'You have to cock it. You press this button here, that's called the "safety", and then hold the stock here, and pull the barrel down like this until it clicks.'

He lifted the gun up and handed it to Miriam.

'So I press this?'

'Yes.'

'And then pull this down?' She grasped the barrel halfway along and pulled. 'It's quite tough.'

Her face creased with effort as she pulled the metal barrel down.

A month had passed since she had agreed to learn how to use the air rifle; a month of protestations and prevarications on Miriam's behalf until, at last, she could put it off no longer. Whereas before she had always been able to tell Joseph that she didn't have time to learn how to shoot because there were so many other more important things to do, now there was more than enough time. Time was the most abundant commodity in the world now.

The month had passed slowly but safely. The media were reporting less frequently. Several commercial television stations had disappeared entirely. The illness was still killing people and there was still no way of stopping it. The cities were decaying and chaotic, the main highways up and down the country were the hiding places of vicious gangs of bandits, refugee camps had sprung up spontaneously as people evacuated the cities, and the army had declared, at an official level, martial law. They listened to the news reports and the sick feeling in their stomachs never really went away but there was a degree of separation between them and the disaster. They had not seen an infected person since they had come to Cornwall. In fact, they had seen hardly anybody. Occasionally people would come to the house, but the sight of the barbed-wire fencing and Joseph's cold behaviour soon saw them on their way. Sometimes they would carry on down the hill and spend the night in the large car park behind the beach, but they never stayed there for long. There was nothing there for them. Had the illness not killed as many people as it had, Joseph knew there would be more people coming their way, along with a greater fight for remaining food supplies.

But Joseph didn't care about the other people. The only thing he cared about was the security of the house and its inhabitants. He enjoyed the new silence that had fallen over the world. He hadn't seen an aeroplane vapour trail cross the sky in weeks and the air was still without the constant vibrations of cars and trucks. The green of early summer swayed softly in the trees and it seemed to him that the world was purging itself of the toxins that had for so long smothered it. The last month had been a good one.

As he lay on the grassland in front of the house, right out near the tip of the headland, the sun warmed his back. Miriam struggled with the barrel for a few seconds, easing it towards the right angle. Finally there was a mechanical click and she exhaled.

'Got it.'

'OK, now you take a pellet' – he fished one from the jar – 'and put it into the chamber, nose first.'

He indicated the curved end of the little pellet. She took it from him, turned it round in her fingers and slid it into the chamber.

'Now you need to bring the barrel back up until it clicks shut.'

She did this quickly.

'OK, and we're ready to fire. You just need to disengage the safety, here.'

He leaned across and placed his finger on the small metal hook next to the trigger.

'Here?'

'Yeah.'

'OK.'

With her forefinger she worked the lever into its position.

'So if you pull the trigger now, it will fire.'

'Shall I do it?'

'Just wait. I need to show you how to hold the gun properly.'

A gust of wind washed across the grass, blowing the tips in a wave before them. As the grass moved it caught the sunlight and they could see the movement of the wind across the land.

'You push the butt of the rifle into your shoulder.'

He helped her turn the gun round.

'Like this?'

He took hold of the stock and pushed it gently into her, making sure it was set firm.

'That's fine. It doesn't make much difference, but it helps to keep your aim steady. If it was a shotgun it would stop you getting bruised from the recoil.'

'OK.'

'Now cradle the gun in your left hand and use your right to fire.'

Miriam followed his instructions. Her hair blew in front of her face. She took her left hand from beneath the gun, rested the barrel on the towel and tucked her hair behind her ear. She brought the gun back up.

'Now look through the sight. Look through it with your left eye.'

'It's out of focus.'

'Use this.'

He tapped the focus wheel with his index finger and she turned it slowly between her thumb and forefinger.

'That's better.'

'Can you see the tins?'

'Uh-huh.'

'Aim for the one closest to us. Get it between the two black lines.'

'The crosshairs you mean.'

He smiled. 'Yeah. Before you fire take a small breath and pull the trigger with a steady, deliberate motion. OK?'

She relaxed. He heard her take a breath. She closed her mouth and there was a snap. And then a ping. Forty yards away the tin popped up and fell backwards.

'Bloody hell!' he exclaimed.

She looked at him and smiled. 'I'm a natural.'

'Go for the next one.'

The second can was twenty yards back from the first one.

'No problem.'

She lifted the gun up and looked through the sight. She pulled the trigger and made a disgruntled face when nothing happened.

'You might want to load it before you shoot.'

She flicked him with the back of her hand and went through the process again, checking with him that she was doing it correctly. She fired but missed the tin. Without the metallic ping of contact it seemed like the bullet was still out there somewhere, flying through the air.

'Bad luck.'

'Let me try again.'

She hit it on her fourth attempt.

'Very good. Now you need to go for the third one.' The third tin can was another twenty yards back.

'I can hardly see it.'

'Just take it nice and steady.'

She fired off six pellets but they all missed.

'This is difficult,' she said.

The sun was getting lower in the sky now. They had been out there practising for over an hour.

'If we wait for a little longer the rabbits will be out,' he said.

'I don't know if I'm ready for that.'

'You should do it. They're just rabbits.'

'Maybe.'

'I don't know why you're happy to eat them, but not to kill them.'

Miriam didn't answer that. She laid the gun down and looked at the towel on the grass in front of them.

'Joseph,' she said, 'can we talk about something?'

Joseph paused. Her face had adopted its serious countenance.

'What?'

'This thing about us going into the cellar every time somebody comes to the door.'

'What about it?'

'It scares the children.'

A small fly fluttered in front of his face. He batted it away with the back of his hand.

'It's safer if we do it.'

'It's overkill.'

There was that word again. 'Maybe we should let the kids answer the door to whoever it might be. Is that what you would like?'

He got the feeling this whole shooting exercise had been nothing more than a ruse to disarm him so she could broach this subject. An unhappy disappointment formed in his head. He should have known better.

'Why have you always got to be like this?' she said.

'Like what?'

'Like . . . this.' She held her arms up towards him.

'I'm looking out for us.'

'We've been here for three months now. I want to try something new. I don't want us to be like prisoners whenever anybody comes our way. And I don't want my kids to be afraid of other people, either.'

'So what would you suggest?'

'Just that we be normal, Joseph. And don't assume the people coming our way are going to kill us. We don't need to go into the cellar when people come. We can carry on as normal. We're too paranoid.'

Joseph sighed. He wished she would trust him.

'The trouble is . . .' He paused, thinking of how to say it. 'I know that most people don't need to be feared, and I wish we could act as if everything was normal, but it will only take one thing to go wrong and it will be all over. Is it worth taking the risk?'

She didn't even consider what he'd said. 'I think so. It has to be better than the way things are now. If we have to hide from people indefinitely then I think I'd rather things ended.'

'What?'

She waved her hand. 'I'm sorry, I didn't mean that. What I mean is we can't go on acting like this. It's not healthy.'

'I know you don't believe me when I say it, but one day something bad will come to the door. It will.'

'Don't be so dramatic.'

He shook his head.

'Let's just try it.'

'OK, I'll make a deal with you.' He thought about making her promise that she would leave him if he became ill, but knew that now was not the time. 'We'll try it, as long as you let me teach Edward how to shoot rabbits.'

Miriam lifted her head upwards in exasperation and sighed loudly. 'God, you're so difficult!'

'Do we have a deal?'

She puffed out her cheeks.

'You've seen that it's not hard. And it's not dangerous either.' He looked at her face, trying to decipher her thoughts. 'I need to teach him, Miri. You won't shoot a live rabbit and you know it. I don't know what the big deal is—'

'OK,' she said quickly. 'It's a deal.'

'Really?'

'Sure. But no more hiding in the cellar.'

'Fine.'

She lifted her hand up for him to shake. He took it and they both shook. He looked back into the direction of the cans and saw the first of the rabbits come skipping out of its hole.

III

The house was deserted and the garden overgrown. The large, grey bricks were crumbling and the white paint of the wooden window frames had peeled away into brown scratch marks. The grass had grown above the levels of the window ledges and the brambles in front of the faded front door were thick coils.

The house had been empty for as long as Joseph could remember. He led Miriam and the children, who carried the baskets, past it and down a gentle slope to the walled garden. He had always wanted to live in this house, away from the rest of civilization, but it was just another thing that had never happened.

There had been a wooden gate guarding the entrance to the garden but over the years it had split and fallen away and now there was no evidence of it ever having existed at all. But the cherry trees were still there, as they had been when he was a kid. The wall of the garden stood well above their heads but it had cracked in places and mosses and grasses had grown into the cracks so that it seemed alive. The grass here was tall, up to the children's chests, but they pushed through and stopped at the first tree.

Joseph looked up into the branches at the little red cherries. Nobody had been here. Through the branches he caught glimpses of the warm blue sky. He set the step ladder, climbed up into the tree and snapped the fruits away.

'Can you catch, Mary?' he called down, holding a handful of cherries out into mid-air.

The little girl nodded, set her basket down and cupped her hands. Joseph smiled.

'Pick the basket up. I mean catch it in there.'

Miriam laughed.

From where he was standing the family appeared as a triangle. He smiled at Miriam but when he did it triggered a type of guilt because this was not his family. It was Henry who should have been there, not him. He was an impostor.

They collected the cherries for what was left of the morning, each of them taking it in turns to climb the ladder. Edward had scrambled up into the trees and along the branches. He had a gift for it and with his help they managed a good harvest.

Just before lunch they went to the largest of the trees, right up in the corner of the garden. Its lowermost branches were out of reach for Edward and so Joseph took his place on the ladder. Standing on the metal platform at the top of the steps he reached up towards the thin branch that lay just beyond the reach of his fingertips.

'Careful, Joseph,' Miriam said, but just as she said it he felt the ladder topple sideways. Instinctively he leaped for the branch and closed his fingers around it as the ladder fell away. Mary screamed with delight as the thin branch bent under his weight. Joseph lifted his feet and reached for the tree's trunk but the branch was too thin and, with a loud crack, it snapped. He thumped awkwardly into the long grass on his backside and with a small yelp.

He closed his eyes in pain and peals of laughter filled his ears. He looked up and was greeted by the sight of Miriam and the children leaning over him, the blue sky beyond them, and as they laughed he grabbed Mary by the arm and pulled her gently into the grass. She squealed and tried to wriggle away from him.

'Not so funny now, is it?' He laughed.

He got to his feet and dusted himself down with a smile on his lips.

They went and sat under the shade of the large tree with their backs against the wall, and ate the bread and cheese that Miriam's mother had packed for them. When the children had finished their food they ran off into the long grass and disappeared from view. The only sound was of the leaves of the cherry trees rustling calmly in the low breeze.

'So I've been thinking,' he said. The wall was warm against his back. 'About my father's bedroom.' As soon as he said it the image of his father's white face flashed uninvited across his mind. 'I thought that maybe your mother would like to sleep there.'

He turned to face her. There was a brief silence and then the edges of her mouth stretched into a melancholic smile.

'I think it's been long enough now. So' – he ensured he did not break eye contact – 'what do you think?'

A warm glow grew between them. She nodded her agreement and, in silence, they turned their heads forwards and stared at the swaying grass.

|||

The family went about their nightly rituals as usual. The children were washed and had cleaned their teeth. They changed into their nightclothes and were tucked into their new bed in the long room at the back of the house.

Miriam and her mother kissed them goodnight, turned off the light and closed the door.

'Edward?' whispered Mary.

'What?'

'Does your side still hurt?'

'No.' He could feel his sister's breath on him.

'Do you like Uncle Joseph?' she asked.

He turned the question over in his head. 'Yes.'

'Do you think he's grumpy?'

'No, I think he's cool.'

Mary ruminated on this for a few seconds.

'He is grumpy though.'

Edward sighed. 'He was nice today though, wasn't he?'

Mary didn't say anything and was silent for a few moments.

'Do you prefer him to Dad?'

'Shush. I want to go to sleep.'

'I'm not tired.'

'You will be tomorrow if you don't sleep.'

'I miss my friends.'

'Me too.'

'Do you think they're safe?'

He wanted to say no, just to annoy her, but he knew she might burst into tears if he did. A few months before he would have relished the chance to play such a joke on her but he no longer had the heart.

'Yeah. They're safe.'

'How do you know?'

'I just do, OK?'

'You don't know for sure.'

Edward rolled over and pulled his pillow over his head.

||||

Miriam's mother waited outside with her ear to the door. She could hear them whispering. Just. For a moment she considered in all of its true colours the lives her grandchildren would probably be forced to lead. The thought made her afraid so she cleared her mind and went to her new bedroom. As she moved across the landing, she thought of Joseph and what him giving her the room meant. He was good really. Maybe he would turn a corner now.

The room was spotlessly clean. Everything had a home. She sat down at the dressing table that was set into a small alcove in the back wall, and brushed her hair in the mirror. She had arranged her makeup and perfumes into a small city of tubs and pots on the right. She had never used much makeup in the past but now, with so much time, she had found herself spending thirty minutes or more each morning arranging her appearance, savouring the process.

There was a photograph of Joseph's mother on the table, in a silver picture frame. It was black and white and she looked young in it. Joseph's mother had always been so elegant. She had not known her for long before she died, but she had dealt with her illness with such grace.

She laid her hands on the tabletop. A smooth patina of varnish sat atop the deep, rich mahogany. It was a beautiful table. The legs arced gracefully down to the floor like the necks of swans, concluding at the carpet in smooth bulbs. Rose vines were etched into the wood, wrapping themselves around the legs, culminating in the flower, which had been elegantly worked into the stanchions.

Three thin drawers ran down the left-hand side of the table. She pulled them open and pushed them closed. They ran smoothly on their runners and their insides were lined with vellum. The top two drawers were empty but in the third one she found a writing pad, a pen and a sheaf of envelopes. On top of the writing set she found a letter. She picked it from the drawer and turned it over in her hands. It was addressed to Joseph.

III

He needed to check the outside of the house before he went to bed. He made his way slowly around the walls. It had been a good day. He sat and leaned against the front wall and looked out towards the sea. In the darkness it appeared to him as a dark void but he could hear it out there, in the bay, whispering against the sand.

The house was quiet inside. He climbed the stairs slowly. He didn't like to show it but the fall from the ladder had hurt his back. He was getting too old to take falls like that. He went to his room but before he went inside a voice came from his left.

'Joseph.'

Miriam's mother was standing in the doorway of his father's bedroom, framed in a rectangle of dim yellow light, wearing a white nightdress.

'I found this in one of your father's drawers,' she said quietly. She held out to him a rectangle of white paper. He crossed the landing and took it from her.

'It's addressed to you.'

Something shot up the back of his neck. His mouth was suddenly dry. He took the envelope from Miriam's mother. She looked up at him expectantly.

'Thank you,' he said.

In the darkness he could see the black, inky swirls of the handwriting on the envelope. He placed a corner of it at his lips. His mind was jumbled. He turned away from Miriam's mother and slowly descended the stairs.

He went to the kitchen and poured some water into the kettle, setting the envelope down on the counter. He did not know if he should open it. The image flickered in his mind again, of the powdered white face and the lips red with blood.

His fingers tapped the unit restlessly as he waited for the kettle to boil. The writing on the envelope clearly belonged to his father; he knew its elegance. The kettle whistled on the hob. He made himself a cup of tea and made his way through to the living room. It was dark but he knew his way around the house without light. He sat in the armchair near the window, his father's chair, and turned on the small reading light at his shoulder. It threw long shadows over the surface of the envelope. He could see his own reflection in the glass of the window, a spectre in the blackness – a head and two dark holes for eyes. Placing his thumb at the corner of the envelope he felt its edge press into his skin. Bringing his thumb under and cracking the paper along the envelope's apex he pulled out its contents and held them up to the light. Two sheets of paper.

His father had always liked nice writing paper. Seeing the script made his throat heavy. It was as if he was reading beyond time and his father was there in the room. He sensed somebody behind him but when he looked there was nobody there, just shadows and gentle light playing across the furniture. But he sensed something there, something being drawn out of the room through an unknown fabric, two worlds merging.

Son,
It feels strange writing this letter. It is not something I ever thought I would be doing. You probably know why I am writing and I know the circumstances under which you must be reading.

Maybe I shouldn't be writing this at all, but since your brother died I have been feeling the regret of never having said the things that I should have. I'm sure he knew, but it's just not the same. I should have said those things. It's funny how you always think back at times when you should really be concentrating on the future. But still.

Over the last few days I've been thinking about the night you were born. It's all still so vivid. I went outside the hospital for some air and as I was standing there I saw a shooting star in the sky and then when I went back inside there you were. I remember seeing you for the first time. You might find this funny but the thing that really struck me was the colour of your skin. You were as pink as a salmon! But the colour was aliveness and I remember you crying and wriggling in your mother's arms – a tiny unit of life. And then there was a very deep-seated feeling of joy and achievement.

Everything changed after you came along; it all opens up when you become a father for the first time. Everything starts to make sense. Those first few years, when it was just you, me and your mother, are still cherished. I used to love being in work and thinking of you at home, and knowing that I had you to look forward to at the end of the day.

I know that you sometimes felt I doted on your little brother, and perhaps I did, but I am writing this now to put the record straight. I loved both of you equally, with all of my heart.

Henry was the sort of kid who needed love demonstrated to him. You were not like that. I always thought that you were more instinctive and that you always knew how much I loved you. In recent years I have started to see that maybe I was wrong and it has perhaps driven you further away than I ever wanted but I hope this letter will put an end to that. I was not the perfect father.

Henry was always like me and you were like your mum. Henry was openly (and brashly!) affectionate whilst you were always so staid. But you were the most sensitive and caring of the two. You were always the most thoughtful and generous. All you wanted to do was be good and do the right thing, ever since you were a kid. These characteristics made me very, very proud of you but, more than this, they brought me great happiness. In this respect you gave me more than Henry ever did. I always felt a depth of bond between us because you were the shooting star. I want you to know that this was how I felt even if you didn't realize it.

You can be the man you think you should be, Joseph. You very nearly are. If you are reading this letter then take care of Miriam and the kids because they will be relying on you. Do not let them come to any harm.

I'm going to finish now. There are things I need to do. Take care, son, and always remember that I love you.

Yours,

Dad

|||

On clear days the sea would appear as a deep green. The different layers of current interlocked behind one another until they became a solid, uniform mass.

'Do you think about him much?'

'Sometimes,' he said. 'Not much.'

A tanker was crossing the horizon, the first they had seen in a month. Pele had ventured out in front of them to the edge of the cliff, his ears standing to attention.

'I think about him,' she said, 'about what happened.'

The face flashed before him again, stark and vivid.

'It's in the past,' he said coldly.

Miriam nodded and wrapped her hands around her body.

'It's all in the past,' she repeated.

And then there was a sound, faint and thin, a sound that neither of them had heard in a long time. They looked up towards the house, at the open front door. The sound was coming from there. The telephone was ringing.

|||

'It's Father Moore,' said Miriam's mother, immediately and without warning, the phone hanging loose in her hands.

She was crying. She looked at Joseph as he closed the front door. Miriam stepped forwards.

'What about him?'

Her mother nodded slowly, her cheeks wet.

'Is he dead?' Miriam clasped the top of her head in her right hand. 'What happened?' she said, her voice high.

'He was' – the old woman reached out her hand to the banister – 'oh God.'

'Mum? What happened to him?'

Her mother looked up at her. Joseph felt he shouldn't be there, that this was a personal thing between Miriam and her mother.

'They . . . he was stabbed.'

A cold creep slumped into the room.

'So he wasn't ill?' he said.

His voice was loud. But he wanted the information. He knew the type of man Father Moore had been. He had to know.

'What?'

Miriam's mother looked at him in confusion. She had to think for a second. 'No, he was ill.' She rubbed her nose with a tissue. The skin prickled on Joseph's arms. 'They killed him to save themselves,' she said. 'They had no choice.'

|||

Joseph went upstairs and lay on his back. As a boy he would lie and stare up into that same patch of space that he stared at now. He was no more sure of anything than he had been then. At no point had his mind finally clunked into the smooth rails. Had the adults of his youth, the people who seemed so assured, been the same? He wondered whether some people were able to find a footing in life whilst others spent their whole time fumbling in the dark. Was that how it worked? Or did everybody feel the same as him but was able to hide it better? Was it a little secret that everybody felt but never discussed?

Father Moore had become violent. Whatever trait was responsible for turning people into monsters had been in the old priest and Joseph knew now what it was. The illness amplified the kernel of every individual it invaded. Gentle people became more gentle, violent people became more violent; a distillation of people's innermost ways. It turned you into who you really were. How it did it, the dissection of its epidemiology, no longer mattered; with each passing day, its nature and origin had grown in the collective unconsciousness into something legendary, mythic and unholy.

He knew the thing that had been in the priest was inside him too: a black orb in his centre, a circle of badness. It was the thing that made him do the things he did, the reason he was stubborn, conceited, intense. It had always been there, that underburn of aggression. It was the thing that made him petulant, made him hold a grudge, made him tell too much truth. He knew when he was behaving a certain way because the black orb would vibrate inside him, cancerous and malignant. He had too much hate in him, hated too many things. There was a discontentment, a resentment that was too strong. It was the reason he could never get close to people, the reason he didn't have any real friends, the reason he had not called anybody when the illness first struck. Its presence was as clear to him in some as its absence was in others. He knew immediately if a similar blackness was in somebody else because the people who had it were the people he disliked. He had it, Father Moore had had it. It was that simple, it was a truth.

The image of Miriam and the kids smiling happily up at him in the branches of the cherry tree came to him and he closed his eyes. *Why am I trying to be something I'm not?*

|||

He took Edward out to the grass at the front of the house. There were no rabbits out but Joseph could sense that when the time came, Edward would not feel the same guilt towards killing that his mother did. When he had been young he had always been able to tell which of his friends would be willing to pull the trigger and which wouldn't. The people who wouldn't pull the trigger were the ones who asked all the questions. Edward listened to Joseph's instructions and carried them out in near silence.

They fired at empty tins for over an hour. It was cloudy and cold, the sea was in high swell. There was more bad weather on the way.

'Did my father used to like shooting?'

'No.'

Edward had taken to speaking of his father more regularly in the past month, as if by filling in gaps in his knowledge, he could keep the memory of him closer.

'Did he like bunny burgers?'

'Yes.'

'But he didn't like hunting?'

Joseph turned to his nephew and placed his hand on his head. A quick decision was made.

'You should stop thinking about your father all the time.'

The boy's head was tiny. His long hair was soft, like feathers. He had large brown eyes, the same colour as Miriam's. They looked out at Joseph questioningly, phrased with a confused hurt.

'Thinking about your dad will not bring him back. Now let's try again.' Joseph nodded towards the cans. 'Try to stay still or you'll never hit anything.'

As he watched Edward lower his head to look through the sight he remembered how he had been as a child when he had fired at tin cans – the weight of the weapon, the exhilaration. It never really went away.

'Uncle Joseph, what's Pele doing?'

Joseph turned towards the sea. Pele had moved all the way to the cliff edge, to the few feet of grass that sloped down to the precipice. He was staring out over the water. His mouth was open and his tongue lolled. Joseph followed Pele's eyes out to sea but there was nothing there.

'Wait here, Edward,' he said. He rose awkwardly to his knees. 'I'll go and fetch him.'

As he stood a gust of wind caught his coat and he had to steady himself. The physical work he had been doing in the garden and on the house was taking its toll on his body. His collar flapped loudly against his neck.

'Pele,' he called.

The dog turned its head inland. Upon seeing its master it lowered its mouth to the floor and looked at Joseph with sad eyes.

'What's the matter, boy?'

He knelt in front of the dog and placed his hands on either side of Pele's head. He stroked underneath his chin and the dog responded with a loud panting.

'Uncle Joseph.'

Edward looked small and distant on the square of blanket. The grass around him blew in the wind, cutting currents. The boy was pointing towards the house. His voice came in and out on the wind in half sentences.

There was a man there, hunched over and wrapped in a dirty

blanket, at the garden gate. The front door was wide open. Joseph was caught for a second, unsure, and then his mind was clear, and he ran towards Edward, towards the gun.

|||

The man was already in the garden. Beneath the blanket he wore a pack that made him look like a hunchback. Joseph thought about shouting but stopped himself. If the man knew he was there he might make a run for the house and lock himself inside.

His breath burst out of him with each stride. The oxygen burned his lungs. He was almost at the gate. The man was feet from the door. He was going to go inside.

Joseph opened his mouth and shouted at the top of his voice.

The figure in the blanket turned round. His eyes widened. His face was filthy, the bottom half covered in a dirty beard. Through the grime Joseph could see the yellowy-whites of his eyes.

'Take one more step towards that house and you're a fucking dead man,' he said loudly.

He stepped cautiously towards him and raised the gun. The gravel of the garden path crunched under his shoes. The gun was not loaded but the bearded man did not know that. He lifted his hands into the air and his dirty, dark blanket fell away.

'Please,' he said quietly. 'Don't shoot me.'

He turned his face away and closed his eyes tight shut.

'Get away from the door.'

He did as he was told. He moved out towards the middle of the garden. Joseph kept the gun trained on him. The man's clothes were stinking. He was thin, emaciated, the skin of his face stretched tight over his cheeks and jaw. His skeletal appearance was shocking. This was the first time somebody had come to the house looking like this.

Joseph tried to breathe. His chest was tight. Adrenalin surged through him. He moved up the path, twisting his body to keep the gun on the stranger. At last he was between the man and the door. There was a squall of noise behind him and then Miriam was standing in the doorway.

'Put the gun down,' she said.

'Stay out of this, Miriam.'

All he cared about was keeping the house safe. He didn't take his eyes off the stranger, who had folded his arms into his body, making himself as small as possible.

'You promised me we weren't going to do this any more. We had a deal.'

'This is different.'

'Don't be afraid.'

He swung his head round to her. She was talking to the stranger, who looked back at her through darting, sunken eyes. The stranger turned to Joseph and their eyes met.

He could feel the volatility of the situation. The man standing before him was wasted to such an extent that he might do anything. Joseph did not lower the gun.

The stranger smiled at him, his teeth gleaming out from between dry, grey lips.

'I don't mean any harm,' he said. 'Please.'

Joseph raised his rifle higher.

'Please,' said the man, again. But now he said it more lightly. He was less afraid. His back had straightened.

Joseph could feel Miriam's eyes on him. He wanted to smash the stranger's skull in. Something at the back of his head told him that the threat he had been expecting since they moved to Cornwall had finally arrived.

Miriam went into the garden and placed her body between Joseph and the stranger.

'Put it down.'

He expected her to be angry, but there was something else in anger's place. It was almost as if she felt sorry for Joseph. Her eyes were open wide and pleading. They sucked the energy out of him.

He lowered the gun and looked over Miriam's shoulder to the stranger. His teeth were yellow, his face vaguely rat-like with a long, thin, triangular nose and a weak chin. His eyes were jaundiced. Joseph knew that some people were bad from the start and you could tell who they were just by looking at them.

'Let me deal with it this time,' he heard Miriam say at the corner of his mind.

Joseph held his breath.

'Joseph,' she said to him.

Her hair had blown in front of her face and she had to squint to see as she pulled it to one side and held it there in a fist.

'You promised,' she said.

III

The sun had almost set and the light in the house was dim. They went into the kitchen. Joseph did not want this man in his father's house. It felt like an invasion, a surrender.

'I'm sorry if I caused any offence,' said the stranger.

His voice was ragged and throaty. There was an odd timbre in it, something that Joseph could not place. Miriam placed a cup of tea in front of him and sat down opposite. There was an agelessness about him. He could have been twenty or he could have been fifty.

'Joseph is just a little wary.'

The stranger's eyes moved across to Joseph.

'I'm sorry.'

'What would you have done if I hadn't stopped you?' he said bluntly.

The man cocked his head to one side. 'I don't know what you mean.'

'You were just going to go inside? As easy as that?'

'No.'

'Yes.'

The stranger paused. He looked at Miriam.

'My name is Paul. Paul Crowder.'

He had realized that it was Miriam who was going to listen. Joseph had been dismissed.

'Where have you come from?' she said.

'London.'

'What happened to you?' She gestured to his filthy clothes.

'I've been living rough. I didn't have anywhere to go.'

He said it in such a way that Joseph knew Miriam would take pity. It was so obvious what this man was trying to do.

'Where are you heading?' he said coldly.

'I don't know. I thought I would decide when I reached the sea.' He laughed nervously.

His shoulders slumped forwards. The line of his collarbone was prominent below his neck. The skin around it was tight, as if the bone had been shrink-wrapped in skin. His wrists were the same: thin, bony. Beneath his beard his cheeks were sunken. The beard itself was coarse and patchy. There were bald gaps at the chin where he had pulled it out. For a moment Joseph felt sorry for him. The man's body had wasted away, was wasting away still, and Joseph reminded himself that sympathy was dangerous.

'Well, you've reached the sea,' Miriam said, with a laugh.

'Yeah.'

He didn't add anything. He had nothing else to say. The idea that he was lost was given space to sink into their consciences.

'Do you have any family?'

Crowder looked at the table and shook his head.

'No friends?'

'They all died. My family and my friends,' he said.

Suddenly the door to the kitchen burst open. There was a shock of energy around the table as the children ran into the room. Edward was chasing Mary. When they saw the stranger, they stopped instantly and their backs straightened.

'Can you wait outside, kids?' Joseph said.

'It's OK,' said Miriam.

Joseph looked at her.

'Come and sit down.' She glanced at Joseph. 'This is Mr Crowder.'

The children looked at the man in the filthy clothes but did not move from their spot. They were uneasy with the new presence.

'We'll go outside and play,' said Edward quietly.

He looked at Joseph, who nodded with approval. 'Good idea,' he said.

He could sense Miriam's annoyance but Joseph didn't care. She shouldn't try to prove a point by putting her children at risk.

'You run along,' he said.

The children left behind them a wake of silence. Joseph's right foot tapped the floor.

'So,' said Miriam, breaking the tension. 'You're welcome to use the bathroom if you want. And we're having vegetable stew for dinner. Is that OK?'

Crowder looked at Miriam and smiled. The skin at the corners of his eyes creased and his eyes flickered to Joseph for an instant and then back to Miriam.

'Thank you.'

|||

Joseph waited in his bedroom whilst Crowder used the bathroom. He stood at the small window and looked out to the west, the direction from which Crowder had walked to the house. He wondered how he had come that way. Logically he would have come from the east, from the direction of the village. There was nothing to the west – just the unmanned lighthouse and the woods.

He listened to the hiss of the shower coming through the wall and imagined the evening that lay ahead – dinner, awkward conversation, and then what? Joseph would have to tell him to leave. He knew that such a moment would arrive. Inviting him into the house was unfair on the stranger. Miriam had given him false hope. He could not stay with them. That much was certain. Joseph would not allow that. If they let him stay, even for one night, getting rid of him would be more difficult.

He thought about what his father would have done if he was still alive, but didn't have to think for long. He would have done the same thing as Miriam – unthinking and instinctive.

The mental photograph of his father dying came to him again. It triggered a sudden, deep anger inside him. The memory grew then, for the first time since it had happened. The mental image pulled back and the scene was there in its whole. He had knelt at his father's side and hooked his arms beneath his back. His bones were light and small. He had sat him up in the street, the sound of gunfire and helicopter blades and screaming all around. There had been no last words, no messages of good will. It was just death. He had just died. His father's biology had betrayed him and he had died. He was just skin and bones and hair after all. A machine. Approximation to sentience was just that. The magic was gone and all that had been left behind was an atrophying carcass.

The hiss of the shower in the room next door stopped. There was movement, sound, Crowder climbing out of the shower, a towel being drawn from its rail. Joseph looked again through his window at the road that stretched over the hill, out of sight, leading nowhere.

III

He was still dirty, even after his shower. It was ingrained in his skin. It had become a part of him. He hunched over his bowl of food and slurped it from his spoon.

'I'm sorry,' he said between greedy mouthfuls. 'I haven't had hot food in days.'

'When did you leave London?' asked Joseph in a voice neither friendly nor hostile.

'I don't know exactly. Three weeks ago. Four, maybe.'

'Where were you living?'

'South. But I was in Highbury when it wiped everyone out. I worked there.' He stared into his bowl as he spoke. 'I went back home and stayed in my flat for a week, just watching the TV and looking out of the window. What else was there to do, you know? There were dead bodies in the street under my window. Nobody came to collect them. I barricaded myself in so that the . . . violent . . . ones couldn't get in.' His eyes flitted around the room. 'You should have seen what they were doing.' The spoon in his hand, which had been moving towards his mouth, stopped. 'They were ripping the dead to pieces.'

Miriam glanced at Joseph. She directed her eyes towards the kids.

'You'll scare the kids,' he said.

Crowder shrugged. 'I'm just telling you what happened,' he said, not listening. He shovelled more food into his mouth. It ran down his chin, through his beard and back into the bowl. 'You don't need to hide things from children,' he said authoritatively.

Edward and Mary, their heads a foot lower than the others' at the table, sat with their arms at their sides.

Joseph sensed the change in the man; his confidence was growing.

'I felt like the last man on Earth, you know? Like the old legends. It was weird seeing a whole city disintegrate into shit—'

'Hey! That's enough.'

He wasn't listening. 'Nobody's got any hope any more. That's why we're all fucked.'

Miriam stood up and went round the table to the children. Crowder carried on, senseless to the frost in the room. Joseph let him speak so Miriam could understand what he had been saying about letting strangers into the house.

'This thing's not going away. It's coming for us all. We're just waiting for it – don't pretend you don't already know this. You know it's true.'

Miriam whispered to the children and they climbed down from their seats. The three of them left the room. Miriam's mother dropped her spoon loudly into her bowl before following her daughter and grandchildren. She put her hand on Joseph's shoulder as she passed behind him in a gesture of power transferral.

Crowder looked at Joseph. His small black eyes gleamed in the light.

'Why are they burying their heads in the sand?'

He half shouted it, wanting them to hear him.

'How did you find your way to this house?'

'I know the village. I used to come here on holidays when I was a kid.'

'So you thought you'd come here and cause trouble?'

'I'm not causing trouble.'

Joseph leaned slowly across the table to the man sitting opposite. He placed each of his hands on either side of Crowder's bowl and slid it gently back across the table towards himself. Crowder's eyes followed the bowl and continued on up until he and Joseph were staring into each other's eyes.

'This is my food now,' said Joseph.

Crowder's eyes welled up instantly.

'Please,' he said. His body began to shake. He covered his face with his long, skeletal fingers. The sleeves of his dirty sweater slid down his bone-thin wrist. 'I'm sorry. Please just let me finish my food. I don't know what I'm doing any more.' His voice wavered. 'I don't know where I'm going.'

Joseph watched Crowder's change half in disbelief and half in pity. Somewhere along the line something had broken this man. In just a few months what had once been a normal working, living human being had been reduced to the shadow now sitting before him.

'Paul,' he said.

Crowder's shoulders jerked as he sobbed. Wherever he had been, whatever things he had witnessed, had caught up with him. Perhaps the house itself was the final push; in it he would have seen the very things that he would never, ever have, and so the enormity of his own hopelessness. He cried uncontrollably – a mass of energy in flux, moving from stored state to spent.

'Paul,' said Joseph again.

But he wasn't listening. Joseph pushed the food back across the table. The steam from it rose into the knot of Crowder's arms and face. The heaves slowed and lessened, like a breeze moving away from a swaying tree. At last he stopped. He took his arms away from his head. His face was red, his cheeks soaked. The hairs on his beard glistened like beetle skin.

'I'm sorry. I'm sorry for the way I behaved. I'll leave.'

'You can finish your food.'

The kitchen door eased open and Miriam came back into the room. She stood at Joseph's shoulder.

'I'm sorry,' said Crowder, again. 'I don't know why I was being like that.'

Joseph watched his movements. Only a few threads of sanity were holding this man from chaos.

'We just want to help,' she said. 'Give you a meal, let you wash, you know.'

'I know.' He shovelled a spoonful of stew into his mouth and swallowed loudly. And then he said, seemingly to himself, 'I don't know what to do.'

The darkness was growing in the room as the day ended.

'They're saying the illness is taking people's hope,' said Crowder, quietly. 'Have you heard that? That's what they're saying. But it's stretching further than that.' He dried his cheeks with his muddy sleeves, smudging two grimy marks on the skin. 'So many people losing hope is contagious. I can feel it leaving me even though I'm not ill. You take it away and you start to realize just how powerful despair is.'

He looked at Miriam and Joseph with a quick, knowing smile. As soon as it had left him, Joseph felt his weird confidence return. He had to get rid of this man. He felt sorry for him but he was unstable. His mental state was too precarious to risk having around the family.

Miriam took a seat next to Joseph. She seemed calm. She pulled Mary's bowl over and took a spoonful of food.

'Where will you go?'

'I won't bother you.'

'You can't stay here, Paul,' said Joseph immediately. 'I don't want you to think you can. You will have to leave.'

Crowder breathed out a large bulk of air, as if he had just been punched in the stomach.

'I won't be any trouble,' he pleaded. 'I can help out.'

'It's not going to happen.'

'You said things will get back to normal.' Crowder addressed Miriam. 'Can't I stay here until then?'

'Paul,' said Joseph sternly. 'You're being pathetic.'

Crowder raised his voice suddenly. 'I'm just trying to survive, for God's sake.'

Miriam sat up in her chair.

'No room at the inn,' he said loudly, his head nodding in understanding. 'Is that it?'

Joseph needed to stop this before Miriam said something stupid. 'That is it, yes. There is no room.'

It was hard to believe that the first man they let into the house was so manipulative. But maybe that was to be expected. You'd need to be like that to survive and, that being the case, Joseph thought about just what other attributes this man might have. The thought made him uneasy.

'Perhaps we could take you somewhere,' said Miriam. 'We have a car.'

Crowder stared at the table like a child. 'Everyone I know is dead.' He said it flatly but the statement rang out clear. 'I'm alone.'

'There are camps though.'

Crowder looked up from the table. 'The camps? They're even worse. I went to the one outside Reading – that's the first place I tried.'

Crowder noticed Joseph's attention spike and turned his chest to face him.

'It had been there a fortnight but by the time I got there it was all over. They're not safe havens. They're fine if the army are there to protect you, but these places are massive and they can't be everywhere at once.' He looked down at the table again and put his hands loosely together. 'You know, when there are no laws, people do' – he looked up at them and smiled wanly – 'pretty much whatever they want. When I got there, I saw . . .' He trailed off, waited and started again. 'What I've learned is that when the world was normal we had all these things to try and make people equal, but take them away and it doesn't take long for the old ways to come back.'

Miriam leaned forward. 'But the news reports—'

'Show you what the army let them show you.'

'Why? I mean, what's the point in that?'

Crowder shrugged. 'People are liars. The army don't care about the truth. They just want people to think they're in control and as long as the news reports show things are going well, they keep their power, right? As long as they are powerful in the minds of the people, they are powerful.'

'So how long were you there for?'

'A day. That's all I needed to see how things were there. But there were more problems than just the gangs; far more. Lots of people were ill. Not with the Sadness, just physically ill. There wasn't enough clean water, not enough food.' He paused. 'Anyway,' he said finally, 'I don't want to go to another camp.'

Miriam said nothing. Joseph could feel her thoughts, feel the loosening towards Crowder.

'Maybe we can let you stay for one night,' she said.

His chest deflated. It had happened. He turned his head round to her. 'No,' he said.

'It's just one night, Joseph.'

He stood up from his chair. 'Can I have a word with you outside?'

She held his stare as she rose, and walked out through the kitchen door.

'What are you doing?'

He spoke quietly so his voice wouldn't travel past the closed door.

'You agreed that we try things my way.'

'You heard him earlier on, you saw the way he was with the kids. Forget whether he's good or bad, Miri, he's just not stable. That's the truth. He could do anything in his state.'

'He's lost his family and friends, Joseph. How do you think he should be behaving?'

Joseph sighed. 'I feel sorry for him, I really do, but he is going to be a problem.'

'Stop being so dramatic about everything. He needs love—'

'Oh please,' he scoffed. 'Miri, I know you want to help him, but going about it like this isn't the right way. If we let him stay, even for one night, we're giving him false hope.'

'He needs to get back on his feet, that's all. Then he can think about what he's going to do next.'

'Which will be to stay here. That's what he wants, and it's not going to happen. Look, the way you think; you don't look at things in the long term. Everything you do seems to be on some bizarre impulse—'

'Not true.'

'It is true. You think everything can be solved with quick fixes. You think that if we let him stay one night he'll get up in the morning all fresh as a daisy and ready to pack up his things and move on. It's retarded.'

'Thank you, Joseph.' She stared at him coldly.

'Well it is.' He shrugged. 'What if we let him stay? You're committing yourself to something you cannot deliver on. He'll see it for more than it is, whether you believe it or not. He'll want to stay.'

'It's just one night.'

'Yeah.'

'Don't be sarcastic, Joseph.' The pitch of her voice was higher. 'We have to do this. I have to do this. I believe it's the right thing to do.'

'What do you mean, "believe"?'

'Christ, Joseph. You don't have to have faith to know that helping people is the right thing to do.'

He ran his hand through his hair and leaned against the doorframe.

'This is crazy.' He took a deep breath and lifted his face to the ceiling. Finally composing himself, he said, 'Do you have any idea how annoying you are?'

Miriam smiled. 'It's just one night.'

They looked at one another. He suddenly wanted to kiss her. He tried pulling his thoughts away from the impulse. He hated himself for the thought even creating itself in his mind. He didn't even know what the feeling was.

She put her hand on his arm and squeezed. And then she stood on tiptoes and leaned in towards him. Her scent was warm and sweet. It had been so long since he had smelt perfume that it triggered a surprising and powerful base reaction in him. She moved her head to the side of his and kissed his cheek.

He remembered picking cherries with the children in the walled garden of the deserted house again, and lying on the grass with the sun on their backs, him teaching her how to shoot. As she went past him, back into the kitchen, he thought about grabbing her arm and stopping her. But he didn't. He let her go.

IIII

It was dark outside. Joseph walked around the house with one of the torches. He wanted to be sure that Crowder had not brought anybody else with him. The air rifle was strapped over his shoulder. The surreal prospect entered his head of one day using a gun against another human being.

He thought back to when he was a young man, an ideological

post-grad at the university. He and his friends often asked rhetorically, who has the right to take another human life? The idea was abhorrent. Where had that ideology gone now? Perspectives change like tides over the course of a life. Ideologies shrink when life tells them to. None of his friends, not even the ones with all that verve in them, all that piss and vinegar, had changed the world. Everything was just the same as it always had been.

Even now the only thing that had really changed was that a framework had been taken away. Human behaviour was allowed to amplify. Perhaps he would follow Crowder after he left, wait until they came to a quiet stretch and blow a hole in his chest. He could treat it as an experiment, a test, for the more dangerous men that would come later. That was the sort of man he had become.

Yellow squares of light were set into the dark walls of the house. They made small, luminescent puddles on the garden directly below, cutting deep shadows into the bushes, describing the blackness in absolute. He closed the metal shutters over each of the windows and locked them.

After two revolutions of the house he was happy that nobody was lying in wait. He flashed the torchlight up and down the road. It illuminated the dry grey concrete and the green grass on either side, but it could not reach the huge backdrop of blackness beyond.

|||

They put Crowder in Joseph's room. It was the smallest of the four bedrooms; just a thin wedge between the bathroom and Joseph's father's bedroom that occupied the south-western corner of the house.

It was small and simple but, most importantly, it had a lock with a key that could be turned from the outside.

'Are you going to be OK here?'

Crowder didn't look at him as he rolled on to the bed.

'Just leave me alone,' he pouted.

Joseph paused at the door. 'You know, we're trying to be—'

'What? Trying to what?' He blew air out from between his lips. 'You're locking me in this room?'

Joseph stood with his hand on the door handle. 'If you try anything, anything at all.'

Crowder turned on to his side, facing away. 'Yeah, I get it, tough guy.'

His back was curved, not humped but bowed. He brought his knees up under his chin.

'Listen to me, Paul.'

The man did not move. 'Just leave me alone,' his voice said slowly and sadly. 'You've already said enough.'

IIII

There was a knock at Miriam's door. She went across the room and opened it an inch. It was Joseph. The overhead light in the room flickered, died and came back to life again. Joseph's head snapped up towards it. The glow in its centre burned white holes in his vision.

'What was that?' said Miriam.

The light beamed consistently now in its socket. The moment had passed.

'A power surge maybe?'

There was no generator in the house. Joseph had rigged up some car batteries to electric sockets but if the electricity did die, they wouldn't provide power for long.

'Crowder's in bed,' he said.

He held up the small key to the bedroom lock.

'Thanks for this, Joseph.' She smiled.

Joseph turned the chair at the dressing table round and placed it in the centre of the room, facing Miriam. He could feel the paper of his father's letter folding in his back pocket.

'We have to talk about something,' he said.

Her eyes narrowed.

'I know you don't want to think about it, but we have to.'

'What are you talking about?'

'If I get ill—'

'Not this again.'

'Just listen, will you?'

She threw her hands up in submission.

'All I want you to do is drive me somewhere where we'll all be safe. You could take me to a hospital maybe, I don't know. I know you think it will all be fine, but it won't, and we need to make plans in case something happens. You know what happened to Father Moore, you know it. If I get ill then God knows what I'll do. That man in the other room, he's a wreck. Your instant reaction was to help him. Mine was to be suspicious of him. What do you think that means?'

'You're just being careful.'

He shook his head. 'Why can't you see it?'

'If you're such a bad person, then why are you being so kind? If your nature, or whatever, is so awful, then why have you done so much to protect us?'

He knitted his hands together in his lap. 'You just don't get it, do you? I do those things *despite* my nature, not because of it. I want you to be safe and I will help whilst I can but that doesn't change the facts.'

'You have no idea how stupid you sound when you talk like this.'

'I know I do.'

'Joseph.' She fixed his eyes. 'You helping us is your true nature. You're getting mixed up in your head. You can't tell what part of you is what.'

'Stop trying to sugarcoat things. We both know the truth.'

He spoke loudly now. He was getting annoyed at her refusal to see things.

Miriam leaned forward. 'There's no point in you shouting. We're not going to leave you.'

He closed his mouth and ran his tongue along the surface of his teeth. He waited for her to add something but she didn't. It was up to him.

'Well then, I'm finished.'

He sat back. Her face became suddenly serious.

'What's that supposed to mean?'

'Nothing.' He rose from his chair. 'I'm going to bed.'

'Joseph, wait.'

'What's the point?' He stopped at the door. 'You know what, Miriam?' He glared at her. 'If you don't start wising up you're going to land all of us in the shit.'

A look of hurt streaked across her features. Nothing had changed. She simply had not listened to a word he had said. It was almost as if she was wilfully refusing to accept the truth. It was clear to him now that she was not going to change her mind no matter what he said so he left the room with a shake of the head. He pulled the door closed and as he did the light on the landing began to flicker again.

|||

Joseph lay on his side with his eyes open, staring at the blank wall next to the window. There was no moon tonight. He blinked. His lids were heavy. The children breathed gently in their sleep.

He checked his watch, not willing to believe it was happening. But it was. He heard it again and so he sat up, his muscles tight, glad he had brought the air rifle up here with him. Quietly, so as not to disturb the children, he pulled on his jeans, his shirt and his boots, took up the gun and eased the door open.

The house was silent. He peered along the landing and moved out. He went to his room. The door was open. The lock was hanging off where Crowder had unscrewed the plate. He threw the light and his eyes stung with the brightness. The room was empty.

Slowly, he went down the stairs. The cellar door was open, a thin angle of light spilled into the hallway. There were noises coming from within. Joseph cursed himself for being so foolish. He edged over the few feet of wooden floorboards with his breath held.

The familiar scent of damp and dust drifted between the door and its frame. Crowder was making no effort to be quiet. Joseph could hear the sound of boxes being dragged along the stone floor, being opened, being rifled through. His old anger urged him to charge down the stairs and attack Crowder but he controlled himself. Crowder might now be armed, he knew.

Joseph moved down the steps as quietly as he could. The night-time routines had taught him every creak and he descended in near silence. He looked down the barrel of the air rifle as he went. The room came slowly into view: the shelves of supplies, the sofa, the table. Crowder was kneeling in front of the low table, his back to the stairs, his head dipped into a cardboard box.

Joseph watched him for a few seconds. He could hear the stranger breathing. He knew he had to shoot him. There was no choice. All his talking, all the warnings he had given Miriam about how the time would come to defend themselves were resolving into something real.

The man in the cellar was a threat. He had disobeyed Joseph's orders, ignored them, but that was not the only reason Joseph had to shoot him. Leaning against the table, easily within arm's reach, was one of the shotguns.

The door to the gun cabinet hung open, the broken padlock on the floor in front of it. As he stared at a line of flesh beneath Crowder's hair at the back of his neck, magnified in the crosshairs, all became clear. He thought of the letter his father had written him, of what sort of a man he really was, of how Miriam believed him to be good, of how she would never abandon him, and he pulled the trigger.

Crowder yelped like a dog. He fell forwards on to the box and slapped his hand on to the back of his neck as if crushing a fly. Joseph flew down the stairs. Crowder recovered and instinctively reached for the shotgun. But Joseph was too fast.

His mind detached from any depth it had; any ideas of mercy were blocked. Blood pulsed through the veins inside his skull. He brought the butt of his rifle round like he was swinging a baseball bat, and smashed it into the side of Crowder's head. The wood of the butt cracked under the force of the blow and Crowder's body fell sideways on to the dirty concrete floor, where he lay still. His eyes stared straight ahead like he was in a trance; his mouth opened and closed with breath, like a fish.

Joseph dropped the air rifle on to the sofa and grabbed the shotgun. Crowder had already loaded it.

'Why did you have to do this?' Joseph screamed. His voice sounded high-pitched in his head, distorted by his anger.

He could feel Miriam and her mother's presence behind

him as they watched from the staircase, clutching the banister.

Crowder blinked. He looked spastic. Joseph felt a sudden and shocking pang of guilt. It shot up through the middle of him but he had to ignore it. He knew he was being watched. His body resisted but he moved over to Crowder anyway and put his boot to his neck, pressing down, pinning him in place. He aimed the shotgun at his face. There was blood on the back of Crowder's neck where the pellet had pierced the skin. The man lay prostrate on the floor and Joseph thought that by striking him so savagely he had caused some permanent damage to him. The thought made his whole body feel heavy.

'Focus, focus,' he whispered. He was out of breath. Sweat formed at his forehead and under his chin. 'Why couldn't you just be a nice person?'

There were tears in his eyes. He had to make his point clear, not to Crowder, but to the women standing behind him on the stairs. A single, clear thought consumed his mind: he had to do this. They had to know what sort of a man he really was.

Crowder was making strange noises now. Joseph could feel the bones moving in his neck beneath his boot. They were so thin. The stranger looked pathetic with his arms at his sides, chest pressed into the stone floor, his head still. His face was red with blood and he was spluttering, trying to speak.

Joseph lifted his boot.

'Please,' Crowder begged. He stared straight ahead, at the shelves of boxes. He did not look at Joseph. 'Please.'

'Joseph.' Miriam's mother.

Hearing Crowder's voice calmed him. At least he could still speak. He took his boot away and stepped backwards. He kept the shotgun trained on him.

'What were you doing?'

Crowder blinked. He touched his neck where Joseph had been pinning him down.

'Answer me.'

'I don't know,' Crowder mumbled.

He was breathing heavily, gasping.

'You don't know?'

'I was just . . .' He trailed off. He started to cry again.

'Joseph, please,' said Miriam's mother.

'Stay out of this,' he snapped, not taking his eyes off Crowder.

'But he's hurt.'

It only served to strengthen his resolve. 'He was going to kill us.'

'Don't be so silly.'

'Just stay out of it, for Christ's sake.'

The old woman made a low gasping sound.

'Get up,' he said to Crowder.

Crowder used his hand to cover his face. 'How has it come to this?' he cried dramatically. 'How can things be like this? What have I done? I wasn't a bad person.'

'Get up.'

Crowder sniffed and tried to sit up. Blood trickled down to the ground in quick drips, running down his temple from the gash where Joseph had struck him. He was shaky, supporting himself with one palm pressed against the floor, his arm fully extended. He placed his other hand at his temple. His movements were slow and child-like.

'Stand up,' Joseph said.

He felt Miriam's eyes on him but he couldn't stop. Not this time.

'What are you going to do to me?'

'Don't speak. Just get up.'

Crowder took his hand from his temple and showed it to Joseph. The fingers were shiny with red, slick with it. There was so much blood. It ran down the side of his face in vast, dendritic lines.

There was movement on the stairs behind him.

'No,' he shouted. 'You're not going to help him.' He stepped back from Crowder so that he could not lunge at him, and turned his head quickly towards the stairs.

'We did as you said, and this is what happened.'

'Let me help him,' said Miriam.

'No. You,' he said to Crowder, 'get up now or I will kill you right here.'

Crowder sighed. 'Well, just do it then.' He closed his eyes in submission. His head swayed lightly on its shoulders. Joseph thought he was going to pass out.

'Get up.'

But Crowder said nothing and did nothing. Through his dirty beard and the grime there seemed to be a fractured peace on his face, a new serenity.

He grabbed Crowder roughly by the collar and pulled him to his feet. His body was light with emaciation, easily manipulated. Joseph pulled him towards the staircase. He saw the look of shock on Miriam's face and it made the actions easier. The children had come to the top of the stairs. He could see their shapes in the doorway. It would have been better for them not to see this but there was no turning back now.

He threw Crowder on to the stairs.

'Up,' he said, prodding the shotgun aggressively into his back.

The shock of movement had given Crowder a new lease of energy. He scrambled up the stairs on his hands and legs. The protestations of Miriam and her mother were just background sounds, whirling eddies in the drumbeat pulse.

They reached the hallway and Joseph pushed the gun into Crowder's back again and pressed hard into the skin. The scrawny figure made a break for the front door. He wobbled as he ran, too weak, using his hand against the wall as support. It left lines of his blood on the white paint. The children ran into the kitchen and shut the door.

Joseph followed Crowder out into the front garden. Pele stood at the gate. The dawn was coming. Crowder swayed drunkenly up the path towards the dog, swung open the gate and limped up the road in the direction of the village. His attempted escape would have been comical were it not for the fact that Joseph was not about to let him go like that. He watched the dark figure from the doorway of the house.

'I hope you're happy now,' said Miriam, standing at his side, crying.

Joseph did not answer. He strode out towards the gate.

'What are you doing?' she screamed. 'Haven't you done enough?'

He had stopped listening. He needed to show them who he was. They had to understand. And this was the time to do it. He went round to the garage at the side of the house and pulled open the doors. He climbed into the car and started the engine. Miriam stood in his way and beat the bonnet with the flats of her hands. Her tears gleamed in the headlights. He drove past her and turned left into the road.

|||

Crowder didn't even try to run out on to the grass. When the headlights of the car illuminated his figure in a blaze of colours against the dying night he simply stopped and hunched his shoulders. Joseph eased to a halt in front of him and got out of the car.

'In,' he called, above the sound of the engine.

He didn't move. Joseph remembered Crowder had a bag filled with his possessions and that it was still in the house. He would have to do without it. He couldn't go back to the house now.

'Get in the car or I'll make you get in the car.'

He felt like he was speaking to a child. In the headlights the blood on the man's face was bright red. Dejectedly, Crowder moved towards the passenger door. Before he climbed inside Joseph said, 'I could tie you up and put you in the boot but I won't. Just don't try anything.'

Crowder looked at him as if he was a bully, said nothing and got into the car.

'We did try to help you, you do understand that?'

Crowder stared blankly at the road ahead. The wound on his forehead had stopped bleeding and the blood on his face was starting to dry.

Joseph had put the shotgun flat along the back seat, sure now that Crowder was no longer able to harm him. Crowder was scared of him.

'What are you going to do to me?' His voice was taut with nerves.

'I'm not going to do anything to you,' Joseph lied.

The engine rattled around them. They drove for several more miles. Crowder sobbed quietly into his chest. His hands were placed over his knees and when they passed the amber light of a street lamp, the mini mountain ranges of his knuckles reared up out of the dark. He was so thin.

They came to a widening of the road and Joseph pulled over into a truck stop.

'Oh God,' Crowder said quietly, to himself.

'Out you get.'

Joseph reached behind him and lifted the shotgun.

Crowder was weeping now, but put up no resistance. He clambered out of the car and leaned against the metal crash barrier. Joseph got out the other side and directed Crowder to the front of the car. He did as he was told until he was standing once again in the white cones of the headlights.

The air was silent save for the leaves on the trees that blew in the breeze with quiet, whispering threats. The police would not come. Not any more. The world was over. It felt as if Joseph and Crowder were the last two men alive and this was the parting of the ways. The wind carried in it the essence of the apocalypse as it bent the tops of the trees beneath its weight and lifted swirls of dust off the road. There was nothing human about the world any more.

'Go,' he said.

He lowered the gun and the two men looked at one another. In that moment Joseph felt a sudden connection with the man. Crowder seemed to sense it too. They had both survived this far. One day ago they had not even known of each other's existence, one hour ago they had been trying to kill each other, but now, suddenly and irrationally, at the side of the road, everything had changed.

In the old world Crowder's actions would have been unforgivable but now, with the gloom-laden dawn light and the freezing wind, it became clear that it was nothing more than the sheer will to survive, a will that burned equally fiercely inside his own body.

'You're letting me go.'

'I'm . . .' Joseph paused. 'I'm not a bad man,' he said.

Crowder put his arm up to block the light from the car. The wind intensified in the trees.

'You're letting me go.' He was smiling at him. 'Why are you letting me go?'

Joseph felt the wind on his face, through his hair. 'What else can I do?'

'You could kill me. You're going to have to kill somebody eventually, Joseph, why not get it under your belt? It'll be easier the next time you have to do it.'

He fixed his gaze on Joseph. Gone was the emaciated weakling. In its place stood a dark and tortured soul, too intelligent for what he had been through, too weak to do anything about it.

Joseph raised the shotgun.

'That's it,' said Crowder, his eyes on the gun. 'Put me out of my misery.' He brought his eyes back up to Joseph's. 'This is your chance.'

Joseph took a step towards the car.

'Don't come back to the house. Find a hospital.'

Crowder did not answer. His body was intensely bright in the headlights, his head lowered at a slight angle as he watched Joseph go to the back of the car. Joseph opened the boot and took from it the sleeping bag, torch and bottle of water he had put in there. He placed them a few yards from Crowder, keeping the gun on him.

'I'm giving you these,' he said. 'They'll help you.'

Crowder looked at the items, then back at Joseph. 'Thank you.'

The light was gaining the day, the eastern sky white at its apron, the trees and the road a dark pencil outline.

'Promise me you won't come back to the house.'

'You're going to tell your wife I'm dead, aren't you?'

'She's not – yes. I have to.'

'Why?'

'I just do.'

Crowder collected the water and the torch in his arms. 'So I can go now?'

Joseph hated that Crowder felt the need to ask permission. He did not like that power. Crowder turned and started to walk away.

'Bye then,' he said.

Joseph watched him walk down the deserted road into the darkness. He thought about shouting good luck, but he said nothing.

|||

He stopped in the village on the way back. The old pub was closed. Large wooden boards had been nailed over the windows. He walked down the main street in the dark. The line of street lights had failed. He found his way along by the occasional light from a house, and from habit. He had walked along this street thousands of times.

He wondered how many people in the village were dead. His father would have known. He would have knocked on every door to see who was all right. Not Joseph though. He had not been to visit anybody since coming to Cornwall. He had told himself he didn't care, that it was every man for himself.

A Siamese cat padded down the pavement on the other side of the road. He could see its white body through the gloom. It stopped and looked at him, its eyes gleaming in the dark.

By the time he got back to the house everybody was in bed. He parked the car in the garage and paused at the garden gate to listen to the sea.

He crept up to his bedroom and switched on the light. Crowder's rucksack sat on the floor at the end of the bed. He opened it and looked inside. There was nothing in it apart from some dirty clothes and sheets, and some empty tins. Right at the bottom was a perfectly rounded pebble. In the front compartment he found a sharp piece of broken glass wrapped in a rag. That was the sum of Crowder's life. There were no photographs, no books, no letters, nothing that told of a past. Those things had been discarded.

|||

There was half a week of good weather. On the Sunday, Joseph had driven to an old industrial estate in search of wood. He wanted to board up the conservatory. The metal shutters for the windows were in place but the conservatory was still too exposed.

When he was within half a mile of the industrial estate he had stopped the car. He knew a way in round the back and when he had got to the fence he had seen a line of cars. There were men there, and lots of them. He had watched them for a while. They wore black clothes, he noticed, and they had dogs, and guns, and were organized. They had gone methodically into each of the buildings, collecting things of use, before moving on to the next. Slowly, and with a low feeling of worry, Joseph had made his way back to the car.

Miriam had said nothing to him since that night, and he had said nothing to her. The incident with Crowder hung heavy in the air. It was the first Tuesday since they had come to the house that they had not waited until dark before descending into the cellar.

He woke late the next morning and looked at the clock at the side of his bed but the screen was blank. The red electronic numbers were not there. The electricity had failed at last. He wondered if it would come back or if it was the end of the energy. He saw the deserted power stations, sitting silent, in his head.

He got changed and went downstairs. Four faces stared up at him from the breakfast table. He crossed the room to the refrigerator and marked off the date on his calendar.

'I'm going to go to the supermarket,' he said, and left the room.

In the porch he pulled on his boots and walked round the house. When he reached Dora's grave he stopped. The mud with which he had filled the hole was shot through with tufts of weed and grass. He closed his eyes and stood as still as he could for a moment. He listened for the sound of cars or aeroplanes, or any other human noise, but there was nothing apart from the wind and the sound of the sea.

He thought of those moments when he and Miriam had been standing in the hallway, debating whether or not Crowder would be allowed to stay. He remembered how the scent of her perfume had dislodged those feelings in his gut. The building fibres of healing had all but finished their work and now he had to unstitch those same fibres that he cherished so much.

Miriam was waiting for him in the garage. Scant light filtered in through the small square windows above the door.

'What are you doing?' he said to her.

'I'm coming with you.'

'What for?'

She climbed into the passenger seat without answering him. They pulled out of the garage and followed the roads down which Joseph had driven with Crowder four nights before. In the metal light of the morning the landscape looked different to how it had then. The bright green of the summer made his body feel lighter and cooler.

'What did you do to him?' she said.

Joseph checked his wing mirror and said nothing.

'Did you kill him?'

He still didn't answer.

'So you're not going to say?'

'What difference does it make?'

'I'd like to know if my children are sleeping in the same house as a murderer.'

He glanced across to her. 'And what if they are?' She folded her arms and placed her forehead on the side window. 'You think Crowder wouldn't have killed you? He had unlocked the shotgun for Christ's sake. He had to go. So I got rid of him.'

'Good for you.'

'You should be thanking me.' He drove in silence for a moment, the tension building. 'Fucking hell,' he snapped. 'How can you be so blinkered?'

'I don't know,' she screamed. She sat up in the seat suddenly. 'I don't know what we should have done, OK?' She began to cry.

Joseph kept his eyes on the road. His mind was becoming foggy. All he had to do was tell Miriam he had let Crowder go. He just had to tell her the truth. But he couldn't. He had to see this through.

'Why are you religious?' he said, hating himself inwardly for saying it. He turned his head to her, taking his eyes off the road.

'What?'

'Why are you religious? Still, I mean? There's clearly no God. You must see that now. Your husband's dead, your life has fallen apart, the whole fucking world is descending into shit, you're being protected by a man you hate—'

'Why are you—'

'God would never allow something like this to happen.'

'Please stop it, Joseph.'

'I'm just interested, that's all. In how you could continue believing something when it is so crushingly obvious it's not true.'

She had stopped crying now. He felt her eyes on him.

'If you want to have this conversation, then come on, let's have it. You've been waiting long enough.' She folded her arms.

'Well, go on then. Tell me.'

The engine pitched down as Joseph rounded a bend in the lanes.

'You take the leap of faith,' she said calmly.

'But it's wrong.'

'It doesn't matter. It's up to me to make that choice. It has nothing to do with you. I suppose you're going to tell me that religion causes wars now.'

'Well, doesn't it?'

'No, it doesn't. People cause the bad things in the world, Joseph; people who are sure of themselves and want everyone else to think like them. People like you.'

He forced himself to carry on. 'Your God is a lie,' he said. 'Everything you have based your life around is fake. I want you to admit it.'

'I won't admit it. You don't know.'

'Everyone knows it.'

She laughed. 'No they don't. You just don't get it. You think you're this beacon of intellect and you're not. You don't understand people, Joseph, and because of that you understand nothing. What I don't understand is why you're so down on people who want to be happy.'

'You don't need God to be happy.'

'It has nothing to do with you how people find happiness,' she said. 'Why can't you understand that? I want to have faith in me, and I don't push it outwards. It just sits in me and makes me happy – why do you want to take that away?'

'Because it's fake.'

'So what are you saying? That people should just abandon hope?'

'Hope has nothing to do with it.'

'Of course it does. It all comes from the same place.'

He clutched the wheel firmly. The car slowed and they turned into the supermarket car park. There were three large army trucks parked near the entrance and lots of armed guards standing outside. None of them wore gas masks or surgical masks as they had when the illness first broke out. As they pulled up two of the trucks chugged to life and drove away.

'It's not me who's the idiot,' she said as she unclipped her seatbelt and let it slide up across her torso. 'You're the idiot, Joseph. You always were.'

|||

The car park was half empty. The cloudy sky was beginning to clear, leaving stark patches of blue beyond the giant steel frame of the supermarket entrance. They parked as close to the building as they could get. Joseph looked out of the windscreen at the guards standing at the entrance. They were clean shaven and smart in their uniforms.

'Look at that,' he said.

She leaned forward but couldn't see anything.

'The lights are on inside. They still have power.'

They climbed out of the car and approached the doors. A thin road ran along the front of the store. When they were halfway across it one of the guards walked towards them, a chunky-looking sub-machinegun slung over his shoulder.

'Good morning,' he said, cheerily, stopping in front of them. He was an officer. 'The budget has changed,' he said.

'Changed?'

'It's a twenty-pound limit now.'

He smiled at them when he said it, trying to make the news easier to digest.

'Twenty pounds?' Miriam glanced at Joseph. 'But that's not enough.'

The officer shrugged.

'The orders came through yesterday, I'm afraid. I know it doesn't seem like much, but it's the same for everyone.'

Joseph felt the slow creep of panic. 'How can we live on that?'

'Prices are still frozen.'

At the store entrance somebody walked out carrying two bags of shopping, hurrying towards his car.

'Is there any news?' asked Miriam. 'Anything about a cure yet?'

The officer laughed. 'If there is, they ain't told me about it.'

Joseph tried to guess if the officer was older than him. His hair was grey above the ears and his skin was creased at the eyes.

'Why are there so many guards?'

'Some markets have been forced to close so there're extra men available.' There was a falseness in his voice. But he left his statement at that. 'Just go in, get your stuff and get out. That's your best bet.' He smiled again. 'Before everything runs out.'

Miriam led Joseph into the store. The shelves were almost empty. People wandered slowly up and down the aisles, checking prices, dropping what items they could find into trolleys.

They had visited the supermarket only a few times in the last few months but it had never been like this. The army had supervised how much people bought, obeying the ration orders that had been handed down from the top. It had been a quick fix, a decision made fast, that people's shopping should be rationed through monetary values ahead of goods. Unprecedented events called for unprecedented responses; that was what they said. The people could choose what they wanted and all prices were frozen. Supplies had been channelled into these central hubs instead of being shipped to smaller stores with less capacity to protect the goods, and that system of rationing had always kept the shelves stocked. They had never been empty like this.

They took a trolley and pushed on through the store, saying little, picking items they had to have. They came to each aisle and their silent desperation grew. There was no milk, no eggs, only rotting fruit and vegetables nobody else wanted. There were still bags of sugar and flour, which they put into the trolley. Some aisles remained filled with electrical goods, or toys, or camping gear; things people no longer needed. They found some rice and some pasta. And some boxes of instant mashed potato. There was no bottled water left.

The store was set up like a ribcage – bones lined up off

the central spine that ran adjacent to the front windows.

The bread aisle was towards the back of the store, far away from the entrance. As Miriam and Joseph approached it they heard somebody shouting. There were people gathered there and they were arguing.

Joseph stopped. He knew it would be best to leave the trolley where it was, to get out of there. He had seen how rapidly situations like this could escalate.

'We have to stay here,' said Miriam, reading his thoughts. 'We don't know how much longer this place will stay open.'

'I know.' They kept their voices low. 'Shall we take what we have and pay?'

'But what about the bread?'

'I don't know if going up there is a good idea,' he whispered.

'But we need bread.'

They were looking at two men, both standing behind trolleys. They were facing in the same direction, into the bread aisle, trying to reason with somebody. One of the men was small and timid whilst the other was large, bald and threatening. He pointed at whoever it was he was speaking to with sharp, thrusting jabs of his finger.

'I don't care how many mouths you have to feed, you can't take all that.'

Joseph turned to Miriam. She nodded, and they went forward.

They reached the two men and stopped. An obese woman was standing in front of a row of empty shelves. Her trolley was filled with loaves of bread. Next to her was her husband, rake thin with a small head and dead eyes. He was ill. He had it.

'We're not breaking any rules. We're under twenty quid. We can buy what we want.'

'But you've not left any for anybody else,' said the timid-looking man.

Behind the obese woman and her husband were another group of people. Joseph counted nine loaves in the woman's trolley and felt the rising tide of anger in his body.

'Why don't you give everyone with a trolley a loaf?' he said. 'And you have the rest.'

'Stay out of this, mate,' said the large man.

He looked at Joseph. The top of his bald head shone in the overhead lights.

'I'm just saying that would be a fair deal.'

'Why should you get some? You've only just got here.'

'Nobody's getting any,' argued the woman, in a shrill voice. Her hair was greasy and she was ungroomed. 'We're not doing anything wrong.'

Joseph heard approaching footsteps behind him. Three soldiers were heading quickly their way. The large man saw them and quickly pushed his trolley forward. It slammed into the front of the trolley filled with bread. He rushed round to the side and grabbed two loaves for himself.

The woman lunged to reclaim them. Her husband watched but did nothing. Joseph saw somebody sneak along the lines of shelves behind the back of the obese woman and surreptitiously take a loaf. It was a small, young woman in a thick, fashionable jacket of bright red. She looked at Joseph and he returned her stare. She was ashamed and turned away, but kept the bread.

'Hey,' called one of the soldiers, from behind them.

And then the whole dynamic shifted. The floor moved beneath him and he fell. There was a huge boom and the shelves rattled, lurched forward and spilled their contents on to the floor. The overhanging lights rocked like swings in a playground. Miriam clattered into his back.

|||

His ears were ringing. The sound of people screaming came from somewhere within the store.

'What was that?'

A cloud of smoke appeared near the entrance, tumbling across the tops of the shelves as one great, grey mass. Machinegun fire. Shouting.

Joseph got to his feet and grabbed Miriam. He pulled her towards the back of the store.

'Wait here,' he said.

She crouched down at the end of the far aisle.

Without thinking, Joseph ran back to his trolley and pulled it away. The fat woman was running towards the exit with the trolley full of bread. She was slow. Her husband trailed behind, walking. Then, like an optical illusion, he was taller. The visibility in the place was shrinking with every second as the smoke descended. Small lights appeared through the murk. There was more shouting. Voices ordering.

'Get down on the floor, get down on the floor.'

The voices behind the masks were muffled and alien.

The obese woman's husband broke into a run. At first Joseph thought he was just trying to catch up with his wife but then he noticed that the man was not moving naturally. He was running too fast for the skeleton that carried him. The motion of legs pumping was slow but he ate up the ground as if the floor was moving towards him. He leaped at his wife and lowered his head. The line of his neck impacted with her back and she was sent sprawling into the oncoming smoke and out of sight.

The lights he had seen in the smoke resolved into beams, like lighthouses at night. The forms of people moved behind the smog. They wore mining lights around their foreheads.

A deep, male voice shouted something indecipherable.

The trolley of bread, now deserted, was just twenty feet from him. The people with the lights on their heads were moving slowly and cautiously. He ran out from the protection of the aisle. He couldn't see far in front of him. His eyes started to sting. The husband of the obese woman was nowhere to be seen. Joseph reached the trolley and pulled it back towards Miriam's hiding place. With his head turned back to the direction in which he was running he did not see the set of hands take hold of the trolley at the far end. His arms jerked, a tearing pain shooting up them.

The large, aggressive bald man stood opposite him. Sweat had beaded on the top of his head. He yanked the trolley back towards him but Joseph refused to let go. He lost traction and stumbled. As his hips struck the metal frame he pushed his body forward as hard as he could, sending the front end into the bald man's knees. The metal struck with a satisfying clunk and there was a grunt. Without thinking Joseph grabbed a tin can from a shelf. By now the smoke had pervaded the air. The bald man had hardly had a chance to recover his footing when Joseph pushed the can hard up into his face. His nose ruptured under the blow and Joseph felt the warmth of blood on his hands. He dropped the can.

'I'm sorry,' he whispered to the man, who was doubled over and holding his nose. 'But you should have let go.'

Joseph pulled the trolley away from the aisle. Miriam was crouched where he left her. He left the bread there and went back for his own trolley.

'Come on,' he said.

'What's happening?'

'I think they're looting the place.'

He helped her to her feet. They were in the last aisle, hidden away in the top corner of the supermarket. The exit was a long way away. They reached the corner of the shelves and stopped. Cautiously, Joseph peered into the aisle and turned back to Miriam.

'We're going to have to run for it,' he said.

There was no sign of the looters. Joseph knew that at the end of the opposite aisle were the checkout stalls but they were concealed in the smoke. The initial bursts of gunfire had relented. In their place, voices called to one another through the smoke, filtered by breathing apparatus, the words disconcertingly unfamiliar.

'The little guy with the woman has got it. He's violent,' he said. 'Keep an eye out.'

She looked up at him and said nothing.

'Hide behind your trolley as you go,' he said.

He looked out into the central aisle again. Two beams of light cut through the smoke. The light twisted and swirled in eddies as it crossed through the dense haze. He wondered if the looters would be able to see this far back. There was a flash of light in the ceiling and an electrical crack. One of the overhead lights, held up by two metal chains, fell to the ground. It landed with a heavy smash.

'Now,' said Joseph.

And he ran out into the aisle. He ducked down below his trolley. A voice called out from somewhere inside the smoke. He threw himself across the final yard of open space and into the safety of the far aisle.

Miriam was still waiting on the other side.

The voice called again. Joseph knew that he had been seen.

Miriam looked at him from across the aisle and shook her head. All he could think to do was to nod to her and keep beckoning her with his arm. There was no other option. She had to get across that open space.

'Come on,' he mouthed. 'Run.'

He could see the fear in her face as she pushed her cart to the edge of the shelves. With quick movements she lowered her body down so that it was beneath the line of the top rail of her trolley. He looked at the contents – mostly bread – surely they wouldn't stop bullets. Her eyes flashed in all directions. She was about to lose it.

'Hey,' he whispered. 'We *have* to get out of here.' She looked at him. 'We have to get back to the house.'

She stared at the space of floor at Joseph's feet. It looked like she was counting down in her head. Her forehead creased in concentration. And she ran.

The gunfire blew into the air. Joseph was jolted by the shock. It loosened the image of his father, the white face and the red lips. It was happening again.

'Over here,' he called, not thinking. Directly behind him boxes of cereal exploded open. He shut his eyes and tried to make his body small. Bullets spat at him from the smoke.

A hand grabbed the top of his arm and pulled him back. His legs were weak. As he fell he swung his body round the corner and to safety. The arm that had pulled him backwards released its grip. Miriam's face was close to his. He could feel her breath on his mouth. He opened his eyes.

'Come on,' she said.

The two of them made their way down the length of the aisle at a run, their trolleys before them. Through the smoke they saw the fire exit behind the last checkout.

They reached the end of the aisle. The checkout was ten feet away across open ground. Sunlight fell in great shafts through the huge plate-glass windows. The explosion had shattered some of the panes into spider webs and the wind from outside swept through the windows that had been smashed, blowing the smoke into rolling billows. Joseph lowered himself on to his knees and brought his head down to the level of the floor, easing himself forward to get a view of the open area between the checkouts and the shelves. Through the smoke he saw one of the looters. His trousers were tucked into heavy army boots. He moved through the dust, slowly, a rifle raised, head cocked and looking along the barrel. He looked hardly human. The proboscis of the gas mask and the large, round eyes gave him an insect-like appearance. The light from his headlamp played along the smooth white tiles of the floor.

Joseph watched him for a few seconds. He was sure he was too far away to be seen. Suddenly, the looter stopped. Joseph held his breath. There was no noise.

'Step out.' The filtered voice was calm.

The figure in the smoke stood deathly still.

'Step out,' said the voice again.

Joseph kept his eyes on the looter. His heart was surprisingly still. There was no fear in him. And then, from the next aisle over, a dark figure moved between Joseph and the man in the gas mask. It was the large, bald man he had hit with the can. His hands were held aloft as he stepped silently into the open. The looter scuttled forward, rifle still raised.

The clear sonic crack of a single shot rang out and the man fell to the floor.

Miriam screamed.

The light from the looter's helmet jerked up along the tiles and blinded Joseph. The rifle was freshly aimed. Joseph tried to pull himself back but his face had turned white hot and there was the shock of gunfire and a powerful jarring that paralysed his body.

III

There was a pain in his right cheek, instant and sharp. He blinked his eyes closed and open.

The light from the gunman's lamp changed its trajectory suddenly and there was a grunting sound. I'm not dead, thought Joseph.

The torch was still focused on him but the angle of the beam was more oblique. The gunman had fallen. The light spasmed. In its moving stream Joseph saw a curl of smoke inches away from his face where the bullet had chipped the tiles.

He followed the light back to its source. The gunman was lying on the floor. The scrawny little man, the one who was ill, was on the looter's back, crouched menacingly over him. He was so thin and gangly, and his movements were so swift and stochastic, that he looked like an animal. He was beating the back of the gunman's head with a weapon. Joseph watched it in a daze of slow motion. The large man who had been shot was sitting up against one of the checkout stalls. A line of blood smeared the white tiles. His head lolled to one side and he was panting.

Miriam pulled Joseph back up.

'We need to go.'

His senses returned as if being drawn through a jet engine. He stood up and they streaked across the empty space, carried by nothing more than reckless hope. The smoke was so thick that they could hardly see through it.

Joseph let go of his trolley and threw himself into the fire door. It yielded under his weight but only a few inches. He looked down. Thick metal chains held it closed.

'Agh,' he shouted, unable to control himself. 'What the fuck?'

'The other door.'

'No way. They'll be down there.'

They could see the car park on the other side of the glass. It was so close.

Joseph ran back into the store and towards the fallen gunman. He lay on the floor, unmoving. The infected man was gone. The lamp on the gunman's head was pointed into the metal rafters of the ceiling, the two glass eyes of his gas mask were smashed and there was an expanding circle of blood beneath his head. There were several gashes at the top of his skull.

Joseph unhooked the rifle from around the man's neck and ran back to Miriam. Her shoulders were hunched. She was looking along the archipelago of checkout islands.

Joseph followed her gaze. The infected man, his face and arms covered in blood, was pulling the large, bald man towards the plate-glass windows. The large man's feet scrabbled in struggle. In the clearer light Joseph saw the weapon the infected man had used to kill the gunman. A hammer.

Things were happening so fast. He checked the gun. There was one bullet left. He could shoot the infected man or he could shoot out a plate of glass in the window and save Miriam and himself. He ran round the checkout island to her.

The large man had been hoisted to his knees. His eyes were half closed and blood trickled from his nostrils where Joseph had hit him with the can and there was a red circle in his gut where the gunman had shot him. His head had turned a deep pink. Above him, the scrawny man loomed with the hammer held in the air.

'Shoot him.'

Her voice was quick and loud.

Footsteps. Running. More looters were coming.

Joseph raised the gun to the infected man. He thought of Crowder and paused. His racing mind slowed. He only had one bullet. It could not be wasted. He turned away from the two men and fired into the window. It struck the pane with a thud and a wisp of smoke. There was a fraction of delay and the glass shattered and fell like crystal rain.

'No,' he heard Miriam say.

The infected man smiled. There was nothing they could do.

'Leave him alone,' she screamed. The veins stood out on her neck. She took a step towards him. Joseph went to stop her.

The hammer moved downwards in an arc. Sharp end first. When it struck the top of the bald skull it was with such force that it broke the skin and embedded itself into the bone.

'Run,' Joseph said, under his breath.

The infected man levered the hammer to an angle and wrenched it clear of the skull. The large man let go of a low, thundering scream. Joseph's nervous system convulsed. The hammer fell again into the head. Joseph couldn't look away. He had to see it. The infected man dropped the body to the floor.

The looters came out through the smoke like creatures passing between dimensions.

Joseph fled. A single thought tripped over and over in his mind: this can't be happening.

They still had their trolleys. Outside, they saw the source of the explosion that had rocked the supermarket. The whole of the front entrance was aflame. The steel girders of the atrium were buckled and black. Bodies lay on the floor, black smoke rising from them. The soldiers.

Saying nothing, they ran towards their car in a direct line. They didn't care who saw them now. Joseph could feel the burn of exertion in his lungs. He thought he was going to throw up. He kept looking back. Nobody coming.

They reached the car. Miriam loaded both trolleys, including the loaves of bread, into the boot. Joseph looked around them to check for danger. Miriam's face had greyed in the smoke and he could see her hands shaking as she struggled with the food.

'Hurry up,' he ordered.

She didn't even look at him.

A man had appeared through the glass they had smashed and was running towards them. He held his hammer in his left hand, above his head like a tomahawk. Joseph climbed into the car quickly. With deliberate care he placed the key into the ignition, making sure not to fumble it. The engine roared to life. The boot slammed shut. He saw the shape of Miriam streak past in the rear-view mirror and she climbed into the seat next to him. Joseph hit the accelerator and sped away. There was a loud bang on the roof. Miriam screamed. The hammer bounced down the windscreen and on to the bonnet. Needles of shock tore up Joseph's chest.

Great billowing towers of black smoke curled from the entrance of the supermarket. A group of people ran out, dressed in normal clothes, but blackened with soot. They had somehow escaped. For the first time, Joseph thought about stopping to help.

One of the looters stepped calmly out from behind one of the army trucks where he had been hiding. His gas mask was pulled up off his face on to his forehead. A large pack was strapped to his back and he was holding at his side what looked like a spear.

'Oh no,' said Joseph.

He felt an overwhelming urge to shout to the people.

The looter strode purposefully into the open and then stopped, raising the spear at his hip. The fire spewed out of it in an orange arc and the people went up like tinder sticks. They were engulfed in seconds. Even through the car windows, and above the sound of the engine, they could hear the screams.

The flaming bodies ran out into the car park, spinning, throwing their arms into the air, then falling to their knees and holding their heads up towards the sky in perverse worship, some of them clutching their faces, before falling to the ground and dying right there on the tarmac.

||||

The pitch of the engine changed quickly up through the gears. Joseph was thankful for the steering wheel that gave him something to hold on to. It kept him steady.

'Animals. Fucking animals.'

Miriam held her hands over her face.

They tore out of the car park and sped through the town towards the lanes that would take them home.

'What was the point?' said Miriam. 'It was . . .' She didn't finish her thoughts.

He wanted to say I told you so, to show her once and for all that she had to listen to him.

'We'll never do anything like that,' she said. He glanced across to her. She wasn't talking to him. She was talking to herself. 'No matter what, we'll never do anything like that.'

He wondered if she included him in that 'we'. She didn't know that Crowder was still alive, and he hated the idea that she might put him in the same category as the men who had just butchered those innocent people. He wanted to tell her he wasn't like them. He wanted her to know that for all his abrasiveness, for all his faults, he was still not like those people. He was not a killer. But he couldn't tell her. It would make her think that he was something he wasn't.

'I'm going to take a detour,' he said. 'I want to check we're not being followed.'

He turned the car into a particularly narrow lane. The road surface was rough with a long, unbroken stripe of grass growing up its centre. After a short distance they came to a crossroads.

Joseph turned left. The road widened and the hedges became forest. On the right was a dirt track leading up between the trees. They travelled along it until the car was far enough in that they could no longer see the road. Joseph pushed open his door. The wood was silent. There was no sound of approaching cars. The leaves on the trees rustled and a bird chirped from somewhere nearby. Out here in the wilds you could have been forgiven for thinking the world was peaceful.

Miriam had been gazing straight ahead since they had entered the lanes. Joseph pointed into the woods. A natural footpath led between the trees.

'If you go down there you come to a wooded valley. It's a dried-up riverbed, my dad told me. There was a hut there. Made of stones with a corrugated-iron roof. God knows who built it—'

'Why didn't you shoot that man?' she said suddenly. 'The one who was ill. Why did you let him kill that other man?'

There was disgust on her face.

'I only had one bullet.'

'We could have smashed that window with something else.'

'If I had shot that man we would both be dead now. You saw what they did to those people outside. Do you think they wouldn't have done that to us?'

She opened her mouth and stuck out her jaw.

Joseph shook his head. 'You are unbelievable.'

He pulled the door shut and they headed for home.

|||

He parked in the garage. The engine ticked with heat.

'Don't tell them what happened,' she said. 'They don't need to know.'

'OK.'

He didn't want to relive it anyway. Of all the things he had seen, nothing had been like that. He had seen so many things in London, but they had all been something born of chaos and panic. It was a natural instinct for people to want to survive. But that was not what the looters had been doing. Burning those innocent people was a pointless act. There was no sense in it. No humanity.

He knew that such people existed but this knowledge did nothing to assuage the feeling of creeping despair in his gut. The supermarket was so close to the house. How long, he wondered, would it be before they found them?

Miriam climbed out of the car but Joseph stayed where he was.

They were bound to come to the house eventually. They would move across the lands swiftly. Not even the army had been able to stop them. Seeing them there, seeing what other human beings could really do to each other was no longer just an idea. It was now a truth. He had seen it. The world had become an immeasurable, monstrous thing, a living entity with a gaping, spluttering maw through which it would suck every last thing. All he wanted to do was protect Miriam and her mother, Edward and Mary. But that could not happen. He would never be able to do it because the animals in the supermarket would always be willing to go further.

Miriam had once said that invisible markers placed human beings higher than the other animals, but he had never believed her until he had been unable to kill Crowder. Something had stopped him, something indefinable, and its presence had been like gravity: an unbreakable law. He was incapable of taking another life. As long as that indefinable thing was still in him, whatever it was, he could not pull the trigger.

His father's letter was still in his pocket. He read it again and rested his forehead on the steering wheel.

'We're fucked,' he whispered.

Infinity swelled around him. He felt it, and understood it. He stayed in the car for the rest of the day and nobody came for him. He drifted in and out of sleep. At midnight he went out to the cliff edge. There was nothing out there except the darkness. The waves struck the cliffs as they always had; that elusive rhythm you could never quite guess.

He tried to rationalize his thoughts: if I were to die tomorrow is everything in place? Would they be safe?

There was a panting at his side. He reached down and stroked his dog's head. Pele's tongue lolled out over the edge of his teeth. They stood there for nearly an hour, the two of them, staring out into the dark of the world as it breathed and turned all around them.

|||

Miriam woke with a start. She had been nightmaring about Henry again. The nightmares were happening more regularly now. Always the same. She was walking through a library in silence, past row upon row of books. Henry would scream behind her and when she turned the library would become a beach beneath a deep red sky. A huge beast, a leviathan, would rise up from the waves and take Henry in its jaws before dragging him into the black sea. Miriam would run towards him and pause at the top of the beach. Burning bodies of killer whales were lined all the way along the sand. As she watched the carcasses burn, the sand on the beach would ignite and firestorm from one end to the other. And then she would wake up, gasping for air.

She tried the light switch. Nothing. Still no power. It had been nearly two weeks now; two weeks since they lost energy, since the man had visited the house, since Joseph had followed him out along the road.

Joseph had hardened since then. He was unapologetic. It was almost as if he was glad of what he had done. Since that day he had kept to himself, leaving the house with Pele in the days and disappearing for hours until nightfall, when he would return, eat alone and go to bed.

She threw some cold water on her face and went downstairs. Mary was in the living room with her grandmother. Miriam stood in the doorway.

'Where's Edward?' she asked.

'And good morning to you.'

Miriam's head ached. Her mind could not focus properly. The burning bodies ran across the plains of her mind.

'I'm sorry.'

'He went down to the beach with Joseph.'

'You let him go? Just the two of them?'

Her mother squinted. 'What's wrong, Miri?'

She didn't want Edward being poisoned by Joseph. She opened the front door and went out into the garden. And then she heard it. The crack of gunfire. It reverberated around the cliffs like a great thunderclap. The wind flapped her nightdress against her body. Her bare feet hurt as she ran across the road and picked her way along the line of the cliff, into the shallow spur to the path leading down to the beach.

Fear grew with every step, with every dart of pain that shot up her shins. Huge green ferns grew either side of the path. She had to climb on to the wooden fence to see over them and down to the beach. There were two tiny figures right at the far end, way past the skeletal remains of the fishing boat halfway along, up near the cliffs and the lighthouse.

The sand was difficult to run on. Her throat was raw dry, its flesh retracting, its pores closing. She could make them out, her son and Joseph. He was holding the shotgun up and looking at Edward. He said something to him and fired out to sea. Joseph looked up the beach and saw her coming. Quickly he handed the gun to Edward. She watched in horror as Edward cocked the gun open expertly, leaning the butt in the sand. He placed the cartridges into the loading chamber.

She screamed to him to stop but her voice reached them only as a whisper. Joseph placed his hand on Edward's back and pointed out to sea. The chaotic crash of the air exploding in the bullet's prow pushed Edward's small body backwards. He stuck out a leg for support and did not fall. Joseph ruffled the boy's hair in approval.

Miriam watched as her little boy raised his head to look at his uncle in the same way that she had seen him look at Henry. The roar of the gunfire echoed off the cliffs all around her, its noise total.

III

'What are you doing?' she screamed.

She pushed Joseph in the chest. That same unreadable face stared back at her.

'All these months and you've learned nothing.' She tried to keep her voice steady. She did not want him to see how close to crying she was. 'You're the same person you've always been. You haven't changed at all.'

She pushed him again, unable to control herself.

Joseph hunched his shoulders.

'What are you doing? Teaching my son like this. I *told* you I didn't want you doing this.'

She grabbed Edward by his hand and marched him back across the beach. She could hardly breathe she was so angry. She turned back to Joseph. His head was lowered and he was staring at his feet.

'If I had anywhere else to go I'd take the kids and leave you here on your own.'

Her feelings were so exposed that she could no longer control them. She felt Edward's hand in hers. She was squeezing it too tightly. Releasing her grip she looked down at him and hardly recognized the face staring back.

'Miriam.'

She looked back at Joseph. He was standing side on to her, his head turned in her direction. He looked at her for several seconds, seemingly considering something that needed to be said, then turned away.

|||

Full summer had bloomed, the vegetable patch they had cultivated in the back garden yielded plentiful supplies and life settled into a laconic routine. The water did not run from the taps, the electricity did not return, and the lack of electricity meant no more television reports, no more telephones, no knowledge of a wider world existing beyond the perimeters of their own little subsistence. The radio still worked but there were no more broadcasts.

In that month they had received no visitors and it felt like time was skipping forward, guiding the world to its new state. Nobody came along the single track road in search of anything and Miriam wondered how many people were left alive, and whether or not the illness that had killed Henry was still claiming victims, or whether the greedy monster in his dark cave was at last sated by its bounty.

Joseph had become even more withdrawn. He would still work, tilling the garden, fixing things around the house. He would go out hunting and sometimes take the van in the direction of the village in search of things that might be useful.

Beyond the back garden, in the field behind the house, he had erected a series of animal paddocks to house livestock. He had pinned wire fencing to thick, heavy fence posts that he had found on one of his trips in the van. When asked, for he never volunteered information, he said there were many farms in the area and he hoped to find some chickens or some pigs, though since then he had been on several foraging excursions and returned each time empty-handed.

Miriam had watched him from the back bedroom. The way he worked was nothing like the way Henry had worked. Henry had always been a messy person; he didn't plan far ahead, was a regular taker of breaks and he tended to throw himself thoughtlessly into projects around the house. Joseph was the opposite. He measured each of the quadrants, pinned lines of string in place with wooden stakes that delineated where the wire fencing would go and then he dug small square holes, one by one, without taking a single break, into which fitted the sturdy fence posts with an impressive degree of snugness. He worked slowly but methodically, his mind clear and focused. The whole process took three days and was conducted in a week of fine weather when the first of the summer hazes came.

One thing that Miriam had noticed was that the sky during dawn and dusk became startlingly beautiful. At break or end of day it would redden at the edges and purple overhead in such a way that it seemed as if the contrast and brightness controls of the air had been adjusted. The colours of the sky were crisp and clear and Miriam could not remember whether or not sunsets had always been that way or whether it was the lack of other stimuli that produced a delusional effect.

Her mother thought the children should somehow continue

their schooling. They decided on the simple idea of reading for an hour each morning and then discussing what they'd read afterwards. Henry's father had a good collection of books but most of them were beyond Edward and Mary's range. The book they settled on was *The Once and Future King*, it being the only work remotely resembling a children's book. The children would take it in turns to read a page and a slow pace was set, but after a few days there was a definite improvement.

Joseph showed no interest in the children's education but one morning Miriam noticed that the copy of the book had mysteriously moved from one side of the breakfast counter to the other. Each night she would note where she left the book and each morning it had been returned to a different point, noticeable only because she had marked its original position. Joseph was reading the book at night when everybody had gone to bed, and not telling anyone.

And there were other things that slowly helped her internal workings crank towards forgiveness. His walks with Pele had continued and at first Miriam had thought it irresponsible of him because if somebody dangerous had come to the house then the family would be without Joseph's protection. But one afternoon she had taken the binoculars to watch the birds in the fields behind the house when she noticed a flash of colour in the trees. She focused the lenses and saw Joseph sitting between two tree trunks far in the distance, smoking a cigarette with one hand and ruffling Pele's ear with the other. She had checked again the next day and, just as the day before, he was sitting in the same spot with his old, black dog faithfully at his side, keeping his unseen vigil.

She wanted to say something to him, but not yet. Her father had once told her, a year before he died, that it doesn't matter how a man treats his loved ones because loving one's family is easy; it is how he treats strangers and enemies that really counts. She had always considered this good advice, and it had been one of the reasons she had fallen in love with Henry. But Joseph treated strangers with contempt and that contempt had ultimately led him to murder Crowder.

As the weeks passed, the nightmares occurred more regularly, sometimes two or three times in one night. She would watch helplessly from the head of the flaming beach and listen to Henry scream as the monster crushed the life from his body. She would wake with a start, sweating and out of breath. In those desperate moments of the endless night she would force herself to forget her emotions and paddle into the shallow waters where the terror would subside and she would feel the calm of numbness.

Sometimes, when the sun was out and she was working in the garden alone, something would trickle up her back. She would lose herself for a moment and think that things might just work out OK. Despite everything she had seen, the feeling, the will for things to improve, was something very strong and when she felt it, it was as if she was being filled through some secret portal in her centre by a warm, amber, syrupy fluid that smothered the jagged protrusions of fear and made her whole body thrum with a quiet peace. Perhaps it was love, she thought, but then she knew it wasn't because this thing had more substance than love, was more ubiquitous and less prone to petty fluctuations. This thing was deep and old, consistent and pure, and when it came to her she would take a deep breath, close her eyes and let it tingle along her bloodways to her extremities, then past those into the world itself so that it engulfed and surrounded her as an aura that gave her renewed energy to carry on.

III

The foundations of the house shuddered in the ground. Ornaments and photographs shuffled across the shelves. She opened her eyes. Darkness and light. It was night but there was a light on the walls, piercing the curtains. She could not tell if she was asleep or awake. Sounds, muffled sounds, crept under the door. Somebody was moving outside. Her head throbbed, spun, tried to rest on something knowable that it could not find.

The light was white; powerful and brilliant, as if the moon had fallen out of the sky into the sea.

She had been shaken in her bed. An earthquake. The land had slipped away and the ocean would come for her. Slowly, the cogs of her mind clicked one by one into the shape of consciousness.

She pulled back the curtain and quickly brought her hand up to cover her eyes. There was something in the bay.

She ran to the children's bedroom. They were asleep and she didn't wake them. As she went back across the landing she noticed Joseph's door was open. His bed was made. There was nobody in the room.

Her mother joined Miriam on the landing. The light was so bright that Miriam could see her fragile frame through her thin gown and nightdress.

'What is it?' she whispered.

'I don't know. Where's Joseph?'

'I don't know.'

They heard Pele barking outside. Miriam rushed downstairs and threw open the front door. The light was hanging in the sky off-shore: one solitary, powerful star. The grass shone brilliant green in its beams.

Joseph was out on the cliff edge staring into it, his body a black silhouette casting an immense shadow behind it, extending halfway back to the house. A cold wind blew in Miriam's face and lifted her hair.

The air was silent. She strained to listen for sounds but all she could hear were the distant waves breaking against the cliff. The light did not move. It was not accompanied by a mechanical sound. Tentatively, she took a step towards it.

'What is it?'

From the cliff top all she could see was the light and the darkness around it. It seemed to fill the whole sky and yet there was still blackness, light and dark melting imperceptibly into one another without a seam.

'It's a ship,' he said.

And then, behind them, was the sound of approaching cars.

|||

In the harsh white light they looked strange, all those people, drifting across the land in their nightwear, all different colours; vibrant, little figures coming towards the light. They had parked their cars near the house and were now walking out slowly on to the grass.

There were lots of them. The unfamiliar sight of so many other people after such a long space of time caused a quickening in Miriam's head. The people joined Miriam and her mother at the cliff's edge and together they looked towards the unnatural ball of silent light that hovered above the ocean.

The water glowed a pale blue as if suffused with phosphorescent organisms. Curling and swirling lines of white surf shifted on its surface. Miriam turned round and looked towards the house, which beamed back at her, the light so bright that it sparkled on the barbed-wire loops that lined the garden wall. The house looked so small and shut off; they had cut themselves off from the rest of the world. There had been people in the village just a few miles away and they had not seen or heard from them and looking at the house it was not difficult see why. It looked like a fortress, threatening and cold with its barbed wire and heavy metal shutters.

The low murmur of voices floated on the wind as the people regained themselves and started to muse over what could have happened. She listened to all the different voices, the different volumes, accents, lilts and tilts of cadence. She had grown afraid of the idea of other people but now, standing on the cliff, those doubts paled in comparison to the warmth she felt. There was no sense of danger between them. The common bond of humanness ran strongly through them. She was so hungry for new connections, to share their grief and fears.

The ship must have been massive, a gigantic body of steel behind that one bright light. It had hit the land with such force that it had shuddered the underlying strata of the coastline, sent a shockwave racing through the solid rock so powerful that Miriam had felt it in her bed. The idea of such power made her feel tiny.

They watched the light for half an hour and soon the little groups of people began to form larger groups as the barriers fell and the natural propensity to communicate became stronger.

Miriam saw the groups merging and felt like a child attending school on the first day. She wanted to speak to them but didn't know how. She looked at Joseph. He was standing on his own, away to the west, his shadow like a long, dark cape running behind him.

A woman turned to her. Her face was still puffy with sleep and her hair was a mess. She was younger than Miriam, but not by much. Miriam looked at her and smiled. The woman waited for a moment, trying to recognize her without success, but smiled back anyway.

'Hello,' she said.

A sudden jolt of empathy crashed through Miriam and she was lost. The stranger came towards her without hesitation and threw her arms around her. Miriam's own arms remained at her side, limp and useless. The stranger's body was warm and relaxed. There was an easiness in the embrace.

'Hey, it's OK,' the voice whispered into her ear. 'There's no need to cry.'

|||

At some point they sat down on the dry grass and spoke openly and happily in the illumination. Being together as a group made them stronger than the sum of their parts. She glanced at Joseph occasionally. He was sitting away from the others but when they asked about his father he answered politely and honestly. They offered their condolences to him and he accepted them graciously.

The night drew on but nobody moved. The children had been safely asleep in their beds but Miriam had woken them to bring them on to the grass to share the night with everybody. Mary sat between Miriam's legs and used her mother's arms as a blanket beneath which she fell asleep again but Edward remained awake, sitting next to his grandmother with his head on her shoulder, listening to the people talking but saying nothing.

The night was warm, even with the gentle breeze. They swapped their tales, discussed once more the nature of what had fallen on the world and chatted hypothetically about what the world would be like when all this was over, when the world went back to normal.

The crack of dawn appeared and it was with the fading of the night that they all stood up, some of them on tiptoe, to face the east and the sky of the new day. Soon it would reveal the source of the bright, white light that had drawn them here.

They murmured and joked and talked about what a lovely time they had had that night, the best in months, they said, as the sky lightened with the promise of a sunny summer's day. The sky turned indigo and then violet and then lilac and inch by inch the sun came up over the edge of the land. It burned a line of watery light out across the horizon like a golden meniscus and as it did the lines of the stricken ship appeared from the gloom.

The vessel was massive. The tiny waves lapped the hull that grew from the water hundreds of feet into the air, skewered at an angle. A great shadowy gash had been torn aft. Countless ships had been ruined against those cliffs, but surely none of this size. Hundreds and hundreds of cargo containers stretched along its deck, their colours emerging with the dawn: red, green, blue, yellow.

It was a quarter of a mile out. They watched for an hour more as the tide receded to reveal the full extent of the tear in the ship's side.

'What do you think happened to the crew?' someone said, but nobody needed to answer. They had been watching the ship with the breaking dawn and not one person had appeared on deck.

Far out to sea, just visible above the waves, were rafts of floating debris, some large, some small. The tide had waned but some of the debris had found its way up on to the beach during the night, including one of the large containers.

Miriam looked at the mess and wondered who would clean it up, or whether it would be simply left to rot.

The morning brought new winds with it. The people from the village were tired and cold and ready to leave. They each said their goodbyes and walked to their cars and the brief happiness of being together as one scattered on the breeze. Some of them drove down to the beach to see if there was anything they could salvage; others drove back towards the village and out of sight. They had come and gone like a wave washing up and down the shore. When the last car disappeared from view Miriam watched the line of bare road and felt the melancholy return to her bones. Her mother put her hand on her shoulder. Miriam kept her eyes on the road.

III

Mary did not like the ship. When she saw it in the full light of day she started crying and Miriam lifted her up and rested her head on her collarbone. The scale of the boat was what Mary hated. It was too massive for the bay. It consumed most of the horizon. It listed with an ominous, distressed portent. Miriam wondered if the tide, now that it had turned, would be able to move it. And where it would go.

More flotsam had been washed up on to the beach and she could see eight containers popping their heads above the shallow waters of the bay. Any others that had been washed out must have sunk to the sea floor. Through Joseph's binoculars she could see things in the gash of the ship: floating crates, pieces of wood, cloth.

At eleven o'clock that morning more cars arrived but these were not from the village. News had spread of the ship that had run aground near the lighthouse and people had come to see what they could take. They drove past the house and down the hill towards the beach, parking up in the large car park that had for so many months lain empty.

Joseph went up to his father's bedroom and watched the cars for the rest of the morning. None of the people who had come stopped at the house. A number of campervans passed – families who had come to live on the move.

'What happened to it?' Edward asked.

Miriam ran her hand over the top of his head, through his soft hair.

'It crashed on the rocks.' She was finding it hard to stop herself crying all the time. Just hearing Edward's voice spiked her emotions. 'The rocks are dangerous around here. That's why there's a lighthouse – to warn people. The captain of the ship came too close to the shore.'

'But it's facing straight forward, like it drove in on purpose.'

She couldn't answer that. Edward was right. Either the whole crew were dead and the ship had veered off course or somebody had steered it deliberately into the cliffs.

She took Joseph his lunch and joined him at the window. He didn't look at her when she came. She opened her mouth to speak. It was time.

'Look at them,' he said, cutting her off.

Down on the beach, just in view, crowds of people were wading through the shallows to collect the things that had come off the ship. Some of the containers had cracked open and spilled their loads into the sea. The people ran up and down the sand and loaded the bounty into their vehicles.

'I should go down there, I suppose,' he said. 'See if there's something we can use.'

Miriam watched the tiny frames of the people. They looked like matchstick men.

'There's a lot of them down there.'

Joseph stared out of the window.

'Fucking hell,' he said suddenly. 'Why did it have to happen here?'

'Joseph,' she said.

He turned to her.

'What are we going to do?'

'We'll just have to see what happens.'

'That's not what I mean.'

They looked at each other. The plate of food she had brought for him was heavy in her hand.

'Do you still think I'm a good person? After everything I've done?'

She remembered him how he had been a few weeks before, climbing in the cherry trees and laughing with the kids. He didn't seem like the same person.

'Here.'

She held up his lunch – potatoes and baked beans, cooked on

the gas camping stove. She looked past him and out of the window and her thoughts were cut short. Something out in the bay caught her eye.

'What's that?' she said, pointing.

Joseph picked up the binoculars from the windowsill and peered through them. There was something coming from the crack of the ship's hull, moving quickly. As it emerged from the darkness Joseph could see it was a rowing boat. The man inside it turned the oars in powerful circles. His shirt was soaked red and blood covered the lower half of his face, from the mouth down; the speed with which he moved the boat through the water was like a trick of the light, an illusion.

III

He beat his path through the waves towards the sand. Joseph and Miriam ran out to the edge of the cliff and called down to the people on the beach to warn them but they were too far away for their voices to carry.

They saw him soon enough. Some of them stopped their foraging and watched his approach. When the boat glided to a stop in the sand he jumped down quickly and waded through the water, waist deep, his arms swaying from side to side.

A few of the people walked out to greet him, thinking him a survivor and in need of help.

Miriam told her mother to take the children inside.

Three of them went into the water to help but when they came to within a few yards of the boatman they stopped. Miriam watched not with horror, but curiosity. She was desensitized to it now. The people turned around in the water and headed back to the shore as fast as they could. Their legs were deep and they tried to run too fast. Two of them fell and thrashed around in the surf. Watching from such a distance through the binoculars and not being able to hear them gave what was happening a cartoonish quality.

The oarsman leaped on to the back of his first fleeing victim and they both disappeared into a white froth. The infected man's body emerged. He was holding his victim underwater, pinning him to the seabed with his knees, barely able to keep his head above water himself. After what must have been a minute the white froth calmed and the sea circled around the infected man's waist as a blue plain once again. He stood up and his victim's body bobbed to the surface. He pushed it back down again and looked around.

'Christ,' said Joseph. 'Why didn't anyone help him?'

Miriam smiled at that. She looked through the binoculars again with a calmness she could not understand.

The other two men had reached the shore. They turned to face the sea. Everyone on the beach was looking at the boatman. They had all nudged tentatively towards the waves.

Miriam saw somebody running towards the water, a young-looking man wearing a tracksuit. He paused at the water's edge and lifted his arm up. The sound of the gunshot was loud even up on the cliff top. It cracked up the rocks and over the wind. The infected man didn't fall. He kept coming into shore, waving his arms in the air.

The people standing around him urged the gunman to fire again. It took four shots until the boatman finally fell into the sea. When his body hit the water it darkened with blood around him.

She remembered the first time she had seen an infected person become violent, on the patch of wasteland near Joseph's flat in London. She remembered the speed with which he had run from the bushes. His legs were machine-like. She remembered how he had struck that poor man without hesitation. What had been his name? She remembered his sister, the priest. Her name was Grace. But she could not remember the name of her brother, who had died to protect her. She felt ashamed for forgetting. Her eyes watered. Why couldn't she remember?

'I guess we know what happened to the ship,' said Joseph.

'Did you see the way they goaded that man into shooting him?' She lowered the binoculars until she could feel their weight pulling her arm down.

'He had to do it.'

'I know,' she said, staring at the sea gulls in the sky.

She turned and walked towards the house. Down on the beach

she watched the little matchstick people treading carefully towards the man they had just helped kill, their tiny bodies moving slowly through the waves.

|||

By late afternoon the tide had marched halfway up the beach. More cars had arrived steadily throughout the day and the sea was full of debris.

The dark gash in the cargo ship's hull had disappeared underwater and the entire structure seemed to have listed still further. It was tilted so precariously it looked like the whole thing might topple on to its side. It reminded Miriam of an old poem Henry had loved when they first met. Perhaps it was a trick of the light but it seemed to slump visibly, drunkenly, inch by inch, degree by degree.

Joseph and Miriam were standing in the front doorway.

'If anybody comes don't let them in. No matter what they say,' he said.

'OK.'

She agreed with him. There were so many people that their presence was more intimidating than comforting. Not seeing anyone in so long had almost tricked her into believing there was nobody left. Seeing the people last night had comforted her because they were laconic, sleepy and gentle. But the people who had arrived that morning were not like that. They were hungry for new possessions, and there were lots of them.

'I'll take the car down, have a look around and come straight back,' he said.

'OK.'

There was a moment's silence.

'We can talk when I get back.'

Miriam nodded.

'There are things I need to tell you,' he said.

Miriam watched him go and locked the front door. When it was closed she pressed her forehead against the cool wood and waited for a moment with her hand on the latch. The house was quiet.

She went through to the back where her mother was sitting in the garden. She smiled when she saw her daughter. Miriam sat down next to her. The sky overhead was a rich blue. A few cottonwool clouds drifted beneath it.

'Mum, what do you think Joseph did to that man? Crowder.'

Her mother's eyes were closed and she was enjoying the breeze blowing across her face.

'I think it's best not to know about it.'

'Don't you think it's important?'

She found her eyes wandering to the back corner of the garden, to the patch of wall beyond which lay Dora's grave.

'I think he's gone. It doesn't matter how he went. All that matters is that he's gone.'

'I didn't know you thought that way,' said Miriam.

'I'm tired, Miri. The things we learned before – etiquette, codes, things like that – don't seem to count any more.' She opened one eye and looked at her daughter. 'What difference would it make if I thought any other way?'

'Are you OK, Mum?'

'I'm fine, honey. Just ignore me. Sometimes it all gets on top of you, you know?'

Miriam picked a fleck of dust off her sweater and flicked it off her fingers. 'I know.'

'Still,' said her mother, 'we soldier on.'

||||

She was using the binoculars like a telescope, looking through the left lens with her right eye. She would watch the people on the beach through the magnified lens and then close that eye just as she opened the other so that in a moment the world appeared close, then far away, then close. The wind blew softly against her face and for a moment it seemed like the world was a benevolent place again. The sunlight was warm. It crept into her bones and she could feel them thaw.

Across the cliff top she could just about see the bench where Henry had proposed to her. She had feared that the memory of finding the dead body on it would usurp all the happy memories, but it hadn't. She still remembered more than any other the day that Henry had asked to marry her. That memory was the strong one. Her heart had won it back. She didn't know how or why, but there it was.

She tried to look for patterns on the beach. The people looked like an ant colony streaming up and down the sand in lines, a world in miniature. She watched them in a trance. They were hypnotic. After a few moments they started to look like a big organism moving as one.

At first, when some of them stopped walking, she did not notice. The gears of the organism had cranked down but the thing still operated. There was nothing in the air to suggest a change had taken place. No cloud crossed the sun to block out the light. There was no sudden gust of wind. All that had happened was that some of the people had stopped walking.

It was only when all the others stopped, and then slowly approached those who had fallen still, that she noticed something was wrong. She lifted the binoculars again. In a human wave that swept all along the beach, people started to sit down in the sand. She swallowed but there was no saliva in her mouth. Her mind started to race. She looked frantically for Joseph on the beach but the faces were too small to see. With her heart pounding she dropped the binoculars and ran towards the cliff path as fast as she could.

|||

There were people running to and from the car park. When she ran out on to the beach the sudden increase in volume shocked her. It was so loud. She had forgotten the sound of people.

It was difficult to see how many were ill. The scene changed every second. Some were screaming, some were groaning, some were shouting. Some were on their knees, hugging those who were sitting down, begging them to come back.

She couldn't see Joseph anywhere. She was running across the sand, trying to make her thoughts orderly. She tried to remember what he was wearing. Yes, his gold T-shirt with the burgundy 77 on the front. That was it.

People barged into her. She looked towards the water. At sea level the true enormity of the stricken tanker loomed above her. It was the monster in her nightmare, stretching back for ever and ever, huge and terrifying.

The sand grew wet underfoot and she stopped at last, putting her hands on her knees, willing air into her empty lungs.

'Joseph,' she said under her breath.

Her mind loosened and clouded. She felt like she had floated out of her body and was watching actors playing a scene. Joseph's shoulders were hunched over and he was absolutely still. He was sitting with his hands stretched out to his knees, his head slumped over his chest.

'Joseph,' she said, this time louder, calling to him.

Joseph did not answer.

|||

She had never looked into his eyes in the same way she had Henry's and so she could not tell if the same thing that had been lost from Henry's eyes had been lost from Joseph's. Joseph was ill, the Sadness was through him, but she could only make that connection through Henry's ghost.

Further up the beach there was the bang of gunfire. She looked up just as a body fell to the ground. A man held up a silver pistol, shoulder height, arm's length. He turned his head towards Miriam and smiled. And started walking towards her.

'Joseph,' she said, crouching in front of him and shaking him by both arms. 'Joseph, please.'

He looked at her like he didn't know who she was. Miriam closed her eyes and tried to release the tension in her body. He was gone.

'Want me to do him for you, love?' said a voice. It was dirty and saturated by a discordant timbre.

She opened her eyes and looked at the man with the silver pistol, the same man that had shot the boatman who had come from the tanker. He was so young, little more than a boy. His track-suit was too big for him. His face was pink and grubby, his eyes stupid and dead. He blinked hard. He moved in short, jerky movements.

'I'll fucking do him for you, la. Bang. Easy. Twenty quid.'

She looked across the sand to the man he had just shot. He was lying on his back with his wife crying on his chest. She looked back to the boy with the silver pistol. He stared at her with his mouth half open, waiting for an answer. He shuffled his weight from side to side.

'You're so young,' was all she could say.

'I'm twenty-two, like,' he said defensively. 'You want me to fuck him up or not?'

Miriam stood and put her body between the boy and Joseph. She was scared and angry.

'He's dead anyway. What if he goes mental?' He swung the gun recklessly around him. 'Makes no difference to me, like.' As he finished each sentence he pursed his lips and stuck out his jaw.

'Leave us alone.'

'Look,' he said. He lowered his voice and glanced about him. 'If I do it, you won't have to later. Know what I mean? Fucking hell, I'm trying to do you a favour.'

'You want me to pay you to kill him.'

'I'll shoot him for free, la. It's the bullets you gotta pay for.' He smiled wickedly. 'It's putting him out of his misery.'

A whole series of memories rushed through her head, of Joseph telling her to let him go if this precise scenario ever presented itself. The boy was vile, his actions abhorrent, he made her feel sick, but this was what Joseph would have wanted.

'I haven't got all day. There's plenty of people here who'll pay for these bullets. I asked you 'cos you looked like a nice lady, like.'

'Get away,' Miriam mumbled.

'What's that?'

'I said get away!'

She pushed him in his bony chest and he stumbled back. He twisted his body around and used the momentum to walk away.

'Fuck you then, bitch,' she heard him say.

He threw his hands into the air as if Miriam was the fool who couldn't see. He walked over to another man and woman. She was lying in the sand and her husband was stroking her hair with a bewildered expression on his face. Miriam watched the husband look up when the boy called to him.

She turned back to Joseph, her heart beating, and waited for the sound of the gun to be fired, for the boy to make his deal. But the shot did not come.

III

It had just happened. She suddenly remembered the preacher with the red T-shirt in London. The world will come and swallow our souls. That was what he had said. From up on the cliff that was what it had seemed like. The earth had sucked something out of them. It had come up from beneath the ground, through the rock and sand, and unfurled its tentacles.

She looked at the sea. It was still moving up the beach. Some of the people, the ones without families to help them, already had water lapping at their feet. They made no attempt to move back to safety. Surely they won't let themselves drown, she thought.

'Joseph.'

He was looking at the sand directly in front of him.

'We have to move.'

Still nothing.

A stab of despair across her chest. She tugged at his arm to stir him but he jerked and pulled away.

'Leave me here,' he said in a quiet, low voice.

'No.'

His head dropped again.

'I'm not going to leave you. I said I wouldn't.'

She pulled at his arm again and thought of the day he had bandaged her knees when she had hurt them, and of his face when he played with the children. She tried to think of the good things. But it was just so hard. Her mind suddenly went into freefall.

'Please help us,' she whispered. 'Please.'

The front of her head hurt, as if somebody had stuck a lattice of pins and needles in there. She could no longer tell if she was crying for Joseph or for how lost they would be without him. Hope drained out of her with each falling tear. He was going to die and their history would remain an unclotted wound. In a few days, all that he was would cease to be. The sound of the sea hissed in her ears. Everything, everything had changed in a breath of the wind.

By the time she had recovered herself the water was just feet away. She quickly dried her eyes and reset her mind.

'We have to go.'

She knew Joseph wouldn't answer. He was happy to let the sea drown him. The thing that had made him what he was, the survivor, had been taken from him. There was a brown apron of scum at the prow of each wave. It edged closer and closer with each tired flop. A sheet of tarpaulin floated a few feet away, half submerged. The water came closer.

'Come on,' she said. She was pleading.

A large wave reared up in front of them. It splashed down and ran up the beach all around them. The shock of the cold made her jump to her feet. She grabbed Joseph by the arms and pulled him backwards. But his body was too heavy. It wouldn't move. Miriam groaned with exertion as she pulled. Her feet slipped forwards and Joseph still did not move. Another wave. It fizzled with froth. The coffee brown of the scum swirled about Joseph's prostrate form in delicate patterns. He lay back in it. The water soaked his T-shirt and turned it dark. It slopped in his hair.

'No,' she cried as she lost her grip on him. His head lay in the wet sand looking at the sky. 'No you don't.'

She had to crouch down to pull him, stretching her back too far forwards. The water sloshed over her feet and around her ankles. She could feel the sliminess of the scum between her toes as she tried to pull Joseph out. The muscles of her lower back stretched under the pressure.

The water was past them. She was losing him. The extra buoyancy meant that she could pull him but as each wave receded it would suck Joseph with it. She was losing ground. She lost grip of Joseph's wrists and slipped backwards. Her backside hit the ground and the impact cracked up through her abdomen. She watched with sudden terror as Joseph's body was pulled out into the water. He was like the other bodies in the shallows; just lying there, floating. She turned inland and leaned over to get a clear line of air for her lungs. She put her hands on her knees.

'Somebody help me!' she screamed. Nobody listened. 'Will somebody please help me!'

The despair rose in her. She ran out to Joseph and grabbed hold of his wrists once more. A wave broke in front of them and splashed into her face. She turned away and closed her eyes. The taste of salt was overpowering.

The sound of the wave was immense; a great punch of exploding air. It smashed into her and she felt the sand beneath her suck back, but her knee held in place. She refused to let go of his wrists as the freezing water tried to prise her fingers open. Particles of sand bounced around her. Back again, knee in, pull.

She heaved with every last inch of her. Her clothes were soaked. Her body ached with the effort. The tide was turning. But she had to hold on. There was a bond between her and Joseph that she could not break. Whatever it was that the monster had stolen from Joseph was still in her. She was not giving up. She felt the strength in her arms as they bent, her muscles tensing taut as she pulled him through the sand. They were out of the water again.

'I've got you,' she panted.

The sun had dipped low in the sky. It had taken her an hour to get him safe and her body threw a long shadow behind her. At last she pulled him between the clumps of marram grass that grew at the fringe of the small dunes in front of the car park. They had drifted right across the bay and she hadn't even noticed.

She let go of his wrists and flopped backwards. She drew breath in deep, long gasps. They both lay on their backs and looked at the sky. Ribs of stratus glowed red on one side and indigo on the other. She wondered what Joseph saw when he looked at them. Did he see something beautiful, or was it just chemicals? She panted until her breath came back and tried, just for those few moments, to think about what she should do next.

|||

She went to look for others in the sea but none were left. Black shapes floated out in the water but they were too far away and none of them were moving. She went back to Joseph and looked for the keys to the car that he had left in the car park but they were not in his pockets. He must have thrown them into the sea.

As the light of the day faded the bright light on the front of the ship glimmered again. It no longer shone into the cliffs. The tide had turned the tanker so that the beam struck the coast obliquely.

'I'm going to have to go back to the house so I can get the spare keys. And then we'll take you back home,' she said to him. She stroked his hair. 'Would you like that?'

'Just leave me,' he said. 'I'm fucked.'

She stopped. 'Don't you want to go home?'

His Adam's apple moved up his throat and he didn't answer.

Miriam stood and found her way through the tough grass to the cliff path. She climbed it slowly, her body aching. Her muscles were stiff with acid and she could feel cramp setting in. There was a handrail at the side of the path that she used to pull herself up. Every movement was a struggle.

When she reached the top of the path the house looked distant. She broke into a slow run. The windows of the house were black squares in the dusk. She knew that leaving Joseph was dangerous. He would probably run away but she had no choice. She had to get the car if she was going to get him back up here.

She went in through the front door.

'He's ill,' was all she could say.

Her mother walked slowly towards her down the hallway. A streak of sunlight cut across it and as her mother passed through it her whole body turned gold.

'What do you mean?'

They drove down to the beach in Joseph's van.

'He should never have gone down there,' Miriam said. 'It wouldn't have happened if he'd stayed in the house.'

They parked the van and went along the head of the beach to where she had left him. She had always expected him to have disappeared but when she saw the empty patch of sand her mind emptied of thoughts and she couldn't move.

Her mother called Joseph's name and hurried along the beach, searching. But Joseph had gone. He did not want to be found.

III

That night Miriam slept in the same bed as her mother. Every few minutes the sounds of new cars passing the house and travelling down the hill to the beach washed in through the walls.

'What are we going to do?' she said.

'I don't know,' her mother answered.

They lay awake for a while longer. Miriam looked at the ceiling that glowed dimly in the half-light from the tanker.

'Miriam? Are you still awake?'

'Yes.'

She could feel her mother's warmth lying next to her.

'What if Joseph comes back?'

'What do you mean?'

'You know what I mean.'

Miriam raised her voice above a whisper.

'Then we look after him. What are you suggesting?'

Her mother's voice was calm as she spoke. 'You've seen how he's been acting lately.'

'So? So what? Where would we be without him? We have everything we need up here because of him. And now you think we should just turn our backs on him?'

'It's what he wanted us to do.'

'No it's not. He didn't know what he wanted. He never did.' She stopped. The curtains swayed. 'I was so horrible to him.' Her breath left her. She was back in the car with him, travelling towards the supermarket. 'I said horrible things to him.'

She felt her mother's hand touch hers.

'Ssh,' she said. 'You're upsetting yourself.'

'All he was trying to do was protect us. And maybe he was right.'

'About what?'

'You know what. People.'

Her mother paused. 'Go to sleep, Miri. We'll talk about this in the morning.'

'There was a boy on the beach today, Mum; going around asking for money to shoot the people who were ill, to put them out of their misery.'

Her mother said nothing.

'Is that the sort of person who has good in them? Who can be redeemed? He wasn't broken, or beaten, or confused – he was just doing what came naturally.' She moved her hand away. 'The last time we were at the supermarket somebody took a *flamethrower* and sprayed it all over a crowd of people. For no reason. They didn't care who lived or who died. They just did what they did. These are the people Joseph warned us about. We didn't believe they existed but I've seen them with my own eyes. They're real, and they're out there. And Joseph tried to tell us but we didn't listen.'

'Miri, stop talking like this.'

'You weren't there.' Her skin was hot. She threw off her blankets. 'And now you're telling me you want to desert him, to become like them. What is it exactly you want to do if he comes back? Push him off the cliff?'

'No,' said her mother.

'Well, what then? What do you really think? What will Joseph do if he comes back?'

She sat up in the bed. 'You know what, Miriam.'

'But I don't know what it is you think we should do.'

'I don't know either, so that means we should just ignore it, does it?'

'This is pointless.'

Suddenly her mother spoke sharply.

'Now you listen here. We can't bury our heads in the sand. You don't seriously think the possibility of Joseph becoming violent is not a real one. You saw how he was with the man in the cellar – he was like an animal.'

'He was protecting us.'

'He was like an animal,' she repeated. 'And we all know what happens when these people change. He won't show us any mercy, and he won't show any mercy to the children either.'

'Do you know what Joseph said to me?' said Miriam. 'He said he was protecting us despite himself, not because of himself.'

'I believe that.'

'Doesn't that mean anything? Doesn't that mean he had to be good?'

'We'll continue this conversation in the morning. Things will be clearer then.'

Her mother turned away and rested her head on her pillow.

Reluctantly, Miriam lay down in the bed with her eyes open. Sleep seemed far away. Her body was telling her it might never need sleep again. She no longer felt the urge to plug into that great unconscious. It was only nightmares for her anyway.

III

By morning the ship had turned nearly a full ninety degrees. It had listed further and come to a rest with its deck tilting inland. The containers had slipped along the deck. Many of them had fallen into the sea. Their sheer weight had snapped open the bulwarks like balsawood.

A low, thin cloud had covered the sky during the night and the air was clammy.

Mary and Edward came running into the living room.

'Has anybody seen Pele?' said Mary, out of breath. Her cheeks were flushed.

'He was here this morning,' said Miriam's mother.

Mary bit her lip in puzzlement. 'He's disappeared,' she exclaimed.

The two children dashed out of the house again and a few seconds later they could hear their voices outside calling for the dog. Miriam followed them out. Down the hill towards the beach a few tents had been erected in the field behind the car park. She looked around for any sign of Joseph but there was none. He had vanished.

'Kids,' she called.

Edward and Mary stopped and looked at her.

'If you see Uncle Joseph I want you to come and tell me, OK?'

'Where is he?' asked Mary.

'He's down on the beach.'

'Why?' asked Edward, his head cocked to one side.

'He's gone to help the people down there.'

'Did he take Pele?'

'I don't know. Listen.' She crouched down to their level so that they knew what she was saying was important. 'If you see him coming, you come right to me. Yes?'

'Yes,' they both said together.

'Promise on robin?' she said.

She had heard them mentioning the robin. Mary laughed.

'That's not how it works,' she chirped. 'We're the robins.'

Mary had not picked up on it but Edward was looking at her suspiciously. He didn't say anything. But he knew something was wrong.

|||

The next day it started to rain a light drizzle. It filled the sky and the ship out in the bay became shrouded in mist. Miriam drove into the village but still could not find Joseph. She finally started to think she might never see him again. The rain cleared by evening. A sliver of brilliant orange cut a laser line across the horizon. The children were put to bed and Miriam's mother turned in early.

Miriam sat in the chair next to the window that Henry's father had always used. Pele had still not returned. She looked out of the window and tried to forget all her thoughts. The silence was absolute.

There was a low cabinet underneath the window. She leaned forward and pulled open one of the doors. Inside were stacks of old photograph albums. She took out the topmost, ran her hand across the smooth vellum cover and lifted it open.

The first photograph was of the whole of Henry's family. The two sons were very young. Henry must have been around six years old but his face was still easily recognizable. His mother had her arm around him. Joseph was different though, looked like a different person. He had a mischievous smile.

She turned the page. The next photograph was of Henry and Joseph on a fishing boat. It looked familiar and then she remembered the photograph she had seen in Joseph's flat in London. It had been taken on the same day. The sky was a brilliant, clear blue and their faces glowed orange in the evening light.

She suddenly felt as if somebody was watching her from the corner of the room. She looked around quickly but there was nobody there. Nobody she could see. But she still felt the eyes, like a ghost behind the veil.

The night was closing in. She looked back to the window. The photograph album was held loosely in her hands and it fell to the floor with a heavy thud. Her breath was gone and the metal taste of fear was in her mouth. Joseph was staring back at her, his face close to the window, his open palm resting against the glass.

III

He tapped it once and everything became still. The click of his fingernails on glass. Miriam was brought through what felt like a series of jolts as the realization of what she was looking at crashed through her.

Joseph ran to the door. His body was too fast for itself. It was not natural. He disappeared from sight. Miriam jumped up. She got to the hallway but he was already inside. There was a white aura around his dark silhouette. She could see his body pulse up and down with each breath.

She ran. She pulled open the door to the cellar and slammed it shut behind her. The cellar was the only option; upstairs would lead him right to the children. She went for the lock but felt the handle being pushed down from the other side of the door. He was trying to get in. She couldn't hold the handle up and slide the lock across at the same time. Both hands were needed just to stop him getting in.

'Let me in,' she heard him say.

The voice came through the wood and sounded like it was submerged in water.

Miriam closed her eyes. The metal of the handle was cutting into her palm. It eased slowly downwards under his strength. But she held on.

'Let me in,' came his voice again. 'I'm going to do something awful to you.'

She let go of a low sob. Her head felt light and her eyes started to sting. She used her body against the handle for leverage.

'If you don't let me in I'll kill your mother and your children.'

His voice was utterly without emotion.

'Oh God,' she whispered. 'Please.' Her voice was high. 'Just leave us alone.'

There was a pause. The door handle stopped moving. Miriam held her breath. Quickly, she slid the lock across. His footsteps walked away up the hall. She lifted her face to the ceiling. This could not be happening. She pulled the lock back across and opened the door. Joseph's hand was on the newel post at the bottom of the banister. When he saw Miriam come out of the cellar he stopped. Against the white light in the garden his body was a dark mass of gravity. It swirled about him.

Slowly, he walked towards her. Miriam receded back into the cellar, down the stairs, facing the door, which she left open. Joseph followed her down. He closed the door behind him and locked it.

'We can help you, Joseph,' she pleaded.

The cellar was dark, the only illumination a thin silver beam of light from the tiny window at the apex of the wall and ceiling that was too small for a person to climb through.

'Nobody can help me now,' he said, calmly. His voice came from somewhere in the darkness near the base of the steps. She could not see him.

'When I was on the beach I saw the dunes rise up all around me until I was surrounded by them in a basin of sand.'

The slow, steady timbre made her cry. She knew what it was and what it meant. The chrysalis of withdrawal that the infected victims entered at the start of the illness had cracked open and the end result was peering out at her from within the gloom. Whatever it was that Joseph had feared was in the cellar with her.

'The sky above the hills of sand was the dark blue of a clear night and the dunes were as black as pitch. Horsemen appeared at their heads – three hundred and thirty-three of them – and they looked down to me. I could see their outline against the sky as their riders watched me.'

Miriam sat down on the little sofa. Her mouth was hot. She bit her lower lip and lifted her knees up to make herself small.

'I knew what had happened. I had gone back in time and the horsemen were the ticking days. The eyes of the horses came alive. They glowed in the dark, a different colour for each of them: two red eyes, two green, two blue, two orange. All the way along, all the way around. I could see them breathing, I could hear their snorts.'

'What are you going to do to us?'

'And then the horsemen started to walk away. One by one the laser eyes disappeared until I was in the present again. And here I am now, in the dark, with you.'

The voice was Joseph's, but also not. It was heavier. There was extra substance in it. There was a movement in the dark. He was moving.

'Where is God, Miriam?' said the voice, quietly.

The silence when there was no speaking made the air heavy.

'I don't know.'

The voice said, 'How is he going to save you from what I am about to do? Why didn't he save me?' A pause. 'Am I going to hell for this? I can't stop myself. I have no choice – but does that mean I have to go to hell? Because I am who I am?'

Her whole body trembled. She thought of the children asleep upstairs. She must not scream.

'God is weak,' said the voice. It had moved again. It seemed to come from the back of the cellar. 'He's killing himself, do you know that? I can feel Him. I'm sure of it. Why does He make us hurt each other like this?'

Her muscles tightened. 'I don't know.'

'No, you never do.' Movement. Across the floor. 'Think,' it said. It was closer now. He was closer. 'Maybe it wasn't God at all; maybe it was just the devil all along.'

There was a disturbance in the air. Miriam jumped backwards in the seat. Her skull burst with pain and she screamed, unable to stop herself. Her scalp burned and she was drawn to her feet. He was pulling her up by her hair. I won't scream again, she told herself inside her head.

The force with which he dragged her across the floor was not human. It was like something of the wild world – a wolf, or a wave. She could smell the dirt in the air as she was dragged through it. The children, she thought, nebulously.

And then she was in the air. Her sense of balance was gone and she was weightless with an utter loss of control. She hit the wall.

Pain shot up her left arm. They were at the far end of the cellar, away from the stairs, in the corner. There was no getting out of there now. She felt the control sweep away from her, and with it went something else. That thing she had felt guide and anchor her withdrew from her body and into the air. It was all going to end in that cellar.

Outside of their sphere of movement the cellar was silent. Neither Joseph nor Miriam said anything. They grunted when they had to but the only real sounds were of their kicking bodies on the floor. She was on her back. Her knees were so that he couldn't get a clear line of attack at her. She turned her face to one side and tried to push him away but he was too heavy.

He pressed her down with his weight and she suddenly felt his hands on her bare hips. When his flesh touched hers she kicked harder. His hands moved down and formed claws that hooked over her trousers. She opened her eyes wide. Her heartbeat doubled.

He prised the material down with both hands. She felt the air against her thighs and shook her head.

'No,' she whispered.

'Yes.'

Her knees were still up and he couldn't get her trousers off without straightening her legs. He pinned her body and somehow managed to lever her straight with his thighs. She was lying flat on the floor now. He said nothing as he worked her trousers and underwear down.

And then her mind left the cellar by the window. It floated up into the sky and backwards through time. She was on the beach again. She saw the blank face of the boy who had offered to shoot Joseph. The boy she had turned away. Up and backwards her mind flew, to the bedroom, to Joseph telling her to let him go if he became ill. Suddenly everything reversed, time tumbled. Somewhere in the recesses of her mind she felt pain through her body. She was on the beach again, with the boy, screaming at him to get away from her, and then she was dragging Joseph out of the sea, inch by inch, up the sand. Forward again, to the dark cellar, control gone, guiding sense gone.

She scrabbled with her hands, tried to wriggle away. There was no purchase. Nothing to hold on to. He grabbed her arms and pushed her down. Her eyes were closed.

'Don't you care about Henry?' she said, quickly and urgently. She had to make a connection.

His head was directly over her. A line of saliva dropped from his mouth to her face. Humiliation flooded up her. She was naked from the waist down. Oh my God, she thought. The clear, calm voice in her mind's kernel spoke to her: this is going to happen.

She could feel his breath.

'Joseph Joseph Joseph,' she whispered quickly. She just wanted him to acknowledge her.

She felt him against her thighs.

'Oh no,' she cried. 'Please no.'

Her arms were pinned. So was her neck. He was forcing her legs open.

'No, no.' She struggled. Every muscle was taut. Her bones tried to lock up and protect her. He was just so strong. He prised her thighs apart like he was a machine. The deliberate way he moved, like everything was planned, terrified her. There was no way to fight this tide.

She felt him against her and all of her breath deserted her lungs. And then time skipped. There were heavy shudders in her body. A portal seemed to draw two disparate pieces of time together. One state had changed to another with no transition. Her heart pounded so fast that she struggled to breathe. He was obliterating everything. There was pain in her centre. Her mind fell back in the cave of her skull and waited, its eyes closed, trembling. It listened to the noises he made as he fucked her and tried to think of other things but all that came was the image of a spring, right in the centre of her, running dry of that golden honey-like fluid until it stopped.

And then it was over and they both lay still, her face turned towards the wall; she cried in silent gulps. She could fight him now, but what was the point?

A minute passed and Joseph stood up. She did not look at him and he said nothing to her. He moved back and away into the darkness again. She already felt it trickling out of her and she closed her eyes as tight as she could.

She remembered a day when she was a child, lying on her back like she was now. She was in a cornfield in France during the summer holidays. The tall plants swayed drunkenly overhead and beyond them was the sky as blue as a sapphire. How could time draw together along that same line? How could two such different things happen along one line?

Her body hurt. Her mind jolted down and down. And she fell asleep on the floor.

||||

In the morning she awoke and sunlight shone in through the tiny solitary window in the cellar. Particles of dust drifted down through the air. She sat up and clothed herself. Already she was crying. The cellar was silent. Inside her head the melody played of an old music box she had owned as a child. She remembered the ballerina figurine that turned around as the music chimed.

Joseph's body was at the bottom of the stairs. He had died sitting there at some unknown moment in the night.

She stood in front of him, over him, and looked down. His head was slumped over, his dead eyes staring at her feet. She felt she should do something, say something, take some action to release the knotted bundle of emotion in her chest. But as she stood there she could think of nothing. He was gone. Only his husk remained.

She passed the body and climbed the steps. The hallway was empty and the house was quiet. She wondered what time it was – early or late.

As she moved along the corridor her memory brought her the events of the night. She felt like her heart was a magnet and what had happened was its opposite. Whenever she went close to it, ready to accept, it slid away. She wanted the poles to reverse and the magnets to fly together, to allow the healing to begin, but that was not how magnets worked. They were always so close but never quite there.

She went upstairs and into her children's bedroom. They were both asleep when she entered the room but Edward sensed her presence and woke up. He lifted his head above the sheets and looked at his mother.

'Mum?'

'Go back to sleep,' she whispered.

He laid his head back down on the pillow.

Her mother was the first of the family to come downstairs. She found her daughter in the back garden, at the wall, peering over to the grave on the other side.

'Miri?'

Miriam puffed out her cheeks and expelled the warm air, emptying her lungs as far as they would go. Her eyes were red from crying.

'Joseph's in the cellar.'

She couldn't look at her mother.

'Is he all right?'

She shook her head. It was difficult to see the lines in the grass where Dora's grave had been dug. Only the very top of the pebble they had found on the beach was visible over the grass.

'What's happened?' her mother asked.

Miriam took a deep breath. The early morning sun shone brightly and it was warm enough to be unpleasant.

'He's dead.'

There was a long silence. The music box music played in her head again. She forced herself to look at her mother. Her face was so thin. And then she saw it in her mother's eyes. It was right there, the thing that Henry had lost, the thing that the monster stole from everybody it touched, the thing that had swept away from her last night in the cellar. Her mother looked so alive with it all of a sudden. She couldn't tell her.

Miriam turned away, the still air hot on her face, and she looked at Dora's grave again. She sensed an alien hollowness in her chest. Her body hurt, her mind was exhausted, and something closed inside her and she felt shut off from something, as if she was on the other side of a locked door.

PART THREE

OF HOPE

'We're not going to make it! We're not going to make it!' Charlie screamed.

Emily laughed and hit him. 'It's not funny.'

The campervan rolled decrepitly on to the grass at the side of the road and stopped. If it wasn't so frustrating, having come all that way and having to stop so close to their destination, it would have been funny. After several seconds of silence he looked across to Emily and scrunched his face up.

'Can you actually believe it?'

Emily laughed in that sudden, off-guard way of hers.

'There's a house over there,' she said, pointing.

Charlie followed the line of her finger until it came to a rest on a cold-looking, fortress-like house on the other side of the road. Grey tangles of barbed wire wrapped itself unwelcomingly around the garden walls and thick metal shutters were closed over the windows.

'Looks friendly enough,' he said.

Emily smacked his chest with the back of her hand again. 'Get your cute little ass up there.'

Charlie raised an eyebrow. 'Excuse me?'

'Go and see if they have a jack.'

'And you just stay here, nice and safe?'

She laughed again. 'Yup.'

Charlie deliberated on this and shrugged his skinny shoulders. 'OK.'

He threw open the door to the campervan and jumped down. Just before he pushed the door closed he turned back to her and smiled.

'Don't forget,' he said. 'If something bad happens to me

remember that I loved you to the ends of the world and beyond.'

Emily watched him skip along the road and open the garden gate.

Saturnine clouds hung heavily in the early morning sky and the house underneath them looked damp and forbidding. Charlie didn't care though. He went up the garden path with the same spring in his step that he always had. He didn't want her to see that he was nervous.

He knocked on the door and looked back to the campervan. When he saw Emily smile at him he raised his thumb and turned back to the door and knocked again, listening for movements inside.

'Hello?' he called. 'Is anybody in there?'

He looked back to the van and shrugged.

There was a thin concrete path leading around the side of the house, still splattered in damp patches after last night's rain. Charlie looked at it and sighed.

'Here we go,' he said.

The path was dark with shadow. Past the far end he could see the edge of a vegetable garden. It didn't look wild – there must be somebody living here. There were more of the metal shutters on the windows. Behind, he could see fields of farmland and beyond that, up a gentle slope, a line of trees.

'Hello?' he called again, moving up the path.

The garden was bigger than he expected. The vegetable patch stretched all the way to the stone wall at the back. The plants grew in neat lines and columns, in quadrants between gravel paths, some tied to beanpoles, others growing in thick green clumps near the ground. A tree stood in the far left corner and the first breaths of autumn had blown some of the leaves from its branches. They had drifted far enough to reach the small patio in front of the conservatory. The blinds were drawn.

Charlie wondered why somebody had gone to the effort of fixing shutters to the windows when the conservatory was so completely exposed. The glass doors were closed. He peered inside through a crack in the blinds but there was nobody there. The room was neat and clean. Behind it, a wide doorway led to an empty kitchen. He knocked on the glass, leaning his head in to get a clearer view. Something moved at the back of the kitchen; a dark form, hiding behind the wall of the doorway. He could make out an arm.

'Hello?' he called again. 'It's all right, I'm not dangerous. My van has broken down, that's all.'

He kept his eyes on the form. Cautiously, it stepped out into the open and came towards him. It was an old woman. She moved slowly into the conservatory and squinted to see the person in the garden staring back at her. Her gait was hunched and her skin looked grey; ghost-like, unnatural.

Charlie smiled and slowly lifted his hand and started to wave.

'Hi,' he said, loudly, so that she could hear. 'How are you?'

She came into the light and he could see how thin she was. The skin on her face was loose. Charlie felt uneasy. When she was a few feet from the door she stopped.

'What do you want?' she said through the glass.

'Um, my van's got a flat tyre but I don't have a jack.'

The woman stepped towards him. From around her neck she took a set of keys and turned one of them in the lock. There was a moment of silence and a pause between them that Charlie had experienced many times before: the wait. The wait to see how somebody would react when a wall of security had been taken down in good faith.

He smiled as widely as he could.

'I'm not a baddie,' he said. 'Honest.'

And he raised his hands up. Miriam's mother smiled.

'You're full of energy, aren't you?' she said, opening the door inwards towards her.

Charlie nodded and laughed, the tension diffusing.

'Sorry, it's just I've been driving for ages and I needed the fresh air.'

'Where did you come from?'

'Nowhere really. Well, I'm from Reading but I was in Europe when it all happened.'

The old woman nodded. 'You've had a long journey.' She was far less scary when she was talking. 'How old are you?'

'Twenty-one.'

'Are you with your family?'

'Nah.' He paused so that she understood. 'It's just me and my girlfriend. She's out the front.'

The old woman swallowed. Her eyes were two tiny dots in her head.

'Are you here on your own?' he said.

He felt the switch in her straight away. She tightened her grip on the door handle and her body moved imperceptibly away from him.

'I didn't mean it like that. Please don't be scared.'

The old woman's face softened as quickly as it had hardened and the moment passed.

'I just wanted to make sure you were OK up here,' he added. 'You know there's a camp at the bottom of the hill? That's where we're going. It's supposed to be safe.'

There was a noise in the kitchen behind the old woman.

Charlie looked past her shoulder and through the conservatory but there was nobody in sight. He sensed somebody hiding. He lowered his head conspiratorially.

'Are you sure you're OK?' he whispered, flicking his eyes past her to the kitchen.

The old woman smiled.

'You're a nice boy,' she said. 'Go and get your girlfriend and come in for some soup.'

He felt a tingle on the back of his neck. These were the best things to have come out of the mess, these little moments of kindness, of trust.

'Really?'

'Are you hungry?'

Charlie laughed. He looked into her eyes, two dark marbles with a square of light in the middle.

'I'm starving.'

|||

He could never have thought that such a meal would be so welcome. It was just a vegetable mush with some salt and pepper but as he swallowed each mouthful he was sure he could feel the nourishing goodness of it seep into his flesh and bones.

Emily ladled the soup on to her spoon in dainty, ladylike amounts, blew on it and ate. She always said that grace would be the last thing she would let go of, but Charlie was past that. He shovelled the food in as fast as he could.

He looked around at each of the faces at the table: the old woman, her daughter and two little kids. He guessed the husband must have died because there had been no sign or mention of him.

'So,' said the old woman, 'what's your plan?'

'We're going to the camp at the bottom of the hill,' said Emily. 'We've heard it's safe.'

'It seems that way,' said the old woman. 'It's been there for months and we've not heard any trouble.'

The younger woman shifted in her seat.

'Do you know the people?' Charlie asked.

The old woman considered his question. 'We don't have much to do with them.'

'Don't you get lonely up here on your own?' said Charlie, not thinking.

The two women paused as if waiting for the other to answer. It was the younger woman who finally spoke.

'We think it's safer to be on our own.'

Charlie nodded and looked into his soup.

The old woman's daughter had said hardly anything the whole time they had been in there. He knew who she was. She was one of the people who had been broken. He had seen it lots of times.

'We heard,' he said, 'that the government are getting close to a cure.'

Miriam's mother smiled. 'You never know.'

'You don't think so?'

'We've heard similar things from people passing through on their way to the camp.'

Charlie's voice became animated.

'We spoke to a guy – didn't we, Em? – who said they've been doing experiments all this time. They haven't given up. There's a small group that are working and when this is all over they'll come back and get things started again.'

The old woman listened to him with patient silence. Charlie took a breath and looked at the little boy and girl.

'I bet you two are loving not having to go to school,' he said cheerfully.

The two kids stared blankly back at him.

'Oh-kay,' he said, and looked at their mother. 'Sorry.'

He stopped suddenly when their eyes met. He broke contact and stared into his soup bowl again, not knowing what to say. He had said something wrong. The room became uncomfortably silent. Tears had formed in her eyes.

|||

'Thanks again for the food.'

The old woman lurched forward and pulled him into a hug. He awkwardly tapped her on the back.

'You be careful,' she said.

'I will be.'

She released him and they looked at each other. He handed her back the car jack they had borrowed to change the tyre and as Charlie let go he wondered what would happen if another tyre went because he didn't have any spares now.

'Are you sure you're OK up here? It's pretty exposed, and there are some bad people around.'

The old woman tilted her head and smiled.

'We're OK,' her daughter said quickly.

It cut the conversation dead.

Charlie and Emily climbed into the campervan and waved as they pulled away.

Below them wisps of smoke rose into the sky from the camp. In the rear-view mirror, the old woman and her daughter stood side by side in front of the garden gate, watching the campervan, until they shrank behind the hill and were gone from sight.

|||

Two men were sitting in deckchairs on either side of the road. Behind them was a line of tall metal fencing that stretched up the hill and down towards the sea. It was not one unbroken fence, but rather thick steel frames with wire meshing across them, linked together by clasps and held in place by heavy concrete feet. The only gap was the road that ran between it that the men were guarding. The deckchairs were so out of context with their surroundings that Charlie laughed.

'Guards,' he said dramatically.

The two men rose and gestured for Charlie to slow down. He rolled down the window and placed his arm over the side.

'Hi there,' he said. 'Any room at the inn?'

The guards looked at each other quizzically.

'Surely is, my man,' said the first guard in a gentle northern lilt. 'Park your van over there.' He pointed past the open gate to an empty space of tarmac.

'Sure thing.'

They pulled into the large expanse of the car park. The first half was given over to cars. Behind those were lines of caravans and some other structures that looked like portakabins. People were walking around casually.

'This is OK,' Emily said.

He reached over and touched her hair. She leaned in for him and Charlie kissed the top of her head reassuringly. So this was the place they had been told about. They were finally here.

Directly in front of them were three of the portakabins. Long ramps with wooden hand rails led along their front walls towards a door. The door to the middle cabin opened and two men stepped out. They approached the campervan, both pulling their trousers up, one around a particularly substantial girth.

'Well, he's not starving,' Charlie said.

Emily laughed and Charlie jumped down from his seat.

'Afternoon,' he said.

The larger man saluted informally. A rim of hair grew around his bald head.

'You just pitching up?'

He spoke with a broad Scottish accent. His face had friendly, rounded features: a small nose, ruddy complexion, podgy cheeks and little eyes that held in them a subtle, disarming sorrow.

Charlie squinted in the low sun that glowed now as a splattering of yellow light behind the drifting clouds.

'Yeah. If that's OK.'

'You don't mind a bit of work? You'll have to pull your weight, comrade.'

Charlie looked down at his skeletal frame. 'No problem.'

The Scottish man laughed and looked at Charlie's body.

'We'll get some fat on that,' and he held out a giant hand with thick, chubby fingers. The index finger was missing from the first knuckle up. 'George McAvennie.'

Charlie's hand disappeared inside the giant fingers and he felt a powerful squeeze against his bones.

'My name's Charlie.'

'Just Charlie?'

'Charlie Oldham.'

McAvennie turned to the man at his shoulder, a tall, thin man with a scratchy beard and an old pair of plastic-framed glasses.

'It's the bonnie prince himself, eh, Andrew?' And then he said something so quickly and with such a thick accent that Charlie couldn't catch it. He just smiled and nodded. McAvennie slapped Charlie on the arm. 'Have you come far, son?'

'Kind of. In a roundabout way.'

McAvennie nodded. 'Who've you got with you, kidda?'

He looked back at the van.

'It's just me and my girlfriend.'

McAvennie's friendly face straightened.

'We won't allow no funny business here.'

Charlie didn't know what to say to that, until McAvennie let go of an almighty booming laugh that made Charlie jump. He slapped him on the arm again, this time harder.

'I'm just shitting you, comrade.'

The tall, thin man next to McAvennie grinned quietly. He had shoulder-length hair but it was thinning and greasy.

'Just ignore him, kid,' he said in an American accent.

Charlie laughed, more with relief than anything else.

'Right,' he said.

'OK.' McAvennie's voice became businesslike. 'You go with

Mr Andrew Fields here. He'll show you to your new home.'

Charlie thought he liked the large Scottish man. He had a lot of energy at least – something that had waned in most people.

The American man, Fields, walked towards Charlie's campervan.

'You coming?'

The sense of ending struck him; of a journey coming to a conclusion.

He watched in silence as Emily moved along in the seat so that Fields could climb aboard. It's going to be OK now, Charlie said in his head, and walked quickly over to the van.

He turned the key and the engine rumbled noisily to life. The American shook hands with them both, introduced himself formally and they pulled into the camp.

|||

'We try to keep all the important things here in the car park. The fields get muddy in the rain, so it makes sense to try and keep the vital things on the blacktop.'

They went down a thin thoroughfare running diagonally through the centre of the car park between lines of cabins, trucks and stacks of what Charlie guessed were supplies covered in light blue tarpaulins.

At the bottom of the car park they came to a small, squat brick building outside which a small queue of people waited. It was the old public toilet building. Next to it was a line of plastic portable toilets and a cabin raised on stilts that Charlie recognized as shower blocks similar to the ones he had seen at the music festivals of the old world.

'It's so organized,' Emily said quietly.

'We keep on top of it. Makes life easier if we work towards the common goal.'

'Common goal?' said Charlie

'To get through this steaming pile of shit in one piece.' He pushed his glasses up his nose. 'To survive. Listen, kids, this thing ain't gonna work if nobody knows what to do.'

The smell of burning wood came in through the open window.

They drove slowly to the corner of the car park. There was an exit at the far end, with two ornate pillars of grey stone standing on either side of the road that led back up a slope to the lighthouse on the point. Branching off the main road a hundred yards along was a mud track cutting a line between two large encampments. Charlie's van rolled slowly on to it and up. On the left was a city of tents. There must have been hundreds of them, erected all across the grassland up the gentle slope, their colours like a rainbow splashed against the ground.

On the right-hand side were more tents. The hillside was steeper and the tents were arranged in tiers. Lines of washing flapped in the breeze. Behind the tents were further tiers made up of more caravans or campervans that looked out over the campsite like spectators at a firework show.

'My God, how many people are here?' said Emily, peering out through the windscreen.

'With you, one thousand, three hundred and eighty-six.' He laughed. 'It's better to know who's here and who's not.'

Charlie was comforted that there was a chain of command at the camp, an order, and that they seemed to know what they were doing. But he knew Emily would not feel the same way.

'Will we make it up this hill OK?'

The mud looked churned up and sticky.

'It'll be fine,' Fields replied.

His accent didn't seem as strong when he spoke quietly. Charlie liked it. It wasn't hard like a New Yorker's. He was probably around forty years of age but his long hair and patchy beard made him look older than that. Charlie pictured Fields as a boy riding a horse through the mountains of Montana beneath a massive sky, crossing a brook, stopping for a lunch of bread and cheese under an apple tree. The rumble of the engine came back to him as a flock of children ran out into the track and, as one, turned and darted away up the hill.

'Follow them?'

'Yup.'

The campervan sank a few inches but held its traction. On the left, the city of domed and peaked tents became more clearly visible. The bases of the tents at the side of the track were rimmed with mud that had splattered up on to the flysheets. Each sat in a circle of brown where trampling feet had killed any grass. Up close things did not look so cosy.

A line of wooden poles, like telegraph poles, lined the left-hand side of the track, sunk into the ground at fifty-yard intervals. Strung along them was an electrical wire dotted with large, round lightbulbs.

As Charlie looked past the lines of tents to the little communal camp areas that had been set up, he saw a young man of about his own age sitting on a log wearing mud-stained boots, strumming a guitar.

'There's a future friend,' he said to Emily. In the rear-view mirror he caught her smile. 'Yup. Me and him are going to become very good friends,' he said categorically.

'You always this cheerful, kid?'

Charlie laughed and gave the answer he always gave: 'Being any other way isn't going to change anything, is it?'

Fields pointed off to a narrower, less defined track that curled snake-like between the tents. It wasn't as muddy as the main track.

'Through there,' he said.

Charlie pulled into the gap. The tyres gained better traction against the more stable grass. They passed a caravan. A woman was sitting on the step in front of the small door, smoking a cigarette and staring blankly at the passing campervan. Painted on the white door was a green lizard with a red stripe running up its back. When Charlie made eye contact with the woman, he instinctively raised his hand. The woman's face became suddenly animated and she smiled to him, waving back with a roll of her eyes.

'Can I ask a question?' said Emily.

'Sure.'

'Who are those women living in that house at the top of the hill?'

Fields grunted.

'Just people.'

'Don't they have anything to do with this place?'

'Not really,' he said quickly. 'We wish they would. We could use that house to see . . . you know, certain types of people

. . . coming. I guess some people are just selfish. Even now.'

Emily didn't reply. Charlie changed up a gear as the hill levelled out.

'Here we go,' Fields chirped brightly, changing the subject. 'Home, sweet home.'

||||

They reached the end of a row of caravans. There was a space between the final caravan and the tall wire fence that looped around the camp. Beyond it was a stretch of farmland perhaps a hundred yards across before it turned to forest. The green leaves of the trees were on the turn, paling, starting to lose their lushness. Winter was on its way.

'I like this camp,' said Charlie. 'It's like a little town, but with tents instead of houses. And mud instead of roads.'

'Jeez, does this guy ever give you a break?' Fields said to Emily.

'He's mildly autistic,' she said, deadpan.

Charlie pulled into the space and turned off the engine. There was a stagnant pause. The engine clicked as it cooled. Each of them waited for somebody else to say something.

'OK,' said Fields. 'Listen up. This is how it works: if we're going to keep this place alive you need to remember the three most important things. One: cleanliness. Do not just throw your food away, do not piss against the fence. Use the bathrooms in the car park. Take your trash to the garbage cans down there as well. Sometimes a truck will come and collect it but don't rely on it. Two: water. We'll bring you water. We collect it from the rain, but you should boil it before you use it. You never know what's in it. And don't pour it away. If you need to get rid of it, put it in a bucket and take it down to the sea at the far end of the beach. Do you have a bucket?'

'No,' they said together.

'I'll get one brought to you.' He looked at them. 'Honestly, guys, I can't stress this enough. Clean water and sewage. It's so important you wouldn't believe. Everyone sticks to the rules because they know how fucked we'd be without them, OK? But there's something more than that.' He was speaking quietly now, kindly. 'We've got ourselves a real community here. You'll see as you go along, and we've all learned that if we do things for the benefit of everyone we can get things done a hell of a lot better, and a hell of a lot faster. That's why people stay here, why we're not all hiding out in houses. Community over individuals. That's what we got here. I'm sorry to say it so bluntly, but it's best to lay it on the line. You'll see it for yourselves. We're all in this together. The rest of the world might be going to shit but we're surviving and it's because everybody knows that what they do, even on the smallest level, is important. Every one of us is a vital cog. It doesn't take much for the system to fail. Just one person not sticking to the rules could cause the whole thing to collapse. Stay positive, stay focused. If you do need to go wizz in the middle of the night, think about it. Right?'

They both nodded slowly. Charlie felt the information warm his insides. They had come so far, seen so many things, and this camp was the one thing they had aimed for. And now that they were here, right away the hope they had held seemed to have been vindicated. There were good men in charge.

'What's rule number three?' said Emily.

'Yeah,' said Fields. He shifted round in the seat to face them. 'Number three.' He ran his hand through his thin hair. 'The illness.'

The atmosphere in the van changed suddenly. The silence grew denser.

'If one of you gets sick, you have to tell someone. Right away. No waiting. You just do it. For the community.'

He stared at Emily and she held his gaze.

'And then what?' she said.

||||

Edward remembered watching his little sister riding her first bike. His dad had fixed stabilizers to the back wheel so she wouldn't fall off. He remembered finding the way her legs moved funny. They beat in such fast circles but the bike went so slowly. Then the day had come when his dad had taken the stabilizers off. He had run behind her, holding her saddle and reassured her, 'I've got you, I've got you.' But he didn't. He had let go and she was riding on her own.

Edward had watched it all from the kerb. He had been sitting in his favourite spot where the men who had made the road had dropped a penny into the hot tar and it was still there, stuck in the gutter. He remembered his dad doing the same thing to him when he had first learned to ride a bike. He remembered the feeling of security he got from his dad when he was near. He had looked over his shoulder on that day and had seen his father a few feet behind him, not holding on to the saddle as he had promised. His dad smiled. 'Just keep going,' he had said. And he did. He moved his legs through the motions of a circle and on he went, not falling. He was doing it. It was so easy.

No bikes any more though. The day after Mary had the stabilizers taken off, his dad had got sick and turned into a zombie. Seeing him help Mary that day was really the last memory he had of him.

'Mary,' he called to her.

She was wearing a red bobble hat and mittens. The grey sea behind her intensified the colour. The hat bobbed up when he called.

'What?'

'What are you doing?'

'Ssh.'

Edward went over to his sister. In front of her was a large mole-hill. He stood by her side and looked at it.

'He's there,' she whispered. 'I just saw it moving.'

As soon as she said it the molehill shuddered. A few lumps of mud rolled down its banks.

Edward's heart started beating quicker. The mud became still again and there was a long silence as they held their breath and waited for a further movement that never came.

'He's gone,' said Edward, eventually.

'You scared him away,' his little sister said angrily. 'With your clomping.'

Edward said nothing. He imagined the mole burrowing under-ground through his tunnels.

'I wonder if they ever dig their tunnels and fall off the cliff,' Mary said seriously.

'I doubt it.'

'It would be funny.'

Edward couldn't see how that would be funny. His sister was just being stupid again. He looked across the bay to the lighthouse. He could make out the small specks of people walking along the road towards it.

His uncle's binoculars were strapped around his neck. He liked to keep them close to him during the day. They came in handy when he wanted to spy on the other children down in the camp. Lifting the binoculars to his eyes he focused in on the white wall surrounding the lighthouse and all the little outbuildings around it. The wall was waist high and he could only see the top halves of the people leaning against it. There were two of them, a man and a woman. Both of them were old. Neither of them were speaking. The man had a white beard and he reminded Edward of Father Christmas.

'Let me look,' his sister moaned, grabbing at the binoculars. The strap pulled on his neck.

'Ow,' he snapped, and pushed her.

She let go immediately. He unhooked the binoculars and handed them to her.

They looked gigantic in her tiny hands. They were bigger than her head. He felt a strange surge of love as she peered through. He got this once or twice a day.

'What were you looking at?'

'The lighthouse.'

Mary tutted. 'You're always looking at the lighthouse.'

'They keep them up there.'

The bottom few inches of her hair flapped about in the cold wind, lifting up around her hat.

'Keep what there?'

The surge of love he had felt had energized him. He dug the ends of his fingers into her ribs.

'The zombies!' he shouted.

Mary squealed with delight as Edward lifted her off the ground. The binoculars fell to the floor. He used to be able to lift her up easily but now it was more difficult, probably because he was so much skinnier.

'They're coming to get you,' he said in a spooky voice.

'No,' she cried.

He put her down and she ran away, wanting him to give chase. He started laughing at the way she ran. Her legs were going fast but her arms didn't move. He chased her around in a wide circle until she was running back towards the house and then he stopped. Mary sensed the chase had ended and turned back to him.

'You can't catch me,' she said, out of breath.

Edward turned away and went to collect the binoculars. His energy had suddenly vaporized. He hated the sight of the house, so sad-looking and cold with its dirty walls and barbed-wire fence. It was so different from their home in London.

A clod of mud had stuck to one of the binocular lenses. He peeled it off and used his handkerchief to clean the glass. He looked back across the bay to the lighthouse once again but the man and the woman he had been looking at had disappeared inside.

III

The atmosphere of the camp changed at dusk. In both light and dark there was a quietude, but the loss of the light took something with it. When the sun went down the place felt more desperate, more like the reality of what it really was: a large collection of people holding on.

'There's more truth about this place when the light is stripped away,' said Charlie dramatically.

He and Emily had spent the afternoon walking around the camp and getting acquainted with its layout. They had seen the huge water collectors in the far corner, had seen the men up towards the lighthouse building a wooden structure that would be more permanent than the tents. Some of the farm fields were tended by hand behind the steel fences. The people working in them looked like the old cotton workers, dotted sporadically amongst the plants. The camp, they had been told, had struck a deal with the farmer who lived in a house somewhere on the other side of the forest.

Emily rested her head on Charlie's shoulder.

'We should go soon.'

'Do you want to go?'

'They said it would be a good idea.'

They were looking out of the little square window next to the door. Charlie stroked her hair.

'You're not tired?'

Emily shook her head. 'We should go.'

'It's so quiet up here.'

'Everybody's gone down already.'

They went outside and listened to the silence. He looked at Emily and tried to visualize past her skull and into her thoughts. He could never tell what she was thinking deep inside there. He closed his eyes and felt sleep come up his body, savouring its chemicals. Rarely now did he sleep well at night. He mourned for the depth of rest that had for so long eluded him. The familiar darkness swept around the corners of his mind like a cloak of mist and he snapped his eyes open immediately.

'OK.' He clapped his hands together with forced energy. 'Come on, you, let's get that cute little butt of yours down to the Great Leader.'

She sighed, her eyes half closed and sleepy. She pushed her hand into his and they made their way down to the beach through the dusk.

|||

The smell of smoke in the air was strong. As they approached the beach the sound of people talking grew. They passed the ornate stone pillars that led into the car park just as a stampede of kids ran out from behind the low toilet building on the right, shouting and laughing as they went. Some of them made strange whooping sounds.

Charlie and Emily stopped to let them pass. Emily leaned her head against him.

'They're so cute.'

The cliffs up by the lighthouse were flickering with orange firelight. Great gusts of smoke swept up into the air in curling torrents. Within them bright orange embers darted and swirled like shoals of fish.

The entrance to the beach was through a small valley cut between the low sand dunes and it was through this valley that the people of the camp were flowing. The air became much colder here as the winds from the sea blasted their bodies.

On their right-hand side, up against the head of the beach, was a line of containers that must have come from the ocean tanker out in the bay. Their doors were open and Charlie could see inside the nearest few. People had set up homes in them. There were various items of furniture and trinkets and lights inside and the people sat around in them as if it was a perfectly normal thing to be doing. To his left, further up the beach near the house where the two women lived, was another, similar line of the containers. A small bonfire burned away in front of them, around which the residents sat on plastic chairs.

Charlie had half expected a kind of party atmosphere but this was nothing like that. People were standing around, talking quietly in small groups. The sheer mass of people was overwhelming. They stretched right down the beach towards the water, and left and right towards the lighthouse on one side and the stricken tanker on the other, the huge outline of which was just visible against the fading light of the dusk sky.

'Look at the size of that thing,' said Charlie. He felt Emily's grip tighten around his hand, and he turned his attention away from the ship to the beach.

'There're so many people,' she said.

The sound of the crowd was very strange. The combined voices talking so quietly was a low but powerful drone; many sounds becoming one. Charlie and Emily walked out into the sand and threaded themselves aimlessly between the group. There were several bonfires burning and they stopped at one of them, glad for the warmth.

The man standing next to them took a step towards the fire and crouched down on to his hams. He was holding a long stick that he poked into the fire and tumbled out of the flames some small, round objects that looked like rocks.

'Perfect,' he said, cheerily.

He looked around fifty, and as he stepped in closer he rolled the rocks on to a plate. Charlie saw that they were in fact baked potatoes wrapped in foil. His stomach rumbled.

The man turned to him in a quick, jerky movement and held up the plate.

'Spud?' He leaned over so he could see past Charlie to Emily. 'How about you?'

Charlie felt a lump in his throat. He tried to say thank you, but his mouth was too dry. He cleared his throat.

'Thanks.'

He took two of the potatoes in his fingers. They were searing. The man laughed.

'Use your sleeves, son.'

Charlie pulled the sleeves of his sweater over his hands.

'That's so kind of you,' he said.

The man nodded. The fire crackled and his face was lit up orange.

'We've all got to eat,' he replied casually.

A voice suddenly rang out across the beach, much louder than the low murmurs of the people.

'Hello?' it said. It seemed to be coming from a speaker system set into the cliffs. 'Can you hear me?'

A collective, unsteady 'yes' chanted out from the crowd. They were making their way slowly towards the lighthouse at the western edge of the beach.

'Gather round, gather round,' said the voice.

'That's him,' Charlie said. 'The Scottish guy on the gate.'

The gaps in the crowd were shrinking as the people converged. It was like being at a concert. The people pushed Charlie and Emily in their direction. When they came to a halt they were just a hundred yards from a stage up near the cliffs. Charlie turned a full circle, looking out over the crowd. A thousand people suddenly didn't seem so large a number now they were all huddled together.

Emily took a baked potato from him and peeled a hole in the

foil before handing it back. He was starving. He bit into it and rolled it around in his open mouth to let it cool. It was soft and sweet and badly needed. When he swallowed it he felt its warmth roll down his neck into his belly.

'OK, OK.'

McAvennie was on the stage, standing behind a microphone and holding a silencing hand in the air. His voice echoed around the cliffs. The crowd became hushed and Charlie watched as McAvennie surveyed them for a moment before speaking.

'Thanks. OK. Thanks to everyone for coming down again, and for your continued hard work.' He spoke matter-of-factly, his accent not as strong as when he had been speaking informally. 'We had a good day today.' He paused. Through the silence the sound of a generator thrummed. 'We have been to the farmer and he has given us permission to go to one of the woods on his land for firewood.' He looked down awkwardly at a slip of white card. 'As long as we're responsible,' he added. 'We'll go and collect it as soon as the weather's good. Maybe tomorrow.' He looked down again at the card. 'The new building's coming along. It won't be long before we can move the school there. Hopefully by Christmas.'

The crowd murmured with approval.

'A school?' Charlie said quietly to Emily.

'What else? Andrew is going away tomorrow on a salvage. He'll be taking the usual team. I say again that if anybody knows of somewhere, or can think of somewhere we can go to find something of worth, let us know, aye? We've got food, and enough, but we can always do with more. And the same goes for supplies. If more people find us and they need help we've got to be ready to take them.'

Charlie put his arm around Emily and felt her move closer to him.

'Some of you may not know this, but today is a special day.' He lifted his head to the crowd. 'The camp is three months old today.'

The crowd started to clap. Emily and Charlie looked at each other and joined in. There were some cheers and shouts and the volume of the clapping increased.

'Empathy. Compassion. Trust,' said McAvennie, emphatically, his voice louder. 'Yes?'

The crowd quietened and nodded their agreement. The low drone of the collective voice returned.

'It's been nearly eight months since this thing started, but we're still here, you hear me? Remember the start of it? The panic?' He waited for a long moment. 'But the bad news is further apart now. Things are quietening down. Have you noticed that?'

Charlie whispered to Emily. 'Is it?'

Emily shrugged.

Charlie watched how McAvennie looked at the crowd and how they looked back at him. He sensed something collective in them, like a spirit. There was a strange connection between everybody.

'We can get through this,' he said, emotion creeping into his voice. 'If you just remember the triangle: empathy, compassion, trust. It won't be long now. We just need to hold together. Together we're bigger than we are on our own. The sum of our parts. We are kind and good and that's all we need.'

There was something even awe-like in the faces of the crowd.

'I for one am proud to be part of this. Just look at what we've achieved, and nobody hurt anyone in getting here. If we had believed what we had been told, we'd have all been hiding away in caves by now, terrified of each other, aye? But we didn't believe it. It wasn't true, was it? Because we've proved it.'

The hum of the crowd rose.

'Am I right?'

The crowd chanted 'Yes' in unison.

The volume with which they said it made Charlie's bones shake. There was something in McAvennie's words, hidden between the vowels and pauses and inflections. The crowd behaving like this, like automatons, was sinister; the way they hung on his every word and the way in which he commanded them was not what Charlie was used to. A woman in front of him was crying. The tears shone on her cheeks in the orange light.

Emily whispered, 'This is weird.'

'The illness will stop one day,' called McAvennie. 'We just have to hold on. We need to keep our hope alive. Each and every one of us.' The energy grew. 'There is darkness –'

Charlie felt the hairs on the back of his neck bristle.

'– but darkness is nothing more than the absence of light.' McAvennie's voice was almost drowned by the crowd but his next words rang out loud and clear. 'And we will light it up.'

Inexplicable goose pimples spiked up all over Charlie's body. He looked down at the half-eaten baked potato in his hand that had been given to him by a complete stranger and he felt his eyes sting.

Just for a moment the desperation and despair had lifted and the whole crowd broke water to take a deep, plentiful breath. Emily stepped in front of Charlie to face him. Her wavy brown hair fell in front of her eyes. In the orange firelight the tips had turned auburn.

'That was good, wasn't it?' she said.

He looked back at the stage, at McAvennie, who was staring out over the crowd with a determined expression on his face. He was just standing there, looking out.

|||

They were having a fire again. Edward watched it passively from his grandmother's bedroom window. He could never make out individual people but he liked to watch the orange light play against the cliffs near the lighthouse. He gazed at it emotionlessly. His uncle had taught him to be frightened of people and Edward fought back the urge to go down and talk to the other kids he so often saw running and playing on the beach or on the fields between the house and the camp.

Behind him he heard his mum come into the room. The darkness disappeared as the light from the candle she was holding chased away the shadows.

'It's bedtime, Henry,' she said.

Edward didn't correct her. She did it sometimes if she was tired. He turned to face the room and saw Mary standing at their mother's side.

They went through to the back bedroom. They didn't need the candlelight because their uncle had made them learn the layout of the house in the darkness.

The children slept beneath two blankets and wore hats to keep their heads warm. Miriam could have used the electric heaters, powering them through the car battery rigs Joseph had set up, but she didn't know for how long they would last and was loath to use them until they absolutely could not hold out any longer. The weather was only going to get colder.

The children sat on the edge of the bed as their mum crouched down in front of them in the same way she did every night. They said their prayers and then she grabbed them both into a tight hug.

She always seemed so sad these days. She had never recovered from Uncle Joseph's death. Tomorrow, he thought, he would try to do something to make her happy.

She blew out the candle and it was dark again. The sheets were freezing as they climbed under them. The bedroom door closed and the children were alone.

Edward lay on his back with his eyes open, determined to stay awake. He did the same thing every night because he didn't want his sister to be awake in the dark on her own. She sometimes wanted to speak and Edward had made a promise to himself that he would always be there for her. He secretly liked the fact that he made these small gestures for Mary without her knowing.

Tonight though she drifted into sleep quickly and without speaking. She slept on her back and always with one leg sticking out of the end of the blanket no matter how cold it was. Edward waited for a few moments to make sure she had drifted off and threw some of the blanket over the protruding limb. He didn't know why because by morning it would be sticking out again. It always was.

'I won't let anything bad happen to you,' he whispered.

He said it every night, mostly for luck. So far nothing bad had happened to her, but he worried about what might happen if he stopped saying it, and he was not prepared to take the risk.

|||

The cold in the air intensified outside the fire's warm bubble. The lambent embers beneath the blackened wood breathed slowly in and slowly out. The crowd that had gathered on the beach had all but disappeared and Charlie sat with Emily alone on one of the logs. Needles of cold pierced the fire's warmth.

'Come on. Let's go back.'

'Hold on,' she said.

Charlie sniffed. 'You OK?'

Emily nodded and said nothing. They stared into the fire a little while longer before mustering the energy to stand.

The line of lightbulbs shining along the edge of the mud track leading back to their van glowed dimly. Beneath them, on the left, they made out the shapes of tent tops in the gloom.

'It feels like one of those refugee camps.'

Emily looked straight ahead. 'Like?'

The track was soft underfoot, the mud churned by countless sets of feet. Charlie was struck with a sudden thought: this is the place where we'll die. He felt the familiar blackness gathering in his mind. Quickly he turned to Emily.

'Did you feel something in the crowd tonight?' he asked urgently.

'What do you mean?'

'Like, some connection.'

'I think so.' She breathed loudly between sentences to recover her breath. 'We just need it.'

'Yeah.'

'Do you know what I mean?'

'I think so.'

'Everybody's been so scared for so long that when we get the scent of hope we –' she thought about the right word – 'over-compensate? There's nothing wrong with doing it. I guess it's just what happens,' she said. 'But it doesn't seem quite natural I guess is what I'm trying to say.'

The going was difficult enough to make their legs ache.

'Do you think you'll be happy here?' Charlie asked.

Emily didn't reply. He let the silence answer for her.

'The people seem nice,' he said.

'Yeah.'

'That man who gave us the potatoes was nice.'

'Yeah.'

They walked on in silence.

'I wonder why the women in that house up there don't come down here,' Charlie said. 'It's got to be safer here than up there.'

'Maybe they just want to be on their own.'

'It's a shame. Did it seem like there was something . . . off . . . with them?'

'They've probably had some bad things happen.'

'Yeah.' Like everyone. 'We should go and see them again. If they won't come down here we should go up there. Wouldn't it be better for them if they knew there was always someone there for them?'

'Maybe.'

'You don't think so? Or you don't want to go?'

'I don't know. It's up to you.'

She stopped and looked at him. Her eyes were glazed in the cold, and the dim reflections of the lightbulbs shone in them. They hugged each other and kissed.

'Shit.' He sighed. His guard dropped. 'Shit, shit, shit.'

'It's OK,' she whispered, holding him. His head was on her shoulder and she placed her fingers through the loose curls of his dark hair. 'It's going to be OK.'

|||

It felt like the fluttering of butterfly wings. She lay on her back and ran through the familiar thoughts that came at night time. The light from the tanker was long since dead and the room was dark, save for the watery glimmer of moonlight. When the skies were clear, the stars were so bright now.

Strange mixtures of fear and joy, panic and calm broke over her one after the other, none of them lasting for more than a few moments. There was no way to hold on to a feeling for long.

Butterfly wings again. Somewhere inside her. She put her hand to her stomach and waited. Her mind wandered to the next day and to the food they would eat. As time went on and as the garden yielded less and the supplies waned, so too did the ability to plan further ahead. It had become so difficult to think more than a day in advance. To contemplate something far away would lead to despair. Food was running out. The bottled water had been used up months ago and they now relied solely on the rainwater from the two large rain collectors Joseph had built.

She closed her eyes even tighter. There were so many things he had done that they so utterly relied on. In daylight it was easier to cope with the fact. In daylight the water collectors were nothing more than practical things that held no deeper meaning than the functions they were built to perform. But at night she could not fight back the resentment of using things he had made.

The butterflies again. This time the tiny sensors in her hands felt them. There it was. Real. She fanned her fingers out across her belly and imagined the tiny foetus on the other side reaching out its hand and touching it against the side of the womb to its mother's, separated only by a few inches of flesh. Not really separated at all. It kicked again and Miriam's heartbeat quickened. She thought for a moment that it might even have been excitement. Maybe that was what it was.

Bringing life into the world seemed like insanity, but if that was true, then the depth of emotion she felt when the baby kicked would not be there. But it was. She had already worked that through in her mind weeks ago. It was like a white pulse of electricity that ran in a band up her body that felt, simply, amazing. That was the truth. It was her baby, not his.

The kicking stopped and Miriam found herself out of breath. But then the light feeling dissipated as fast as it had emerged because that was how her body worked nowadays, and the reality of what was happening returned. With it came the undercurrent of panic.

The camp in the hollow down below was still growing. There were too many people. It would be like a microcosm of the world before the Sadness had struck. And in so much, it was doomed to fail. It didn't matter how many of them were good people. It would only take a handful to ruin everything. She closed her eyes and waited again, with her hand on her stomach, for another butterfly.

|||

The darkness in him was worse at night. Charlie would lie there and feel it mist up around him. He had hoped that getting to the camp would keep it at bay, but they had been here for a week now and it was coming back stronger.

He slept on his side, facing away from Emily, and when he did he could feel his heart beating in his chest. Sleep was a precipice. As he approached its edge and peered over he could sense the cessation of his heart. It seemed too ephemeral, nothing more than a slab of meat held precariously in place by fleshy webs in the dark casket of his ribs. If he fell asleep he would die.

Vertigo swirled in his head and he snapped awake with a jolt, stepping back from the precipice. It was not death itself he feared, it was more its constant proximity. It never went away, it was always so close. Life was so easy to snuff out. That was the frightening part. He tried to blot out the things he had seen happen to his family. The memory was there, staring at him, but instead of confronting it, it was easier to turn away and gaze instead into the black, a membrane that could filter out those thoughts.

He threw off the covers and let the cold air soothe his skin. He could hear the faint sound of Emily breathing next to him. She had never lost the ability to sleep. No matter what happened Emily was always able to absorb it and move on. He envied her. Her ability to deal with anything that life threw at her was both incredible and annoying. She slept on her back with her head tilted to one side and he looked at her face in the darkness for a moment. The knowledge of her presence always made him feel better. Quickly he sat up and pulled on his jeans. The air was so cold that his skin bristled with goose pimples. The final piece of clothing was his trusty deer-stalker hat that he had been given as a Christmas present last year. He thought how blissful life had been back then, of how nobody in the whole world knew what was about to happen. Everybody had assumed as part of their instinct that things would last.

|||

Charlie slipped through the door and closed it behind him as quietly as he could. The fence that separated the camp from the fields beyond was directly in front of him. A delicate low mist hung just above the ground. This wasn't the first time Charlie had walked the camp at night, but he had never seen a mist like this. The moonlight caught in it and seemed to give it a magical quality. Since the arrival of the Sadness the world's properties had intensified. Whereas before a sunset had been pretty to look at for a few moments, it was now something much more. What in the old days had been nearly beautiful had now been returned to its full glory. It was as if the world itself had become more alive.

He walked carefully down the hill and found the main mud track by keeping his eyes on and following the line of lightbulbs that ran along it. The camp was so quiet. He pictured everybody in their caravans and tents, sleeping soundly. He liked that there was nobody around. It gave him space to think.

After seeing so many awful things happen, the fact that a place like this camp could exist, and had existed for many months, was miraculous.

The mist occupied the slice of air from knee to waist height. He could see it moving in the light. In some parts, where it was thicker, it glimmered as though fireflies were in it.

He reached the road and turned left. Through the darkness, with the mist still clinging low to the ground, he saw a dark figure up ahead between the two ornate stone pillars at the car park's entrance.

Without breaking stride he continued onwards. As he approached the pillars the figure resolved into the shape of a man wearing a dark cloak. The mist flowed around him. The thin crescent of a new moon hung in the clear night behind the figure and the idea that he was already dead and this was some final test became suddenly more real. Charlie slowed and waited to see if it would move.

Standing there, hooded, still in the blackness, the figure looked at Charlie. Charlie stopped, unwilling to go any further.

The man spoke. 'You want to pass?'

His voice was quiet but easily audible through the silence. The 's' was drawn out into a snake's hiss.

Charlie wanted to turn and run.

'Where are you going?'

Charlie went to speak but his voice deserted him. He cleared his throat and said, understanding how foolish he sounded, 'Toilet.'

The man in the dark cloak was still. 'I don't think I can allow that.' He breathed deeply. 'So what now?'

Charlie didn't like the way his 's's were elongated.

'I'll go back,' he said.

'Why go back? What is "back"?'

Charlie had no answer. The danger he felt from the man was palpable and growing.

'If,' he said, 'you had seen what I have seen you would understand.' He moved forward a step and when he did, the mist around him became animated, flowing into the space in which he had been standing. 'The great road of truth opened up in front of me and the carcasses of the ages were strewn along it,' he said in the slow, quiet, steady voice that the ill people used, though this man was not ill: the accompanying sense was not there. 'This is what it looks like. A world without hope. We have reached the crack of doom.' The cloak was so dark it might not have been there at all.

'Who are you?' Charlie said.

No, the man wasn't ill. But he wasn't normal either. There was something in him, as if he was halfway between sick and healthy.

'It is the prism you stare through when hope has gone that truly matters. We can each of us look upon the same thing and see something different; it is a filter of many colours. Would you like me to tell you what I saw in the world? When I was hopeless –' the man lifted a hand into the air, and Charlie felt something very old pass through him – 'I saw a lack of *reason*.'

The cloaked figure took one final step forward in silence and Charlie saw at last that it was not a cloak he was wearing at all. Nothing more than a thin blanket was thrown around him. The hood was just a part of the blanket. The dark void where the face should be started to materialize into substance. A thin, pallid oval of skin grew out of it. Slowly, the man reached up to his hood and pulled it away to reveal a skeletal head. The skin around the face was taut and unblemished. He wore a thin smile with narrow lips. A clump of dark hair at the dome of the skull looked blue in the moonlight.

'I saw it all,' he said again. And he opened his mouth. His tongue emerged from the gaping maw and Charlie took his first step backwards.

The reality of what he was seeing did not click into place immediately. His brain needed to align the physical sight of it with how the tongue could possibly have come to be like that. At first it looked like there were two tongues inside the mouth, like two fat snakes in their nest. But that was not so. The tongue was forked. The moonlight revealed that an untidy V had been cut out of its centre to create two distinct tips that tapered to thin points. The man stared at Charlie to watch his reaction. There was something like glee on his face. The eyes seared into him from their sunken depressions. Charlie felt their malevolence and the contempt in which they held him.

'I'm going to go,' said Charlie.

'You think this,' the man gestured around him, 'is going to save you?'

Charlie turned to leave.

'You think this is paradise?'

As Charlie walked away he heard the footsteps behind him, following. He stopped and turned back.

'Bad things will come here. Bad people. You know who I'm talking about. You've seen them and the things they do. We all have.' He smiled again. 'I'm here already. And when others arrive you will see what will happen. You will tear yourselves apart. It is in our nature. Nothing more than savages.'

'Who are you?'

The night came to life and threw itself around them. There was an invisible barrier between Charlie and the rest of the camp. He felt isolated. The wild vibrancy of the world howled all around him.

The figure turned and walked away but his voice carried on the air when he spoke.

'I am the man who returned.'

III

Her mother had gone down to the camp and returned with the two eggs.

'I like the Scottish man.'

'He's being nice because he wants the house, Mum.'

Her mother turned the cake mixture between her fingers. For a moment Miriam thought she was going to let the comment pass.

'What's happened to you, Miri?'

'Nothing,' she answered quietly. She took the bowl from her mother and poured in some more of the powdered milk. Mary's would be the first birthday since the illness had struck. Apart from Henry's. His birthday had been last April but had passed by unobserved.

The cake mix was ready. The oven had been hooked up to one of Joseph's car-battery generators. It was worth the effort. Mary was going to love it. Today, she was eight. Miriam dripped some bottled lemon juice into the mixture. Her mother circled around the edge of the mixing bowl with a wooden spoon and folded the mixture in on itself.

'Pass me the baking tin,' she said.

Miriam slid the tin over and sprinkled some flour into it. Her mother poured in the mixture and the cake was slid into the oven. After ten minutes its smell tapped into senses the two women had not used in months. Miriam dried her hands in the hand towel and opened the drawers to find some birthday candles.

Cutlery in the top drawer, cooking equipment in the second, clean towels in the third, miscellaneous in the bottom. She rummaged around between chopsticks, sandwich bags, dusty old paper napkins. There were no candles.

'Try the dresser,' her mother suggested.

She went out of the kitchen area and into the adjoining room. A long, narrow drawer opened to reveal some boxes where Henry's mother had stored the good silver, a tablecloth and a small box. The baby kicked and Miriam put her hand to the dresser to support herself. She opened the little box and there they were. A small pack of yellow candles. She looked at them and stopped.

Her mother had started washing the dishes in the sink, using the water from one of the buckets.

Miriam lifted the candles and brought them up to the level of her face. She thought of Henry's father and how he must have kept the candles here just in case they would ever be needed, in the hope of the children coming here for their birthday. She went back into the kitchen and threw them on to the counter.

'You know,' she said, casually, 'I never thought I would ever be able to kill somebody, but now I think I could do it.'

Her mother stood up straight and looked at her daughter.

'If it came down to it, I think I'm finally ready. If somebody threatened the kids, I don't think I'd be able to stop myself. I'd get the shotgun, and do it.'

Her mother was not smiling any more. 'You shouldn't say things like that in case they come true.'

'But I don't care if they come true. I've learned enough to know what sometimes needs to be done.'

She caught a glimpse of hurt on her mother's face.

'I never thought I'd hear you say something like that.'

Miriam shrugged and looked away dismissively, folding her arms across the baby and saying nothing.

IIII

Edward jumped out of bed and wobbled over to the window to see what the weather was going to be like for his sister's birthday. He pulled the heavy curtains across and stepped back from the thin rain that didn't make a sound as it landed on the window. He looked past the back garden to the forest behind the fields. The remaining leaves on the trees were a deep red or a bright orange.

He tiptoed back over to the bed and stood there for a moment, looking at his sister. Then, quickly, he yanked off the blankets and her eyes snapped open.

'Happy birthday!' he screamed at the top of his voice.

Mary leaped up in shock and her head rocked back and forth on her neck. She opened her mouth to say something but then closed it again. Edward jumped up on to the bed and started to bounce, tossing her body up and down.

'Happy birthday, happy birthday, happy birthday,' he cried.

Mary still seemed like she did not know what was going on. Edward hopped off the bed and ran to the drawers where he kept his clothes. He grabbed something and ran back just as Mary was starting to come round.

'Here.'

He threw a balled-up piece of paper in front of her. She picked it up.

'It's your present,' he said, eagerly.

He watched her face change from one of tiredness into a smile. Her face in the mornings always looked creased. Her eyes widened as she ripped the paper wrapping off. Inside was what looked like a clump of fur.

'What is it?' she said, twisting it around.

'It's a rabbit's foot.'

Mary furrowed her brow. 'Er, what would I want this for?'

Edward smiled at her. She was so stupid. He took the foot from her and whispered, 'It will bring you luck.'

Mary took the rabbit's foot back and looked at it again.

'It's a lucky foot?'

'All rabbit's feet are lucky,' he said.

Mary took a breath to say something, stopped, then decided to say it after all.

'The rabbit this came from wasn't very lucky, was he?'

III

The flatbed truck rumbled to a stop and the jostling bodies in the cab sat still for a moment.

'Out we get.'

Charlie was sitting right up against the door and could feel the other men pushing into him. He slipped the handle and jumped down to the ground. He looked around. The air was freezing but alive with the smell of coming winter. The trees that lined the thin lane leaned over to form a natural, golden archway that looked like the inside of a church. It had rained nearly every day in that first month since he had arrived; a consistent drizzle so fine that it hardly seemed to land at all, but today the sky was crisp. A single crow squawked from somewhere within the wood.

He went round to the front of the van and waited for the others. They had come to collect him earlier that morning. McAvennie himself had knocked at his door. This was Charlie's first day of work.

There were six of them in all and they had driven out of the camp for a few miles through untidy lanes to this spot where the farmer had said they could take firewood.

McAvennie joined Charlie. He was holding a small handsaw.

'Here you go, kiddo.' His eyes darted towards the trees. 'Let's get started.'

Charlie took the saw. It seemed a little small for tree-felling. He held it up in front of him to inspect it.

'It's not great, but it'll have to do,' McAvennie said.

He slapped him on the shoulder and Charlie turned and walked into the woods. He went straight up to a smallish tree. It looked as though it wouldn't take as much effort as some of its older, larger brothers. He had never cut down a tree before but he did not want to look like a fool in front of the other men. He wanted to be just as productive as everybody else. In the last month he had learned that a person's willingness to work was held in high regard. He placed the saw against the smooth, grey bark and made a cut. At first he worked slowly to ensure the saw didn't slip from its groove but when he was far enough in he sawed a little harder and tried to set himself into a rhythm.

He sawed for around half a minute before realizing that none of the other men had joined him in the woods. He stopped and turned to the truck.

The men were staring at him, smirking, each of them holding a large chainsaw. When they saw him turn round they all started laughing.

'How's the saw working out for you?' McAvennie howled, doubled over in the joy of his own joke.

Charlie nodded and smiled. 'I see,' he said quietly. 'Pick on the little one, eh?'

His initial annoyance fell away quickly and his smile broadened. They were accepting him. They laughed louder.

'Christ, boy,' puffed McAvennie, 'you're taller than all of us, man.'

He stepped off the road and into the woods. Great billowing puffs of steam chugged out of his mouth.

'Come on, comrades,' he said. 'Sooner we do this, the sooner we can go home.'

They worked for most of the morning. Charlie's job was to stack the wood into manageable piles that could be transported back to the van. It was hard work. His muscles were unused to it and they ached. They had shrunk over the months and the wood was heavier than it would have been had Charlie been at full strength.

At lunchtime they downed tools and decided to take their food, a flask of soup, a flask of tea and some bread, into the woods. The air felt Christmassy. It was early November and although the prospect of the coming winter was frightening, the day itself held some magic.

The wood followed the path of a valley. A river had dried up in the ages past, its only remnant being the flat, auburn, leaf-strewn carpet along which the six men walked in convoy. Charlie felt contented there. The darkness was far off. It was difficult to know how it could even exist at times like this.

He fell in step alongside one of the other men, a man of maybe thirty years. A big bushy beard covered the lower half of his face and he had a woolly hat on his head. He acknowledged Charlie with a nod.

'How are you finding the work?' he said in a soft, northern voice.

'It's OK.'

'You're new?'

'Yeah. Got here a couple of weeks ago.'

'You don't remember me, do you?' said the man.

Charlie looked at him. He was sure he had never seen him before.

'It's the beard,' said the man, stroking his chin. 'I was the guy at the gates on the day you got here.'

'God, you look so different.'

'Yeah, the beard'll do that to you.' They walked in silence for a while. 'My name's David,' he said, without offering a handshake.

'Charlie.'

'Nice to meet you.'

'Cheers.'

David laughed. Somewhere in the distance the sound of running water babbled.

'Have you got any family left, Charlie?'

Charlie hesitated. 'No.' He stepped on a damp twig that disintegrated beneath his boot. 'You know.'

David sucked a stream of air in through his teeth. 'I'm on my own as well.' A flurry of wind whistled through the trees and a few of the orange leaves drifted from their branches and swung in invisible cradles to the forest floor. 'It's pretty fucked up, right?'

Charlie laughed. The man's gentle voice didn't sound right swearing. 'Yeah.'

'I mean, I was on my own anyway,' David went on, returning to the subject of family. 'I'm not married. And I don't have any brothers or sisters.'

'What happened to your parents?'

'No idea. They lived in Spain. I tried calling them when it happened but, well, it was crazy then, you know. The phone wouldn't even connect on the first day.'

'Shit.'

'I kept trying them for the first few weeks but they never answered.'

'And they didn't call you?'

'No.' He paused. 'They didn't even have my number. Right?'

Charlie was surprised by the openness of the man and he understood what he had meant. He felt sorry for him. At least when the Sadness had come for Charlie's family it hadn't left anything open-ended. There were no wounds needing to be healed, no rifts that needed to be closed.

'So they could still be out there.'

'Maybe. Who knows?'

'Do you think you'll ever go and look for them?'

David sniffed in the air. 'I doubt it. There's no way of getting over there anyway.'

'Yes there is,' said Charlie, suddenly. 'You can go through the tunnel. That's how me and Em got across.' He was speaking in his overly quick style he used when he thought he could help someone. 'We were in Europe when the Sadness hit.'

'Really?'

'Yeah.'

'And you came through the tunnel?'

'Yeah. They'd got the service tunnels open by then. There weren't any trains or anything, obviously. It was pretty grim there, but we had to come back.'

'Why?'

'Because—' He stopped. 'I don't know. It just felt like the right thing to do. The only thing, really.'

'I can see that.' David turned to Charlie. 'It's easier when you have something to aim for, isn't it?'

'I guess so.'

'That's why this camp is doing so well. Just the running of it, the keeping it together, it keeps everyone's minds active. We've got something to do and it keeps our minds off all the shit.'

'You think so?'

David nodded. 'It's probably a way of dealing with things. I mean, if you think about it, how could a camp like ours be so successful? It's not human nature to get along so well in such large numbers. Not without laws and police and stuff. We're not used to working together for the sake of the "greater good" or whatever. If it weren't for the depth of the shit we're in, the whole thing would have collapsed before it even got off the ground.'

'You think?'

'A lot of people see this camp as something magical, right? George helps with that, with his speeches. He probably even believes it himself a little bit.'

'And you don't.'

'It is magical, no doubt. Well, it's amazing at least. But there's nothing spiritual about it. It's just survival. It's human resilience.

After the Sadness first came and everything fell apart, everybody just ran for their lives. We scattered and looked after ourselves. But look at it now. A few months on and we're starting to get a perspective on what has happened and what we have to do to get things back to normal.'

'We heard,' Charlie interrupted, 'that the government are getting things ready to start again. They've got a base up near Derby, or somewhere.'

David's lips curled upwards beneath his beard.

'Maybe. Well, probably not, but I don't think it matters. We're already doing it. We've realized that we have to work together. Hoarding things in little groups won't work. But what I'm saying is that we haven't really had to work hard to keep the camp. It's all just happened naturally. It's instinctive. It's in us to survive. It's not that we wanted to do it, we *had* to do it.'

Charlie nodded. The riverbed snaked around a low spur.

'It's how all life works, if you think about it. Everything always falls into place. We came together because that ship out in the bay ran aground. We all worked at getting the stuff from it, organizing ourselves, because it kept our minds away from the darker things. And then the camp just started to flourish. We survived.

'George gives his speeches and says that what's happened isn't natural, but it is. You just need to follow the thought through to its conclusion. Things did fall apart at first but we were always going to recover. There's nothing magical about it. It's just human resilience.'

'Human resilience,' Charlie repeated to himself.

'Of course, we don't have many guns here so we can't go around killing each other as much as in other countries,' he laughed.

Charlie smiled. It might be true that the camp was not magical, that it was something to do with evolution and an animal's inbuilt will to survive. But he didn't believe there was no magic in the world. David had not taken the Sadness itself into account. There was something magical about that, of this Charlie was in no doubt. And it wasn't good magic.

III

The dried-up riverbed led around several bends and they came to a small, deserted hut. It was only a few feet high, made of brick that was covered in moss and lichens. The roof was gone and in its place somebody had thrown some sheets of corrugated iron, the edges of which were rusty and jagged. A sapling grew through a gap in the iron. Some large stones were standing around the structure that the men used as seats.

The soup had retained some of its heat during the morning and the steam from it rose in perfect cylinders into the still air. Charlie ate quickly and savoured the goodness of the food.

The other men laughed and joked but he did not feel he was one of them enough to join in yet. He was happy to just sit and listen. It had been so long since things had seemed so normal.

After a few minutes McAvennie eased himself awkwardly up from his stone seat and went over to Charlie. His plastic soup bowl was tiny in his gigantic hands. He sat down next to him and released an almighty belch.

'That's better,' he said, patting his chest.

He tilted his buttocks slightly and broke wind with a high-pitched rasp.

'Nice one,' congratulated Charlie.

McAvennie ignored him. 'So you had a good chat with David?'

Charlie looked across to the man with the beard and woolly hat. David smiled and saluted at him.

'Yes,' he answered warily.

'Relax, kiddo. We just want you to . . . understand . . . what the camp is, from all angles. So, what do you think?'

'About what?'

'Everything. Your first day's work.'

'I've enjoyed it.'

'Good lad.'

'Is that why you've brought me here?' He was starting to realize something. 'As a kind of initiation?'

McAvennie nodded.

'You could say that, aye.'

They both stared ahead.

'I like to spend time with the new arrivals. We don't have that many these days.' He sounded almost sad when he said it, as if the more people that came the better. 'I hope you understand why we've brought you out here today. We really are just here to help everyone, Charlie. We know that people get a bit funny when they first come to the camp but there's nothing sinister about the place, ya ken? We just like to tell people that. We know and understand the nature of the camp and so we like to tell folks all about it when they first come here. So there's no confusion.'

'You don't need to say that to me. I trust you.'

McAvennie blew into his soup. 'Thank you, Charlie. That means a lot. Most people aren't so trusting so early on.'

'It's a fault of mine, apparently.'

'A fault?'

'Being naive.'

'Trusting and naive aren't the same, Charlie boy. Not now, and not in the old world. Understand? Do you know what I used to do, kid?'

'A politician or something? A teacher? I don't kn—'

'I was a union man. In the port. Bristol?'

'Oh. OK.'

'People trusted me then, Charlie, and you can believe me when I say that the guys on the docks weren't naive. But I always told them the truth, no matter how hard it was. And it was hard a lot of the time. In return, they trusted me. Trust. It's so important. And it comes from being honest and not fucking around. I will never lie to you.'

'OK.'

'Do you believe me?'

'Yes.' He had seen and heard enough of the large Scot to make his decision by now. 'I actually really do.'

'Have you been to the beach at night? Have you heard what we say about empathy, compassion and trust?'

Charlie nodded.

'It's just a wee motto we thought up. And it's what's kept the camp together. We keep trying to drum it in so that it's always at the front of folks' minds. Maybe it'll become second nature, who can say? But we'll keep on saying it for now. Getting the message out there, you know. Do you know what empathy is?'

'Yes.' He laughed.

'Good. Can you do it?'

'What? Empathize?'

'Aye.'

'Definitely.'

'Compassion?'

'It's my middle name.'

McAvennie smiled. 'Your girl's getting told the same thing.'

'She's a tougher cookie than me.'

'If she can tell good from bad she'll understand. That's what we always say.'

'She'll be fine. Emily's amazing.'

'Where's she from?'

'Nottingham?'

'Oh aye.'

'She's got me through this really. If she hadn't been around then . . . I don't know.'

McAvennie patted Charlie's leg.

'You both seem like nice kids. We need people like you.'

McAvennie's face was so round and funny looking, with his soft, hooded eyes. He had the sort of look people trusted instinctively. Charlie liked to think he was a good judge of character. A small chamber inside him was still wary, but he was getting there.

'So,' said Charlie. 'Have you been here from the start?'

McAvennie spat a little piece of food on to the ground.

'Pretty much. First day I got here was the day after the Cambodian struck. We heard about it and came down to see if there was anything doing.'

'We?'

'Aye, me and the wife like.'

Charlie hadn't pictured him having a wife.

'What do you mean by the Cambodian?'

'The ship. It's her name. *Cambodian Empress*. Aye, and when we got here there was . . . how do you say it? Like, a *wave* of it. The illness. I saw it plain as the nose on your face: one minute everyone was going about their business, next minute, wham.' His voice had become flat and serious. 'About fifty of the poor fuckers. Just stopped dead.'

'Where was this? On the beach?'

'On the beach, aye,' he said quietly. 'After that' – he turned to Charlie – 'you want to help, you know? So,' he sighed, 'we tried to get them off the beach. I had my caravan so we had a couple in there. You know, Charlie, a lot of people tried to help. They weren't all out for themselves no more. They were a wee bit panicked, but then they came back. And that's how it all started really, after those people got sick.'

Charlie didn't say anything.

'There were already lots of people down on the beach. Lots of cargo had washed up from the boat, you see. Things just happen naturally. Me and a few of the guys who knew about ships went out to her and managed to get a fair haul. We still go back when the sea's all right.'

'Do you—' Charlie had to clear his throat. 'Do you know what happened to it? The boat.'

'One of them was violent.' He spat another morsel of food to the ground. He didn't need to say any more than that. 'I shared what I found and after that everything just happened. A wee bit of kindness can go a long way.'

'It's a great thing though,' said Charlie. 'You'd have thought someone would have ruined it by now.'

'Aye.'

'But they didn't.'

'There were a few that tried it on but what could they do? We'd managed to get a bit of a structure together and it's amazing what that'll do, Charlie. It takes away a lot of the fear, for one.' He changed tack. 'Look, the pricks among us, and they are always there, even they know when something makes sense.'

'So what happened?'

'We talked them down,' he said simply. 'Didn't need to do no more than that. You'd be surprised. You can find some good in most people, kiddo. It's in there somewhere. They knew what we were trying to do and in the end they accepted it. You know, they're still in the camp now. And they're fine.'

What David had said about the nature of human resilience came back to him.

'I saw a man on one of the first nights I got here,' said Charlie. 'I needed a piss and on my way down he was just standing there in the middle of the path.'

McAvennie nodded but said nothing.

'Do you know what I'm talking about?'

'Nope,' said McAvennie, casually.

'He had, like a –' Charlie pushed out his tongue and pointed to the tip. 'You know?'

McAvennie nodded his comprehension. 'What happened?' His eyes became suddenly interested.

'Nothing,' said Charlie, guardedly. 'Not really. It was just a bit . . . weird.'

'I know who you're talking about. He's new; came here the same day as you.' McAvennie shook his head and made a groaning sound. 'He's going to be a problem. That's why he's not out here cutting wood with you,' he said, candidly. 'What did he say to you?'

'Um, weird stuff. He was talking like he was ill, but he wasn't.'

'He says he was cured,' McAvennie said slowly.

Charlie went to say something but was cut short. 'What?'

McAvennie stood quickly. The air changed.

Charlie looked across to one of the stones opposite, just as one of the workmen dropped his soup. As it hit the ground the steam from it rose off the leaves with a scalding hiss. The man fell sideways from his stone seat.

McAvennie was on his feet and over to him faster than his frame should have made possible.

'Phillip,' Charlie heard him say urgently.

He fell to his knees and cradled the man's head in his arm. The other workmen were moving forward with looks of puzzlement and shock on their faces.

The man who had fallen ill looked old and tired. His mouth opened slightly. Charlie could just about make out what he was saying.

'No. I can't. I think I'm—' The man stopped. His body tensed as the eyes changed in an instant. They switched from alive to not alive in that way everybody could sense but nobody could explain, as if their bodies had become heavy and the air around them started to swirl.

One of the workmen stood in front of him, blocking Charlie's view. They had gathered in a crescent around the stricken man. McAvennie was looking up at them from his kneeling position, helpless. David had his hands knitted together on top of his head. His eyes were closed tightly and he was saying something under his breath.

Charlie's body felt light, his head faint. He wanted Emily.

'What are we going to do?' he heard one of the workmen say.

'Has he got any kids?' said another voice.

'No,' came the answer. 'Not any more. Nor a wife.'

Charlie fell away from the scene. A tunnel of vision was the only link between him and the woods. The workman who had been blocking his view moved to one side and all he saw was a man lying on the ground, staring vacantly into space, his essence sucked out.

|||

They carried the old man back to the truck and loaded him on to the wooden, open-top deck at the back. He started crying hysterically and opening and closing his fists like a baby. They tried to comfort him but he would not stop crying.

'Come on, Phil,' they said. 'Ssh. It's OK.'

The tears ran freely over his face.

Charlie had never seen this type of reaction to it before. He watched the man cry and felt an enormous sense of uselessness.

They loaded their tools alongside the man and one of them stayed on the back with him, holding him down, as they drove back to the camp. They left the wood they had chopped at the roadside.

|||

They flew past the old, damp house at the top of the hill, almost losing control on the way down. The tyres spat wildly when they skidded into the mud. They sped through the car park as McAvennie ratcheted through the gears with great metal crunches.

Then the truck started up the hill to the lighthouse. People looked at them with their arms at their sides when they passed. They knew what was happening. The truck came to the low white wall that rimmed the lighthouse and the brakes screeched. They stopped and McAvennie turned to Charlie.

'This isn't for you.'

Then the truck was pulling away from him up the road to the lighthouse and Charlie was alone. He could hear the old man crying, even over the sound of the engine. He stood there, at the side of the road, watching the back of the truck, his head numb.

||||

He felt foolish standing there; unimportant. He wanted to help. They needn't have dumped him unceremoniously like that. An old feeling of being unwanted rose in him. Quickly, he turned and went back to the campervan but Emily wasn't there.

He sat on the end of the unmade bed and put his head in his hands. It was the first time Charlie had seen the illness in the camp. For some stupid reason he had assumed that people did not get ill inside the protective forcefield of the place. Something had left his body. The lightness he had felt since arriving had gone.

His body hurt from the work he had done. The image of the man falling from the stone replayed in his head and with each repeat the darkness edged further from its corners.

And then, quickly, his mind took him back to the street on which he had spent his childhood. He was there again. It was quiet and eerie, a strange atmosphere in the air. How he had known what it was he could not say but it was from the same reservoir from which all people could tell the ill from the well. It was an ancient instinct that had crept imperceptibly back to the world, speaking silent messages through the forgotten senses. The atmosphere on the street was of death. That was what it was. Emily had held his hand.

The sound of somebody approaching brought Charlie back to the real world. He went over to the small window set into the door of the campervan. Emily was walking up the hill between the caravans. When he saw her, his heart lifted a little. He pushed open the door and stepped down to the ground to greet her. She smiled wearily when she saw him.

'Hello,' she chirped.

'You look tired.'

She kissed him. 'I'm OK. How was it?'

'OK,' he answered.

She looked at him. 'What's wrong?'

'Nothing. It was OK.'

'What's the matter, Charlie?'

He turned away. 'Nothing. Just leave it.'

Emily's eyes burned into him. Sometimes the way she could tell what he was thinking just by looking at him was horrible.

'Fine,' she said at last, and walked past him quickly, slamming the door of the van behind her.

Charlie stood in the cold for a minute. He looked down the hill at the tents in the distance. The camp was always so quiet. He went into the van where Emily was making the bed.

'We're fucked,' he said.

She stopped.

'We're still getting sick. The Sadness is going to wipe us all out. It doesn't matter where we go, whether we're running or staying in a place like this. It's still killing us and there's nothing anyone can do. Do you know what that means?'

Emily said nothing.

'It means we're fucked.' He could hear the emotion in his own voice. 'I don't want –' he stopped for breath – 'I don't want to lose you.'

She sat down on the bed. He felt so trapped, like the walls of the world were moving in from all directions.

'There's this thing out there and nobody knows what it is and it's coming for us. All of us. It's unstoppable.'

'Be quiet, Charlie,' she said.

'I want to leave.'

'What?'

'I want to go somewhere where it's just me and you.'

'Charlie, no.' Her voice faltered.

'Why not?'

'I don't like you being like this.'

He covered his face with his hands and shook his head. 'I'm sorry, Em,' he said. 'I'm sorry.' He tried to gain himself. He was usually so good at fighting back the demons in the daytime but now they were loose.

'Charlie,' she said. 'Charlie,' she said again, this time more forcefully.

He took his hands away.

'Come here,' she said.

He paused. She was staring at him with a gentle intensity.

'Come . . . here.'

He crossed the space to the bed and kissed her. She prised his lips apart and he felt the soft thinness of her tongue. She pulled him backwards roughly so he was lying on top of her. He grabbed her hair in a tight grasp. They stopped kissing and he unzipped his coat and pulled his sweater and T-shirt over his head. His heart thumped. They kissed again and he moved down to her neck and as he did so he felt the darkness in him intensify and solidify and form into a dense mass.

||||

Pop! The rabbit circled and fell to the ground. Edward got to his feet and ran across the grass to collect his quarry, slinging the air rifle across his back so that it bounced against him as he ran. He was desensitized to the sight of dead rabbits by now. He kicked the body gently to check it was definitely dead and lifted it up by its ears. It was a big rabbit.

Somebody was watching him. He could sense it. He turned slowly, not wanting whoever it was to know he was on to them. The boy took the rifle from his shoulder and loaded some pellets into the chamber. He was sure there was somebody there. It was possible to sense such things. He had always been able to do it, and his powers had grown since they moved out to the country. Sometimes he even felt invincible, like a superhero.

They were behind the gorse bushes near the cliff edge. He could see them now. He kept his head facing forwards and watched them from the sides of his eyes. One of them was the blond boy he had seen when he watched the kids from the cliff top. He had noticed him at the time because he seemed to be the leader.

All Edward wanted was some friends to play with. He still wished Pele would come back but it had been such a long time since his disappearance that it didn't seem likely. He had never known the kids to come up the cliff path to the top before, and he wasn't allowed down to the beach on his own. It seemed impossible to make friends. But now an opportunity had presented itself. The kids were here, even if they were spying on him.

Maybe he should say hello. How dangerous could they be? As he considered this the image of his uncle came into his mind: the old-looking face, the wrinkles in the skin around his eyes, the dirty stubble on his chin. He always knew what to do. He always knew what was going on. And so Edward ignored the children, just as he had been taught, and walked straight past them towards the house.

IIII

They lay in bed. The dawn light cut a crack of white down the centre of the curtains. Charlie sat up and stretched his back.

'Morning,' he said, seeing Emily's eyes flicker open.

She made her morning groan and smiled.

'Hi.' Her fingers reached out from under the covers and she touched his chin. 'Stubble,' she said.

Charlie yawned. 'Not stubble. Beard.'

Emily laughed. 'You're not growing a beard.'

'Why not?'

'You're just not.'

'Haven't you noticed how many of the men have them? It's all the rage down on the camp.'

Emily giggled. 'I forbid you to grow a beard.'

'Don't you want me to get along with the guys? Hmm? Do you want me to be unhappy?'

Emily rolled on to her front and reached up to kiss him. 'Do you want me to be unhappy?'

Charlie frowned seriously. 'If that's the price of a beard – yes!'

She dropped her face into the pillow and muffled something.

'What's that?' He stroked her hair.

Emily lifted her head up and looked at the headboard in front of her. 'I said, you're horrible.'

'I see.'

They looked at each other for a long time. Her hair fell in front of her face and she blew it away.

'I want to go to the lighthouse,' she said.

Charlie rolled his eyes. 'Why?'

'I don't know. Don't you think it's weird how we're not allowed up there?'

Charlie groaned. 'What does it matter?'

'Are you serious?'

'Why can't you just trust them?'

'It's not that I don't trust them, it's just . . .' She trailed off.

'What?'

'Don't you think it's weird?'

'What?'

'This place.' She pulled the covers right up to her neck. 'It's too perfect.'

'Too perfect?'

'Something isn't right, Charles. You must have sensed it.'

'Something isn't right, Charles,' he mocked. 'Why are you so cynical?'

'I'm not. You know what I mean.'

'Honestly, Em, I was with George all day yesterday and he seems really genuine. It just takes getting used to.'

'It's like everyone's been brainwashed.'

'Brainwashed,' he repeated.

'You can mock me,' she said, 'but everyone is a bit weird.'

A few strands of hair fell in front of her face again.

'That's not weirdness,' he said, placing the outside of his hand against the hair and brushing it away. 'It's called people being nice.'

'It's weird.'

He shook his head slowly. 'What do you think they're doing at the lighthouse? Some evil experiment or something?'

'I don't know but if they don't want us going up there then there must be something, surely.'

'Maybe they just want to give the people up there some space.'

'Yeah? So why wouldn't they let you in yesterday? When they took that man there?'

'I don't know,' he said.

There was a knock at the door.

'Charlie,' a voice called.

Emily and Charlie looked at one another.

'Come on, comrade. Time for work.'

Charlie grinned. He lowered his voice and said in a thick cod-Scottish accent to Emily, 'Och, man, will ya nae leave me alone for the love of William Wallace!'

Emily laughed.

|||

Emily had been sent to work in a place called the Hall of Records. It was a static caravan lined with shelves of paper documents. There were credit card bills, phone bills, medical appointments, sales letters, all the types of correspondence that might have fallen through any typical letterbox.

The job of the women who worked there was to file the documents alphabetically according to surname. The letters came from the salvages the men went on. The documents were kept for posterity, according to the woman in charge; to retain a semblance of what humanity once was. She liked the work, she told Charlie. She had worked in offices before, during her summer holidays, and it wasn't that different. But Charlie knew that it was. Emily would come back from work tired and quiet, as if the shadows of the people she filed away every day were getting into her soul, darkening it.

In the evenings, meals were collected from a tent in the main car park. You could choose to eat at the tent on the large tables that had been brought in, or you could take it away with you. Vitamin tablets were taken with every meal.

Because the population levels had dropped to such an extent, they lacked for little in terms of utilities. Vans, cabins, tents, tables, hardware – all were in plentiful supply. Petrol was the rarest commodity but McAvennie had the foresight to make a store of it. It was collected in large canisters and stored in a brick structure they had made themselves at the far wall of the car park, away from the wire fences. The petrol was guarded at all times.

As winter settled into its machinations the temperatures dropped. Charlie spent the first few weeks working in the woods. They cut the firewood and loaded it on to the back of the truck and nobody ever mentioned the man who had died that day. Every time he passed the old house at the top of the hill Charlie would think of the two women and two children inside.

Sometimes word would spread around the camp that a salvage team had been sent but had not come back. But they always came back in the end. Because of the nature of the salvages, the teams would have to spread further afield. This meant they spent progressively longer away from the camp with each journey.

Rumours of raiders and marauders had gained momentum. The main arterial roads of the country, the motorways and A roads, were seen as off limits. Travelling along them was not safe any more. When new people arrived at the camp, increasingly they came with tales of being attacked, or having seen the aftermath of a violent incident. Sometimes they had even seen human remains at the sides of roads. The people at the camp listened to the stories. They had no connection now with the outside world and so the only news was hearsay and whisperings. The fragility of the knowledge was in itself enough to unnerve them; it described to them just how cut off they really were. Inversely, it made the safe running of the camp an ever more precious thing to preserve.

At the end of each day Charlie and Emily would return to the cold of the campervan. They had taped cardboard over all but one of the windows, following the advice of one of the women who worked with Emily. It made little difference – it was still freezing in their flimsy husk. They slept in their clothes and when they woke in the mornings they would find that some parts of their bodies were warm and other parts ice cold.

At some point Charlie stopped showering in the mornings. The showers in the car park were too hard a prospect to confront in the cold dawns and so he started going to work unwashed. He had always been meticulously clean but his body was so weary on waking that the long walk to the bottom of the slope was too much. His mind was tired. The food they ate was enough but no more than that.

They had seen McAvennie speak on the beach on several occasions and now his words resonated far more deeply than they had on the first night at the camp. His reassurances penetrated further now that their bodies were weak. Emily admitted to having felt it but said it was because their minds were tired, more malleable, she said. Charlie was not so sure. He saw it more like an alignment. They were a part of something. They belonged to something again. With the old world gone, they had found a new place. And this time he knew how important it was to hold on to it. He felt in his fellow refugees the same will. They were tired, but they were aligned.

|||

The children and their mother waited in the cellar in silence. They were sitting on the sofa beneath the small, thin window – Miriam in the middle, one child on either side. She had her arm around each of them and the feelings in her stomach made her think that she shouldn't be doing this. But it was best to hide in the cellar. People were not to be trusted. In the darkness they waited until the door creaked open at the top of the stairs and the call came.

'It's OK. You can come up.'

Miriam expelled the air that had been waiting in her lungs. They rose to their feet and went upstairs.

'Who was it?' she said. She looked down the hallway. They

weren't alone. Two figures, a boy and a girl, were standing there. They held in their hands plastic carrier bags. Miriam recognized them immediately.

'We have guests,' Miriam's mother said happily.

The boy stepped forwards.

'Hi,' he said. 'Remember me?'

|||

'I've come past this house quite a lot since we moved to the camp, and I've always wanted to call in, but I've always been with my colleagues' – he noticed Emily smirk when he said the word colleague – 'so we couldn't stop.'

'Was the potato soup really that good?' Miriam's mother said, with a smile.

Her voice had become high-pitched with the excitement of entertaining guests. Even if the guests had supplied all the food. They had brought with them something near a feast: two cooked chickens, potatoes, carrots, peas, a parsnip. But the *pièce de résistance* was a dry packet mix of *coq au vin* sauce. Added to this were some freshly baked loaves and for dessert they had brought a large bar of chocolate. They cooked the vegetables, prepared the sauce and were now sitting around the dining table, illuminated by candles.

Charlie laughed. 'I don't know. You were the first people we met when we got here. Since things started looking up.'

'Looking up?' said Miriam. She failed to see how the situation could have improved.

Charlie took the serving spoon and dropped some peas on to his plate. She noticed he had rings around his eyes. He wasn't sleeping.

'I know it might sound weird, but yeah, things are looking up I'd say. It was really strange when we first got there but you get used to it. It's a bit . . . different.'

'Different?' Miriam leaned over the table on her elbows, her empty wine glass dangling over her plate. A few glasses of wine wouldn't hurt.

'The people there are just so . . . nice.'

He turned to Emily, who nodded her agreement.

'It's better than we'd hoped for,' she said.

'But it's funny,' Charlie went on. 'I got there and I thought it was safe because there were people there. It was such a shock when we saw that people are still—' Charlie stopped. Their children were there. 'You know, getting the s-a-d-n-e-s-s.'

Edward looked at his mother and made a funny face as if to say, does this person really not realize how old I am? Charlie looked down at his food.

'But I guess that just is what it is.'

There was a pause.

'Well, you certainly don't seem to be lacking for food down there. My goodness, look at this,' said Miriam's mother.

'This is all from George. We don't normally eat as well as this, but it's not bad down there.'

'Who's George?' asked Miriam.

'I guess he's the leader. Big bald chap? Scottish?'

Miriam nodded. Him.

'So why has he given us all this food?'

'It's supposed to be a gesture,' Emily said. 'He told us to bring it. He wanted to let you know you have nothing to worry about from us.'

Miriam looked at the girl. She spoke with the same faint confidence she herself had cultivated as a young woman. Her dark complexion and chestnut brown hair were different but she didn't look unlike Dora. She had the same small, pointed nose and dark eyes.

'That's very kind.'

Miriam's mother smiled at Emily, little orange dots flickering in her eyes. Miriam said nothing. She watched the girl glance across nervously to her boyfriend.

'To tell the truth,' said Emily. And then she looked directly at Miriam. 'He was wondering if you wouldn't feel safer at the camp.'

The air in the room changed as soon as she said it. Miriam felt herself seize.

'We're fine up here, thanks,' she answered slowly, trying to keep herself calm.

Charlie held up his hand. 'What he means is that you might feel exposed up here on your own.'

Miriam nodded and leaned in. She needed to make herself clear.

'I know you two are not to blame for this, but you can tell your George that if he wants something then he should come and ask for it himself.'

Charlie shook his head. 'It's not like that.'

'No?' She cocked her head.

'No.'

'So what would happen to the house if we left?'

'They want to use it as a lookout,' said Emily, honestly. 'That's what he said.'

'A lookout.'

'To see if people are coming this way,' Charlie explained.

Miriam shook her head. She could sense how awkward the two of them felt. They were too young for this kind of conversation. The Scottish man who had come to her house a few months ago should never have sent them to do his bidding.

'It was only a suggestion,' Charlie said quickly.

'Did you ask him why he didn't come himself?'

Emily answered as politely as she could. 'He said he's tried before.'

Miriam sat back and thought. 'What happens if I say no?'

Charlie and Emily shifted awkwardly. The air was getting increasingly heavy.

'What do you mean?'

'What if we want to stay here?'

Charlie shrugged. 'Then you stay here. I don't . . . I don't know what you mean.'

She had been waiting for this moment for months, ever since the camp had first assembled a few days after the arrival of the stricken tanker. It was bound to happen.

'Is he going to take the house off me?'

'What? No!' Charlie coughed with the absurdity of Miriam's thoughts. 'Definitely not. It's not like that down there. It's really not.'

He genuinely believed it to be true, but Miriam also noticed the girl was looking at the boy with surprise.

'Is it, Em?' he said.

Emily waited for a moment.

'No,' she said. 'It's not.' She turned to Miriam. 'I was sceptical of the camp, I still am probably, but I really don't think they would do something like that.'

'I know they wouldn't,' added Charlie, speaking quickly and defensively. 'They've realized that we have to do things together. They've even got speeches for it and everything.' He stopped.

Miriam finished the wine in her glass. Perhaps she would have another one. What harm could it do?

'Tell George we're fine where we are,' she said, and leaned forwards for the bottle.

|||

They finished their meal and the children were put to bed. They drank the wine and Miriam brought out extra bottles from the cellar before taking them through to the living room where they were now sitting in the light from the candles Charlie had carried from the kitchen.

Her mother was dozing in the chair with her head tilted to one side, her mouth half open.

'When it first started,' said Miriam, 'I tried to, I don't know what, pretend it wasn't happening, something like that. It's kind of hard to accept, do you know what I mean? Probably not,' she said. 'You're still so young. When you get to my age you get so settled you think the little life you've built is indestructible.' She was sitting in her father-in-law's chair at the window. 'My husband got it so early on. We didn't even know what it was. He was one of the first.'

Emily and Charlie, sitting side by side on the sofa, said nothing.

'When I finally did come to terms with the fact that it was real, and that took a long time, I always thought things would be OK in the end. I don't how, or why I would even think that. It's funny, isn't it: why we would think that. My brother-in-law brought us here.' She turned her head to the window. 'He never trusted other people. That's why he wanted us to come all the way out here, away from London. He didn't believe in happy endings.' Her words caught on something and she had to stop.

'Things will get better,' said Charlie. 'If you came down to the camp you'd see it.'

'Maybe,' she said, rolling her head around on her neck.

'You will,' he said, and hesitated. 'I suffer from depression,' he blurted. And then he paused again, thinking about what he had just said. He looked at his wine glass and closed one eye to focus. 'Er, yeah.' He swallowed. 'But since I got to the camp I've been a lot better, haven't I, Em?'

'You suffer from depression?' He seemed so jolly all the time.

He waved his hand up and down in front of him. 'I actually have to make an effort to be this happy.' He smiled sarcastically. 'I actually have to make an effort!'

Miriam laughed at his light-heartedness.

'It's a shame you don't trust any more. But it's an easy thing to lose, I guess,' he said.

Miriam didn't say anything to that. In truth, she wished she could trust again. She just couldn't see how.

'But if you do feel like that then I guess you'd not like the camp. George says this thing about trust. It's one of the things that keep things going down there. We have to trust each other. It is hard, and sometimes we're expected to trust him, and it doesn't seem right, but if you don't trust then who knows what will happen?'

'That sounds sinister.'

'It's difficult to explain.'

'The lighthouse,' Emily said, quickly. 'It's where they take the sick. But we're not allowed to go up there.'

'Why not?'

They made eye contact.

'I don't know. We're just not. We're expected to "trust",' she finished.

Miriam took a sip of her wine.

'I'm sure they know what they're doing,' Charlie interrupted, his words mildly slurred. 'I don't know why you're so obsessed with the place.'

'I'm just not entirely convinced by all this Great Leader stuff.'

'I don't think he claims to be anything he's not,' said Charlie. 'It just kind of happens, doesn't it? Some people are just good leaders. You naturally get used to it. You shouldn't be so down on him. He's a good guy. Anyway, I for one am happy to fall in line.'

Emily lowered her head. 'Charlie's a naturally trusting person,' she said, as if he wasn't sitting right next to her, 'but I, maybe, am not. Well, not as much as him.'

'It's good to question things,' said Miriam.

'But the thing is,' Emily went on, 'although I can't say I fully understand what it is that's going on down there, I have to say I've never seen anything, um, untoward there. Yeah.'

The room fell into a silent hollow and they each drank from their wine glasses.

'So what do you think it is?' Charlie asked.

Miriam looked at her sleeping mother across the room. 'The illness?'

'Uh-huh.'

Miriam sighed. 'A virus? Who knows?'

'I don't think it's a virus,' he said with *faux*-confidence. 'The scientists have already said that.'

'It could be a new type of virus.'

Charlie shrugged. His pupils were great black orbs.

'Have you noticed how, since it's happened, the world seems . . . different, somehow? I don't mean because people are dead and the world has ended,' he said quickly. 'I mean how everything seems, like, quieter. And, I don't know, more clear.'

'It's because there are fewer people. Fewer cars. No factories. It changes things.'

'So you have noticed it?'

'Of course.' She had assumed everybody had. She'd never questioned it.

'So what you're saying is the world is healing itself, is that right? Now that there are less people.'

'I don't know if that's happening.' She tilted her head. 'What do you think?'

'Well, I have given it quite a lot of thought,' he said, jokingly. 'Are you religious?'

He said it suddenly and casually. Miriam felt her mind stumble.

'Yes,' she said, slowly.

'Well, what if it really is something to do with, you know?' and he pointed upwards with raised eyebrows.

Miriam shook her head and smiled.

'I'm serious,' he said. 'Lots of people are saying it. We've all scoffed, but why not? It could be. Don't you think so?'

'I don't know.'

'But if you really are religious then you have to admit it's a possibility.'

Miriam looked at him. 'But if it is true, why did he take my husband? And what happened to your family?'

Charlie raised his finger drunkenly. 'My family are gone too. But I've thought about that.'

'Oh you have, have you?'

'Yes,' he declared. 'He's not taking "bad" people or "good" people; maybe He just doesn't think like that. Like us. Just because He made us – if He made us,' he added as a caveat, 'then it doesn't necessarily mean that He has, like, human sensibilities.' He stopped for her reaction.

'OK.'

'Maybe it's not even a punishment or anything like that. I don't know why we have to see it as being a punishment anyway – if it's God doing all this, then people will be going to heaven anyway.' He slowed himself as his thoughts ran away. 'Maybe it's just restoring an order. An old order. And that's what this new world is. That's why we're having these weird sunsets and things. And why things happen like they do now. Haven't you noticed how everyone seems to go through these tests if they want to survive? I've spoken to so many people about this and they've all said the same thing.' He was speaking quickly again. He sat up in his seat. 'Think of everything you've been through since it happened, right?'

Miriam nodded.

'It's long periods of nothing, punctuated by big events, right?'

'Sure. That's the nature of everything.'

'Yeah, but each big event always involves you making a big moral choice, yes? Do you help someone, or leave them? Do you steal or do you ask? Do you fight or do you run? It's been the same for everyone. And then, when it's over, there's a lesson learned. About yourself, or about the world. I think about it when I can't sleep. Don't you feel like you're going through a gauntlet, and it's getting narrower and narrower? You're constantly questioning who you are. I don't know, maybe that's just me, I'm just saying that it seems similar to all the old Bible stories.'

Miriam's mind jumped back in time. What Charlie was saying did make sense. She remembered London; going back to help the priest; volunteering at the hospital; helping Dora; coming to Cornwall and letting Paul Crowder stay; the boy who had offered to kill Joseph when he had fallen ill on the beach. All choices. And she had made the same one every time. And she was alive.

'And when each test is over, it all goes away. You don't have to worry about things coming back to you and biting you on the –' he cleared his throat – 'on the bottom. The choices are yours, and yours alone. You don't have to worry about the police, or getting caught, or society or anything like that any more. You can do what you want. It's just as easy now to make the bad choice as it is to make the good one. Easier, even. Because the bad choice is usually the easier one.'

'You've given this a lot of thought.'

'Depression does that – makes you think too much.' He laughed drily. 'But I think everyone's thought about it. Maybe they've arrived at a different conclusion but everyone's thought about it. That's another of the things that comes with the new world – more time to think. Haven't you found that? Now that things are slower I've felt more –' he hummed in thought – 'attuned. Like I've found my correct pace.'

What seemed like many years ago she had been part of a similar conversation with Joseph and Father Moore. Father Moore had thought the same thing as Charlie, that the Sadness was divine, but when it had come from his lips he made it sound ugly and dangerous, and absurd. Charlie had said the same thing but it was different. Coming from the young man with his girlfriend fallen asleep on his shoulder, what he said had a far stronger veracity. It was not what was being said, she realized, it was the type of person who said it. Charlie made the illness sound almost like something she needn't fear. She looked at him looking at her with his big, dark, shadowed eyes, and she felt strong emotions that, since that day in the cellar, had gone. Something was coming back. She was remembering something.

'It's getting late,' she said.

Charlie blinked and nodded. 'You're right. We'd better be going.' He turned his body around to face his sleeping girlfriend.

'Wait,' she whispered. Something that had bound itself very tight around her was loosening. 'Leave her. You can both stay here tonight.'

|||

Charlie slept well. It was the first time he had slept in a proper bed in almost a year. The house was so much drier than their van. No freezing particles of floating moisture were in the air. He thought about making use of the bed with Emily but decided it would be disrespectful. He lay awake for a short time but it was to enjoy the warmth underneath the covers. There was no swirling darkness.

When he woke up the next day he felt as if he had been given an elixir. His body felt lighter and his mind was alert. He wished he could stay in the bed for ever. Emily was already awake. She had found on the bookshelf an old trashy horror novel. The speed with which she read had always been something he could not fathom. The yellowing pages of the book flopped down either side of her supporting thumb.

'Any good?' he asked.

'Sssh,' she said.

He rolled on to his stomach and closed his eyes.

There was a knock at the door.

'Hello?' said Emily.

'Are you decent?' the muffled reply came through the door.

'Yes.'

Miriam's mother came into the room with two glasses of orange juice and some toasted bacon sandwiches.

She sat on the edge of the bed as they ate and explained to them that the electricity for cooking came from a car battery that a man named Joseph had rigged up to an electricity adaptor. They used them on special occasions, she said.

They went downstairs and sat in the living room for nearly an hour. Miriam was far quieter than she had been last night, Charlie thought. She was sitting in the armchair by the window again. The faint smile that had been on her face the previous night had disappeared. There was no eye contact.

At last, Charlie and Emily went to leave. Miriam's mother let them out into the fresh air of the morning. Wind blew through the grassland in front of the house, the bending tips of the grass marking its path.

'It's been so lovely having somebody to speak to,' Miriam's mother said.

Emily was looking up the road to the left. 'What's that?' she said.

There was something in the road on the brow of the hill.

'It's a person,' Charlie said.

The man came slowly. He was walking with a limp. More than a limp; his left leg was dragging behind him.

'He's hurt,' said Miriam's mother.

'Hang on,' said Charlie, squinting. 'That's Andrew.' He looked at Emily. 'The American.'

Fields was holding his left arm across his chest, supporting it with his right.

Charlie ran up the road towards him, his body needling with a sudden, strange fear. The lightness that had seemed so strong and unassailable just minutes before was darkening, and he felt it propelling him forwards.

III

The house was dark and cold. Charlie hadn't noticed it before, but it now seemed oppressive. His eyes couldn't adjust to the dimness.

Fields lay on the same sofa which he and Emily had sat on the night before. A wet cloth had been folded on his forehead. At the neck, his shirt was red with the blood that clotted his beard. His injured arm lay diagonally across his chest and his glasses were missing. His face looked somehow altered – pulpy.

McAvennie barged into the room and stopped when he saw him. Behind him, David, the man with whom Charlie had chopped wood, peered over his shoulder.

'Fields,' he said. 'Jesus. What happened?'

Fields brought his good hand up to his forehead. The other arm looked as if it had been twisted in its socket. The hand was facing the wrong way.

'We . . .' His throat was dry and he coughed. 'We were attacked.'

McAvennie stepped further into the room, standing at the end of the sofa.

'Who attacked you?'

Fields turned his head to one side. A deep purple bruise ran along his cheekbone from his ear to his chin.

'Bandits. They –' he inhaled a breath – 'just came out of nowhere.'

||||

Silence. Miriam stood in the doorway with her arms casually folded, but her heart was beating fast.

'Where are the others?' said McAvennie.

'All dead,' said Fields quickly. 'They would have killed me too, but they –' he winced with pain – 'told me to go.'

David made a sound from the window. He pulled the curtains to one side and looked out. Then he turned back to the room. 'He might have led them here.'

McAvennie raised his hand to silence him in a gesture that said, not now.

'When did it happen?'

Fields opened his eyes halfway. 'I don't know. Two days ago. I think.'

Miriam's mother brought a glass of water into the room.

'And you've spent that time walking back.'

Fields nodded slowly and allowed Miriam's mother to bring the water to his lips.

'Where are you hurt?'

'It's my ribs. And my arm. I think they're broken.'

'We'll get you help.'

'My leg hurts as well.'

Miriam noticed that McAvennie was sweating. She watched the conversation so intently that it had not occurred to her that so many strangers were in her living room after so many months of it being empty.

'Come on.'

McAvennie moved to the centre of the sofa and went on to one knee to help Fields to his feet.

'Wait,' said the American.

McAvennie stopped.

'Thompson. They said they were going to Thompson's.'

McAvennie looked up to David.

'The farmer,' he said.

David turned his head and looked again out of the window, in the direction of the village. McAvennie put his hands on his belt and pulled his trousers further up his waist. He looked at Miriam.

'Can you take Andrew here down to the camp?'

She froze. She was not involved in this. It wasn't her business.

'Of course,' her mother said for her.

Fields grabbed McAvennie's leg. Miriam saw a flicker of something run across his face: an amalgamation of pity, concern, fear and despair. His voice sounded heavy.

'What is it, Andrew?'

'We saw –' He swallowed. He closed his eyes and ran his tongue along his lips. 'They've been burning crops.' He sighed. 'Whole fields. We saw them.'

The room fell silent. Miriam felt her throat become heavy. She remembered the looters in the supermarket who had been wearing the gas masks.

'We have to go,' said McAvennie. He looked quickly at Miriam and nodded his thanks before leaving. David went after him. Miriam, Charlie and Emily followed.

'Where are you going?' said Charlie.

McAvennie didn't turn back. 'We have to check on the farm.'

'It could be an ambush,' said David.

'They'll be gone by now.'

'We could go and get help from the camp.'

'No,' he said sternly. He had reached the car and stopped. 'We've got a weapon with us. We don't need to risk more people.'

'We're coming with you,' said Charlie.

'No you're not.'

Charlie grabbed McAvennie's arm. 'I want to come.'

McAvennie frowned at him, and nodded.

'OK. Get in,' he said. He turned back to Miriam. 'Thank you for doing this. Just take him down the hill and say you need to get him to the lighthouse. Someone will go with you.'

Emily climbed into the back seat after Charlie. McAvennie jumped in behind the wheel and pulled away from the grass verge, into the road and into the distance.

Miriam and her mother watched from the garden gate. Soon the car and the sound of its engine faded to nothing. Miriam's mother turned to her daughter. Her expression changed just as Miriam tasted the saltiness at the edges of her lips. She lifted her fingers to her nose and when she brought her hand away, her fingertips were daubed in red.

'Your nose is bleeding,' her mother said.

'It's nothing.'

She felt suddenly guilty and tried to hide the blood by covering her nose with her hands. Her mother was looking at her suspiciously. Miriam didn't even know why she would hide such a thing from her mother. Maybe she should tell her the truth. But not now. Not yet.

|||

Fields helped himself into the back of the car. Miriam started the engine and, through habit, checked the petrol gauge. Nearly empty. Her body pulsed with adrenalin. For so long she had looked down on the camp with dread and fear, and now she was about to drive straight into its heart. The fear of the camp had become something nearly irrational. But she needed to get the man in the back seat to safety.

The tide in the bay was far out. The tanker had listed as it always did in low tide. A veil of rain hung over the horizon, moving inland.

The guard at the gate stopped her. He was younger than she was, tall and skinny. A patchy beard grew around his chin. He recognized her immediately as the woman who lived at the top of the hill.

'What's been happening up there?' he said, leaning down to her.

Before she had time to answer he saw Fields on the back seat and was rushing round the front of the car. He opened the passenger-side door and got in.

'Down there,' he said, pointing.

III

Just keep your hands on the wheel and your eyes on the road ahead, she said. Just get the job done and get back to the house. Her neck felt like it was being squeezed to the point of pain. They passed through the car park and she threaded the car between the two stone pillars at the bottom.

'Up there.' The man sitting next to her pointed to the road ahead. 'We're going to the lighthouse.'

She accelerated up the hill, trying not to look at the tents to the right. Some people looked up from whatever it was they were doing to see, and she ignored those as well.

The lighthouse grew up out of the hill until it came into plain view. Its surrounding wall was broken where the road passed through it. Miriam drove up to the low stone building that joined the cylindrical tower of the lighthouse and stopped.

An older man came out. He had short white hair and a white beard. He wore a pair of large, unfashionable glasses.

Miriam watched the two men speak with a detached mind. She remembered what Emily had said about the lighthouse. The tower was imposing, a lot taller than it looked from the opposite side of the bay. Beneath the white paint she could see the outline of the giant bricks that had made it. Its plain, windowless face was threatening.

The old man helped Fields out of the car.

'Dear, dear, dear,' he said. His voice was quiet, hardly audible. There was a faint hint of an accent. 'What have you been up to?'

Miriam got out and stood clear to give the men space.

Fields groaned as he stood. The man who had directed her to the lighthouse placed Fields's good arm around his shoulder and helped him towards the long, whitewashed building.

The old man watched them go. 'Thank you very much for your help,' he said quietly.

Miriam smiled. 'It's OK.'

There was a questioning look on the man's face, as if he was considering something.

'I am Isaiah. Doctor Isaiah Balad.' He held out his hand for her to shake. Two small black eyes were hidden deep in their sockets behind his glasses. He smiled and his face became smaller and crumpled.

She took his hand and it was small and soft. He tilted his head to one side, gauging her reaction to him.

'Miriam,' she said.

'And you are the woman who lives on the top of the hill?'

His accent was German. Or maybe Belgian. It was only faintly discernible.

'I am.'

'Please, come.' He motioned for her to go into the building.

Miriam paused.

'There is nothing to worry about,' he said. 'Please.'

Miriam walked past him. Inside was a small, closed-off foyer. Fields had already been taken inside and the foyer was empty. There was a desk on the left-hand side and a painting of a lifeboat sailing through stormy seas hanging on the wall. A set of large, wooden doors was in front of her.

'We keep the lighthouse for the sick,' said Dr Balad calmly.

He curled his hand round the long metal bar of the door handle as he spoke.

'Would you like to see it?'

Miriam felt as if she was about to be shown something she should not see. According to Emily, this lighthouse was a secret place, and yet the doctor in front of her was being very open.

She thought about the question. Did she want to see? Behind

the doors lay death. By sick, the doctor had meant infected. She found it difficult to understand why he should want to show her. She felt as though she could *feel* the room beyond the doors. She could sense it. Dr Balad read her thoughts and he pulled the door open.

|||

The lane that led up to the farmhouse was thin and lined with tall hedgerows. Potholes were filled with muddy rainwater. Charlie sensed immediately the same thing in the air that he had felt so many months ago when he had returned to his parents' house. The old senses were spiking keenly. They were in danger.

'Be careful,' he said needlessly.

The lane widened and became a road. A line of houses on either side came into view, three on the right, three on the left. Beyond them stood the large farmhouse. Nobody said anything. They swerved slowly around the charred remains of a burned-out Land Rover and came out on to the street.

And then there was a high-pitched hiss, growing in volume, outside the car. Charlie went to turn his head towards the direction of the noise, but he was being shunted forward and upwards. There was a loud, deafening boom. He saw flames lick against the windscreen and instinctively grabbed for Emily.

The world turned sideways, the horizon shifted up through angles. Everything became still and slow. A glimpse of a man dressed in black clothes. Shouting in the street. Charlie's body floated for a second in the absence of gravity, and then the car was on its roof. There was a metal-on-concrete smash. His back rolled up against the roof and he tucked his head instinctively towards his chest. The car rocked back and forth and then they were still.

'What happened?' David yelled from the front passenger seat. A trickle of blood ran down the side of his face into his beard.

The rattle of gunfire came on the breeze and an instant later the clang of the bodywork being peppered with bullets roared all around them, striking the underside of the car.

'Out,' he heard someone call.

He pushed against the door nearest him but it was stuck. The frame was buckled. Tilting his body sideways he tried to right himself. Emily had stopped moving next to him. He prodded her.

'Em.'

Nothing.

His door was yanked open from the outside and McAvennie's arms pulled him out of the car. Charlie fell flat on to the wet road. A bullet ricocheted off the base of the car with a metal scream.

'Come on,' someone called.

David was running for the nearest house. He threw himself into the front door and it splintered open. A bullet smashed the ornate light next to him. McAvennie grabbed Charlie and they ran for the house. Bullets spat into the mud of the garden with dull thuds. Charlie covered his head with his hands and ran blindly. Emily, he thought. He slowed but McAvennie pushed him on.

'Go,' he said.

They were inside the house, in a dark hallway.

'There's someone in the back,' David called from the far room of the house.

'Upstairs. Get upstairs.'

'I need to get Emily,' Charlie said.

'No.' McAvennie's face was fixed as he looked at Charlie.

A line of bullets spat into the hallway.

McAvennie grabbed Charlie and physically forced him up the stairs.

They went into a bedroom at the back of the house. Two skeletons were lying on the double bed, above the sheets. They were fully clothed. Plastic bags had been tied over their heads, sealed at the neck. What had been a woman lay with her arms tied to the rails of the headboard. The man had chained himself with handcuffs. Around them were damp green rings of what looked like mould. The place stank. Charlie stumbled backwards into the corner and vomited.

'We've got to go back,' he heard himself say. The sound of his own blood pumping pulsed in his ears. 'Emily's still—'

'Wait here,' said McAvennie. 'I'm going to get her.'

He ran out of the room. Charlie followed. There was a man at the top of the stairs, wearing black trousers and a black sweater. He was holding an assault rifle. His face was covered by a small, insectoid mask. When McAvennie came out of the room they were just feet apart. The man in black hesitated for a second. But McAvennie did not. He threw himself bodily at the gunman and they tumbled down the stairs. There was a short crack of gunfire. The plaster on the ceiling rained down in thin, dusty columns.

McAvennie got to his feet and leaned over the gunman, who was trying to free his weapon. McAvennie struck him hard in the face.

There was shouting outside. More of them. No time.

The gunman shouted something but through his mask it was just a formless noise. McAvennie struck him again. And then again. The body of the man in black went limp and McAvennie unhooked the gun. He looked up the stairs to Charlie.

There was a movement in the front garden.

'Look out,' Charlie called.

McAvennie swung around just as the front door was kicked open. The Scotsman fired without hesitation and the noise of it in the small space was blistering. The man he had shot stood in the doorway for a moment, three waterfalls of blood trickling out of holes in his chest. That man was also wearing a gas mask. He pulled it off and there was a confused expression on his face.

'We left the girl,' he said, slowly, measured.

His right knee gave and he went on to it, his head slumped forward as if he was genuflecting to the man who had killed him.

Charlie ran down the stairs. McAvennie had gone out into the garden and made it to the garden wall. He was crouched behind it, firing randomly at the houses across the street. Charlie could not see anybody firing back.

Emily was in the car. The wheels were still spinning and he could hear the engine. There were flames coming from beneath the upturned bonnet, flowing out of the side and up into the sky.

Charlie could wait no longer. He ran out into the garden and immediately something struck him. It smacked into his leg and he fell where he was. Pain started to radiate from a single, tiny point in searing shockwaves. He put his hand on his leg and when he looked at it, the hand was covered in blood. The pain strengthened so intensely that white flakes filled his eyes.

McAvennie came to him and pulled him up against the wall.

'Here,' he said.

Charlie groaned. He felt warm metal in his hand. 'What?' he said, groggily.

'Just fire.'

'What?'

'Charlie,' he said. His voice was angry.

Charlie tried to focus. He opened his eyes. McAvennie was upside down.

'You have to cover me,' he said.

'Cover you?'

His bald head was bleeding. 'Come on, kiddo.'

Charlie nodded and took the rifle in both hands.

'Just fire. And don't stop until you're empty.'

His mind returned. Quickly, as if through a tunnel, he could think clearly. It felt fleeting, as if the clarity would soon pass. He turned his body and brought the rifle up above the level of the wall. And fired. There was nobody in sight but the gunfire was returned. More of it struck the upturned car in which Emily still lay. They were upstairs.

Sparks flew from the underside of the car as bullets rained down. The pain from his leg had spread to his skull, the nerves that connected the two pulsing like pregnant spider sacs.

McAvennie ran recklessly out into the road. He crouched down and disappeared inside the car, his backside sticking up into the air. More gunfire. The flames at the bonnet were spreading. The driver's seat was on fire.

Charlie fired again. McAvennie did not stop. His body pulled at something with great yanks. He brought a foot up and put it flat against the concrete ground as a lever and then re-emerged. He had Emily in his hands.

The sight of her set off a firestorm inside of him.

'Stop shooting,' he called.

Though he did not stop himself. And then he saw it. The house across the street, on the roof. He could see the head popping up above the angle, the gun aimed down towards the car. Charlie pointed his rifle at the sniper's head and pulled the trigger. Chunks of slate exploded off the roof low and to the left of his target. Coolly, he brought the gun around to adjust, fired and saw the head jerk backwards violently.

McAvennie rose to his feet with Emily in his arms and stumbled into the garden. There was no more gunfire. He sat down next to Charlie, gasping for breath. His head was slick with sweat and blood. His chest heaved as he laid Emily down. Her head moved and her eyes opened.

Charlie pulled her into his chest and as he did so he looked at McAvennie, who was still trying to recover his breath. David came out of the house. The cut on his forehead had bled all over his face.

'The other one did a runner,' he said.

Emily's breath was hot on his neck but he could not take his eyes off McAvennie. He couldn't believe he had got Emily back. The large Scot's eyes were closed and his mouth was open in a grimace as his breathing steadied.

'Fuck me,' he panted. 'I'm so unfit it's ridiculous.'

The room was much longer than it had looked from the outside. Two large windows on the leeward wall were set into the brick. White light flooded through them. Miriam's mind was flung instantly back to the hospital in London.

Two rows of beds, each perpendicular to the walls, spread into the distance. Down the centre was a line of fluorescent lights. Right at the far end, perhaps fifty yards away, was another set of doors. Apart from the windows in the one wall, the room attained a perfect symmetry.

White nets hung over each bed. Miriam had seen similar things in the government facility she had been taken to.

She hardly flinched at the sight of all the people. The density that had been so heavy when the illness first arrived, that had pressed in on her, was much lighter now. She was desensitized to it. She looked at the room, at the shapes of the people just visible behind the white veils. Nearly all of them were lying on their backs. Some of them, though, had sat up in their beds, where they remained now, motionless.

'It's just so strange,' she said.

'Yes,' she heard the doctor say over her shoulder. 'But when they react like this, so sad, it is more than a little beautiful, is it not?'

She felt something vibrate inside her. There was something beautiful in the darkness of it. When people just *stopped* being they had their protective shells stripped away to reveal their innermost delicacy and fragility. She saw it. The thing the ill people had become when everything else had left them was the one thing worth protecting in them. Seeing it there in the room, feeling it, restored something in her that she had not felt in months: a tiny, indefinable flicker that had been sucked out of her that day in the cellar.

'Why are you showing me this?' she said.

'Why not?' He walked past her and down the central aisle between the ends of the beds, his shoes clicking on the painted stone floor. 'I like to keep the rooms clean,' he said. 'When people on the camp tell us somebody they love has become ill, we like to assure them their final days will be comfortable.'

His accent, now that she had placed it roughly, came through stronger.

'It is for the best for everyone. In this camp, we have realized it is important to maintain the things that allowed us to get where we got to as a civilization. We are always compassionate.'

'What about the people who become . . .'

'Violent?'

Miriam nodded.

'We keep them in the lighthouse itself.'

'You lock them in?'

'Yes. We have to. Their families always understand. Is that what you were thinking?'

'I wasn't thinking anything.'

'Have you seen them? With their strength? Would you like to know what it is?'

Dr Balad didn't turn back to her as he walked. His voice hooked her. The thought of the injured American man who had been in her house, the fear she had felt when she entered the camp: all of that was dissipating.

'It is called hysterical strength. There is nothing more magical about it than a shooting star. It is strange, but it is normal. That is to say, it is within the realms of possibility. The muscles in the body are rarely used to their full potential. When somebody is electrocuted their muscles become rigid and strong. They grip.' He lifted his hand up and clenched his fist. 'In the olden days, the Vikings had fighters they called Berserkers. They were men who would fight in a fierce rage, a frenzy. You know the word "berserk"?'

'Yes.'

She could feel eyes on her, peering out from behind the white veils, and she could see the heads of their owners turning as they walked past. She didn't know if she believed what Dr Balad was saying. It was too arbitrary. She understood the doctor's need to find a rational answer for why people were able to act as they did when ill, but the true answer was beyond rationality, beyond science; it was something outside human knowledge, something new.

'There are theories,' he went on, 'that it was a psychotropic state, brought on by the plants they used to make their drinks.'

'I thought those stories were old wives' tales.'

'Perhaps, perhaps,' he said. He reached the far door at the end of the room and stopped. 'But how else can we explain it? We have animal DNA in us, Miriam, which was locked off millennia ago. But it is there, inside us. It is all written in our genes. We do not use our bodies to their full potential. Now,' he said quickly, 'I would like to show you something else. But you must prepare yourself.'

'What are you going to show me?'

'There is a man in here. He will say things that might frighten you, and you must not listen to that. But you should see him.'

'Wait,' she said. 'Why are you showing me all this when you keep other people away?'

Dr Balad smiled.

'You are our neighbour, Miriam. You have a right to know what is happening here.'

III

They waited behind the wall for several minutes. The gunfire had stopped but they didn't know if there were more snipers lying in wait. Slowly, the beating of Charlie's heart levelled out. His leg throbbed. He looked down at Emily and could just see her face as the mouth turned downwards and her eyes scrunched shut.

'Charlie,' she said.

She was crying. She never cried. He put his hand on the top of her head.

'All right,' he said. 'It's over now.'

He made sure his head was below the level of the wall. He was too scared to move. They were so vulnerable where they were.

'I think they're gone,' said David.

'Aye, well, they're not fuckin' shooting at you, are they, you daft twat?' said McAvennie.

The realization that David was standing up in the centre of the garden in full view of the street struck Charlie, and he laughed with shock at the insanity of it. When he did, pain shot through his leg.

'We'd better check the houses,' wheezed McAvennie. 'See if anyone's alive.'

Charlie stayed where he was. He knew that if he stood up his legs would fail him. He watched McAvennie's face. An expression of saddened disbelief was across it.

'You OK, Charlie?' McAvennie said, turning his head.

'I'm fine. Just give us a minute.'

'How's the leg?'

Charlie smiled. 'Shot.'

'Do you think you can walk, kiddo?'

Charlie closed his eyes and took a deep breath. 'Yeah. Just give me a minute.'

The two men walked out of the garden and out of sight.

'Emily?'

She was sobbing into his chest.

'It's OK. They're gone.'

'I'm sorry,' she said. 'I don't want you to see me cry.'

He pulled her closer. From behind the wall, McAvennie called to Charlie. Emily let go of him.

'You'd better go.'

Charlie looked at her. 'He saved you,' he said. 'He just ran out into the street and saved you.'

Emily dried the tears from her cheeks. 'I know.'

Charlie braced and pulled himself up. White pain flashed through his body but he ignored it. McAvennie wanted him and he was not going to let him down. He had to stand up. He put his weight on the good leg and looked down the street into the lane, at the end of which lay the dark and forbidding structure of the large farmhouse. That was why they had come here. The street appeared deserted. Weeds had started to grow up between the kerb and the gutter. His eyes moved upwards, to the roofs. He looked at the spot where he had fired at one of the attackers. A sudden and intense plume of darkness billowed up from beneath him and he physically shook his head to disperse it. He had shot Charlie in the leg, and if Charlie had not killed him then Emily would have still been inside the car, burned alive. There had been no choice.

He noticed one of the large blue water tanks that had appeared when the government was still operating. There was a gash ripped out of its side. Just past it, McAvennie appeared from a house.

'Anybody in there?'

He shook his head despondently.

'Dead,' he said simply.

They found nobody alive. Every one of the houses had been raided. The only place left to check was the farmhouse. The four of them went up the short lane. The hedgerow on either side was laced with brown sinews of dead honeysuckle. Charlie and Emily moved slowly.

There was a large garden in front of the house, covered in gravel. Charlie noticed there were no cars. The front door hung open. McAvennie and David went inside. In silence, Charlie and Emily stood on the gravel courtyard.

They waited. They could see the men moving around through the large windows. The house was in good condition. The windows were new, the brickwork had been restored. Small conifer trees lay on the ground, fallen from pots that had been pushed over.

'What's that?' said Emily. She was peering down a thin alleyway at the side of the house. 'The grass is dead.'

The gravel crunched under her feet as she went towards the edge of the house, craning her neck to see. Charlie followed. At the far end of the alleyway was a lawn with a black line across it where a streak of the grass had died.

The air was colder at the side of the house. Slime had grown along the path and they had to be careful to keep their footing. Slowly, the back garden came into view. The black line in the grass fanned out. The shape was like a funnel, the wide end opening up as it got near the house.

Further into view the garden came. Emily saw it first. She let go of Charlie and screamed. Pain bolted up his leg and he fell against the wall. Emily had jumped back into the alley, her feet sliding in the slime.

Charlie peered out into the garden, worried that another of the snipers was there. But the garden was still. He looked at the thing Emily had seen and his mind froze.

The sliding doors at the back of the house were open and thin white curtains were blowing out into the garden. The blackened grass was like a bulb in front of the windows. In the middle of the blackness, lying on its back, its arms upturned and the fingers of black bone pointing upwards to the sky, was the charred corpse of a human being. The body was as black as coal in most places but in a few patches it was a deep pink, where the flesh underneath had been exposed from animals feeding on the carcass. The mouth was agape in agony. A long metal pole the height of a person had been thrust into its belly. The skeleton had concaved itself where its owner had been trying to reach up to the pole to pull it out.

Charlie tried to understand how a person could ignite somebody like that and then skewer them so grotesquely, but his mind could not assimilate the idea. He went towards the body, unable to stop himself.

Closer, he could see that the black skin had thin striations across it. It looked like fibreglass. There were small needles of pink visible where the surface of the skin had split away. Charlie looked at the body impassively. The eyeballs were gone. The clothes had been burned to nothing, the hair on the skull frazzled into the texture of thin fishing line, contracted and shrunken.

He could see that the person had been a woman. Breasts were discernible on the ribcage, though they were distorted and flattened. He could taste the vomit in his mouth again. He went to throw up but there was nothing left in his stomach. His diaphragm folded inside of him. The darkness swelled all around.

III

A curling stairwell led both up into the lighthouse and down into the ground. On the right was another door leading to an unseen room. The air was cold. A strange sensation came over her. She felt somehow empty, as if her worries were being taken away. Dr Balad seemed to have something that everybody had been in search of for months: answers.

'We go down,' he said, closing the door to the stairwell behind him.

He flicked a switch and bright white light flickered to life with a hum. The walls were thick and secure; the painted red steps gleamed in the light. They came to a single wooden door at which Dr Balad stopped.

'Don't go too close to him.'

He knocked on the door and announced himself before entering.

Cautiously, Miriam stepped forward.

The room was square. Some chairs were stacked in the left-hand corner. In the near corner, just inside the door, was a neatly made camp bed. A desk was set up on the right-hand side. A man was sitting behind it. His face was deathly white, whiter still in the harsh overhead light. A thick clump of unkempt black hair covered the top of his head. His eyes were sunken and his face drawn as if he hadn't eaten enough food for a long time. Miriam had seen many of those faces now.

There was something different about this man, though, something altered. Miriam recognized it as soon as she saw him. The same unexplained feeling that allowed people to tell the sick apart from the well. He looked ill. He looked infected.

His eyes turned on her and she caught his gaze. He stared at her for a few seconds and his lips broke into a grin. His skin stretched and wrinkled at the edges of his mouth like taut cellophane.

'What do you want?' he said.

'Christopher, I'd like you to meet Miriam.'

The man looked at Miriam, maintaining his smile. 'Miriam,' he said quietly. 'The woman from the top of the hill.'

He spoke with a lisp-like speech impediment. He nodded to the empty chair on the other side of the desk.

'Sit,' he said.

There was no paper on the desk. The reason for the man being down here in a near empty room, alone, was difficult to guess. The overhead light was so powerful that the shadows were small and crisp. The man behind the desk had a mass about him that sucked her in. He was dense. She sat down in front of him.

'Christopher came to the camp very recently,' said Dr Balad. 'He offers us great hope.'

As the doctor spoke, the man sitting opposite her lowered his head slightly and looked at Miriam from underneath his brow. The faint grin remained all the while, lips slightly parted, pink tongue moving slowly behind them.

'I am the man who returned,' he said.

'He has a certain way with words,' said Dr Balad with an awkward laugh. He put his hand in his trouser pocket, brushing the hem of his white doctor's coat to one side. 'Christopher was ill. But now he is not.'

It was a few moments before Miriam decoded what the doctor had said. She found herself trying to remain calm but was unable to prevent a quickening of her breath. The front of her head, just behind the eyes, felt light.

The man on the other side of the desk widened his grin as he watched her reaction. He parted his lips far enough to allow his tongue to emerge. Slowly, he ran it across the apron of his top lip.

Miriam jolted backwards in shock. The tongue was forked. It had two points where there should have been one. In the harsh light it looked overly fleshy. The scars in the fork were visible as deep shadowless pits. Its underside was whitish and dry.

'I was ill,' said the man. When he formed an 's' sound it oozed out as a hiss. 'I saw it all. I saw where we stand now – at the cusp of entropy.' He closed his mouth and his grin returned. 'You want to know how I made my tongue?' he said. 'It is a new story. After they cured me, I needed the pain I had been shown.'

Pain. The way in which he said it gave it extra meaning. He punched it out.

'It is nothing more than that. I did not mutilate myself before I was ill. Only after. And it is as simple as that. It is no . . . great . . . shakes. I cut my own tongue out because I longed for the pain. That is what I was shown. We think,' he said, 'that all we want is happiness but that is not true. We are snakes eating our own tails, Miriam.' He said her name slowly. 'We want pain just as much as we want pleasure. The pain defines us in the same way. If it was taken away, you see, we would find it in another form.'

He spoke like he was still infected.

'Is it true that he was ill?' she asked Dr Balad.

The man opposite tilted his head as he looked at her. He appeared to be interested that she was asking questions about him as if he was not there.

'We have no medical way of telling, of course. But . . . we think so. Can you not feel it?'

She hesitated, sensing the doctor's eager anticipation. She could feel it, just as she had felt so many other strange truths through the filter of her new sense.

'Yes,' she answered.

'I feel it also,' he said quietly. 'Take off your shirt, Christopher.'

Slowly, the man rose from his seat. It took several seconds for him to stand fully upright. He was tall and the motion was one akin to unfurling rather than standing. He crossed his arms over each other and grasped the bottom of his shirt. With his eyes trained on Miriam he pulled it up and over his head.

His whole upper torso was covered in surgical stitches. His body had been slashed open and sewn back together. But the dark purple lines were not random. They ran from the area around his kidneys, symmetrically, up his sides to the collarbone, in towards the centre of the chest where they almost joined before snaking back down like train tracks over his heart into his abdomen and then into widening swirls that curled back in towards the middle of the pubic bone, where they finally joined. Instantly, the two swirls at the bottom of his stomach reminded her of inverted devil horns. She knew that her eyes were wide open and her hand had covered her mouth, but her actions were no longer voluntary.

'It's beautiful, isn't it?' he hissed. 'Look at me. I am the man who returned. This is my map.'

'Show her your arms,' said Dr Balad.

'Did you do that to yourself?' she said.

At the back of her mind was the idea that she should not be here, that what she was seeing was something that did not have anything to do with her, but she could not hold the thought. The pattern of the scars was formed in such a way that it sucked her thoughts towards them.

Christopher smiled. 'I did not.'

Miriam swallowed. 'Who?'

He pulled his shirt back over his body and sat down.

'Your arms,' said Dr Balad again.

The man behind the desk was now bored of this conversation. He no longer seemed to relish the way he was being treated by the doctor as an exhibit. Miriam picked up on it, saw his frustration and saw him control his feelings. Their eyes caught and they shared a moment. With reluctance, the man rolled his shirt sleeves up.

'You don't have to.'

'I know I don't,' he said, but continued to roll the sleeves. He placed his hands on the desk and turned his arms over so they were palm upwards, revealing the fleshy underside of his forearms.

She saw the holes, three on each arm, and leaned over for closer inspection. Cylinders of skin and flesh had been removed from his arm. They looked like miniature version of holes in a golf course. The diameter of each circle was that of a pencil. Miriam wondered with horror just what type of a machine could make such a wound.

'How did this happen?'

She looked directly into the tiny holes. They seemed to go right into the centre of the arms, right to the bone. They were so deep that even in the harsh light they were clouded in shadow. The incisions were so smooth and clinical. She could feel Dr Balad watching her.

'The powerful men of the world did it,' said Christopher. 'In their desperation for a solution they decided they would do anything.'

The dynamic in the room had shifted. He was talking more normally. The malevolence she had felt from him had not gone, but it had waned.

'Well, they found their solution,' he said.

'Why did they need to do this to you?'

'It worked, didn't it?'

He glowered at her and she felt instantly vulnerable again.

Dr Balad spoke. 'I have never seen such a thing done to a person before.'

Miriam ignored him.

'Was it the government?'

'It was done at a . . . facility.'

She remembered the place she had been taken to after Henry's father was killed. There was the doctor who had freed her. And there was something else: the feeling of unease, of being trapped, of seeing all the ill people there, collected up from the streets by spacemen in suits from the future. They were unknowing and unwilling. She remembered the doctor's shock when he realized she was not ill, his determination to let her go, to get her away from the place. And then she remembered something that in all the times she had thought back on the moment she had not recollected: the screaming that echoed down the corridors. She looked at the man opposite once more.

'We are all doomed,' he said. 'This camp, it is nothing. You saw what happened the first time the world was decimated. It will happen again. A little push this way, or a little push that way, and this camp will all come tumbling down. Badness is too strong a force. It is too destructive. Goodness is too passive. The time will come.' He looked at her deeply. 'You know it will.'

She held his stare.

'Why do you think you are here?' he said. 'Hmm?' He tilted his head but she was not frightened of him. 'Why are you the guest of honour?'

'Christopher, that's enough,' said Dr Balad.

'They want your house,' he said.

'Do not listen to him, Miriam, he says these things for effect.'

Christopher smiled. His tongue emerged from his lips again.

Miriam stood slowly and they went to leave.

'Who are you going to trust?' said the man, as the door to the room swung shut. 'Them? Or me?'

III

When they reached ground level again they stopped.

'Can we go up there?' she said.

'No.'

Above them, up in the upper heights of the lighthouse, she could hear footsteps moving over a wooden floor. A voice called out. It sounded like an order, but the words were muffled.

'You have to understand,' said Dr Balad. 'The people up there are doomed. They *will* die.'

'Can you not cure them? Now that you have –' she failed to find the words – 'that man?'

'We do not know how he was cured. We do not know the process, or the drugs. I showed you the man only because of what he means. And that is that the illness does not have to win. We do have a chance, Miriam.'

'Why do you keep him down there?'

'We didn't at first. When he came to the camp he was living with everybody else, but he was . . . a nuisance. He would walk around the camp at night and frighten people. And so we offered him the room in the lighthouse. It is funny because nobody had known about the door that led beneath the lighthouse until he arrived. It seems strange now, does it not? That we had not seen something as clear as a door in the wall?'

She could hear the rumbling of a generator from somewhere outside.

'You know,' said Dr Balad, 'what he just said? About who will you trust? It is always difficult for people to trust us here because it seems so strange, that we exist so peacefully. We know this. But I will tell you that we can be trusted. I hope you will come to realize this, because trust is so important a thing.'

|||

When she got back to the house it did not look the same. She saw just how cold and damp it had become. She went to the back garden and looked over the wall at the grave. It wasn't even there any more. It was just grass now. Joseph's animal paddocks were still empty. Placing her hand on her stomach she waited for a kick but nothing came.

As she moved slowly back into the conservatory she heard a knock at the front door. Her mother was standing in the hallway.

'It's the Scottish man from the camp,' she said. 'He's back.'

Miriam went towards the door but her mother stopped her.

'You know you can tell me what happened,' she said.

Miriam turned away and went down the hall. She thought of the man with the forked tongue, sitting inside the earth, in the little room beneath the lighthouse. Is that what her mother had meant? She opened the door.

'Can I come in?' McAvennie said.

They sat down at the kitchen table.

'We were attacked,' he said.

Miriam tried not to show emotion. She was not part of the camp; it had nothing to do with her.

'They . . .' he paused. 'They killed everyone – the farmer who owns all the land behind your house, his wife, all of the folk who lived in the wee hamlet there.'

Miriam faltered. 'There are terrible people out there,' she muttered.

'This was different,' he said. 'They weren't killing for protection, or to steal.' He looked at her, hoping she would understand his meaning. He was sitting with his back to the window, his face in shadow. 'They just . . . did it.'

'And so why come to me?'

McAvennie composed himself.

'You're not safe up here.' He knitted his hands together, put them on the table and leaned forward. 'These . . . men. They've been burning farmland, ruining crops. And there's a lot of them. We'd heard they were out there. There've been rumours of them for months: men dressed in black clothes and gas masks.'

He noticed the change in her.

'It's their *thing*. Look.' He fished something out of his pocket. It was an Ordnance Survey map of the area. McAvennie unfolded it with his large hands, laid it out on the table and spun it round so it was the right way up for her.

'Here.' He tapped the map with a chubby forefinger. Black shapes circled fields, hand-drawn in ink, with crosses marked out. The shapes formed a semi-circle. It began ten miles to the west of the lighthouse and swept round to a few miles east of Miriam's house. 'They're closing in on us.'

Miriam shook her head. She thought about the sick feeling she had felt in the supermarket that day, when the aisles had been filled with smoke and the looters had crept through it, moving like insects.

'They'll hit you first,' said McAvennie.

'They'd be pretty stupid to come round here, with all the people living down on the camp.'

'They're not doing this to survive,' he said. 'And they're not scared of us. They've burned whole fields. What kind of a person does that, eh?' He leaned back in his chair. 'There's something else I need to tell you, Miriam. You got your two bairns, yes?'

'What about them?'

McAvennie scratched the back of his head. 'We know the folks who lived down in the hamlet had children. I'd seen them myself.'

Her body went cold.

'We couldnae find any kids in the houses. We found their parents, aye, but the kids?' He shook his head and looked at her. 'No sign. They must've been there – they had their wee bedrooms all made up.' He tapped the table with a nervous finger. 'No kids.'

She couldn't look at him. 'What do you think happened to them?'

McAvennie shrugged. 'Your guess is as good as mine.' He left it at that.

Miriam looked out into the hallway to check the children were not hiding outside. Her brain could not pinpoint any one idea.

'What do you think we should do?'

McAvennie breathed out heavily through his nose. 'Come to the camp.'

She shook her head. 'I can't.'

'Why not, Miriam?'

'I just can't.'

'You can trust us.'

She allowed the words to hang in the air. He clearly didn't understand that she could not risk her family's safety down at the camp. There were just too many people down there. She didn't want to be amongst them.

'Do you have kids?' she said.

'I did. I had a son who died,' he said plainly.

She went to say something, opened her mouth, but nothing came out.

'He got ill. My wife too.' His face was impassive. 'But they both died in the camp, aye? I know what you're thinking, Miriam. You're thinking you cannae trust so many people. You came from London? You saw what happened. But I trusted the folk down on the camp. I took my family there.'

'I'm so sorry,' she whispered.

He waved his hand. 'It's in the past now.'

She waited.

'I do think about them but what good does it do? I can think all I want, they ain't coming back.'

'George,' she said. 'I want you to understand.' She put her hand on the table. 'I used to have faith in people, I really did. Joseph, my brother-in-law, used to hate it. He said I was naive and all that stuff, but I always thought it was important to give people the benefit of the doubt.'

'If you show people kindness, you can gain their trust,' he said.

'But I was wrong,' she said, gaining strength. 'If there's one thing I know now, it's that people are dangerous. I don't mean people like you, I mean people on the whole. They're just too . . . selfish, I guess.'

McAvennie made a clicking noise with his mouth. 'It's funny,' he said. 'You don't seem like the sort of person who'd say something like that.'

'I'm not. I wasn't.'

McAvennie leaned forward. 'You can trust us.'

Something flashed in her head. The man in the lighthouse. He had said something to her: who will you trust? She looked at the man sitting across from her, and at the map on the table. They want your house – that was what he had said.

She folded her arms across her chest. 'We'll stay here.'

McAvennie sighed.

'Just for the time being. We'll see what happens.'

'I think you're making a mistake,' he said.

'I know.'

He folded the map back up from the table and went to stand. 'You know what I heard?'

Miriam shook her head.

'It was something my first boss used to say. He used to say smile and the world smiles with you.' With surprising delicacy he tucked the chair silently under the table.

'My grandfather used to say that to me.'

They looked at each other.

'Do you believe it?'

Miriam blinked. She was tired and needed to sleep. 'Maybe,' she said. 'Sometimes.'

McAvennie became still. 'You know,' he said. 'We had a guy come in to my work once to tell us about teamwork. He told us about this experiment they did in America. They had five thousand people in a dark room and in front of them was a giant screen and every person had an electric wand in their hand.' He leaned on the back of the chair. 'The screen showed a view from the cockpit of an aeroplane coming in to land. So, the people in the crowd, all five thousand of them, had to land the plane together. Their wands had wee sensors in them linked up to a computer that controlled the plane. None of them had any experience, none of them were allowed to speak. All they knew was the left side of the crowd was left and the right side was right. The people at the front could dip the nose and the people at the back could pull it up. So in they went and do you know what happened?'

Miriam shook her head.

'They went in and they went too steep and at an angle. They were missing the runway. But they didn't crash. When they realized they were missing, all of them, without saying anything, pulled up into the air. Then they circled round and flew in a few more times, never making it, but never crashing either. And they did it as one. There were five thousand of them but they were one pilot. And they did it. They got it down in the end. They landed it. I mean, don't you think that's incredible?'

'I guess so.'

'See, people think they have to struggle alone, that they're not linked, but that ain't true, Miriam. It really isn't.'

|||

It was so dark. The clouds had settled low over the fields and the night sky was nothing but a black void. Miriam was standing on the road in front of the house, looking in the direction of the village to the east. She could see nothing, not even the line between the land and the sky. She could have been blind. The darkness could have been just in front of her face, or hundreds of yards away.

The night before she had dreamed again of Henry being pulled into the sea by a monster and the beach catching fire. But the dream had changed. It had a new beginning. She was no longer standing in a library. It now began in the cellar, with her lying on the floor, a dark figure standing over her. Behind the figure she could make out a line of light where the door at the top of the stairs was ajar.

She put a hand on her belly. Soon there would be no hiding it. The bulge was beginning to show. Perhaps it would be a boy, she thought. The image of the line of light in the cellar cut through the darkness. Whenever the memory of what had happened came back to her, she would toss it aside. Memory was just something in her head. It had no physical basis. It could play tricks, it was unreliable. And if it did not exist, then there was no need to concern herself about it.

She looked again into the darkness. She tried to focus on the distance. Where was it? The idea of men lurking in the dark, circling the house, waiting to attack, chilled her. The point where she had cared about her own safety was long since past but she still felt it so strongly for her children. How could she possibly keep them safe?

She had seen the men who were out there, the things they had done. Dread crept through her veins and between the bones of her skeleton. Everything was about to change. She turned towards the house.

When they had first started dating, Henry had brought Miriam to Cornwall. It was the first time she had met Joseph. She still remembered how funny he had been, how charming. The sun had been shining and the walls of the house had been recently painted. Joseph was with his partner at the time – Deborah, or Diana, wasn't it? They had sat in the back garden in the shade of the old tree. Their mother was still alive and she had made fresh lemonade. Miriam had thought at the time how perfectly quaint their way of life seemed. Life was so full of hope and prospects then. Everything seemed so solid, so unassailable.

She pulled her hat down over her head. Sometimes she still thought she would wake up in that same bed in London and Henry would be there, still alive and still himself. She was aware that she was crying only because the wind made her tears cold on her face.

Crouching down in the road, she lost her balance and rolled on to her side. And there she lay. She brought her legs up into the foetal position to keep the baby warm. She imagined it doing the same thing inside her. That the life in her womb would experience the world in this state brought a wave of desperation.

'Miri?'

Her mother's voice was behind her, her hand was on her side.

Miriam didn't reply.

She saw the line of the light in the cellar doorway and felt

Joseph's cold, rough hands on her. His strength pressed down on her and she was pinned against the floor.

'He raped me, Mum,' she said.

When the words came out her whole body felt empty. A vacuum was left where the words had waited.

Her mother sat her up in the road and put her arms round her neck.

'I'm pregnant.'

She was sure her mother already knew, but she said it anyway.

Her mother squeezed her and she was transported back to her childhood. There was a level of safety in the embrace that she had not remembered her whole adult life. It was the safety that could only come from having complete, unthinking trust. Her mother held her tight.

In the cellar, Joseph pulled away from her and receded into the darkness to die. And at the top of the stairs she saw it: a line of golden light at the edge of the doorway, slowly widening, opening, to reveal the flames of the burning beach.

III

Rumours were already going around that something bad had happened. Faint whispers ebbed between the lines of tents and caravans. Charlie, Emily and Fields were sitting on chairs behind the stage, down on the beach. McAvennie was sitting at a table next to them, looking over the map. Beyond the stage Charlie heard the drone of people talking quietly. He could feel the pain in his leg trying to hurt him but the anaesthetic he had been given when they took the bullet out had not yet worn off.

McAvennie stood up and walked off to the side of the stage to look out on the beach.

Emily leaned in to Charlie. 'What do you think he'll say?'

'I don't know,' he answered.

McAvennie ran his hand over the top of his bald head. There were some metal steps at the back of the stage. He put his hand on the flimsy handrail and pulled himself up. The steps wobbled precariously under his weight as he ascended. He walked to the centre of the stage and his body turned orange as he went into the glow of the firelight. The sound of the people changed. Their volume dropped. He tapped the microphone. Dull thuds rang out around the cliffs.

'Is it on? OK. Hello,' he said.

Charlie smiled. This was the fifth time he had seen the big man speak and every time he started in this nervous way.

'So,' he said.

And stopped. He surveyed the crowd of people in front of him. Charlie struggled to his feet so he could see out over the top of the low stage. He looked at the orange faces of the crowd in the darkness, looking upwards expectantly at their leader. He could feel the tension striking between them.

'Most of you have probably heard by now about what happened to one of the salvage missions.'

The crowd stayed silent.

'It is true,' he said. 'They were ambushed. The attack was planned and it was efficient. Five men were killed.'

Charlie heard somebody in the crowd moan. Many of those in the front row dropped their heads. He turned around to see Emily. She caught his eye and smiled nervously.

'They let one of them go. Our man Andrew Fields. He came back.'

The crowd waited for more.

McAvennie's gait was slouched.

'What those . . . people . . . did. It is frightening,' he said.

Charlie swallowed hard. McAvennie was telling the truth.

'There are people out there who would wish us harm.' The intensity of the silence between sentences was almost palpable. 'I am going to be honest with you. But I must state again that it is my utmost belief that if we stick together then we can make it through this. I say it now because it may be that soon that belief is something you will question. When we are pushed into danger it is easy to fall apart, but if we fall apart, we fall. You understand?' He paused for breath. 'Many of you have heard rumours of this band of criminals. I had heard about them, moving around, stealing, burning, making harm. But they're not rumours any more, OK? These people are real. And they've sent us a message.' He adjusted the way he was standing. 'By sending Andrew back, they wanted us to know what had happened. They wanted us to know what they had done.'

The crowd had started moving. The people were uncomfortable. There was murmuring.

'They've been attacking places around the area for months now. They attacked the supermarket in town, they've raided villages, burned whole fields of crops. And they killed Farmer Thompson and his wife.'

'It's pointless,' somebody shouted through the silence.

'Aye, aye. It is,' McAvennie agreed. 'It is pointless. They are cruel.' He stopped again. 'But we are not. And that is why we will survive.'

The crowd was becoming agitated.

'Hold on a moment, now hold on,' he said, raising his hand. 'We've made a map of the places we know they've hit. They've been attacking places all around the camp, moving inwards.'

The whole crowd made a deep, discordant sound of shock. McAvennie allowed them to take a moment for the news to sink in. They needed it. He waited patiently.

'Where are they now?' a woman shouted.

'We don't know.'

More talking.

'How can you not know?' came another voice.

'Just stop,' said McAvennie.

Charlie felt a sense of growing chaos in the air. He was losing the crowd. They were buckling.

'Sssh,' McAvennie said into the microphone. 'Quieten down now.'

But the voices grew. Charlie watched in disbelief.

'Please,' McAvennie said again. 'Just wait.' His voice was sterner.

The people in the front few rows looked up at him again and stopped talking. The volume of the crowd fell away.

'I know how you are feeling. I feel it too. It's only natural to be worried. But we must work together.'

'Fuck that – we need a plan,' somebody shouted angrily.

'Aye, we do,' McAvennie reassured them. 'And we will make

one. But you must understand that it is not so easy. We don't know where they are. Should we go looking for them?'

'Yes,' said the angry voice.

'Who? Who should go looking?'

To this, there was no answer.

'They are dangerous, cruel people. If we were to send people out to look for them, they would be killed. There are more of us, this is what we have on our side. If we send people out then we give up that advantage.'

'So what? We just wait for them to come to us?'

'Perhaps,' answered McAvennie. 'What have we always said? Empathy, compassion, trust, aye?'

The crowd mumbled. It was obvious to Charlie that this was the last thing they wanted to hear.

'What's wrong?' said McAvennie. His voice was louder. It rang out. 'What? Now that things are getting tougher it won't work?'

The crowd was silent.

'That it worked while things were good but it won't work when things are bad? Your solution is to fight back, just have a fight – is that it?' He looked at them, his head shaking from side to side. 'This is a sight I didnae want to see. Has nothing I said meant anything to you? Hmm? Have you really only stayed here because you get food and shelter and be damned with the rest?' He tapped his finger to his head. 'Think,' he said. 'Think about it. I can't just guide you through this. I'm not your guardian angel. We're all in this together. If something good happens, it is because of all of us, not me. If something bad happens, it is not my fault; there's no room for blame any more. That's part of the old world.' He gestured at the space behind him, the past. 'Remember what I said before to you? About darkness being the absence of light? Well, think about that. We are the light. We are not going to become like them,' he said, sweeping his arm into the air. 'We are not going to burn things, or needlessly kill people. You think I'm not a realist? I am. You think I lack courage?' He looked at the crowd but nobody answered. 'I promise you I don't. But consider this: everything we have done here, everything, has been based on the idea of kindness. And look at what we've got. Would you really be so willing to go back to the old ways so easily? We don't need to start fighting. Not yet. It has to be the very last resort. And if we compromise these new ways once, what then? It's backsliding, and I do nae want to do that. If we go back to the old ways, this place will fall apart. I guarantee you that.'

The crowd were hushed. There was an electric buzz in the air. He seemed to have won them over. For now. He turned away from the microphone and came towards the back of the stage. As he descended the metal steps Charlie could see the look of worry on his face.

Emily stood up from her chair.

'George,' she called.

The Scot saw her and stood there at the bottom of the steps. The image of him pulling Emily out of the burning car blazed up in Charlie's mind.

He came over to her and the bond between them was immediate and strong. Emily stepped forwards. McAvennie was unable to hide how upset he was.

'Thank you,' she said.

McAvennie's smile was weak. 'I was just doing what anyone else would have done.'

'You saved me.' She lowered her head. 'And I want to say that what you're doing here –' she nodded to the camp – 'I think it's amazing.'

'Thank you, Emily.'

Something flickered across his face and when it was gone his energy had started to kindle in his eyes again. Emily touched Charlie's hand. He linked his fingers through hers.

'It makes you proud to be a part of something like this, you know, after everything that's happened. And I just wanted to say it. Because that's how I feel.'

|||

Two weeks passed. New salvage teams were sent out and all returned home safely. Nothing was heard of the men in black clothes. There had been no fresh attacks. Some people had left the camp out of fear, whilst others arrived with meagre possessions and gaunt bodies and tales of how they had found themselves still alive in this new, dangerous world.

A week after McAvennie's speech the sun had set through a veil of purple haze hanging over the horizon. Hundreds of people went down to the beach to watch it. Miriam and her family were joined on the cliff top by what people remained in the village to the east – the same people who had come when the tanker first ran aground that night. When the sun sank into the haze it turned from orange to red. It became massive in the sky; its corona flickered and spat. As Miriam looked at it she thought of her baby and the life it could have if things would only work out well. It would be born into a strange world, but it needn't be a hopeless one. There is always that see-saw, she thought: hope on one side, despair on the other.

Emily had stood next to Charlie outside their campervan and he had put his arm around her. Her mind became light and she thought of a day in her childhood when she had watched a boy sitting underneath the apple tree that grew in the field behind her house. There had been a stillness in that day she had fallen in love with, and she had looked for it since, for that pocket of serenity in the hustle and bustle of life, but she'd never found it again.

McAvennie had been on the main gates when the sun moved into the haze. He had sat down in one of the plastic chairs, turned it towards the sea and let the gentle heat of it warm his face. He closed his eyes and thought of the harbour in the village where he had been brought up, and remembered his father coming home on the fishing boats.

When Miriam's mother saw it she thought of her wedding day, of confetti flakes drifting slowly before her eyes, of the sound of people laughing and clapping. Life had looked so full.

Mary had run to the edge of the cliff, right out to where the grass fell away to nothing. The sun looked as if it was so close that if she ran fast enough and jumped far enough she might be able to land on its surface and walk on the mountains there and lie amongst the red flowers her father had told her about.

Edward had followed her. He had walked slowly, with his hands in his pockets, not thinking of anything. He wanted to make sure Mary didn't go too close to the edge.

When Charlie saw it he thought for a moment that its sight would burn away the black clouds of darkness, but it didn't. The clouds remained. The deep orange sky and the huge red orb made him feel desperate. His heart scratched against his ribs and he thought of the man he had killed in the small hamlet next to the farmhouse. He kept seeing the silhouette of the man's head appear at the roof. He hadn't even thought about what he was about to do – he just did it. That was perhaps the hardest thing to accept. The image was becoming seared on to him.

||||

Charlie was waking up early. The cold made his leg ache. The wound had recovered well for the first week; there had been no infection and when the pain came, as it did at times, it was easily bearable. But now the aching was worse and he was still unable to put normal pressure on it. When he walked without his crutch it was with a limp, and the limp was becoming more pronounced.

A recent salvage had brought back rolls of plastic, formed into grids that could be laid down as walkways. There were several areas of pathway that had become almost impassable with mud. The work the men were doing was exhausting and dirty. But it was good work. The pathways were welcomed.

They were working near the top of the hill, near Charlie's camper-van. At the far end of the village of tents was the structure of the school that was being built. It was almost finished. Charlie watched a man straddle the roof and hammer tacks into the roofing material.

Fields came and stood next to him.

'You OK, Charlie?'

Charlie nodded. 'I'm fine.'

'You don't seem it.'

The man on the roof of the school building shimmied along it. Charlie watched vacantly as he reached into a cloth sack tied to his belt, pulled out a tack and hammered it into the roof. He was so far away that the sound of the hammer blow was inaudible.

'You don't seem yourself.'

'I'm OK.'

'You can't let things consume you, man,' said Fields.

'I'm not.'

'When you came here you were full of beans. You need to get it back. Get your mojo back.'

Charlie sniffed.

'Wanna talk about it?'

'I'm fine, honestly. I'm just tired.'

The man down below shimmied across the apex of the school roof again and started hammering. When he did it reminded Charlie of the man on the roof in the hamlet; his head snapping back violently, a tiny black stain against white sky, there and then gone. The sound of slapping footsteps echoed up the hill and one of the little kids came running towards them. He had a mop of blond hair that he had to brush out of his eyes.

'Mr Fields, Mr Fields,' he said, breathlessly.

Fields and Charlie stared at the child.

'My dad said to fetch you,' he managed to pant. 'Can you come down?'

|||

They followed the boy down the slope and into the middle of the tented village. Charlie had never been in between the tents before. Only when you were in amongst them did it become clear just how many there were. There was just a foot or two of space between one flysheet and the next. The guy ropes criss-crossed like spider webs, making it impossible to navigate a path through without stepping over them. The place was a mud bath near the centre. Charlie realized just how easy he and Emily had it living up near the top of the camp.

Somewhere behind the canvas walls of the tents he could hear raised voices. Two men were arguing. One of them was holding a bucket. He was short and squat with a red face.

'You did, I saw you do it,' said the other man, who was taller with thin blond hair and glasses.

'Why have you got to be such a dick about it?' said the squat man.

Fields strode up to them. 'Oh-kay, what's going on here?'

The man with the bucket turned to him. 'You stay out of this, Yankee.'

'He was pouring his piss away,' said the blond man.

The squat man raised his face to the sky in exasperation. 'So what?' he said, impatiently. 'What difference does it make?'

'It's the rules.'

'Yeah? Whose rules, Benjamin? Not mine.'

Fields spoke. 'You can leave if you don't like the rules.'

The man snapped his head around. 'I told you to stay out of this.' He seemed more agitated than he should have been. There was a volatility that Charlie could sense was about to overflow. 'So I poured it away, big deal.'

'It is a big deal,' Fields replied calmly.

But Fields's calm only served to heighten the squat man's agitation. He looked at Fields, and Charlie thought for a moment he was about to lash out.

'It's not even that far to the toilet,' said the blond man.

The squat man shook his head and then, slowly, dropped the bucket and put his hands over his face. The moment froze.

'You know what?' he said. 'Fine.'

He picked up his bucket and walked away from the group, round to the front of the tent. Charlie heard him rummaging inside. They went round to the front and Fields looked inside.

'Come on, man, don't do this.'

'Leave me alone.'

Charlie noticed that the little blond kid who had fetched them was standing in the near distance, watching the scene.

'What are you doing?' said Fields.

'What does it look like?'

Fields turned to Charlie and the blond man. 'He's packing up.'

The blond man snorted. 'Good riddance,' he said, loud enough for the man inside the tent to hear. 'As if we haven't got enough problems here already.'

Fields sighed.

Charlie looked at the blond man. He had bad skin and watery blue eyes. The squat man had been in the wrong but Charlie found himself siding with him. The way his body had relaxed when he had dropped his bucket spoke loudly to him.

He emerged from the tent flustered and out of breath. He had packed his things into a large suitcase with an extendable handle that was clearly never intended for a camping holiday and when Charlie saw it he caught a glimpse of the man's past life. In that one out-of-place object he saw how much the man had lost, how much everybody had lost.

The blond man watched him impassively, arms folded, as he went about disassembling his tent.

'Please stop,' Fields pleaded, his shoulders hunched. 'Where are you going to go?'

'I don't know.'

Charlie could not stay quiet any more. 'Don't go.'

'It's OK, mate,' he said, his eyes flicking to him. Everybody knew he was the kid who had been shot in the leg. 'I'll be all right.'

'Why don't you just pitch up somewhere else? Somewhere away from him?' Charlie said. He felt emboldened by the way the blond man was behaving. 'Wouldn't that be better than just leaving?'

But the squat man was stubborn and could not be persuaded. He packed his tent and rolled it up.

'You can't last out there,' said Fields, finally.

'I can't last in here, either,' he said. 'I'm fed up with it. I'm fed up of living like this, getting covered in shit every day. It's no way to live.'

'Life is harder out there,' said Fields, pointing.

'I'm sorry for calling you a Yankee,' said the man.

Fields laughed. 'Believe me, buddy, I've been called a lot worse. Come on. Don't go.'

He shook his head. 'I have to.' He went to leave.

Charlie stepped in front of him. 'Wait,' he said. He put his two arms out and placed them on the man's shoulders. 'Please don't do this.' The man's eyes were dark green and they stared at him without the emotion Charlie had expected to see. 'You don't know what's out there,' he said quickly, his mind flushing hot. 'The raiders that are out there . . .'

'Kid, I'm not scared any more.'

He went to step around Charlie, but Charlie moved to block him.

'They won't just kill you,' he said.

The deep green eyes flickered. Charlie thought about all the things the man in front of him had seen during the course of his life, and how nobody would ever know about them because if he left he would fade into history like he had never been there. Nobody would remember him. The darkness shunted forward.

'Let him go,' said the blond man, uncaringly.

'Shut up,' Charlie said, losing himself. His brain was losing its grip.

'We all stick to the rules,' the blond man continued, 'because we know it's the right thing to do.'

The squat man brushed Charlie's hands off his shoulders. 'Ben's right, mate,' he said.

'He's not.' Charlie's voice had faded to a whisper.

'Charlie.' Fields's tone was filled with kindness. 'If he wants to leave he can leave.'

'But you'll die,' he whispered.

He was fully aware now that everybody there was looking at him.

The squat man smiled. 'It doesn't matter.'

How could it not matter? Charlie could not understand it.

The blond man put his hands in his pockets. Charlie looked at Fields, and the tall American nodded to him. He lowered his head and stepped aside for the squat man to pass, and as he wheeled his suitcase through the mud along the only path with no guy ropes Charlie heard him say, 'Take care, Charlie,' before he disappeared.

The three remaining men stood there for a moment until, at last, the blond man said, 'Well it's good riddance as far as I'm concerned. He was always going to be trouble.'

|||

They found the Christmas decorations in the attic of the house and had trimmed up as usual. The decorations were dated and reminded Miriam of how Christmas had been when she was a child. But there was no tree. Henry's father had always used a real tree and the decorations they hung about the house seemed without substance with no focal point.

Edward had got into trouble a few days ago when he had gone into the woods behind the house and returned with carrier bags filled with holly sprigs. The holly now adorned the tops of the picture frames around the house.

The baby was getting heavier. Her back hurt and she found herself getting tired easily. She had to sit down to put on her shoes. That was something she had forgotten. Sometimes she could feel bony protrusions pushing against her stomach, rolling along underneath its surface as the baby moved. She needed more food than she ate but there was none available. The vegetable patch yielded little in the winter and the stores of tinned food in the cellar were almost gone.

Miriam and her mother had rationed the food they had left to last until the end of January. They would have liked to ration it further because winter would not be over by then but it was impossible. There was hardly enough as it was. When she was having Edward and Mary she had gained weight. But not this time. The baby was taking too much of the food for itself and leaving Miriam hungry.

It was not until Christmas Eve that Mary first mentioned presents. When she asked she did so in a guilty way, as if she knew it was not right but she couldn't resist.

'Things are going to be a little different this year,' Miriam told her daughter.

Mary's large, round eyes surveyed her mother.

'Christmas is not always about presents,' she went on. 'It's about being with your family – with me, and Gran, and Edward.' The words were not going to be enough, Miriam could tell.

The shifting lines on her daughter's face described her disappointment.

'Is Father Christmas OK?'

Miriam smiled inwardly. If Mary were not eight years old she would have thought the question was phrased in such a way that it would force a concession from her.

'He's OK, but he might be stuck at the North Pole this year.'

'So he's not dead?'

Miriam brushed Mary's hair away from her face. 'No,' she said.

That evening they sat on the floor around the coffee table in the living room and had a large open fire as a special treat. They had made a loaf of bread, which they toasted with the toasting fork over the hot flames.

'This is how people would spend Christmas in the olden days,' their grandmother told the children.

They took the board games out of the airing cupboard and played until past midnight. The excitement of Christmas kept the children wide awake and Miriam let them stay up. The fire was warm and it soothed her body. She was tired but the children's enthusiasm was infectious enough to keep her awake.

They went to bed at just after one o'clock in the morning. Miriam sat down on the edge of her bed and hoisted her feet up. She pulled the blanket over her, right up to her neck, and fell asleep instantly.

When she awoke, it was to the smiling faces of her whispering children. They wanted to go downstairs. The old custom in London had been for them to wait in their bedrooms until they were told it was OK to go downstairs, where their presents would lie, underneath the tree and hung in stockings above the fireplace, and though the setting had changed they had not broken with tradition.

When she threw the blankets off the dull pain of cold settled over her skin.

'But you know that Father Christmas couldn't come, don't you?' she said, addressing Mary.

Edward stepped in. 'It doesn't matter,' he said.

They went downstairs and into the kitchen. There had been a frost again. The sky was filled with a thin grey mist leading up into a thick white soup of cloud. The whole world was without colour.

Mary ran out to the living room and returned a few minutes later, looking despondent. Miriam thought of how if Henry had still been alive he would have done something for the kids. He would have made sure of it. She thought she might start crying and so she stood up from the table and went to the front door for air. She pulled it open and looked out at the big grey sea. The tide was in and the swell was high. And then her eyes were drawn to the front step and her breath faltered.

On the ground was a cloth sack the size of an old dustbin bag.

It had not been tied at the top and she could see that the sack was stuffed full of wrapped presents. She looked around to see if there was anybody near, but the road running past the house was empty. She was crying now. She went to call the kids but her voice failed her. She looked down towards the camp, at all the little tents popping up out of the hillside, and thought of the people inside them, and then stared back down at the sack of presents.

III

The new year came. It rained on the first day and on the second day the rain in the road turned to ice. In the camp, the slippery mud in the pathways between the tents became hard and irregular. McAvennie had told Charlie that in the time between Christmas Day and new year, seventeen people had died. Sixteen of the illness. One had died of exposure; an old man who had been found in his tent. He had lived on his own since his wife had succumbed to the illness. His body had frozen into a solid block.

The cold snap made Charlie's leg hurt. Despite the pain he continued helping Fields and the other men with the laying of the plastic walkways. Christmas had come and gone and the depth of winter thickened all around them. And still there was no sign of the raiders who had attacked the farmhouse.

Charlie looked, as he so often did when he was standing around watching the men work, down to the camp. The bright colours of the tents were fading as layers of dust and mud slowly settled on them. The progress of the school building was slow. He couldn't see any difference in it from one day to the next.

He turned back to the workers. One of the men, who had been shovelling out a muddy pool, threw down his spade and put his hands on his knees.

'Fuck it,' he said.

Charlie was standing further down the hill on his own, holding some of the long metal stakes used to pin the tracks to the ground. He looked at the man.

'I can't do this any more,' he said.

Fields limped over to him and put his hand on his back. He was talking to him quietly, out of Charlie's earshot. The man shook his head. Charlie turned away.

Further down the hill he caught a glimpse of something passing between a gap in the tents. His eyes followed the direction of the movement. A man emerged. Charlie recognized him immediately. It was the man with the forked tongue. He was wearing a pair of old, ill-fitting trousers and a tattered shirt. He looked different in the daylight. He looked more human, but there was still something overtly dangerous in him; in the way he moved, swaggered. His body was long and thin and fluid.

Charlie looked back up the hill towards Fields. He was still talking to the man who had thrown his shovel down, and when he turned back his chest tightened. The man with the forked tongue was standing in the centre of the path just yards away.

'I hear you got shot,' he said, and walked towards him. 'In the leg.'

His face was so white, his eyes a translucent green.

Charlie's mouth went dry. He became aware of the ever decreasing space between him and the approaching man.

'In the leg,' Charlie repeated in agreement. 'Your name is Mims, right?' He tried to sound casual, or friendly, or both.

'You're scared of me, aren't you?'

'What? No,' he said with a half-laugh.

'I guess there are a lot of rumours going around about me.'

Until he had started speaking, Charlie had forgotten how Mims's 's's came out as a hiss because of the way his tongue had been cut.

'I haven't heard any rumours,' he lied.

'I know what you're thinking,' said Mims.

'I'm not thinking anything.'

'You're thinking, does he remember me?'

Charlie felt his skin condense in fear. He didn't want to be afraid of him.

'I don't like you, Charlie. That's just the way it is. I have singled you out, from all the people in the camp, for no reason other than I can, and there's nothing you can do about it. I've been watching you a lot recently.' He stepped forward again. 'But today is the day.'

Charlie looked back up the hill towards Fields. The American saw Mims and turned. There was a pause.

'Hey,' called Fields.

The fist struck Charlie at his temple without him even seeing it. His body spun round and he stuck out his bad leg instinctively for support. When his weight went on to it a pulse of pain shuddered up him and he fell to the floor. He turned his head just as Mims leaped at him, his face filling his whole field of vision. Charlie caught a glimpse of the forked tongue between his lips.

'I'm going to kill you,' he whispered.

Charlie's brain tried to process what was happening. Another fist landed, this time on the other side of the face.

'I haven't done anything to you,' he said, quickly and clearly.

'Doesn't matter. There is no *reason*. Remember?'

When he was struck the third time a high-pitched tinnitus rang in his ears. His arms were pinned at his side and his face was exposed. He closed his eyes.

The weight of the body on top of him was suddenly gone. There was shouting and the sound of a scuffle. Charlie opened his eyes. Three of the men who had been helping lay the matting were struggling with Mims. When he saw that Charlie was looking at him, he stopped struggling and smiled at him menacingly. His green eyes glinted in the white light of the clouds.

'I bet you didn't expect that,' he said, grinning. 'Look at you all. You'll see. You'll see what happens when the bad people come.'

Fields helped Charlie up.

'You're cut,' he said.

The three men pulled Mims down the hill towards the car park. Charlie used his sleeve to clear the blood away from the corner of his eye. His thoughts were slowing but his body felt energized. A dull throb had started in his head. He looked up at the grey sky and at the tiny white flakes drifting slowly downwards, black against the clouds.

'Oh my God,' he said. 'It's snowing.'

|||

The snow floated gently down in small flakes. The sea wind caught it in its breeze and spun it into swirling columns drifting inland. Edward and Mary watched it from their grandmother's bedroom window.

Edward took Joseph's binoculars from the sill and peered through them. He had heard something in school about how snow was rare near the sea. They watched for a little while longer and soon the colours of the landscape began to fade. The green of the grass was bleached as the snow started to settle.

'Come on,' said Edward, 'let's go outside.'

They ran downstairs and pulled on their overcoats and wellington boots and ran out of the front door into the snow. The wind had dissipated and now the snow fell directly down in straight, silent lines.

'Listen to how quiet it is,' Edward said.

His little sister craned her neck forward and turned her head to listen.

There was no sound of anything at all. Edward thought the fact that snow was silent was a wonderful thing. He looked up into the sky, leaning back so far that he had to put his leg out to stop himself falling. The snowflakes landed on his face, their only signal being the little cold patches on his cheeks. He opened his mouth and tried to catch them.

'Look at that,' she said. 'They're out again.'

She was pointing down to the beach.

Edward looked through the binoculars. The kids from the camp were playing football. A crashing sense of loneliness and boredom fired through him out of nowhere. He was starting to recognize more of them. As well as the tall blond one who seemed to be the leader, there was the fat one with brown hair and glasses who always went in goal, the little red-haired one who was the fastest of the kids, the skinny black-haired one who never tried, the black kid who was the best player.

'Shall we go down there?'

'Edward,' she said in a high-pitched voice, 'we're not allowed.'

Edward sighed. 'Let's just go.'

Mary's eyes widened at the suggestion. 'Mum will kill us.'

Edward shook his head. 'Mum's gone weird.'

The little girl turned one corner of her mouth down when he said that.

'Haven't you noticed it? Come on, let's just go. She won't mind.'

Mary was thinking it over. He grabbed her arm and pulled her towards the cliff path.

'Come on.' Mary gave little resistance. It told him that she wanted to go as well. 'Just trust me,' he said.

|||

The snow on the mud looked like sugar on coffee. Charlie's face felt numb. Mims had caught him just above the brow and he could feel the blood pooling, pushing the skin out. He felt a sense of recklessness in him that wasn't wholly unpleasant.

There was a movement inside the campervan; Emily was home. He pulled the door open and she was standing over the small counter, flicking through the pages of an old magazine, her back to him.

'You'll never guess what's just happened to me,' he said.

She didn't move from the counter. 'What?'

'I've just had a fight. Remember that freak I told you about? He . . . Em?'

Emily closed the magazine and went over to the bed, throwing herself on to it without looking at him.

'What's the matter?' he said. 'Have you been crying?'

She rolled away from him. 'I'm OK.'

Charlie sat on the edge of the bed and put his hand on the centre of her back. 'What's happened?'

'Nothing.'

'Have you seen the snow?'

She didn't answer.

'Hey,' he whispered, and leaned in closer.

Emily brought her face around, letting him see. Her eyes were red and her cheeks glistened in the pale light. He knew she didn't like people seeing her like this and as she tried to smile, Charlie felt his chest stir. She looked so vulnerable.

'I love you,' she said, simply.

'What's happened?'

Emily shook her head. 'Nothing. I just . . . you know. Sometimes it just hits you.' She sat up quickly and turned away from him again. 'So,' she said, pressing the balls of her hands to her eyes and sniffing. 'I've got a present for you.'

She went back over to the counter, leaving Charlie alone. He moved his body up against the headboard. He wished she would open up like this more often. They still hadn't spoken about her family, even after all this time. She just shrugged it off; it doesn't matter, we'll never know.

She came back holding something wrapped in a paper towel.

'Here,' she said, trying to sound cheery. Her face looked different somehow, more lumpy.

'What is it?'

'Open it.'

He took it from her and unfolded the bundle. 'What's this?'

He held up a round, flat cake. It had a dusting of sugar on it that spilled on to his fingernails.

'It's a Welsh cake,' she said proudly.

'Well this is a nice surprise,' he said.

Emily laughed. She nodded to the cake expectantly.

'Eat it.'

'Where did you get it from?'

'I made it with the girls this afternoon.'

'What does it taste like?'

'Eat it and find out.'

There was a sad smile on her face. Charlie brought the cake to his mouth. 'Wait,' he said. 'Is this the only one?'

'Uh-huh.'

Charlie paused. 'Have you had one?'

Emily nodded and blinked quickly.

'Liar,' he said.

'It's a present for you.'

Charlie sat up straighter. 'Why are you so kind?'

Emily brought her left hand up, put her middle finger and thumb together, into a circle, placed it near Charlie's forehead and flicked.

'Oi!' said Charlie.

'I'm kind to you because you're my little retard,' she cooed.

Charlie laughed with an involuntary gasp. 'Thanks a lot.'

Emily sniffed again and wiped away the residue of her tears with her finger. Her eyes were clearing. She looked hungrily at the Welsh cake.

'Half each?' she said.

Charlie felt a sudden emotion surge right through him, and he snapped the cake in two. It was delicious: buttery and sweet, soft and crumbly. There were currants in it that gave it a tangy edge.

'Oh my God,' he said with his mouth full, 'that's amazing.' He adopted a Welsh accent. 'It's bloody marvellous, mun, dew dew dew.'

Emily threw her head back quickly with a giggle, putting her hand over her mouth as she chewed.

'Nice, aren't they?' she said.

Charlie grabbed her and pulled her against him. She turned her body around so her back was to his chest. He kissed her cheek and they fell into a stillness, watching the flakes of snow land as grey blotches on the surface of the skylight. He had forgotten all about his fight with Mims.

'Charlie,' Emily whispered conspiratorially.

'Yeah?' he whispered back.

She put her hand softly against his face.

'That really was your Welsh cake,' she said. 'I ate mine before you came back.'

||||

They walked nervously out on to the sand. The snow was falling more heavily now and had started to gather up at the head of the beach in a thin white covering. The kids playing football saw the two children approaching and the tall blond boy looked at them for a moment. Edward felt the nerves jangling inside his body. This was the boy Edward had spent months watching through the binoculars.

The boy seemed to be thinking about something, and then he held his arm into the air.

'Fancy a game?'

Edward's relief came in a big sigh.

'Come on, Mary,' he said.

The two children ran towards the makeshift football pitch, leaving footprints in the snow behind them. The blond boy walked over to greet them. The game had come to a stop. Some of the kids watched what was happening. Others stood around and talked amongst themselves.

'Hey,' he said.

He sounded as if he was trying to be friendly but now, close up, Edward felt something cold about the way he was. He was taller than Edward and he looked at them through half-closed eyes that were watery and cool.

'Hello,' they answered together.

'I'm Adam,' said the blond boy.

'I'm Edward and this is Mary,' he said.

'I'm Mary,' Mary echoed.

'Yeah, listen. Girls can't play,' Adam said, looking straight at Edward.

It caught the boy off guard. Adam stood there, waiting for his reaction.

The guilt for what he had done crept up inside him. It wasn't just that he had disobeyed his mother by coming here; he had also betrayed his uncle, who had told him not to trust strangers. He had ignored both of them. He suddenly wished he hadn't come down here.

'Do you still want to play?' said Adam.

'Why can't I play?' said Mary in a sulky voice.

'Because you're a girl.'

'But there are girls over there,' Edward pointed out.

'They're watching. Your girlfriend can watch,' said Adam. He tried to contain his smirk. His clear blue eyes regarded the two children.

Edward turned to his sister.

'Will you watch?'

'I want to play,' she moaned, and stuck out her bottom lip.

'Come on, Ad, hurry up, for fuck's sake,' one of the kids called, the little red-haired one.

Edward blushed. He didn't like it when kids swore in front of Mary. Adam twisted the upper half of his body around.

'In a minute.' He turned back to Edward. 'Are you playing or what?'

He so much wanted to play. He'd spent months and months looking after his sister and he deserved a break. He wanted new friends. If Mary wanted, she could go and play with the other girls. She didn't even like football anyway. She was just being contrary. These mechanisms of justification, reeling in the guilt, turned in his head until at last he was able to make his decision. He wouldn't play for long.

'Yeah,' he said, and he took the first few steps away from Mary. 'I'll play.'

IIII

They played for over an hour but Edward couldn't enjoy himself. He was torn between guilt and frustration. His sister could have played with the girls, but she had to try and spoil it for him by going back home. He was also thinking about the promise he had made to protect her. He did not know if that promise had been broken. He peered up to the top of the cliff, to see if she was up there, looking down on him, but there was no sign of her.

He wanted to leave so he could check that she was all right. He kept thinking of a reason to excuse himself but nothing came. There was something about the boys that unsettled him. They weren't like the kids from home. They were faster and stronger and bigger.

The snow fell more slowly, then turned to drizzle, and then stopped. Something was happening. The clouds in the sky started to thin and ribs of blue appeared. The kids looked up at it in wonder.

Another of the strange sunsets was in progress, this one more startling than anything they had seen before. The sun was behind a thin bank of clouds that cut horizontally across the sky, the top and bottommost edges in perfect alignment with the sun's own edges. It appeared behind the cloud as a chrome disc in the sky, bright but not bright enough that the children could not look directly at it. Edward couldn't understand what he was seeing. There was something next to the sun.

'What are they?' said one of the kids.

'It's the colours of the rainbow.'

The shadows behind the children were long and deep.

'It's so weird,' said Adam.

Edward watched in silence. He could not take his eyes off it. Next to the sun, strung out alongside it, were seven hoops of colour. They made hazy circles, each one the same size as the sun, each one touching the edge of the last. Seven hoops of colour.

Some of the children started to cry in fear and ran back to the camp.

'The marauders won't like that,' said Adam.

'What are the marauders?' said Edward.

Adam gazed at him through his cool blue eyes, the lids low and smug.

'The baddies,' he said.

Edward stared at Adam. Some of the other kids gathered round.

'They live in the woods and eat human flesh,' he went on.

'And if they catch you, they cut your face off,' said the little red-haired kid, whose name, Edward had learned, was Michael. He was twelve, like Adam, but he was much shorter than them, and he spoke with a very high voice, and very quickly.

Adam said, 'They only ever wear black clothes, and they have gas masks they never take off.'

Edward was frightened now.

'Do you know why they can't take them off?' said Adam. 'Because if they do, their skin will catch fire.'

'He doesn't know what that means,' Michael, the red-haired kid, said.

'You're lying,' said Edward.

'Vampires.' Adam paused, and allowed the word to settle in.

'There's no such thing.'

'Yeah?' Adam laughed. 'So who killed Saul's dad?'

Edward looked at the little black kid. His head dropped when Adam mentioned his father.

'He was on the salvage team that got attacked by them. In the middle of the night. We heard McAvennie – he's our leader – say that they could fly, and they flew out of the trees.'

'They ripped his head off,' said Michael gleefully. 'And drank his blood out of the stump.'

Edward shivered. He looked at Saul again. The little boy, who was much younger than Adam and Michael, just stood there and let them say it.

'They came from Transylvania as well.'

'That's why we're having these sunsets,' Michael said. 'To scare them off.'

'Have you not heard of them?' said Adam.

Edward had had enough. The seven circles of colour were fading.

'I'd better go,' he said. 'My mum said I had to get back for tea.'

Adam and Michael glanced at one another and smiled.

'See you later, Eddie,' Adam said coolly.

Edward turned back to the cliff face and ran up the path to the house. His skin was hot and he felt sick. He thought of the marauders and imagined them hovering outside his bedroom window in the middle of the night. He imagined their long fingernails tapping on the glass, testing it for weaknesses, and he ran faster.

His family were standing at the garden wall, looking at the sky. Their faces were glowing in the light. The colours on their faces kept shifting. Edward stopped on the other side of the road. He looked at Mary but she turned her eyes away from him. Edward shifted back to the sun, to see the hoops of light one last time, but they had already disappeared.

III

Miriam was woken the next morning by the sound of cars. At first the noises did not register. She laid her head down on the cold pillow and tried to fall asleep. But then, as the minutes ticked past, she remembered the absence. The absence of sounds like that. The sound of so many cars was not normal. They just kept passing. As the clarity of wakefulness clicked through her she rolled on to her stomach and pulled herself up. The baby was so heavy now. Pulling the curtain back, out of breath from just the motion of rising to her knees, she looked out. There were two cars coming up the hill from the camp, both with great bundles covered in blue tarpaulin strapped to their roofs. The people were leaving. Something had happened. Miriam's eyes followed the line on which the two cars were headed. She looked and as she did so she felt panic seize. Four columns of black smoke were rising into the sky, from the direction of the village.

From this distance the bases of the black columns were nothing more than thin lines, but the higher into the sky they went, the wider they became, spreading out like great funnels. Her instincts told her immediately what had happened. What was happening. The men with gas masks were coming.

The image of the man holding the flamethrower flashed across her. She remembered what Edward had said to her last night, what the kids were calling these men who were pressing inwards, who were almost here, and she closed her eyes: vampires.

III

When the village came into sight, Charlie sat forward in the passenger seat and put his hands on the dashboard. He had never seen anything like it. This could not be Britain, he thought. The main street that ran through the centre of the village was lined with debris and burnt-out cars. The fronts of the houses were charred with black scars. The windows, the ones that weren't covered with wooden boards, were smashed.

On the right-hand side of the street a house still burned. Flames spewed out of the windows, the walls only just discernible beyond the upward-flowing rivers of smoke. A few of the men who had come from the camp to help were caught in the fire's trance. They were just staring at it. Even above the car's engine, Charlie could hear the low, powerful breathing of the fire in full power.

On the other side of the road, what looked like a newspaper shop had had its windows put through and the contents incinerated. The inside looked like a great, dark mouth. There was a long, black, crumpled mass lying half in the shop and half out. It would not have looked human were it not for the outstretched arm on the pavement.

They saw McAvennie up ahead. In the kerb a weed had grown so high that it came up to his waist. The plants were moving back into the areas that had for so long been human domain. Slowly, Charlie thought, they were slipping to nothing, like a puddle drying up.

Fields stopped next to the Scot. Charlie got out of the car and went up to the tall weed. He put his fist around it and wrapped one of the fronds around his hand. He went to pull it up but something stopped him. An internal part of him said to leave it.

'You were supposed to stay in the camp,' said McAvennie in a tired voice. He looked at Fields. 'How many?'

'Twenty-five families,' answered the American.

'You couldn't persuade any of them to stay?'

Fields shook his head. 'Every one of them who wanted to leave, left. I couldn't talk them down. What about here?'

'Carnage.'

McAvennie's face was redder than usual and his clothes were darkened by smoke. Fields placed his hands on his hips. His injured arm still didn't look right in its socket.

'They killed them all,' McAvennie said.

Charlie's gut tightened.

'How many of them are there?' Fields asked.

'Christ knows. They've just disappeared again. They come in and they go out like the fucking wind.'

Charlie looked around him. 'There must be a lot,' he said.

'A lot more than we think.' McAvennie blew out a lungful of air. 'For them to do something like this . . .' He trailed off. 'There're fifty houses here,' he said.

Not seeing them was the worst part. He found it hard to picture it, hard to think where they might be hiding. All they left behind them was death and destruction.

'What's the plan?'

McAvennie stared into the middle distance. 'We're going to burn the bodies. We have to. Forty of them.'

Fields hesitated before asking, 'Kids?'

McAvennie pulled his trousers up around his waist. 'Killed them this time.'

Charlie's skin went taut. 'What are they doing?' he said.

'They're trying to scare us. Freak us out,' said Fields.

McAvennie nodded soberly.

Charlie's grip tightened around the plant. 'It's just fucking ridiculous. Fucking pricks.' He could feel his body's reaction hard now. 'How can they do this? We'd never do something like this.'

'That's 'cause we're civilized.' McAvennie snorted.

'No.' Charlie shook his head. His legs were shaking. 'They were civilized too.'

'Jesus, Charlie man, think of the underbelly. The sex traffickers, the drug dealers, the gangs, aye? They were in the cities before. But there ain't no cities now so they've had to move, right?'

'But killing kids—'

'Come off it, are you kidding? Charlie, these are bad men on a different level. They'll do anything. They do bad things for the fucking sake of it. Compassion is a weakness to them.'

'So what can we do?' Fields said.

'I don't know yet,' said McAvennie, glancing at him. 'Bad is more powerful, always will be. You stick five good people in a room of a hundred bad people and they'll get ripped apart. But you put five bad people in a room of a hundred good people, and it's still the good people who'll lose.'

The wind blew the scent of burning wood across the street.

'Should we fight them?'

McAvennie blew some air from between his lips. 'We could.'

'It'd be a difficult thing,' said Fields. 'These guys don't fuck around. They really know what they're doing. And what have we got? We don't know how to fight.'

'We've got a few people. There's that guy who was in the army, and a few cops. We have weapons.'

'It doesn't matter anyway,' said McAvennie. 'We've got something they don't have.'

Charlie nodded. 'We're the good guys.'

McAvennie shook his head. 'Not that, no. I wish that counted but it doesn't. Nah.' He swatted a fly from his face. 'However many people they have, we have a lot more.'

|||

McAvennie took them down an alleyway between two of the houses. High wooden fences had been erected on either side. More of the tall, ugly weeds had cracked the pavement and grown up with their hardened fronds.

The alleyway led into a children's play area. A handful of men from the camp were standing around a pile of human carcasses, heaped motionless, side by side, two deep. A strange image of vacuum-wrapped hot dog sausages came into Charlie's head. He had seen many corpses since the Sadness arrived but they still did not look real. There was no physical difference between a dead body and a live one, and yet there was a difference. Dead bodies looked faulty, animalistic. Without the spark to animate them it was difficult to imagine how such a thing could harbour something like life.

Charlie watched the men in the play area. Two of them struggled between a wooden kissing gate on the far side of the park. Between them, curved like a hammock, was another carcass, this one female.

Charlie looked at the man holding the legs and a trickle of anger dripped into his stomach.

'He wanted to help,' said McAvennie.

The white face of Mims reflected the colour of the sky.

'But he's bad,' said Charlie.

McAvennie was standing behind him. 'We have to keep him on side.'

'Why?'

'Would you rather fight against him, if the time comes?'

That was not good enough for Charlie. 'It's not right.'

'He wanted to help.'

'No he doesn't. He's just here to get a good look. Because he's sick.'

'Easy, Charlie.'

'I'm right.'

'Really? So why are you up here?'

Whatever McAvennie said, Charlie would not agree. It was only yesterday that Mims had attacked him.

'He's been through a lot, Charlie. It's bound to mess you up.'

Mims and the man with him dropped the dead woman at the end of the line of corpses. Her body slumped to a rest, her arm falling awkwardly underneath her body, and the scale of what had happened to the village shunted into Charlie. These people had been massacred. He imagined the screams and the pain, the despair and submission as the black wave swept through the streets. The fibres in his bones hardened, the marrow inside them toughened, the darkness surrounding him calcified.

'Any more?' McAvennie called.

Mims saw Charlie. As the other man answered McAvennie, Charlie watched the silent grin expand on Mims's face.

'One more that we can see, Mr McAvennie.'

McAvennie nodded.

'Bring it here and then check the cul-de-sac.'

'Yes, sir,' came the answer.

Still smiling at Charlie, Mims turned and left the park at the far side.

|||

The hinges of the old front door creaked open. They could do with some oil, Miriam thought absently.

'What's happened?'

'They killed everyone in the village,' McAvennie said.

The latch was still in her hand and she was glad for the weight of the door. It supported her as her legs became weak. Deep down she knew what had happened. It was always the worst outcome when people were involved.

'You can't stay here,' McAvennie said. 'If you do, they'll come for you too. And then they'll come for us.'

She knew what he was saying was the truth but she could not

register his words. Her mind returned over and over to the same memory: the flailing arms of people on fire.

'I'll tell you everything we know,' he said.

She moved her hand from the latch to the edge of the door.

'We don't know where they come from or why they're doing what they're doing. They're like ghosts. All we really know is that they've been taking kids.' He spoke plainly, in short, precise sentences. 'Probably for a long time.'

Slowly, the words started to make sense.

'The folks over near the farm had kids. We know this, and we know there were no kids left after they had been there.' He stopped and stooped, looked up into her eyes. 'Are you OK?'

Miriam turned and ran to the back of the house with her hand over her mouth. Kneeling in front of the toilet she threw up into the bowl. Her throat stung and cool sweat appeared at her brow. The air was cold in the room and felt good against her face. Shakily, she drew herself to her feet.

McAvennie waited patiently at the front door. Uninvited, he had not stepped inside.

'I'm sorry,' she said. Her voice sounded croaky.

'What do you want to do?' he asked.

She closed her eyes and leaned her forehead against the wall. She was tired. 'I don't know.'

'Will you come to the camp?'

'Do you really think it will make any difference?'

'I do.'

Miriam swallowed. Her mouth was full of mucus. 'This is . . . insane.'

McAvennie said nothing.

'Why . . . why do you think they're taking kids?'

'They're not normal people, Miriam, they're animals. Kids are easy to train, easy to scare. They're just slaves.'

Her mind could still not process it properly. The idea was too far removed.

'When do you think they'll come?' she said. There it was, she thought. She was going to give up the house.

'They won't come tonight,' he said. 'They know we'll be on guard. But after tonight –' McAvennie shrugged – 'who knows?'

She opened her eyes a little. McAvennie's face looked like it had become faintly lopsided. His large head looked less symmetrical than it had.

'Can you protect us tonight? Just in case?' She tried to smile.

'Of course.'

The baby moved in her stomach, twisted itself around and rubbed against the womb. 'I'd like one more night here,' she said.

III

Fields and Charlie were checking the remainder of the houses in the village. Entry was not difficult – all the front doors had been smashed in. The sky was darkening. They needed to check every house before the bodies could be burnt.

A surprising number of the houses were empty. The old occupants had either left their homes at the start of the outbreak and escaped to an unknown fate, or had been killed by the marauders somewhere outside, whilst fleeing.

Charlie was standing in front of a small white house. The lawn had grown untidily to knee height. There were no burn marks on the walls and the windows were intact.

Going inside the houses was a strange experience. In the long-since-evacuated places a thin veneer of pristine dust had accumulated on the hard surfaces. The houses without people were strangely cold. It was like looking at an old photograph, a snapshot of how things were.

Once inside the small white house he called out. No answer was returned and so he went into the living room. A television was in the far corner, near the window. There was an old-fashioned gas fire fastened to the wall where a fireplace had once been. On the mantelpiece was a glass-faced carriage clock. Its gold-plated mechanism had stopped turning and the time was permanently set at a quarter past six. A china figure of a ballerina, sitting down and tying the strings of her ballet slippers, was next to the clock, and next to her was a small teddy bear. There was a photograph of a young girl in a standing frame.

The staircase creaked under his weight. The ceiling on the

landing was low. He thought he heard a noise downstairs. He called out again but there was no answer. Outside, he thought he could hear shouting. He listened closely but there was nothing.

The front bedroom housed a large, wooden bed. The mattress was gone and the springs sagged in the centre. Underneath the only window was a dressing table. A large yellow powder puff sat next to an array of metal trinkets. Charlie felt an overwhelming sense of melancholy. He lifted the powder puff off the dressing table. Flecks of white makeup had hardened on its surface. I shouldn't be in here, he thought. He wanted to go back to Emily, to hide out in their van and pretend the world didn't exist.

He sensed something behind him. The old woman's ghost, he thought. He stopped and put the yellow powder puff down. No, not a ghost. He turned round.

Mims smiled at him and lifted a sharp knife up in front of his face. He twirled it so the edges glinted white in the dying of the daylight.

'I told you I was going to kill you,' he said.

Charlie backed into the dressing table. It shuddered under his weight.

Mims stepped into the room and rolled his tongue across his upper lip. The fork in it looked plump, distended. Even from across the room Charlie could see the scars of ulceration.

'You see, they think my "treatment" made me like this. But that's my great secret. It didn't.' He smiled. 'That's the thing about the end of the world – it's a perfect leveller. All our histories were wiped. Look at me. I am a murderer, and yet when I was doomed, they saved me. Me. The only one they saved. Crazy, isn't it?'

Charlie fumbled behind him for one of the metal trinkets on the dressing table. They clattered on to their sides.

'Are you seriously thinking of fighting me off with a makeup pot?' He paused and smiled again. 'I bet you didn't think you'd ever meet somebody like me, did you?' He snapped his lips. 'Look at what I can do when there's nobody to stop me. I can . . . revel . . . in it.'

Shouting outside. He turned his head and looked out of

the window. Below, Fields and another man were running up the garden path into the house.

Mims cricked his neck and sighed. Charlie could see he was making a decision. His movement was quick.

'Charlie.'

They were calling to him. They were running up the stairs.

The knife was in the air. Charlie turned away. He saw Mims straighten. The knife missed and slammed into the wall an inch from the window.

When Fields saw Mims he stopped.

'What the hell are you doing here?' he said.

David joined him on the landing outside. He was looking at Charlie in a strange way. Charlie couldn't tell what was going on. Mims was standing in the room as if nothing had happened.

'Charlie,' said David. 'You need to come.'

Charlie looked at him. He was stunned by what had just happened. Mims just stood there. There was too much going on.

David stepped into the room, into the light.

'Come on,' he said. 'We have to go.'

Outside there was the loud roar of a car engine.

|||

Fields sat in the back with him. They drove quickly through the side streets and on to the road that led out of the village and back to the camp.

'What's happening?' he said. 'Are they back?'

He looked out of the windows on every side, twisting his body left and right, searching for a sign of the marauders. But he couldn't see anything.

Nobody spoke. They came to the camp and slowed. He expected the car to stop in the car park. That was where the cars stopped normally, surely. His heart was beating fast. He was realizing something. He shook his head. His mouth filled with water and he started to feel sick.

'Is she dead?'

It was all he could say. His body was restless. There was an energy building inside him that had nowhere to go. He looked at Fields. The American refused to look back.

The car passed through the car park and ascended the hill towards the lighthouse.

|||

He had met her at university, in their very first term. There had been an Indian summer that year and he had happened to be sitting next to her on the lawn outside the main campus building one day. There were perhaps fifteen or twenty people sitting in the circle, all of them nervous about meeting new people, all of them trying to say something interesting or funny. The lawn was dotted with daisies; that was what he remembered. And clover rings. He remembered it because she had made a daisy chain. She didn't say much as she threaded the stalks of the flowers together.

Her vacant eyes didn't even recognize him.

'Oh no,' he said. There was no power in his legs. He slumped to his knees and put the palms of his hands on either side of his face. 'Oh no,' he said again. 'Oh no, no, no.'

He could feel Fields and David standing behind him. His mouth opened wide and he drew breath. She was looking at the ceiling. The old doctor with white hair and a white beard was sitting on a plastic chair on the other side of the bed. Shouldn't he be doing something? Shouldn't he be getting ready to take a reading, or filling up a syringe, or preparing a drip? He was just sitting there.

Once, there had been a knock at the door. Somebody was on the phone. He got out of the little single bed in his dorm and went to the door. He turned back and she was looking at him. The sun was shining through the crack in the curtains. Her hair was spread across the white pillow and he felt a flicker in his stomach.

The room they were in now was cold. Her hair was on the pillow but it wasn't like it had been. He stood up again. She moved her head and looked at him. It wasn't her. She had her body but it wasn't her.

'What can we do?'

The doctor looked at him from across the bed with terrible eyes.

'There must be something.'

'You can only accept it,' said the doctor, with a voice so gentle that it hardly reached him.

'You must be able to put it off at least?' His voice wavered. 'Mims. They fixed him, didn't they? That's what they said. So do the same.'

All that came back was silence. Silence from the doctor, from the two men standing behind him, from the walls and the floor and the ceiling.

She had been there on the day he had returned to his home. She had been there when he found his family. She had been the one who had held him when he cried. And she had never doubted him. It had become that they were just an extension of one another. Many hours had passed when they were in the van and not a word had been spoken. He had never been like that with anybody else. She made him calm. She took away the dangers. And she fended off the darkness. He couldn't handle the thought of her not being there. She was too good to go.

'Emily?'

She didn't answer him. She turned her head away. Her neck looked pale. He could see the veins just underneath the skin. The bottom of her ear was poking out from beneath her hair; she was wearing her tiny pearl earring.

'Emily,' he said again. 'It's me, Charlie.'

He leaned over her and took her hand and gripped it. She did not grip back.

The doctor was a blur in the background. He was moving away. Three sets of footsteps faded away as they left Charlie.

'Can you hear me?' he said. 'Emily?'

III

Three men were in the house. They would sleep downstairs. A blockade had been set up further down the road. Fencing had been erected as far as possible and the house was now within that perimeter. The fence stretched far enough either side of the road to stop cars or other vehicles getting around it. The fields were too rough and too wet. Twenty men guarded the new defences.

Miriam had packed some things, as much as she could fit, into the car. Most of the family things had been left in London: photograph albums, old videos, school reports. They were probably still there, in the house with the front door still ajar, in the carcass of a dead city. This was the second purge. Anything she wanted to keep but couldn't fit into the car was packed up into boxes and placed in the airing cupboard upstairs where Henry's father kept the board games. As she closed the door she wondered if this really was the last time she would see them.

At the top of the stairs she paused. She put her hand on the newel post and rested. Whenever she stopped she could feel the restorative power of stillness. In her legs, in her back.

What remained of the food in the cellar was loaded into a truck, as were the battery packs they used for electricity, and the bottles of rainwater. The camp would make use of them.

That evening they ate a meal of tinned baked beans and mashed potato. It felt to Miriam a little like the Last Supper. Earlier she had told the children of the move and they were quiet as they ate. Edward was sullen. Mary was still not talking to him after he had abandoned her down on the beach. Miriam's mother pushed the food around her plate but ate little. Her appetite had left her weeks ago, ever since Miriam had told her about what Joseph had done.

After dinner she asked the guards if they would leave the house for an hour so she could put the children to bed for the last time.

Miriam looked at the sky. There was nothing magical about it tonight; no hoops of colour, no oversized moon. The stars were bright, but that was just the way they were now.

She tucked Edward and Mary into the large double bed in the back bedroom, savouring the moment, knowing it would be the last time she would do it in this house for a while. Maybe it would never happen again. If the marauders never came, would McAvennie be willing to give the house back to her?

Mary was scared and Miriam stayed until she fell asleep. Neither Miriam nor her daughter were aware of the silent vigil Edward kept every night. It took nearly an hour for Mary to fall asleep. She cried for a while, and Miriam hugged her. Edward lay still, on his back, pretending to be asleep.

Miriam left the two children just as the guards returned. Her mother was sitting at the kitchen table in silence. There was nothing more to be done. They were ready to leave. All they had to do was wait as the minutes ticked down.

|||

She woke up. There was a noise outside the house. A rasping, heavy breathing. Clicking. The muted sound of slapping against something soft. Perhaps she was still asleep and this was a new dream. The monster that had killed her husband had come to the house. The light from the stars illuminated the bedroom; she could see the outline of the furniture as she sat up and listened. She was not asleep.

She pulled herself on to her knees and looked out of the window. The grass leading to the cliff edge was silver. There was nobody in the garden.

She must have been imagining it. Nobody could have got past the outer perimeter. There were too many guards. There would have been noise: gunfire, or shouting. She looked down to the garden again, this time moving her head into the glass so she could see the whole of the wall beneath her.

Instantly she fell back on to her bed. Her body went stiff. There were people down there, hugging the walls. Her throat went dry and she stifled a cough. Gas masks.

She looked again. Their backs were pressed against the wall, moving slowly, crab-like. There it was again: the rasping sound. Along the wall, near the corner of the house, was a man on a horse. Silver breath floated into the air from the animal's nostrils. The rider patted its neck.

They must have come from the woods beyond the farmers' fields. Or maybe they had just gone around the outer perimeter. It didn't matter. They were here. They had come. McAvennie was wrong.

Miriam got to her feet. The landing was pitch black but that didn't matter. She knew the house just as well in the darkness as she did in the light. As she moved along the banister she became aware of who it was that had insisted on them learning how to do this.

She went as quietly as she could into the children's bedroom and woke them from their sleep. They waited for her at the top of the staircase whilst she went to wake her mother.

The old woman took over a minute to come round. Miriam was crying. They were losing time. Just as they had done dozens of times before, the family made their way down the stairs in darkness and silence.

Edward went first. Miriam could see him moving. His footing was assured. He moved the same way that Henry had: the same lightness of foot, the same confidence in his movements. The boy went silently along the hallway to the cellar. He knew what to do. Holding the door open, he ushered Mary downstairs, then his grandmother, then Miriam.

'You first,' she whispered.

Without hesitation he did as he was told. She went to close the door after them. The three guards were asleep in the living room. She needed to wake them. They were their only hope.

A quick, high-pitched metal sound. She stopped and held her breath. The letterbox was opening. A thin line of torchlight played across the floor, moving upwards, towards her.

'Wake up!' she screamed. Her voice came out much louder than she had expected. 'They're here!'

There was shouting outside. Muffled and distorted.

She pulled the door to the cellar open and ran down the steps. She stopped halfway. She hadn't locked the door. Cursing, she turned and clambered back up the steps and slid the lock across. Oh God, she thought. This can't be happening.

A burst of gunfire tore the air in half.

Miriam screamed with shock.

'Mum,' she heard Edward call. The sound of Mary crying came up the stairs. Miriam went down into the cellar, trying to hold the baby steady as she went. She was so immobile.

The small window near the ceiling let in just enough light for her to make out the three shapes sitting on the sofa. They listened to the noises upstairs. More gunfire and then a thud. A man screamed and there was more shouting. And then the sound of distant gunfire, coming from the direction of the village, from the direction of the outer perimeter. And then there was a great boom that shook the molecules in the air.

'What's happening, Mum?' Edward jumped to his feet. In his pyjamas he looked like a skeleton.

Upstairs there was more shouting. The cellar door banged under the weight of something heavy being smashed into it. The door was thick but they would get through it.

'Let us in,' a cold, deep voice called.

'Get the shotguns,' she whispered to him, taking the keys from around her neck.

His head bobbed away into the darkness as he ran to the gun cabinet.

'Get two,' she said.

'Let us in,' called the voice again. She knew that the guards would have been overrun by now. She saw them sleeping in the living room, only just stirring when she called out to them. Far too late. And now they were dead.

Edward came back. The guns were nearly three-quarters his own length.

'I loaded them,' he said.

'Come on,' she whispered. 'Over to the window.'

Her mother and Mary stood up.

There was a wooden stool in the corner that she fetched over. She tried to climb up on to it but it was too difficult. Her mother took her place and looked out through the window.

Somewhere out of sight a wild report of many guns being fired rang out.

'I can't see anyone,' her mother said.

'Open the window,' she said.

'We can't fit.'

'The kids can.'

She caught her mother's eyes. They glimmered in the half light. The old woman turned back and struggled to get the rusty catch across. It slid with a metal groan and she pushed the frame open.

Miriam crouched down in front of Edward and grabbed his arms.

'Run to the cliff path. Don't look back. Get to the camp. If anyone gets in your way, shoot them.'

He stared at her impassively, listening to the instructions.

'Mary.' She turned to her daughter. She took one of her hands off Edward's arm and held it out to her. Mary ran across the few feet of space and held her mother's hand. Her cheeks were drenched in tears.

Another bang at the top of the stairs and the crack of wood. The frame was splitting. The lock was about to give.

'You go with your brother.'

Mary shook her head and sucked air between her lips.

'You'll be safe with him,' said Miriam.

'No.'

Miriam stood up and lifted her daughter. Mary started to scream and kick.

'Mary,' Miriam said as sternly as her voice would allow. Her head was hot. 'You have to go,' she said urgently. 'I'll follow you later.'

The little girl stopped kicking and Miriam and her mother pushed her through the tiny window. Her head fitted with two inches to spare. She rolled away and was gone. Miriam halted. Her daughter was gone. She could not see her.

Edward was already up on the wooden stool. He pushed one of the shotguns through the window and turned back to his mother.

'Here,' he whispered, holding the second gun out to her. 'Don't worry, Mum,' he said. 'I'll make sure she's all right.'

Miriam put her hand over her mouth. She couldn't look at him. Her mother took the gun from Edward.

The boy scrambled easily up the wall. He steadied himself on the ledge and eased his head through. It just made it. He dragged the rest of his body through and, like Mary, rolled out of sight.

Miriam looked up at the window. The stars were so bright. They seemed to suck her upwards towards them. She watched for a moment. She hadn't even said goodbye to him. She had just let her children go. That was what had just happened.

But then the stars were covered again. Edward's head came back into view. It was sideways and his hair flopped down.

'Promise me you'll meet us in the camp,' he said. There was hardly any emotion in his voice.

The two women stared at him. He just waited.

'We promise,' said Miriam's mother.

Edward nodded seriously, and disappeared again.

Miriam and her mother swung around. The door shattered open and the beam from a helmet lamp cut a circle of white out of the darkness.

The man came down the stairs slowly. Miriam lifted the shotgun and aimed. She remembered the lesson Joseph had taught her about firing the air rifle: sure and steady. She heard his voice telling her. She moved her eye over the barrel to aim. The man coming down the stairs was fucked. She held her breath.

|||

It was just a simple movement. A mere curling inwards of the finger. That was enough to blow a life apart. Something so tiny could cause something so massive, like the splitting of an atom. The light from the helmet on the man's head swung across the room. She had to fire. She had to kill him.

The light kept coming, further and further across the floor, fast. She felt as if everything that had happened in the last year had led here, as if the whole thing had been engineered to allow this situation to be. She wanted to fire. She became aware she was not breathing. The light was on her. She squinted. And her finger did not move. Her body would not allow it. Her mind slowed. Everything in the room came towards her, she could feel everything in there. Slowly, she lowered the gun and waited.

She dropped the gun on to the sofa behind her and put her hands in the air. She turned her face away in anticipation. And then she realized something. She was still alive.

'You are pregnant,' said the voice.

A momentary pause, and, 'Yes.'

The voice sounded non-human, like a robot. There was a disconnection in its static fuzziness. Through the murk she could make out the shape of the man's gas mask. It had two snouts and two large insect eyes.

'There are no more of you here?'

'No,' she said.

A voice, distended with gain, indecipherable, called from upstairs. The man on the steps called something back. He had a small gun strapped over his shoulder, pointed at her, like the guns she had seen police carry at airports.

Something stirred in her. Something was coming back. She was still alive.

'Please,' said the man. 'Come with me.'

The two women did not hesitate. Both of them sensed the hope and were willing for it to lead them wherever it would. They went up the stairs and the man waited behind the door. He pulled the mask away from his face so they could hear his voice more clearly.

'Wait right here until I come for you.'

He left, and Miriam and her mother waited. Through the door they heard moving around, the sound of people running. There was no more gunfire from the house but it was still firing in short, sharp blasts in the distance.

Neither of them spoke. The baby was moving inside her, sensing its mother's fear. Through the darkness her mother's hand touched her shoulder. The door opened quietly.

'OK, come.'

They followed him out into the deserted hallway. The front door was wide open and they could see the silvery expanse of grass beyond.

'Go,' he said.

He pulled his mask all the way off so they could see his face. The two women hurried past him.

'Thank you,' Miriam said with a shaky voice. She didn't even look at him. She didn't look back. Behind them, they heard the front door slam shut.

Out into the open they ran, Miriam using both hands to support the baby. The going was painfully slow. Blind panic coursed through her. They were so exposed. There was no choice but to keep going, one leg after the other. Her lungs clutched for oxygen. She turned her head to the right, expecting to see a convoy of vehicles coming up the hill from the camp, but there were none. It was just a dark ribbon of road.

She swung her head the other way, to the direction of the village.

'Go,' she called to her mother.

A line of horses was galloping towards the house. They appeared as a blur of legs. The deep echoing hoof stamps rumbled across the grass.

The two women could go no faster. The cliff path was not far now. Another fifty yards maybe. She tried to imagine how their shapes would appear to the horsemen. Maybe they were small enough to go unnoticed, or too small a target to hit.

Suddenly the grass hissed all around them. The sound of exploding, splattering mud. And then, a fraction of a second later, gunfire. They had been spotted.

Her mother was behind her. Miriam had almost reached the cliff path. She stopped and turned. She expected to see her mother lying on the ground. But she was still going. Her run was awkward, more of a walk. Miriam remembered things from her childhood, happy memories, blazing like angels.

She looked back towards the house. It was far away. They couldn't be accurate from that range, surely. More gunfire. It missed by a good fifteen feet, but arced inwards towards them, spraying over the grassland.

The sound of horses' hoofs was louder now.

'Oh Christ,' she whispered. 'Come on, Mum.'

One of the horsemen had broken away from the pack and was streaming across the grassland towards them. In the moonlight he cut a dark figure. His head was low.

The old woman drew alongside Miriam. They came to the cliff path. The ground was unstable on the first part. Only then did she realize she was not wearing any shoes. She looked for a place to hide but the ferns and brambles on either side of the path would not give. They had to go down.

The thunder of the horse grew and grew. And then stopped. The horseman had reached the path.

Miriam and her mother rounded the first bend.

'Be careful,' her mother said.

Miriam stopped. Their way was blocked. A group of men were coming up the path towards them. She could see their heads and shoulders in the moonlight.

'It's the women from the house,' a voice whispered.

'Jesus,' said the man in the front. 'You made it.'

Miriam hurried towards them. An immense wave of relief broke up her and her whole body went weak.

'One of them's followed us.'

She looked up the path towards the bend. The man's silver face became stern.

He mouthed, 'Just one?'

She nodded.

He turned back to the men and urgently put his hand up to silence them.

The breeze moved in the dead ferns. Around the bend were quick moving footsteps. Miriam could see the torchlight from the horseman playing over the ferns and brambles. The animal whinnied hauntingly from the top of the cliff as its rider descended the path.

When the light came into full view, the lead man lunged up the path. Miriam heard a grunt and some thuds. More of the men moved forward. The horseman groaned as they attacked him. Miriam listened to the sound of rubble scratching beneath feet, of disturbed movement, of violence, and all she could think about was the fact that somehow she would see her children again. She turned away and put her hands together. Under her breath, she said quickly, 'Thank you,' and opened her eyes again and the silvery beach that shone below her had never looked so beautiful.

|||

He was aware of the bodies around him. Some were whimpering in the dark. It was a peculiar trait of the stricken that they would always lie on their back with their faces straight up. Their families sat around the beds in the same way that Charlie sat with Emily. The sound of gunfire was a distant boom and nobody cared.

Emily was sleeping. He had been there for nearly ten hours and she had said nothing to him. In the recesses of his mind, behind the swirling darkness, he wondered how long he had left with her.

The lights had been shut off but he could see quite clearly, by the moonlight, the whiteness of the veils that hung over each of the beds.

He thought about the world as it would be in three days, when she was gone. Without the central pivot on which all his actions hinged he would spin off into darkness. He wished that time could be stretched so that three days were smoothed out into six, or nine. Three was not enough.

The door at the far end of the long, thin room creaked open. Charlie didn't look to see who it was. He remained in the cold plastic chair at the side of Emily's bed. Behind the white veil she would have looked already dead were it not for the slow rise and fall of her sleeping chest.

The doctor with the white hair and beard came and stood next to him. He spoke with a gentle, faintly accented voice. 'How is your leg?'

Charlie didn't answer.

'Please, Charlie, I need to speak with you.'

'Go on then.'

'Shall we go into the next room?'

Charlie did not want to move.

'Charlie, it is difficult. I know this. But you should come with me.'

'You know,' Charlie said, his eyes not moving from Emily, 'she could have been killed a few weeks ago. Our car was attacked and she got herself trapped. George ran out into the middle of the street, someone was shooting at him, and he pulled her out. It was a miracle.' He laughed. 'That's what I thought at the time. I really did.'

'I know the story.'

'But it was pointless. The whole thing was pointless. Look at her now. I mean, what was the point in saving her then only to take her now?'

Dr Balad said nothing to this.

'I guess you've heard all this before. People wondering why, trying to justify it.'

'It is in our nature to seek out meaning. It is one of our chief driving factors.'

Charlie looked up at the doctor.

'Please,' said Dr Balad, 'come with me.'

|||

She walked across the sand barefoot, the freezing wind cutting easily through her nightdress. From the camp she and her mother would have looked like two ghosts drifting along the beach from the sea. Miriam had not felt this light in years. It eclipsed the darkness of the year past, eclipsed any feelings of anything in her life, in fact. She had been given an impossible second chance.

Much further behind them the men from the camp carried the horseman they had captured by the arms and legs. There was hope in the air. She could feel it on the wind, could hear it in the crashing of the waves against the shore. The extra weight of the baby was nothing any more.

They walked past the metal containers. The doors were just ajar and they could see the occupants peeping nervously out of the gaps. The men from the camp told them they had caught one of the marauders. There was joy in their voices.

The beach thinned at the far end where the cliff curved in towards the water. The entrance to the camp was just beyond the marram grass, where the car park had been. More of the metal containers punctuated the silver sand as black oblongs.

When they saw their mother, the children bolted out of the shadows and scuttled across the beach. Miriam could see the tracks their feet left. The sand spat up around their ankles in white clouds. Edward was still carrying the shotgun in his hands. Miriam and her mother went down to their knees and opened their arms.

|||

They went through the far door, deeper into the lighthouse building. Charlie looked up into the darkness of the tower. Dr Balad led him through a door into another part of the building. They were on a thin stone corridor. The walls were whitewashed and small square windows let in the moon.

They came to a square room with a table and four chairs in it. There were some cupboards there and a sink. It looked like a first-aid room.

'Just a little further,' said Dr Balad.

The final room was small and cramped. Dr Balad flicked on a weak light. There was a steel desk, behind which he sat himself down. There were some books on the desk and along one wall stood a bank of filing cabinets.

'Sit down,' he said.

There was a cheap plastic chair in front of the desk. A bundle of white dust sheets were on it, which Charlie lifted up.

Dr Balad spoke in clear, declarative sentences.

'There is no easy way of saying this. Your girlfriend is very sick. She is going to die, and there is nothing we can do about it. We all know that people react differently to the illness and so I ask you: is Emily safe? And before you answer, please remember that other people's safety is at stake.'

The chair was cold. The room was freezing.

'She won't do anything,' he said.

He fidgeted to make himself comfortable. He understood the doctor was merely doing what had to be done but that did not help. Deep down, Charlie suspected he was hoping to hear this man tell him of a magical cure. He thought about what he had said to Miriam, about the arrival of the illness presenting people with a series of tests against which they were forced to pit their wits. Words had never felt so hollow to him.

He sat forward.

'So can I go now?'

'Please,' said Dr Balad. 'There is something else I would like to talk to you about.' The doctor put his palm on one of the books. 'We have, I suppose the best way to describe it is, an initiative.'

The dim overhead light accentuated tiny rivers of red veins running across the doctor's cheeks. He shifted in his seat. 'I am talking about euthanasia.' The legs of his chair scraped against the floor in the pause. 'I am sorry to speak so directly to you but let us not circle around the facts. We have a man here at the camp who can help you.'

Charlie's arms felt cold. He folded them over into his chest. His mind started to revolve.

'What's that for?' He nodded to some electrical boxes on the wall on Dr Balad's left-hand side.

'Excuse me?' Dr Balad looked at the boxes. 'Something to do with the lighthouse, I guess.'

'Does it work?'

'I don't know. We wish to conserve power here, not waste it. I know this is difficult for you, Charlie, and it may seem monstrous, but you will not be the first to accept. If I may suggest, think of it rationally. We do not really know what happens when the people become infected but they seem to suffer the most terrible torment.'

'I don't want to hear this,' Charlie mumbled.

'Perhaps not, but the choice is yours to make. It is not so monstrous as you might suspect. Consider this: the food we have saved alone through our initiative has fed the entire camp for one day.'

'Stop calling it that,' he said. 'And is that all that matters? How much food you can save?'

'You know it is not.'

Charlie hung his head.

'You should think about it seriously before you make a decision. Think of what is best for Emily.'

I know what's best for her, he thought. 'How do you do it?' he asked.

'That is not important. Do not burden yourse—'

'It is important.'

'Why?'

'Where is the person who does it?'

'We keep him out of sight. He prefers it that way.'

'So this is why you keep people away from the lighthouse?'

'Keep people away?' Dr Balad's brow became creased. 'I do not know what you are talking about.'

Charlie felt repulsed.

'So as we go happily about the camp, thinking everything is going fine, we are just a moment away from death.'

'We always leave the choice to the family.'

'Yeah? What about that man I saw getting ill in the woods? His family were already dead. Who made the choice for him?'

'Please, Charlie, do not get angry. What is the difference between one day and three?'

'What happened to him?'

Dr Balad did not look away. 'He was euthanized.' He stared at Charlie with moral certitude.

'So where was his choice?'

'I have spent far longer in the company of the sick than you have, to be blunt. The suffering some of the people experience is truly terrible. I wish you could understand.'

Charlie shook his head in disbelief. He felt like he had been betrayed.

'So all that stuff about trust – that really means nothing.'

'We do not tell people about it because there are some things that are more important.'

'Right.'

'We need to maintain our collective hope. What we offer is ugly and difficult and will erode hope. But we must at least offer it. Do you not see that?'

Charlie did see it. But that did not make it acceptable.

'We did not arrive at this choice with any easiness.'

'I don't want to do it,' he said categorically.

Dr Balad nodded once.

'Thank you,' he said. 'Then it will be so.'

||||

She slept deep and late. When she woke she lifted her head from her pillow and looked at her sleeping family. She was in McAvennie's trailer. He had brought her here last night, made sure they were comfortable, and left again.

Miriam knew the danger all around her was growing in, but the gratification of being with her family blocked it out. She had been away from them for twenty minutes at the most, but that short distance had a depth far greater than ordinary time. The reality of never seeing her children again had reared up high before her. She knew now what it meant.

The door to the trailer opened and the children stirred as cold air washed into the room. They lifted their heads groggily and then dropped them back down into the blankets.

McAvennie hadn't slept. The rim of hair around his head was sticking out even more than usual. Large bags had appeared beneath his eyes.

Miriam looked at him and smiled. 'What's happening?' she said.

McAvennie sighed. 'Hard to tell.'

'Are we safe here?'

He stretched his back and there was a loud click of bones aligning. 'I don't know.'

Another wash of cold air and a second man stepped up into the trailer. Miriam recognized him as the American who had come to her house after being attacked. She nodded to him.

'Hey,' he said absently. To McAvennie he said, 'We've locked him in the lighthouse.'

'OK.'

McAvennie turned to Miriam. 'Can you tell us what happened last night?'

She tried to explain but the events had become unreal. She remembered seeing the man on a horse up against the wall of the house.

'We crept down to the cellar.'

McAvennie didn't take his eyes off her. He was waiting to hear about his men, about how she had done nothing to alert them of the danger.

'I didn't think to . . .' She trailed off. 'Your men. Do you know what happened to them?'

He shook his head.

The American spoke. 'We haven't been able to go up there.'

'But there's no more fighting?'

McAvennie sat down in a plastic chair near the door. 'We have one of their friends. The man who chased you. It should buy us some time.'

'So you're going to try and talk to them?'

'I don't know. We're not exactly used to this sort of thing.' The stresses were starting to show as red blotches and grey stubble. 'The people are scared and jumpy.'

'And there's nowhere to run,' added Fields.

'We could go out past the lighthouse,' Miriam offered.

'There're no roads there. It's all forest,' replied Fields.

McAvennie slapped the arm of his chair gently.

'We don't want to run away.' He looked at Miriam. 'I need you to do me a favour,' he said.

|||

She looked out over the sea of faces. McAvennie was standing next to her, waiting to start speaking. He had brought her to a semi-constructed building. It looked like it was going to be some sort of long hall. Beams of timber were stacked in piles behind them and the front porch of the building acted as a low stage.

People were coming up and asking quickly what was happening, what had happened last night, what they were going to do. Worried expressions creased their faces as McAvennie told them as calmly as he could that he would explain everything. Their eyes flickered to Miriam and then back to McAvennie.

McAvennie turned to Fields, who was standing at the side of the stage. He nodded to him. McAvennie stepped forward to the microphone.

'Hello?' he said. 'Can you hear me?' He tapped the head of the microphone. 'OK.'

The crowd fell completely silent.

'So last night was a bad night.'

The people moaned as one voice. The sound resonated through her body.

'The marauders attacked us again.'

The noise of the crowd rose. Everybody knew what had happened but they somehow expected their leader to be able to offer them something more than the truth.

'We don't know what's going to happen. So we need to make decisions.'

A voice rang out from somewhere near the centre of the crowd.

'We do know. They're coming to kill us and use the kids as slaves.'

Miriam looked around for the source of the voice. There was a commotion near the middle. Some people were shouting.

'OK, calm down,' said McAvennie.

The volume of sound was increasing. People were turning away from the stage to see what was happening. To the far right, Miriam saw some men moving towards the commotion. And then the crowd started to move. It looked like a tide. Heads bobbed up and down as one shape and the shouting was louder. A fight had broken out.

McAvennie shook his head and stepped back from the microphone. It was falling apart. The camp was disintegrating.

A circular gap in the crowd had formed, in the centre of which two men fought.

Miriam squinted when she saw their faces. One of them she did not recognize but the other was unmistakable. It was the man with the forked tongue who lived beneath the lighthouse. There was a thin line of red running down from either edge of his mouth and, as the men dragged him off, she could see he was smiling.

McAvennie covered the microphone with his hand and called across to Fields, 'That's it. That's it for him.' He took his hand away. 'Stop it,' he called. His voice was loud now. 'You're behaving like animals.' He said the word animals with menace. 'Still. After everything.'

The crowd turned slowly back towards the stage.

'It's unbelievable,' he said.

The people watched but were not silent. There was something dangerous about them, something latent and threatening.

'We must not lose our heads now. Of all the times we have to stick together, now is that time.'

Miriam glanced across to Fields at the side of the stage. He was staring out over the crowd, trying to see who was doing what. She felt many eyes on her. She was exposed.

'This woman,' said McAvennie. He swung his left arm in an arc towards her. 'She was the one who lived up in the house on the top of the hill, aye? She's lost everything. It's a miracle she even made it out alive. But she did.'

The crowd's interest had been caught now. The muffled voices were desisting.

'This woman is pregnant,' he declared.

McAvennie turned to her and put his hand over the microphone again.

'You OK?' he asked with a reaffirming nod.

The eyes of the hundreds of people were on her belly. She could see people near the back standing on tiptoe, their heads swaying back and forth to see, like the heavy tops of wheat blowing in a field. She nodded gently to McAvennie.

Every voice had fallen silent. It was so quiet that the sound of the sea lapping the beach in the far distance could be heard beyond the low bluff. The danger that had been hanging so pervasively had dissipated in an instant.

'You see now?' said McAvennie.

The hush said they did. Miriam tried not to focus on anybody. They seemed themselves to be like children, willing to follow, easy to shape. It was not the normal way that people behaved.

'There is hope,' he said. 'We are still not like them.' He pointed off up the hill.

A woman at the front of the crowd leaned forwards. 'But we're scared, George,' she said. Her eyes glanced at Miriam and then fell away.

'I know that.'

A man made his way to the front and threw his hand up into the air.

'Come on, George, this has gone far enough. This empathy crap is fine when you haven't got . . . psychopaths bearing down on you. We've got one of their men, right? Where is he?'

'No.' McAvennie shook his hand. 'We're not going to do anything rash.'

'Says who? Look, you're a nice guy, George, we all know that, but you're not the leader. Those people have been coming closer for weeks. They've killed our friends. If we don't do something then they are going to come down here and they're going to kill us as well. Mims might be a prick, but what he said is true. They won't just leave us be.'

The others around him agreed.

'So what are you saying we should do?'

The man shrugged. 'We get that guy and we string him up so they can see him. We talk to them, tell them to leave or we'll kill him.'

McAvennie shook his head. 'That's insanity.'

'It's better than nothing.'

'You think they'll just leave us alone?'

'All I know is that while we're standing around having meetings, they're actually doing stuff. Planning stuff.'

McAvennie looked out over the crowd. 'We'll have a vote.'

He gestured for the man who had been speaking to come on to the stage. His clothes were caked in mud, but the mud was smeared in straight lines, as if he had tried to brush it off. The skin on his face was loose through loss of weight. He stood alongside McAvennie, looking out over the people.

'If we do something stupid now – and we don't really know what we're doing – then it might be disastrous.'

The other man leaned into the microphone. 'The powerful always win. That's all I'm saying. Everybody knows that. And it's even more true since the Sadness came.'

'I agree,' said McAvennie. 'They do, aye. But it's us that are the most powerful.'

The man shook his head. 'Not this time.'

'OK, look.' McAvennie was addressing the crowd now. 'They might have minds worse than ours, be capable of going further into depravity than us. In the past we would have lost against them. But not now. Now we have a whole new society and it's different from the old society. They might have better weapons and be more brutal but they can't beat us because if we do what we've been doing since this camp started, which is sticking together, we can't lose. My friend here said the powerful always win. Now even if you just look at the numbers, there's nearly eleven hundred of us. We are the most powerful. In every single way. But only, only, if we keep going like we have done. Together.' He paused.

Miriam watched the man standing next to McAvennie. His head was lowered, almost as if in shame.

'OK, let's vote.' McAvennie hitched his trousers up around his waist. 'If you agree with me, put your hand up.'

There was a pause. Everybody remained still. Nobody raised their hands. Miriam felt nervous for McAvennie. She had spoken to him only a handful of times but she trusted him. What he said made sense. She looked at all the frightened faces. Still nobody moving. She could hear the sea again. The sky was the dull grey of steel. She glanced across to Fields. He had his good arm raised in the air. She thought for a moment and then raised her own arm.

A few heads turned towards her. She kept her hand in the air. McAvennie looked at her. His face widened into a gentle smile and he turned back to the crowd. The hands were going up. One by one, thin spikes of flesh pointing at the sky. From left to right more arms were raised. One of the women in the crowd held one arm up whilst she used the other to dig her husband in the ribs until he too fell in line. Nearly everybody had lifted their hands.

McAvennie put his hand over the microphone. 'OK?' he said to the man.

The man's shoulders slumped and he patted McAvennie on the back.

Miriam stared out over the sea of raised arms. And the eyes looked back at her.

||||

She thought he was going to squeeze her to death with the power of his hug.

'I just voted. Nobody wanted to go first was all,' she said.

He released his bear-like grip and looked at her. He was a completely different person when he smiled. She remembered how he had told her his family had been killed. It was funny how history could be hidden away inside people's heads.

'Why don't we just leave?' she said.

'Because we can't. This is bigger than the camp,' he said. 'If we lose this place then who knows where this thing'll stop.'

They walked along one of the muddy paths away from the school building.

'We've got you and your family a place to stay,' he said.

'Hey,' she said, stopping. She was looking at something between the tents. McAvennie craned his head round to one of the open communal areas.

'I know that man,' she said. Her mind scrambled. Her memory chugged into motion. 'Oh my God,' she whispered.

He said he had killed him. She had castigated him for it. She had pushed him away because of it. A long time ago a man had come to the house. He had tried to kill them. That was what Joseph had told her, and he said he had killed the man for it. After that, everything had snapped.

She was standing behind him. He was sitting on a folding chair in a circle of people.

'Paul,' she said.

The man did not move.

'Paul Crowder?' she said.

He turned round. It was him. It was the man who had come to the house all those months ago. His thin face with the long nose, the sunken cheeks, the weak chin. It was him. He was alive. The thing that had driven Joseph further away than anything else had never happened. Joseph had let him live. Her mind fired hot with flashing synapses.

'Excuse me?' said Crowder. A half-smile, half-grimace cracked across his face.

'It's me.'

There was recognition in his eyes. He stared at her and she saw his face visibly whiten. There were ten or so other people sitting around in a little circle, all of whom had turned their attention to the strange, pregnant woman they had seen on the front steps of the school building.

McAvennie came and stood beside her.

'I'm sorry, you must have me mistaken for somebody else.' His eyes regarded her vacantly.

Miriam stood there, not blinking.

'This is Zachary,' she heard McAvennie say.

The man she thought was Crowder smiled at her and turned

back to the circle. She knew her memory had changed, that she did not trust it as she had, but she was sure it was the same man.

'Zachary,' said McAvennie.

The man turned around again, glancing slyly at Miriam.

'Are you OK?'

Crowder's face stiffened and he nodded.

'I can't remember who she is,' he said, slowly, as if scanning old memories.

McAvennie put his arm around Miriam and led her back between the tents to the muddy path.

'I know that man,' she said quietly. 'He came to my house. Months ago. His name's not Zachary.'

'I know.'

She could think of no reason why he would try to be someone he wasn't. Or perhaps he really was Zachary and Paul Crowder was the fraud.

'He came here a few months ago. He was the one who brought Mims here.'

She went to turn but McAvennie stopped her.

'Miriam,' he said. 'I need to tell you something. About your two wee friends, Charlie and Emily.'

|||

Emily had said not one word. Charlie sat at the edge of her bed and there, sleepless and exhausted, the darkness came. It curled around him like a whirlpool. He tried to think of the happy times with Emily, but all the memories were behind. This was the fact that kept coming back round. There would be no new memories with her. In front of him was the great blackness. After Emily, there was nobody. Everyone he loved would be dead. He had forgotten about what had happened at the village, forgotten the men who were closing in. None of that mattered.

During the night, as he fought himself back from the precipice of sleep, he had brought the chair right up to the bed and held Emily's hand. His eyes stung with fatigue. Whenever he closed them they became increasingly difficult to reopen. Perhaps he should go outside, he thought. Maybe Emily would like to go for a walk.

The sound of voices filtered through the small, square windows. Charlie stood up from his chair. His bones stretched and clicked. Pulling the white net curtain across, he looked out of the window and put his hand against the glass. Mims was out there. Two men held his arms but he was fighting to break free. A slow, burning hate crackled up to the surface.

There was another shout, further down what must once have been a neat lawn. McAvennie and Fields were there. McAvennie was pointing and shouting. He was pointing to a red wooden door set into a block building up near the lighthouse tower.

The men bundled their prisoner towards the door. His head was swinging wildly from side to side. He was trying to bite them. Charlie felt a new anger now, this time towards McAvennie. His large frame and sorrowful eyes, the way he moved awkwardly, were not so endearing. Not now that Charlie knew what he allowed to happen to helpless people with no choice. You never really know anybody, he thought.

He turned back to Emily's bed. She was still there, supine. He had pegged the veil up on one side so he could be close to her. Her eyes were still open, still staring at the ceiling.

'I have to go,' he said.

Emily didn't acknowledge him.

A balloon of fear rose in his throat. But he had to go.

|||

He went quickly along the ward and out into the wide, circular space that was the base of the lighthouse tower. A thin stairwell with a metal handrail curled up around the wall, leading to a closed door painted green. There were noises coming from behind it. It was the first time he had heard the noises and they made him stop. There were more sick people upstairs. The shouts from behind the door were dull, resonating echoes. They sounded like ghosts.

He went through into the annexe. He could hear Mims's raised voice. It spurred him along the long, thin chamber towards the door at the far end. He thrust it open and went inside.

It was a light room with two large windows. A table and four chairs stood in the middle of it and there was a sink in the corner.

The two men who had Mims threw him on to the floor, where he sprawled out, arms and legs unable to break his fall. He jumped quickly back to his feet and turned to face his captors. He hunched down and it looked like he was about to attack when he stopped. His torso relaxed and he smiled, still unaware of Charlie's presence.

'Well done, men,' he said snidely. 'Good soldiers.'

McAvennie came in with Fields trailing behind him. His body consumed the whole of the doorway, blanking out the light as he passed through.

'What the fuck is the matter with you?'

He moved towards Mims as if he was about to attack him. Suddenly, he became aware of Charlie, and turned to him with a look of shock he quickly tried to disguise.

Mims turned, following McAvennie's gaze.

Charlie was remembering the house in the village, and what Mims had done. The will for revenge was overwhelming. Charlie had never felt the pure anger that was in him now. The framework of who he was was shifting. He could sense dark new avenues opening up inside his mind; new roads to look down that had been closed before.

'What did he do?' Charlie said. He heard his voice but it was as if through a muffling fog. He wiped his eyes and tried to clear the thought of Emily in the next room.

'Charlie, son, why don't you go back inside with Emily, eh?' McAvennie moved towards him.

'Don't,' Charlie said. 'Forget it, George.'

'Charlie.'

'We should kill him.' He looked in the direction of Mims. 'And then go and euthanize all the others in there.'

McAvennie nodded his comprehension. 'I see. I don't think now is the time, Charlie.'

'It's a good time for me,' Mims chirped.

'You shut your fucking mouth,' McAvennie shouted, turning on him. 'Or I'll rip that snake tongue out of it.'

'Well, are you going to "euthanize" those people in there?' he said, mocking Charlie's words. 'Hmm?'

'That's enough.' Fields raised his hand into the air. 'Why did you even come here, man?'

Mims flicked his head back and smiled. 'Because.'

'Because what?'

'Because I want to see what's going to happen here.'

'You're not going to,' McAvennie snapped. His voice was so loud it seemed to shake the room. 'You're out of here. Gone.'

'You won't let me go,' he said. 'Because of your sense of right and wrong, you self-righteous prick. You're weak. That's all it is. You won't send me past that house, past those people.'

'You are such a twat,' McAvennie wheezed.

'They're going to come here. It won't be their first massacre and it won't be their last. They'll take what they need and move on. This is the way things will be from now on. You know, deep down.' He coughed. A dribble of red saliva bubbled at the corners of his mouth from his fight. He spat it into McAvennie's face. 'You know it, and you know there's nothing you can do about it.'

McAvennie grabbed Mims quickly by the throat and smashed his head against the stone wall. Mims grunted under the weight of the blow.

'Fat man,' he said. 'This place will burn.'

McAvennie shaped to punch Mims but stopped himself. He let go of him and, through clenched teeth, made a low, guttural sound. And stopped. He turned to one of the men behind him.

'Lock him up,' he said.

|||

'We should kill him.'

All the heads turned towards Charlie.

He relaxed his body.

'I'm serious. I'll do it. Fuck it.'

McAvennie was looking at Charlie as if he felt sorry for him.

'Give me a gun or something. I've done it before. What difference will it make now?'

He meant every word of what he said. The new roads in his mind were resolving. The darkness rolled through the clouds above them. Killing Mims really did seem like a thing he could do. He didn't care any more.

'What do you mean, what difference?'

'Come on, George, you agree with this sort of thing, right?'

Charlie didn't like the pitiful way everyone was looking at him. They saw him and thought they understood what he was saying, what he was going through. But they didn't. They had no idea.

'Stop it, Charlie.' McAvennie glowered. 'Those people were already dead. You think this is easy? Keeping all these people together? With no easy food, no easy water, no rules to follow? I have to make the tough decisions, yes, but it is never, ever, without compassion. Who else would make them? I didn't choose to lead this place. I had to because nobody else would.'

The direction of Charlie's anger was out of control. The darkness in his head was swirling dangerously close to his centre, moving into channels and corridors he had always succeeded in keeping free. He knew he was behaving like a petulant child.

'Go back in there,' McAvennie said to him in a scolding and unsympathetic voice. 'Before we both say something we regret.'

Charlie stood there for a moment, his head hot and his legs weak. And then he left.

|||

Heavy with rain, the sky darkened towards night. Sandbags were piled into low turrets around the entrances to the camp. Guards were installed at them. They had lots of guns, accrued slowly over the months of salvages. Most of them were loaded but there were also those for which they had not been able to find ammunition. They were taken to the fronts for no reason other than it seemed the right thing to do.

Miriam took the children to the utility blocks near the beach to wash. People walked quickly past them without a passing glance, each readying themselves for what would be the first night on the camp with the horsemen looking down on them from the top of the hill.

During the course of the day eight large trucks had pulled alongside what had been Miriam's house. As each truck arrived men dressed in black appeared from the metallic innards and passed quickly, without ceremony, into the house. Nobody knew how many men there were in total. Some said nearly a hundred had been counted, but there was no reason to think there couldn't be a lot less than that, or a lot more.

The camp itself had fallen into flux. People had been leaving all day, choosing to take the risk of the wide open spaces rather than wait for whatever the horsemen had in mind to do. They had filed across the fields beyond the lighthouse and into the woods, leaving in small groups: young families, couples, clusters of widows, gangs of men. If they had cars then they left them behind.

As Miriam waited in line for the showers she listened to two men standing behind her talking about why they were staying. One of them said there was no choice, that the people who had left the camp would be dead in days and that the best chance of staying alive was here. He said he couldn't keep running any more. What would happen if they did leave? Set up another camp? A smaller one? The other man said they should have made better defences but his friend asked how, when they didn't know what they were doing.

Further up the line, ahead of her, people were turning round and whispering and pointing up the hill. Something was happening.

Miriam craned her neck to see but the trailers in the car park blocked her view. The queue started to disperse in front of her like a vapour trail.

She grabbed someone's arm. 'What's happening?'

'I don't know.'

Miriam felt Edward and Mary grasp her hands. She turned her family round and they followed the crowd towards the entrance of the camp. They had gathered at the tall metal fences that lined the perimeter. Heads bobbed up and down in search of a better view but Miriam didn't need to get any closer. She could see.

The sky was a dirty metal grey so dark it made the grass of the hill beneath it look like a sea of iron filings. There were three dark shapes on the hillside, halfway between the house and the camp. Fear shot through the crowd. The shapes were just there, on the hillside, brazenly unafraid of the hundreds of people looking up at them. Three men on three horses. One of them had pulled his gas mask to the top of his head. He watched the camp through a set of binoculars.

'Look at them,' someone said behind her. 'They don't care. They're not even worried.'

Miriam clenched her hands round the hands of her two children. She couldn't move. The audacity of the horsemen compelled her to watch. The horses were standing in profile to the camp, their riders holding the reins with heads turned sideways.

Those men had taken her house but their tide was not going to stop there. That was clear now. They would keep on coming.

'What do you think?' a voice said behind her. It belonged to the injured American man who had been in her house.

A second voice replied. 'I think that pricks will always spoil everything.'

Miriam turned to McAvennie. He saw her but his eyes could not keep contact. He looked past her and towards the three surveying horsemen on the hillside.

'And there will always be pricks.'

||||

Somebody had died. The old doctor with the white hair and beard had come in with a group of men. The family had cried and screamed and the body was taken from its bed and laid on a stretcher and covered in a white sheet and removed from the ward.

Charlie had watched and tried not to associate it with an echo from his future, something bouncing backwards through time as his own mirror. Emily did not have long and soon that grieving family would be him.

'I'm going to leave the camp,' he said to her. She had eaten nothing in two days. Her eyes gazed steadily and unerringly upwards.

'There's no point in staying here,' he said. 'I just want to be on my own.'

Emily blinked.

'Em?'

Her head tilted on the pillow and her eyes gazed into his, a quarter way closed. His heart came instantly back to life. He leaned in. Was that really Emily?

He could smell something. A faint, low smell. She turned her head back and stared once more at the apex of the white veil that draped over her bed.

'Em?'

He looked at the sheets. The whiteness of them was darkening in an expanding circle around her crotch. Charlie pulled the sheets off her and instantly the smell intensified. He froze. She had soiled herself. She smelt of piss and shit. Quickly, he threw the sheet back over her and looked at the face that did not acknowledge him.

His chest convulsed and he put his hand gently on her forehead. Just by being there he was taking from her the very thing she had always said she would lose last: her grace.

He couldn't let anyone else see her like this. Thinking quickly, he looked about him. There was a disused toilet off the foyer in which they kept stores. He ran into it and found some toilet rolls. In the corner of the room was an empty waste-paper basket.

He sat her up in her bed. She offered no resistance. Lifting her nightdress over her body he made sure the damp patches did not make contact with her skin. Hooking his hands over her underwear he pulled them down over her thighs. The stench of faeces was as heavy as lead in the air. He gagged but kept going. He threw the underwear on to the pile of sheets and unrolled long lengths of toilet paper. Again, he remembered the daisy chain she had threaded on the campus lawn, a whole world away from here. He stopped.

He slumped down in his chair, deflated. She was dying and he was there in the middle of the night cleaning shit off her legs. This could not be right. In the vast machinery of the universe surely these depths had not been intended.

'Come on, Charlie boy,' he said to himself.

He stood again and tore along the perforations of the toilet paper. The moonlight in the windows offered just enough illumination. The faeces had smeared along the insides of her thighs and he started there. He gathered it up in the soft paper, balled it up and dropped it into the waste-paper basket. He then tore off some smaller strips and laid them over her body from her belly button to halfway down her thighs to soak up the glistening urine. He pressed on the paper and his hands became moist and cold. But he had to carry on. He needed to finish before anybody came in.

Rolling up his sleeves he forced his hands under her thighs and lifted her legs up like a mother does a baby. Looking away he finished cleaning. As he threw the final pieces of toilet paper into the bin he started to laugh. This was so ludicrous. He lifted Emily up and pulled off the rest of the sheets. Then he dressed her in a fresh nightgown and laid her down on the bed again.

'I will never tell anyone about this,' he said softly. He breathed in through his mouth to avoid the smell in the warm air.

He was finished. She was clean again. He crossed the room to one of the empty beds of the silent ward. If anybody was awake they didn't say anything. He pulled off the bedding and dropped Emily's soiled sheets down in their place and went back to her. He checked the mattress and it was not as wet as the sheets. He unrolled some more of the toilet paper and dried it as best he could. He made the fresh sheets up, rolling Emily to one side as he tucked the other in until she was lying, once again, in a clean bed.

He took the bin and the dirty sheets outside to the large, metal dumpster. The cold air made him shiver. The moon was nearly full and the stars were so bright they turned the sky purple.

He went back inside and cleaned his hands with some of the water from the tank near the door. When he sat back down in his chair at the side of Emily's bed he looked at his girlfriend.

'There,' he said. 'It never happened.'

'A lot of things have happened,' she answered.

Charlie's breathing stopped and he sat up quickly. Her voice sounded weird, like it was not quite hers. It was deeper and slower. He leaned over her.

'Can you hear me?' he said. She didn't answer. 'Is there –' he swallowed – 'can you come back? Can you fight it?'

Emily stared at the white netting overhead as if the words she had spoken had never existed.

'Come on, Emily,' he pleaded. He stood and leaned right over her face so they were both staring at each other. 'You have to be able to come back,' he said. He felt his chest fill with something. It was like joy. If she was talking, she must still be there. 'I know you feel sad but we can fight this.' He kissed her cheek. His voice was loud in the dark, silent room. 'You don't have to be sad because I love you. Em, please.' He moved his hands on to her arms and shook her gently. 'You don't have to give in. Please don't. You have to stay alive. We need people like you in the world. We need more people like you, not less.' She was looking at him. She wasn't turning away. 'That's it.' He smiled. The weight in his body was lifting. The darkness was retreating. He was getting through to her. He could sense that behind her eyes she was fighting. 'Remember that time when we went for a bike ride in the middle of the night on the last day of term? And we found that bench on the seafront? You said it was the happiest you'd ever been.' He smiled at her. 'Think of that. Think of all the great times you've had. Put them in the front of your head. Think of all the great things still to come. Everything will be better one day; it's not impossible. Just fight it. I think what you have to do is put the happy things right up there, that's how you can beat it. I just have this feeling.' Emily continued to gaze at him. He wished that tears would form in her eyes. That would at least be a sign. Something flickered in her. Charlie lifted his face away from hers. She was going to say something.

'I've seen so many things now. I think they're true, I don't know.'

Charlie nodded, urging her on.

'It's like there's more than one truth,' she said. 'One thing is true if you feel one way, but if you look at the same thing and you feel differently, then another thing is true.'

Charlie nodded again.

'Love is an extension of hope,' she said. 'Not the other way round.' He stopped smiling. Emily swallowed and regarded him as if she did not know, and had never known, who he was; as if he was just some impostor who had invaded her life. 'That's why I don't love you any more.'

|||

The baby was restless. It could sense its mother's unease. It kicked hard against its wall, over and over. Miriam placed her hands on the globe of her stomach.

She was lying in bed, far away from sleep. The children slept next to her. Her mother was sitting up, looking out of the window of their little campervan. Thinking her daughter was asleep she sat over her family and Miriam wondered how often this had happened in the past without her being aware of it. She said nothing. In a way she felt like a child again with her mother keeping vigil like that.

I'm safe, she told herself. There are no noises and I am safe.

The surrounding danger was palpable but it was not moving. In the present was solace. Stretches of time, long-term plans; if you had such concepts then you had not adjusted correctly to the way things now were, and Miriam realized this. Time was immediate. If she was going to worry about the future then she would never stop worrying and the thin lattice of hope around which her whole existence was now precariously balanced would crash.

Into the small hours of the morning she waited for the sound of gunfire, or screaming, or explosions, or some other indicator of violence. The camp held its breath and waited for something that never came. Safety in numbers, she thought.

There was no attack. Miriam was washed into sleep halfway to dawn and there she stood, in the library again, not on the cellar floor, between the shelves and shelves of books, waiting for the beach to her right to burst into flames and for the great black sea monster to devour her husband once again.

|||

Morning came. The temperature had dropped and the sky had lowered itself with dense grey clouds. In the bay the great skeleton of the grounded tanker yawned its metallic song. Its innards were rusted and breaking, the decomposing metal amalgams of its hull raining down to the seabed as they would for centuries until the violence of the day that had marooned it became so great that all other remnants of the machine would be lost to the effortless infinity of the ocean.

The people of the camp awoke from their few scant hours of rest and emerged from their little shelters blinking and with a temporary relief. They had not been attacked. They were still alive. They took the shared air into their lungs and wiped their weary eyes.

||||

Mary was getting much better at holding a grudge. She still hadn't forgiven Edward for not letting her play football, despite the fact that he had pulled her from the cellar of the house and taken her to the safety of the beach. In the olden days she would have got over it in a few hours, but it had been four days now and she still wasn't back to normal. It made him feel bad inside. He had promised to protect her and now he felt he had betrayed her.

When Edward tried to speak to her she would turn dramatically away and look into the air as if she could not hear him.

'I said, are you coming to play?'

Still she refused to answer.

'Fine.' She was so stupid. He stormed off.

'Wait,' she called after him.

Edward turned. Her wellington boots were caked in mud and her dress fluttered around her knees.

'Where are you going?'

'We're going up to the lighthouse,' he answered. A sudden pang of love struck him, as it always did, out of nowhere, and he wished his dad was still alive because Mary needed her dad. 'Why don't you come?'

He could see that she wanted to.

'I'm going to stay here and keep Grandma company,' she said stubbornly. 'She's probably bored,' she added.

He knew what she was doing. She was trying to make him feel bad, and it was working.

'You could stay with us, Edward,' she said, tilting her head and placing her hands behind her back.

'But I told the others I was going to meet them.'

'Why are you so mean?' she said.

'I'm not being mean. I have to go because I said I would.'

Mary turned and ran up the muddy hill to where they were staying. The mud hopped up around her boots as she ran, like a group of slimy frogs jumping all around her. He wanted to go after her. He didn't want to make new friends if it meant she was going to be on her own all the time.

He started back up the hill, following his sister's tracks. If he went after her this time then it might be enough for her to forgive him for what he had done on the beach with the football game.

'Eddie.'

Edward stopped. He recognized the voice as that of Adam, the tall blond kid. Turning back round he saw them there, five of them, standing in the path waiting for him.

III

They went down the muddy track with the line of lightbulbs along its side and into the car park.

'I thought we were going to the lighthouse,' said Edward.

Michael, the short, ginger-haired boy, was walking next to him. 'Change of plan,' he said.

Adam led the way. Behind him were three others. One of them was a kid who, Edward remembered, was called Trio. He remembered because he had long hair down to his shoulders and looked cool. The second boy was the fat one with glasses who had played in goal. His name was John. The last one was the small black kid, Saul. He was the one whose father had apparently been killed by the marauders. He was the youngest.

The boys made their way through the car park. They stopped

when the entrance to the beach came into sight, just past the utility block.

A group of men were sitting in chairs around the low wall. Beyond them a tower of sandbags was piled high to protect the camp in the little valley between the low sand dunes.

Grass-covered sand dunes bulged up on either side of the entrance point. On top of them more of the wire fences had been put up, but they looked a little wonky to Edward's eye because the ground on which they stood was not flat.

'What are we doing?' Edward asked.

'Ssh.' Adam put his finger to his lips and went over to Edward. He smiled slyly. 'We're going to do some spying.' His glassy blue eyes scanned for Edward's reaction.

'What do you mean?'

'I heard my dad talking to some of the others. They reckon McAvennie's a wimp and that he should be doing something to fight back.'

Edward found it hard to believe that Mr McAvennie was a wimp. He was huge. Edward looked at the other children. They all seemed happy with whatever plan Adam had devised.

'So we're going to spy on the vampires,' he said.

'If we know what they're doing,' interrupted the fat kid with glasses, 'we can report back to our dads and they can find a way to beat them. No offence, Saul,' he said to the fatherless black kid as an unnecessary aside.

'Don't you want to help your dad?' said Adam.

Edward looked at him. Did he know?

'My dad's dead,' he said firmly. Something moved in his chest. He had never said that before. His face was burning red and then there was somebody patting his back. Looking round he saw Saul smiling sadly up at him.

Edward knew his mother would kill him if she knew what they were planning. It had been hard enough to get her to let him out in the first place after he had sneaked down to the beach without asking.

'But there's no way to get out of the camp.'

Edward had already decided he did not like Adam. He was cocky and loud-mouthed and there was an aggression bubbling away inside him. This plan only confirmed his feelings. Adam grinned again.

'Follow me.'

'I think I'm going to go back,' Edward said quickly, making his decision.

All the boys looked at him.

'It'll be all right, Eddie,' said Trio. 'Even if we get caught they won't do anything to us. We're just kids to them. That's why we have to do it. It's more dangerous for the grown-ups than it is for us.'

'But still.'

'Come on, man,' Saul said. 'They killed my dad.'

The two boys made eye contact. The marauders were evil. And you do have to fight evil. Something told him this was the right thing to do, even if it was stupid and dangerous. His uncle would have done it.

'Look, Eddie,' said Michael in his fast, high-pitched voice. 'They'll thank us for it.' He pushed Edward gently in the back.

'Are you with us?' said Adam. He was standing right in front of him and Edward suddenly realized just how much bigger Adam was. He no longer felt like he had a choice.

|||

They ducked between the cars in the car park and made their way to the front wall. Edward's heart was thumping. He was remembering climbing out through the little window in the cellar on the night the marauders had come, and the level of fear that had propelled him so quickly across the grass to the cliff path with his little sister.

Beyond the car park was an uneven patch of marram grass hummocks before the tall, wire fences about twenty yards away.

Adam peeked over the wall to check the coast was clear.

'OK, go.'

He jumped easily over and disappeared to the right, towards the beach, into the grass hummocks. The other boys followed. Edward tried to wait until they had all gone but Michael refused to let him go last. Edward felt sick. Over the wall he went. The grass came up past his knees and his feet sank into the soft sand.

He ran as fast as he could after the other boys, adrenalin pushing him on. He caught up with them and overtook the fat kid with glasses. They snaked along the floor of the little valley they were in, between the small, grassy dunes, until they came to the wire fence, where they stopped.

Adam gave them instructions to remain in the tall grass at the back of the beach and to run to the cliff path. The metal containers where there had been people living were now empty and so it should be a clear run.

As he spoke Edward looked at the top of the fence; he couldn't see how they could get over it but Adam crouched down into the grass and parted the tall, bony stems at their base to reveal an open space at the valley floor where the fence did not quite meet the ground. It was just big enough to crawl through.

The fence rattled and the boys had to cover their mouths in case the men further along the beach heard them laughing. Edward started to feel a little better.

They were standing on the precipice of a low bluff and they clambered down on their bottoms until soon they were jogging along through the marram. The tide was far out, but it was just turning inwards. The boys waited at the base of the cliff path to catch their breath. There was no sign of the marauders and Edward's sense of fear was giving way to one of adventure and excitement. It felt like a game.

'Right,' said Adam. 'So now we need to get to the top of the cliff and wait. You got the binoculars, John?'

The fat kid with glasses lifted up his sweater. Strapped to his belt was a pair of binoculars in a hard leather case.

'Cool. OK, ready?'

Adam looked at each of the boys. John removed his glasses and pinched the top of his nose in a dramatic display of stress.

'I don't know about this.'

'What don't you know?' Adam tilted his head.

'I don't know. If this is really a good idea.'

'It's too late now. We have to go.'

'It's dangerous, Adam.'

'So why did you come?'

John shifted his weight from one foot to the other. Edward felt the same way as him. He knew this was stupid.

'Come on, let's just fucking go,' said Michael from the back in his squeaky voice. He passed the boys and hopped up on to the first step of the cliff path. 'We're just wasting time.'

The dead ferns on either side of the path were thick and damp. Water evaporated from them into swirling ghosts of mist that magically disappeared when the boys got too close to them. Whenever they came to a bend in the path they would stop and listen. But it was always quiet. Edward looked out over the bay. The sea was such a long way out.

Adam moved silently behind him and he could hear Saul and Trio talking quietly until Adam told them to shut up. They were near the top of the path. Edward knew the final strait of steps well, with their rocky, clay surfaces.

He strained his ears. There was still no sound. Suddenly he realized something. The marauders would never leave this path unguarded. What they were doing was ridiculous. Even if the marauders were vampires, their masks protected them from sunlight.

They were here. Just as he had known the kids had been watching him from the gorse bushes that day on the cliff top, he knew that alien eyes were on him now. His sixth sense was never wrong. He stopped.

'What?' Adam whispered.

But Edward was watching the damp, brown bracken of the ferns. They were moving. Edward swung his body round to the other side. Another form was rising up out of the undergrowth, this one already further out of the bracken than the first. The movement was sickeningly slow, like a long-dead monster coming up out of a swamp.

The boys turned to run but the path was blocked. A man dressed in black clothes and wearing a black gas mask was standing over them. He aimed a short rifle at them and used its tip to point them up the path.

'Go,' he said, through the mask in a deep, fuzzy voice. 'Up the hill.'

III

Edward had never felt his heart beat as fast as it was beating now. It thumped with such ferocity he thought it might explode out of his chest.

They reached the summit of the path and walked out on to the grassland where four more of the vampires waited for them. The boys had nowhere to go.

The men looked ugly and dangerous. Edward imagined their heavy, thick boots kicking him in the head as he lay helpless on the floor. Up ahead the old house looked cold and dirty. There were lots of big trucks parked in front of the garage and on the grass at its side. He wanted to do something, take some action. His mind raced for an idea that would help them escape. He could smell the damp on the air, the scent of the grass, the salt from the sea. His senses were stronger.

To his left, Saul started to cry. Edward looked at him. Saul was a foot shorter than he was. His clothes were tiny. He must have been years younger than him.

'Please let us go.' Michael looked at the ground as he spoke. 'We won't do it again. We're sorry.'

'What is it that you are doing?' one of the vampires said. With the gas mask pulled over his face the voice sounded like a robot. The big insect eyes of the mask reflected the grey sky.

'You won't do anything to us,' said Adam.

Edward looked at him. 'Adam.'

'If you don't let us go, we'll sue you.'

The largest vampire tilted his head and said something that sounded more like an insect clicking than a voice. All the other vampires started laughing. The large one stepped closer to Adam.

'You will report us to the police, is that right?'

'Yeah.'

'I do not think we will let you go.' He paused. 'Your parents – they have one of my friends down there and so we will keep some of their friends up here.'

'Fuck you,' said Adam. Edward couldn't believe what Adam was doing. 'I'm not afraid of you,' he spat.

'What have we done to you? Have we attacked you, or your family? I don't think so. And so why do your parents have our friend, when we have done nothing to you?'

'That's not my fault,' said Adam.

In a burst of violent movement the faceless vampire rushed Adam and grabbed him roughly by the back of the collar. He yanked him forward. Adam would have fallen if the vampire hadn't held him up.

The boy's face went red.

'Leave him alone,' said Michael. He tried to prise the vampire's fingers from Adam's collar. 'He can't breathe.'

The faceless figure pushed Michael away and the boy fell awkwardly to the ground. 'You must behave while you are with us.' He turned his head to Edward and the other boys. The sound of Saul's quiet sobs drifted on the wind. 'If you don't behave yourself you will be in very big trouble. We are not like your fathers. We come from a more cruel world than you.'

He turned and pulled Adam towards the cliff edge, away from the path, to where the grass ran away to nothing. Adam's legs dangled behind him, trying unsuccessfully to get a grip.

Edward felt his own body grow taut and hollow. The fibres in his flesh went hard.

Adam's red face looked strange against his blond hair.

The vampire stopped and turned back to them. He was five yards from the cliff edge. The grass sloped horribly towards it. Edward looked at the other vampires. They passively watched their leader do whatever it was he was about to do.

'This is your first lesson,' shouted the lead vampire. 'It is called "obeying".'

One of the smaller marauders was close to Edward. He could get the gun off him if the other boys saw him and helped him.

'You will obey me, or I will kill you.'

He swung Adam around like he was made of nothing but feathers, and let go.

Edward watched as the boy ran towards the cliff under the momentum. He tried to stop but his legs were not his own, he was going too fast, the ground was too steep. He fell to the grass but his body continued to roll horribly down the slope. Time moved so slowly. If he could get his body to move, Edward was sure he could reach Adam in time. But his body wouldn't move. Adam started to scream. He wasn't going to stop. The scream disappeared and he fell. His body vanished. He was gone.

|||

Everything came to life. The vampires encircled the boys, shouting instructions through their alien masks. Saul was screaming. John and Michael were standing with their hands on their heads, looking at the spot where Adam had just been. Trio watched the largest vampire lumber back towards them with giant strides.

Edward felt warmth against his legs. He had wet himself. A grown-up hand pushed his back. An angry voice echoed around the inside of his head. His legs stumbled forwards and he fell. Hands picked him up and moved him on. They were heading for the house. He thought of his mother and how she would feel if she never saw him again.

The house looked monstrous. The door was opened and the boys were pushed forcibly into its throat, into the dark.

The vampires had put a large, metal lock on the outside of the cellar door. One of them slid it back and the boys were thrown inside. John was pleading something with them but Edward was unable to comprehend his words. He went obediently down the steps and the door was slammed closed behind them.

The lock on the outside bolted shut.

He reached the bottom step and stopped. There were eyes in the dark. The window through which he had escaped before had been boarded up with wooden planks. He couldn't see properly.

'Hello?' His voice went timidly out in front of him and searched for a reply.

It came back quickly. It was another child's voice. 'Hello?'

|||

'Come in.'

Charlie went in to Dr Balad's office. His desk was empty apart from the pair of glasses that lay upside down in front of the doctor.

'Hello, Charlie.' His quiet, measured voice sounded tired.

'Emily doesn't have long,' he said. He just needed to say what he had to say without thinking too deeply about it. 'She's in her last day.' The doctor's eyes reflected the faded light of the weak lamp. He said nothing. 'I know we can do something,' said Charlie.

Dr Balad nodded. 'I see.'

'Mims. He was cured. He had it and got better, didn't he? Everyone knows. That's why we have him here. Isn't it?'

The doctor sat up in his chair. The wooden frame creaked under his movement. 'It is true,' he said.

'So you can cure Emily.'

'We don't know the cure, Charlie.'

Charlie shook his head, refusing to believe it. 'You can do something for her. Mims has been here for the same length of time as us – you must have learned something.'

'Now you must listen,' said Dr Balad, his voice suddenly tight. 'I am not a scientist, I'm a medical doctor. I have done everything I know but it has led to nothing.'

His eyes seared with desperation that mirrored Charlie's heart. The answer to everything was with them but they could not access it.

'Have you not been able to get anything out of him?'

Dr Balad steepled his long, thin fingers underneath his chin. 'Christopher Mims has no idea what happened to him. They cut his skin up into lines and yet he remembers nothing. And I can find nothing medical in what they did.'

'But who did it? Can't we find them?'

'He doesn't remember. He doesn't know where he came from, or who did it.'

'But –' Charlie put the ball of his hand to his forehead – 'there must be some way.'

'I will tell you everything I know but it will not help you. Just like everything with this disease, the cure, if it happened, would defy logic. I like to see people die no more than you. I can assure you that I have been affected in an equal way to everybody by what has happened.'

'Tell me what he said.'

'He spoke only of a great pain. The people who did what they did . . . they cut him open. There are surgical wounds, all over his body, and they are very clean. They were made by a surgical knife but to what end I have been unable to discern. It makes no sense to me. Really, he should have died from his wounds – they are that extensive. It is a miracle he is still alive.'

Charlie sensed that what the doctor was saying to him was something he had said countless times before, like an actor reciting lines. He wondered to how many families this man had said this, how many times he had been made to quietly crush the hope they held for their loved one's survival. All they wanted was answers, knowledge. Understanding. That would make it easier. But there was none.

'The cuts he said brought him great pain and all he can remember apart from the pain itself is emerging from it into a room with bright lights, the operating theatre. After that, his memory clouds again and then he wakes up not far from here. And that is his story. There is nothing more to it than that.' Dr Balad took a handkerchief from his white jacket pocket and placed it to his nose.

'So you think there's a place near by that did this? A hospital, or a government facility or something?'

'No.'

'There must be.'

'There is no such place, Charlie. We have looked. It does not exist.'

'But—'

'No. Charlie, understand me. We cannot save Emily.'

The two men looked at each other across the desk.

'You know,' said the old man, 'you should feel blessed for your time with her.'

Charlie scoffed and turned his head away. He wasn't looking for consolation.

'I do not say that in a haphazard way. I have seen many people become ill here in this lazaret. Hell –' he laughed – 'I spend all day with them. And I have seen all of the different reactions to the illness. You see, to my own mind, this illness, this "Sadness" as they say, seems like nothing more than something going missing from us. As a doctor this is of course a silly thing to say, because illness is brought about in a typical way by the introduction of something into the body – a virus, a bacterium, a poison – but here we can find no such foreign invader. You know of what I speak, yes? Something is lost in those that become ill.'

Charlie closed his mouth tight shut.

'People think that when somebody falls ill with this disease they become very still and sad, or if not they become angry and violent, you see? But that is not right. It is not one or the other, it is a whole spectrum. A sliding scale. That is what I think, judging by what I have seen. Whatever the illness is, the resulting symptoms are people's reaction to whatever it is being lost from them. There are no tests to prove this, no experiments we can do. It operates entirely outside of our science. But I have seen it. Everybody has.

'And people react in myriad different ways. Some will cry to their deaths, some will talk of their greatest fears, others of the things they never experienced, and others still will run away from everything they love –'

Miriam opened the door of the campervan and stepped down into the cold weather. The smell of salt was strong on the wind.

'– Some will consider the very worst thing they can do, and then, despite every inch of them telling them to stop, they go ahead and do it –'

She pressed her hand against her stomach. The baby moved towards it.

'– There is no loss of consciousness, not even in the violent ones. They do not turn into chaotic, thoughtless killing machines. As they carry out their atrocities, they know inside what they are doing. But they cannot stop –'

As she did every hour of every day, she thought about the night in the cellar. The flash of memories never went away.

'– They do it anyway. They cannot stop because the thing they lost when they fell ill was all that kept them from slipping into their own terrible chaos.'

She was looking at Joseph's dead body sitting on the wooden steps of the cellar. The yellow morning was peering through the tiny window above her head. She breathed in. The air was cold and soothing.

'She told me she doesn't love me any more.'

'That was not Emily speaking. She was telling you something that was not true. She thought it was true because of the thing she had lost, but it is a funny thing, the truth. People always think it is a simple idea. They believe it to be flat, like a piece of paper, and if you shine a light on it you can see it and there is nothing else to be seen. But it is not like that. The truth is like a globe. You shine a light on one side and the thing you see will be different from that which you would see if you shone a light from another angle. Both are the truth, and both are different.' He smiled. 'That really is the truth.'

She went down the hill and sensed something in her chest. The density was returning. She turned her head and looked out of the camp to the old house on the top of the hill.

IIII

The kids in the cellar told them they been kept captive by the vampires for months. As they spoke, a feeling of sickness grew in Edward's belly. The kids were weird. They said the marauders were not vampires at all, they were just normal men. None of them had ever seen any of them drinking blood or anything like that. They spoke very quickly and quietly. Their faces, even in the dimness of the light, could be seen to be thin and grimy and the whites of their eyes gleamed with their own light.

Edward hadn't said anything. He knew that if he spoke he would start crying. The image of Adam being thrown over the cliff replayed in his head but it never seemed real. His brain would not allow him to accept it had happened.

The cellar was full of children. Many of them sat slumped on the floor between the shelves of supplies – lines of bodies disappearing towards the far wall, into the shadows. There was definitely something very odd about them, like they didn't have any energy. They didn't have the Sadness; it was different from that. To Edward, they seemed to be like old people but in children's bodies.

'What do you think they'll do to us?' said John. His voice was higher than normal.

'They'll train you up, probably,' came the reply. 'If you don't mess up, they'll keep you.'

'What do you mean?'

The door at the top of the stairs swung open with a heavy creak and the boys stopped. Light flooded the stairway and a black figure appeared. He clomped down the steps and into the centre of the children. The light from a torch in his hands played over the boys – Edward was aware in a back corner of his mind that there were no girls down here – until it came to a rest on Trio. The boy squinted and held his hand up to block the light.

Edward watched in a detached, emotionless state. His fear was receding and being replaced by nothingness.

The man lurched through the protruding limbs of the boys, grabbed Trio and pulled him up to his feet with a violent tug. Trio tried to struggle, shouted, 'Get off me,' but the man beat him across the side of the face with the handle of his torch and after that Trio went quietly, dragged up the stairs and beyond the closing door.

Nobody said anything. No air was being breathed in the room. The boys waited.

Even through the ceiling Trio's scream rang out clearly. Edward covered his ears to block it out. His heart felt like tiny needles of glass were being fired into it. When the glass shower was finished his pulse emerged as a deep thunderclap, thumping over and over.

Saul started crying loudly. Through the dark he clambered over the bodies towards Edward and sat down next to him. Edward put his arm around the boy but couldn't speak.

Michael went to the bottom of the stairs and looked up at the door. He said something but Edward couldn't hear him. Above, Trio was still screaming. He would stop for a second and then start again. Sitting on the cold stone floor, Edward dropped his head on to his knees and clenched his teeth. He couldn't even imagine what they were doing to him. Beyond his heartbeat he felt again the sickness stirring in his gut. Adults weren't supposed to do these things to children.

'Stop crying.'

Edward paused. The voice was near to him. He looked up. The dark shape of one of the boys was standing before him as an inky, indistinct mass. 'I said shut up.'

He was talking to Saul. Edward pulled the little kid closer to him.

'Leave him alone,' he croaked.

'If he keeps crying like that they'll come back.'

'He's only a little kid.' His voice was shaky. The little boy next to him was trembling.

'I couldn't give a fuck,' said the boy, his voice becoming something more like a growl. It was unstable. Edward was frightened by it. 'If you don't shut him up, I'll do it for him.'

|||

The inwards approach of the sea was like the inwards approach of the marauders. David watched it coming in. Having been stationed at the sandbag lookout turret on the beach there was little else to do. His mind wandered in and out with the movement of the sea's edge. He wondered, as he did most days, about the fate that had befallen his parents, he thought about how hungry he was, he thought about his friend, Charlie, up in the lighthouse with Emily, and then he thought about just what exactly was going to happen to the camp. He tried to remain true to his theory of human resilience being all-powerful. Everybody would stick together because it was the best way to survive. It was pure Darwin really. But faced with an unseen enemy, the only sign of which was in the destruction and violence they left behind them, his theory seemed suddenly very naive.

The waves were big. If you watched them for long enough – the way they rose up, curled over and flopped down one after another – they could hypnotize you. The sound of the crash came after the sight of the wave collapsing; out of time. Wave after wave; he watched them come further and further up the beach.

At first, he thought the black shape in the waves was a log being tossed around in the surf. It was only when the tide came close enough that he thought it was too irregular for a piece of wood. They had a child's telescope to look through. David brought it over and steadied himself by placing his elbows on the sandbags. After a few moments he located the object and centred it in the lens. He held his breath and waited.

A new wave was forming in the bay. It drew the water before it up into its curling wall. It lifted the shape and turned it over and David dropped the telescope.

'Jesus,' he whispered.

He called over to one of the men and pointed out to sea. The man swore and looked down the beach, towards the cliff path. The beach was empty.

'Come on,' he said.

They streaked down the sand and into the frothy white of the surf. They pulled the body to dry land. It was a child. Its body was broken in the middle, the clothes ripped about a great red gash in the ribs. Its face had been folded into the skull on one side. It looked monstrous and inhuman.

'I know who this is,' said the man.

David lost control of his stomach and threw up into the sand.

|||

'That is why I say you have been lucky, Charlie. Because Emily has not acted like anybody else I have seen. It is true that everybody behaves in the quiet, gentle way at the illness's outset, but they undergo at least some level of change over the course of the three days. They progress along the spectrum. Some go far along it, to the end. Others go only a short way along. I speak to families and I understand, Charlie, what seems to decide the trajectory of a particular person, and it is always the people who were the most loved that go on the shortest journey along the spectrum.'

Charlie could not look at him. His throat was hot and there was a pain in his temples.

'And they were loved because of the people they were before they were ill. I cannot explain it in any other way. Some people inspire great love in others. I do not know why any more than I know how many stars there are. But whatever that inexplicable thing is that causes people to be loved, it is very strong in those who remain gentle.

'And I can say to you honestly,' said the doctor to Charlie, who shifted in his seat as the doctor spoke, 'that Emily has taken the shortest journey along the spectrum of anyone I have seen.'

Emily had once told him that sometimes she wanted never to speak again, and that those times came when she was most contented. She said it was as if speaking was not necessary; that sometimes it just made things complicated. Often, when lying in bed in the morning, or when sitting on a bench in a park, or walking along the seafront, she had told Charlie to shut up and stop his incessant talking. And when in silence he looked at the world's sights and smelled its smells and heard its sounds, he started to know what she meant. But she was speaking now. And she was looking at him.

'There is something in us. It is seeded when we are very young and it is buried very deep. We are rarely reminded of it, but when we are we remember it well and feel like we have just been greeted by an old friend. And we think we will never forget it again. But we always do. It's that thing that connects us all. It's like a little stream that flows through us and between us and reminds us that we are part of one big thing.' Emily closed her eyes tight. 'Oh, you don't understand.' Her eyes reopened and she turned her face away from Charlie, the shadows shifting in the clefts of the white pillowcase. The shimmering meniscus of a tear played on her eye. 'You don't know what I mean,' she said.

'I do.'

Charlie looked at her and watched the change that in that instant befell her and he saw the world as it was: a great spinning orb thrusting aimlessly through the void and then he was back on the lawn of the university campus again with the sun on his back and a pair of delicate hands before him.

He held those hands in his own and for the briefest of moments felt serene.

The change he had witnessed was just an infinitesimal thing. So small and so big. He let go of Emily's hand and it fell to the blanket. Only the memories remained now.

|||

Adam's father was halfway down the beach. David held the child in his arms. One side of the body, from the shoulder to the hips, had collapsed in on itself as if it didn't have any bones. It allowed the body to sit in its human cradle as if it had been designed that way.

A group of people had gathered near the sandbags, which had been pushed over to make access to the beach easier.

Adam's father, upon seeing his child's lifeless and broken body, stopped. He looked at it as if it was something obscene. The initial hesitation in his eyes flickered away and David handed the body over.

The man's glasses were steamed up. He saw the child through a mist. He said nothing. His mouth seized into a clenched, vice-like lock.

'I just found him,' said David. He was freezing. His clothes were sodden and the taste of salt was strong in his mouth.

The crowd of people kept their distance as Adam's father went down on to his knees and laid his son's body on the sand. He put his hands over his face in silent agony, sliding his fingers beneath his glasses, over his eyes. His shoulders rounded to a slump and he stayed there in that position for a full minute.

|||

Charlie ran his hand over Emily's face. His mind had started its revolutions again. Those few brief moments with her had ended, the serenity had cracked and the darkness encroached. He felt her cheeks and placed his fingers at her lips. She was still warm and he wanted to make sure that he never forgot the way she felt. Panicked that he might forget something about her, some tiny nuance, made him touch her. He looked at her and tried to take a photograph in his mind.

He became aware of somebody watching him. He looked one last time at Emily and turned back into the room. When he saw Miriam standing there in the centre of the darkening space he opened his mouth to speak but nothing came out. He felt the deep bond of loss between them.

Miriam went to him and threw her arms around him. He hugged back quickly, surprised at himself.

'She only just went,' he whispered.

She put her hand on Charlie's head, through the curls of his hair. He was just a child really. Charlie held on to her. Over her shoulder, he said, 'It's not fair that she's gone.'

An image crossed her mind, of Henry in the rear-view mirror of the car.

'I know,' she said.

'She didn't deserve it.'

Henry had gone to sleep slowly that night. She had stayed with him. He had just looked at her. That was all. They had sat on the bed covers, his back twisted against the headboard and his legs curled under him. She had held his hand and they had looked at one another for a long time until his eyes had shut and he had gone to sleep.

|||

Edward shifted his body so he could shield Saul.

'He's scared,' he said.

'He should be scared – if they hear him. Now are you going to shut him up?'

Edward looked down at the top of Saul's head, just a dark, murky shape. The little boy was sobbing more quietly. He had heard the threat of the boy standing over him and was trying to stop himself.

'Don't worry about it, Saul, we'll be out of here soon.'

'We're not getting out of here,' said the boy in the dark.

Edward tried to pick out Michael and John in the gloom but he couldn't see them. He wished they would come over and help.

'We will get out of here. The people in the camp will come and save us.'

The boy laughed. 'Are you kidding?'

'Or we'll escape,' Edward added.

'Escape?'

'This is my house,' he said. 'I know how to get us out of here.'

There was a hesitation.

'What makes you think I'd let you go?'

Edward felt his skin go cold. His mouth was dry. He realized something. 'How old are you?'

'Older than you are.'

Saul pressed his body closer to Edward in fear.

'Whose side are you on?'

|||

Charlie couldn't look at Miriam. His eyes flitted around the room and rested on anything but her. Inside his head everything felt clear and sharp.

'When we came back from Europe we went to her family first but the place was deserted. There was no sign of a struggle or anything and the house was still intact. It looked like when somebody goes on holiday, you know? They had just vanished. We never found them, but she never mentioned them. Never.'

He hadn't told anybody this since it had happened. The only other person who had known about it was Emily. But his mind focused now in a cool, detached way that allowed him to gain a wider perspective, unblocked by the foggy emotions that had blinded him from the truth.

'So then we went to my family. We got near the house and I got this feeling that something was wrong, do you know what I mean?

Since the illness first broke I've been aware of this thing, like, I don't know, a sixth sense.'

Miriam nodded that she did know.

'I wanted to turn back and run but she stopped me. She said we had to go and see because if I didn't then . . .' He paused and changed tack. 'She just said I was afraid. So we went.'

The memory of it played in his head as he recited to Miriam what had happened. She listened in silence.

'When we got there, the front door was lying in the garden, just torn off. I already knew what had happened. There were no noises inside. It was weird because the living room wasn't trashed. Someone had come in and taken the TV and stuff but apart from that it looked normal. It had all happened in the kitchen. It must have only taken a couple of minutes.'

His throat was dry from speaking and he could hear his voice cracking. The images of the house were still so crisp.

'The first person I saw was my dad and he was just . . . lying . . . there, on the floor. His head, it was just, I don't know, weird. It was all out of shape and scabby. He was lying in a big dried-out circle of blood; my *dad*.' The fog of emotion was coming back. He felt hot. 'You know, you see something like that and something inside you just snaps and it'll never repair itself. My mum was the same. Her head was crushed as well. Oh God—'

Miriam hugged him again. Charlie felt sick. His eyes were stinging.

'It was all flat.'

He envisaged the scene, lived it out in his mind. There was no point holding it back any more.

'It was my brother. He must have got sick. He, you know, he always thought he knew everything, but he wasn't a bad person, Miri. He wasn't the sort of person who could do something like that.'

'I know,' she whispered. 'Don't say any more now.'

'He wasn't a bad person. What he did, he killed my whole family, even my little sister, but he didn't know what he was doing,' he cried.

Miriam bit her lower lip.

'When they get ill, some people do things that aren't them.'

She swallowed.

'You can't say he was bad because of what he did. Once you're ill you're not the same. I *know* he was a good person.'

Miriam said nothing. The baby kicked in its womb.

'He tried to be a good person in life and that's the most important thing. Dr Balad said the illness just strips away the barrier between us and chaos. So if my brother was so close to chaos all the time then surely the most important thing is that he kept it at bay when he was normal. He fought it every day. It didn't control him.'

Miriam looked out of the window. The sky was shifting, the clouds thinning. As Charlie unburdened himself from something that had been wrapped so tightly around him, a crack appeared in the gloom of the dusk and she remembered something somebody had once said to her about how everything had cracks because it was the only way for light to get in.

||||

The kid moved quickly. He grabbed Edward by the chin and pushed his head back against the stone wall. Instinctively Edward leaped forward and wrestled him to the floor. He was surprised by how easily the kid fell. Hands lashed out at Edward but he was able to grip their wrists. His arms bent against the pressure from the other kid but he refused to let go. Slowly, using every muscle in his arms, Edward pushed back. The scuffle took place in silence. Nobody said anything in case the men upstairs heard and came down to take another one of them.

'What are you doing?' Edward panted.

'You're dead,' the kid replied in a whisper.

'But I can get us out of here.'

He was winning the struggle.

'You can't. We're never getting out.'

The kid's strength suddenly died, as if defeated by his own words. He turned his face away and lay still and Edward pinned his arms to the floor.

'I can get us out. I know a way.'

The atmosphere in the cellar had changed. Edward felt the eyes of the children on him, but they were no longer threatening.

'How?' said a voice.

'Shut up, Patrick,' said another.

'Why should I?'

'We're part of the Collective.'

'I'm not part of it.'

'Neither am I,' said another voice.

'They'll kill us.'

'They won't kill us,' said Edward.

'How can we get out?'

Edward released the wrists of the boy he had been fighting. The boy didn't move. Edward felt good; powerful. One thing was for sure and that was that he was not scared. All he wanted to do now was get out and get back to his mum and his sister and his gran.

'We have to wait until it gets dark,' he said.

|||

Miriam's mother watched from the crowd. Mary was standing directly in front of her with her grandmother's hands on her shoulders. The rumours were already spreading that the men who had taken the house had killed a child.

She saw the little boy's father stand up and turn to the group. The man swayed on his feet like he was drunk and then stumbled towards the crowd. He was walking, Miriam's mother could see, towards McAvennie.

'Where is he?' he said. 'Where's the prisoner?'

McAvennie shook his head, breaking ranks from the group and stepping towards the child's father. He said something to him that Miriam's mother couldn't hear.

The boy's father shook his head violently, his face contorting. He grabbed McAvennie's sweater.

'Tell me.' His voice rang out.

McAvennie lowered his head.

A voice came from the crowd.

'They put him in the lighthouse.'

A chaotic instability was stirring. Bodies behind her were bumping Miriam's mother forwards and there was nothing she could do to stop it. She almost knocked Mary over.

'Can we go back?' said the little girl.

A hand grabbed the old woman's shoulder and moved her roughly aside. Its owner stepped past her.

'I'll help you, Benjamin,' he said.

He was a large man with a thick, brown beard. He was looking at the little corpse lying in the sand and Miriam's mother could see the genuine lines of pain across his face.

Some of the women in the crowd were crying. More people were coming on to the beach. Miriam's mother turned her head and looked up towards the house. She could just see the roof and the upstairs windows.

Benjamin, Adam's father, snapped his head round.

'Come on,' said the man with the beard.

'No.' McAvennie held up his palms. 'This is not the way.'

'Forget it, George,' he said. 'Empathy and compassion you say. Well, where's the empathy and compassion for Benjamin? Look at his kid, for Christ's sake.' He gestured to the body. 'I've had it. We need to do something.'

'Revenge won't solve anything.'

'Just shut up,' Adam's father shouted.

Everybody turned to him.

'My son is dead. And somebody has to pay.'

'I'm with you,' someone shouted.

All around her, people started moving back up towards the camp.

Adam's father ran his hand through his thin blond hair. His anger was stronger than his grief and he left the child's body in the sand because he needed his vengeance.

'Please,' McAvennie called after him, but his voice was lost beneath the din. Unmoving, he watched the crowd follow Benjamin.

'What's going on, Gran?'

She didn't answer her granddaughter.

For how much longer could McAvennie hold things together, she thought, as she watched him make his decision and start running up the beach towards the mob.

|||

The wind blew through Charlie's hair and it felt good. His body felt insubstantial. The light of day was fading and soon the night would be on them again.

'Do you ever think about your husband?'

'Every day.'

He looked at her. Her face was white and the skin over it was loose. She always looked tired, her hair was lank and unkempt and the tip of her nose always red. The baby in her belly was huge and it seemed that every time she moved it took a massive effort. All of these things made Charlie think of her as being impossibly strong, with a machine inside her turning interminable rhythms of survival.

'At least you have the baby.'

He noticed something change in her face. He had said something wrong.

'The baby isn't his.'

His mind stumbled as he cursed himself. He lowered his jaw to speak and felt his cheeks redden.

'It's OK. Something happened,' she explained. 'My brother-in-law – you never met him – he looked after us and then one day –' she shrugged – 'he got ill.' She thought of Crowder, of how Joseph had told her he had killed him. 'It's like you said, some people find it easy to be good and some people find it hard. He was a good person, really.' She wondered if Charlie would ever again be the same person who had visited her that night before Christmas. She hoped he would. But it was going to be a long way back. 'It's the ones who find it hard but do it anyway who are the real saints,' she said.

|||

She was standing alone outside the lighthouse as she watched the people approach the outbuilding. There were too many of them to count. They reached the wooden door and tried the handle but it was locked. Some of them went to the small, square windows and peered inside. They were shouting and trying to force the door with their shoulders. There was something in the outbuilding and they wanted it very badly. Miriam stepped forwards and almost toppled with the weight of the baby.

McAvennie appeared from the crowd. He ran around the edge of the group and tried to get near the door. Fields was there too, along with some other men who made up McAvennie's team of helpers.

McAvennie was trying to stop them. He had forced his way through the crowd and taken up position between them and the door. His wide arm-span reached from one side of the door to the other and he wedged each of his palms into the frame so that nobody could get past.

Miriam waited at the back of the crowd. Through the heads and shoulders she found a clear line of sight.

'You mustn't do this,' he shouted. 'We need him.'

The crowd jeered back at him, a mass of distressed noise.

'Out of the way, George.'

There was a patch of space between McAvennie and the rest of the crowd. She could see the profile of a man with thin blond hair and spectacles. He seemed to be crying. A fierce anger was scarred on his face.

'Let us past.'

'Don't you see that if you do anything to him then that makes us as bad as them?'

'How dare you?' screamed the man with thin blond hair.

'They did it first.' This came from a second man, with a thick brown beard and long hair.

'Give him to us, George,' the blond man shouted.

Miriam stood on tiptoe. The crowd started shouting again. Their voices were furious. Something very bad had happened.

McAvennie tried to silence them but it was not working. There were too many of them and they were too volatile. Fields and some of the other men formed a line around McAvennie to keep the crowd out.

Angered by the men's protection of whatever was inside the

building the crowd drove suddenly forward as one, the sound of shouting and screaming heavy on the air.

Miriam grabbed the arm of the woman in front of her. 'What's happening?'

'They've got one of those *pigs* in there.' The woman faced forward and threw an angry fist into the air.

McAvennie had disappeared beneath the swarm of people. The sound of cracking wood crunched out over the noise of people shouting and the door to the outbuilding swung quickly open.

Barging and shouting came from within the small hut and then the crowd reversed itself and began to fan out into a ring, five to ten people deep.

Miriam saw a man thrown into the centre. He stumbled but kept his footing. She only caught a glimpse of him before the crack in the ring of people closed and all she could see were the backs of heads and shoulders. He was wearing black combat trousers tucked into heavy boots, a black shirt and a black army jacket. Around the top of his right arm was tied a red band. Seeing him there, in the daylight, induced a wave of nausea.

His hands were tied behind his back.

This crowd was baying for blood. There was something within their anger that could not have existed before; something wild and uncivilized. Whatever it was that had happened had triggered a ferocious, animalistic blood lust in these people. It was tangible in the air. The danger was intimidating in its immediacy. The crowd was entering something close to a frenzy.

McAvennie pleaded for reason.

'You can't. After all we've done. Please don't do this. If you do this everything will have been pointless.'

'They killed my son.'

The words snagged on Miriam's attention. She looked at the blond man again. Tears stained his face. Something started to make sense.

McAvennie had scrambled into the centre of the ring and was standing between the blond-haired man and the prisoner, who was expressionless in the violence around him.

'Why are you defending him?'

'We're not killers. If you do anything to this man you will have to live with it. It doesn't matter what *he*'s done – that's irrelevant. It's what *you* do that matters.'

'He doesn't deserve to live.'

'He's the only thing keeping them from attacking us. He's the only thing we have to bargain with.'

'I don't care . . . My son is dead, George.' The blond man opened his lips and his teeth clamped together.

The tall man with the brown beard shouted, 'Why are you so worried about them attacking us anyway? There are more of us than there are up there. We're armed. We have men who know what they are doing.'

The crowd started shouting again. Miriam strained to hear the conversation between McAvennie and the men near the front.

'Strength in numbers,' the man in the brown beard added. 'That's what you always say.'

McAvennie shook his head. 'But we don't have to fight. Why does everyone think that's the only way to solve this? The world is a bigger place now, much bigger than it was. There's room enough. We don't need to fight and die.'

The man in the brown beard grabbed his hair in exasperation.

'That's not how those people think, George. Are you being deliberately naive?'

And then, without warning, he pounced. Tired of speaking, he pushed McAvennie aside and lunged at the prisoner. In a tangle of arms and legs they toppled to the floor, where Miriam lost sight of them. The crowd was shouting and cheering. She saw, through the writhing mass of people, the blond-haired man step forward. McAvennie grabbed him and said something and looked at him pleadingly but the blond man broke eye contact, pushed past him and disappeared beneath the crowd of heads and pumping fists.

The crowd was shifting. Bodies collided with Miriam and she was too heavy to get out of the way. The crowd enveloped her as the centre of the ring moved towards her. She caught glimpses of the assault through the bodies. Everybody was attacking him. His body was being dragged around the grass in all directions, everybody taking turns kicking him. They were going to rip him apart.

Miriam tried to get out of the maelstrom but it had its own force and she could not push against it.

'Make room,' somebody called.

From the other side of the ring Miriam saw something that made her feel sick. A large rock was being passed over the heads of the crowd. It was about the size of a skull. Over the aeons the ocean had moulded it into a perfectly smooth egg shape. When they saw it coming, the crowd's cheers ballooned savagely.

The blond-haired man saw it and lifted his arms for receipt. He held it above his head and turned to the prisoner. He paused. The front rows of the crowd became hushed in a collective intake of breath. And then the blond-haired man dropped the rock.

The prisoner tried to shift out of its path. The rock glanced off the top of his head and fell harmlessly to the ground. Miriam breathed all the air from her lungs. She could see everything now. McAvennie was being held back by the man with the brown beard. Fields and the others were being similarly restrained.

'This has to happen. It's only fair,' she heard someone say.

The blond-haired man moved in and lifted the rock once more above his head. The prisoner was more animated now. He wriggled to the edge of the ring but was always rolled back in by the crowd. His face had rivers of blood flowing all over it.

Miriam pushed past the few people in front of her and into the open space. She looked about her, at the crowd goading the blond-haired man on. Their faces were not human. This could not happen. It was too savage.

'Wait.' Her voice was a scream.

The blond-haired man turned to her as if he would listen to what she was going to say, almost as if he wanted a way out of this. And then somebody grabbed her. Strong arms pulled her backwards.

A stranger's voice whispered in her ear, 'Just let it happen. You can't stop it.'

The blond-haired man stepped over and around the squirming prisoner, unable to get a clear shot with his boulder.

The captive said something in a foreign language. This only served to enrage the crowd, who were appalled that this man might plead for his life on English soil but without its language.

A spasm of horror went through Miriam as a middle-aged woman stepped out of the crowd and fell to her knees behind the prisoner's head. She took his skull between her hands. She was screaming at the blond-haired man.

'Now. Go on. Now.'

The blond-haired man steadied himself. He planted his feet on either side of the doomed man's hips and his whole chest rose up as he filled his lungs with air.

The rock came down hard and direct. The sound, the dull thud that was too quiet for its consequences, was the only sense of the incident that Miriam absorbed. When she opened her eyes again the hostage was still, his head facing away from her. The crowd was silent.

A voice was calling from somewhere down the hill. They could hear it now that they were quiet.

'Wait,' it called. 'Don't do anything.'

The words were clear.

A man was running over the grass towards them. He was carrying a child.

'Don't do anything,' the man called again.

The child had its head buried in the man's shoulder. One of its arms dangled limply at its side. As they came closer it became clear that blood was dripping from the child's hand.

'Who is that? Is that little Trio?'

The child's long hair moved and he turned to face the crowd. It was a little boy of eleven or twelve and his face was smeared in tears and blood from his hand.

'They have our kids,' called the man.

A kinetic terror fired through Miriam.

'Don't touch our hostage.' The man ran over to McAvennie and stopped. He was panting. 'They want to trade. We have to give them their man back.'

|||

The boy's hand was wrapped in a blood-soaked handkerchief. The blood had saturated the cloth and was dropping to the ground in viscous globes.

'My God, what have they done to him?'

Fields unwrapped the handkerchief. The corpse of the prisoner lay forgotten near the outbuilding. As Miriam watched her eyes were drawn to the man who carried the boy. He and McAvennie were looking at one another. David looked young, despite his beard. His eyes carried a deep worry that he conveyed in silence to the man standing opposite.

The handkerchief came away from the child's hand and Miriam involuntarily covered her open mouth with the back of her fingers.

The boy's little finger was missing. It had been severed at the second knuckle leaving a bloody, painful stump. A woman behind her screamed.

'Where is he?' asked David.

McAvennie looked at him, unable to answer. Nobody said anything. Their heads turned collectively to the lifeless husk of the hostage the men at the top of the hill wanted returned.

David said nothing when he saw it. The arm around the little boy pushed up so he could get a better grip and that was his only reaction.

McAvennie put his hand on the top of Trio's head, nearly covering it entirely with its immense span.

'It's OK, Trio lad,' he said. 'I've got a finger off and it never harmed me.' He held up his hand and showed the boy. McAvennie smiled at the child. 'Tell me what happened.'

The little boy's voice was lower than Miriam had expected it to be. He told McAvennie about how he and his friends had escaped from the camp and climbed the cliff path, where they had been caught. Fields tried asking which other boys were with him but McAvennie stopped him and said to let the boy finish. Trio told them about the merciless way in which they had killed Adam and of how they had taken them all to the cellar in the house at the top of the hill.

He told them about how they had come for him and how they had sent him back to the camp with their message, and how they had cut off his finger so that the camp knew they were serious, and finally how David had seen him coming down the hill and run out to him and carried him back to safety.

When Trio had finished he put his head back on David's shoulder. The crowd waited for McAvennie's reaction. Just moments before they had betrayed him utterly. They had taken the trust he had in them and scattered it to the wind and now here they were, Miriam observed, following him once again.

He tapped Fields's chest.

'Come on,' he said.

The two men went to leave.

'What are you going to do?' said the blond-haired man, sweating, his voice still saturated with anger.

McAvennie's face twitched at the man who had just killed their only hope and then, at last, he smiled.

'I'm going to talk to them.'

Everybody shook their heads and started mumbling.

'You can't. What can you say to them?' a woman said.

McAvennie just shrugged. 'What I've been saying to you all, all this time. I've got to try and stop this before it goes any further.'

'You don't understand—'

'Stop it,' he said loudly. 'I'm going. Look, I'm not your leader. I didn't ask to be in charge. All I've done since this camp started was what I thought was the right thing to do to make things work. And that's all I'm going to do now. I have to go and talk to them. You say I'm naive –' he looked at the big man with the brown beard – 'but everyone has some good in them, even those men up there. I just need to find it.'

And with that the crowd desisted. McAvennie and Fields walked away over the grass towards the road.

III

Miriam had so far managed to keep her dread under control. What she was thinking had long odds. Surely she would know if it was true; she would feel it inside because everybody had attuned to the new world and developed that nebulous sense that had been dormant before. But then she realized that the dread that engulfed her was that sense. It was telling her that her fears were true.

She struggled to catch up with the man carrying the boy. The baby was so heavy. Adrenalin pushed her body on.

'Wait,' she called out.

When he saw that it was Miriam calling to him, David stopped.

'I need to ask the little boy,' she said.

She looked at Trio and he looked shyly back.

'Who were the boys you were with? What were their names?'

Trio didn't say anything. His large, hazel eyes were glazed with a patina of moisture. He was becoming upset again.

The dread inside her was mushrooming. Her head felt light.

'Was one of them called Edward?'

The little boy turned his face away and placed it back into the shoulder of the man who carried him. He nodded.

IIII

A series of emotions lay before her like a steep, stone staircase: fear for her son, an instant longing to have him back, anger that he would have done something so stupid, despair that he was gone. She needed to move, to find Mary, to find her mother. One leg in front of another, she told herself; don't think.

The crowd left the lighthouse and went down into the flat valley. Hundreds of people had gathered near the main entrance of the camp. By now, everybody knew that something bad was happening, that a child had been killed and that a gang had gone to the lighthouse for vengeance, that more children had been kidnapped and were being held in the house at the top of the hill.

It took nearly half an hour for her to reach the bottom of the camp. The light of day was almost gone. In the hollow it was gloomy and the air was leaden with a fractured electric energy.

A red car was driving along the road, up the hill to the house. McAvennie had left. She watched the car go. It was so far away she couldn't hear the sound of its engine.

'Miri?'

Her mother was holding Mary's hand. In the dusk she could not make out their faces in any detail. Mary let go of her grandmother's hand and ran to her mother. Her wellington boots slapped the concrete like the beating of wings and she threw her arms around Miriam's leg without saying a word. Miriam looked at her mother.

'They've got him.'

|||

McAvennie and Fields were in the house for over half an hour, during which time the gloom of the evening deepened. On the horizon a tall bank of silver mist appeared. The crowd waited and spoke in hushed voices in anticipation of what was about to happen.

Miriam and her mother found a seat near one of the campervans where they had a clear view of the house. Mary sat at their feet. She didn't understand what was happening but knew enough to remain quiet.

At last, McAvennie and Fields reappeared. An audible sigh broke out along the whole crowd. They were still alive. Miriam put her hands together in her lap, out of sight, and said a prayer under her breath.

The two figures were only just visible in the dusk light as they climbed into the car, turned it round in the road and drove slowly back towards the camp. The headlights of the car shone to life.

'That's a good sign,' her mother said.

From the back of the house there was a dark blur of movement and two horsemen appeared in the road. They rode out after the car.

The crowd fell silent.

McAvennie must have seen the horses because the car slowed, then stopped. They were halfway between the house and the camp.

A group of women were standing near Miriam, all of them wearing cloth headscarves.

'What's he doing?' one of them said. 'Why is he stopping?'

'It's a good sign,' Miriam muttered under her breath. Her hands clamped together tightly.

The horsemen split. One went round to the driver's window and the second took position at the other side, further away from the car. They saw McAvennie wind down his window and put his large head out into the open.

Just then, Miriam looked at the second horseman. He threw something small underneath the car, like a tennis ball. Miriam's veins turned to ice as the first horseman drew a handgun from his belt.

The crowd screamed.

The red car jolted forward in a stall.

McAvennie pulled his head back inside the car as the horseman fired his handgun twice into him and his head fell, dangling out of the window. The crowd screamed again, this time in panic. An orange light flashed out from beneath the car and then there was a low, hollow boom and the car was lifted into the air. Its shape changed, the far side folding in on the near with a yawning, metallic moan. The car remained upright but it was in flames. The far side door was somehow thrown open. Fields must have crawled out of the wreckage because the first horseman reared his animal around to the other side of the car and fired again.

There was more gunfire, this time much closer. Some of the camp's guards were firing up the hill at McAvennie's assassins but their bullets missed their mark. The two horsemen joined ranks again and fired their handguns wildly into the crowd.

Like a wave, the crowd turned and scattered. Miriam watched as the horsemen turned and galloped back up to the house.

|||

The human noise was deafening. Everything was falling apart and there was absolutely nothing to stop it. As the crowd scattered people fell to the ground and were trampled. The togetherness had disintegrated. There was no order in their panic. Miriam had seen the camp being born and now she was here to witness its death.

Her family was safe against the wall of the campervan but it was too dangerous to move. Her mind jarred. The flaming car in which McAvennie and Fields had perished rolled a few yards down the road and off on to the grass where it came to a final stop. The flames were already dying into the dark.

Her thoughts shunted to her son.

'Edward.'

The house was almost invisible now. The night had almost fallen.

'We have to get him.'

She pushed herself off the wall and made her way between the people towards the entrance.

'Miri, stop. Damn you, Miriam, just stop.'

Her mother's voice had genuine anger in it. Miriam turned. Her mother was standing in front of the campervan with Mary at her side; two dark figures against the dim white of the wall.

'Mum, I can't just leave him.' Her voice at the end of the sentence crumbled into a whisper.

Mary was crying, her mouth had widened right across her face.

'Come back, Miri. We'll think of something.'

Miriam shook her head. 'I can't.' She coughed.

She had already thought of something, and that was that she could not leave her son to those men. No matter how dangerous, she had to go. Even if she was going to be killed, it would be far worse to remain alive and do nothing. She turned away from her mother.

Her body prickled when she saw the blond-haired man with glasses waiting at the entrance. He was with some of the people who had killed the prisoner. When he saw Miriam he stopped talking and moved towards her.

'Right. Where are you going?'

She didn't want him to see her crying. 'My son is up there. They have him.'

'You can't go,' he said categorically, and with a total lack of sympathy.

'They won't shoot me. I'm a pregnant woman. They wouldn't kill a pregnant woman.'

His face was crossed by a quick emotion. 'They've killed my son,' he said. He spoke slowly, contorting the words into ugly, condensed sounds. 'They took him and threw him off a cliff. So don't fucking tell me what they will or won't do. They'll kill you without even thinking about it.' He crossed his arms. 'George McAvennie is dead. Things are different now. And you're not going anywhere.'

|||

There was activity in the lighthouse. Dr Balad had run up and down the long ward a number of times. He had people with him and outside several vehicles had arrived. A draught washed through the room. The heavy double doors set into the circular tower of the lighthouse had been opened and the loud rumble of a diesel engine filled the room.

Emily's body had been covered with a white sheet from head to toe. Charlie was sitting next to her. He felt numb, as if his emotions had short-circuited. He needed to pull himself away.

He heard gunfire. Two shots, a long way away. Something had been happening down on the camp over the past few days and he had deliberately ignored it.

There was a low boom. And then two more shots. Charlie went to the front of the building and out into the open.

The view stretched for miles but his eyes were drawn immediately to the small circle of orange flame across the valley. As he watched it he became aware of the shouting. It was too dark to see clearly but the sound of human screams was unmistakable.

To his left there was the scrape of thin metal. He knew what it was. People were trying to get out of the camp and in doing so they were destroying the fence. He went to the low white wall that surrounded the lighthouse and its outbuildings and peered over. The back of the camp was closer and he could clearly make out the shapes of people against the tall wire fencing.

The whole thing was shaking from its far end at the top of the slope to the near end by the lighthouse. Its straight line was moving wave-like under the pressure of the people until, at last, the middle section broke away and fell. The steel frames of each panel clattered to the floor and the people streaked over them and away across the farm fields towards the forest.

Charlie turned back to the orange ball of flames. He guessed it must have been a car and that meant, he thought calmly and slowly, that the marauders were about to attack. He breathed deeply and closed his eyes. The air smelled good. The scent of salt from the sea was strong. The horizon was clouded by a tall body of mist, visibly drifting inland. Its prow billowed under itself. It didn't look very thick, it wasn't a soup and its tiny droplets seemed more silver than grey.

He breathed out the hot air from his lungs. Malignant flecks of darkness had formed in it and he needed them gone. He could feel the whole world shifting. Change was everywhere. It was all around him and stretching off into the future in a dense cloud of unknowable fate. The new roads in his head were strong now and the old ones were becoming faded and overgrown.

Life had been so easy, he thought. But now he was on a new trajectory and it was dark and dangerous. Nothing of what had made up his experience was now left. He was a rocket ship being fired into outer space, leaving everything he knew behind.

He went to the other side of the lighthouse. The heavy double doors in the lighthouse tower had been closed. All that remained was a large white van. Whatever they had been doing was now finished. All the cars were gone.

Dr Balad was leaning against the side of the van.

'What's going on?'

The old doctor sighed. 'It looks,' he said philosophically, 'as if the time has finally come.'

'What's in the van?'

'It is a bomb,' he answered plainly. 'With which we will destroy the house at the top of the hill.'

Charlie nodded. 'You're going to take out their base.'

Dr Balad looked at his watch. 'It is five o'clock now. I think perhaps we have set it too late. We need to get it across there in a few hours, and not before.'

'Can't you change it?'

Dr Balad shook his head. 'It's already started.'

|||

The men of the camp ensured their sandbag defences were sturdy. The guns and ammunition were dealt out evenly and they took up their positions.

David found himself halfway along the front fence with a man he had never met before and who said little. They waited in silence as the night came down. All the way along the line nobody said anything.

David could not stop thinking about how this could have been avoided if only he hadn't tried to bandage the boy's hand. If he had taken the child straight to McAvennie, if he had run just that little bit faster, they would not have killed the prisoner and this situation, this waiting in the cold for death to come, might never have happened.

This was not supposed to happen again. In the civilized world men did not wait in battle lines. Yet here he was, a puny rifle resting on the top of a sandbag, the muzzle poking through a little square in the flimsy wire fencing. This was what it had come to. For all of the systems and processes and plans and armies, he was still huddled over a single gun in the dark, not knowing what to do or when to do it.

The mist that had been moving inland flowed over the camp. Leading fingers of it probed in the lines between the tents and caravans, keeping low to the ground before the greater mass of it, with its tall front wall, washed in and threw the camp into a denser, more complete dark. The sky above the mist was clear and after a few moments the mist changed. It started to glow with electric life, as if tiny fireflies were shimmering in and out of the ether.

David stopped holding his gun so tightly and looked up, whilst way up the hill inland, Miriam, her mother and Mary moved to the window of their campervan and gazed out on the silver ocean of air, and Charlie, up near the lighthouse, watched the camp disappear from sight as the low-lying prow swamped it and then he turned and let the main wall of the mist flow through him.

Everybody there, all of the hundreds of people, looked about them. They reached out to touch the mist but when they did it would curl away from them in spinning ribbons. Maybe the attack would never come. Without being able to see, the men at the top of the hill would call off their assault. It seemed inappropriate that something so beautiful should be disturbed by the prospect of violence.

The men of the frontline squinted into it. If the marauders were coming down the hill, they could not see them. David looked left and right to see the men behind their sandbag guard posts but they weren't there. His vision did not stretch that far.

When the gunfire did come, as it surely did, the men on the frontline did not fire back. Cut off from the next station along, nobody knew what to do. They could not orientate themselves to the source of the fire and there were no orange bursts of light in the mist.

'What's going on?' David called.

And then he realized that nobody along the frontline was shouting. Nobody was screaming. Nobody was hurt. And it was because they were not part of the fight. David lifted his gun quickly, yanking the muzzle back through the little square in the fencing.

'They're not here,' he shouted. 'They're behind us.'

|||

They came over the fallen fences at the back of the camp, little flashes of yellow in the mist, like tiny bolts of sideways lightning. There was no pattern in the lightning flashes. They were not moving in a line.

The screams did not take long to carry on the wind to him. They rose up through the mist to Charlie like spectres. Inwards the tiny sparks moved. He wondered if he would last the night to be able to follow his plan and leave the camp. He didn't really care if he lived or died. Being strafed by a swarm of bullets would not hurt for long.

It was a strange sensation, watching it all happen through the bizarre medium of the silver mist. All civilization, every inch of its idea, seemed so false now. It was just a facade to cover up the reality of life – life was hard and cruel and innately not civilized.

He was empty as he watched the lightning flashes move further into the camp. Their advance was not fast, it was not rushed. Charlie watched it passively. The sight of the gun flares was pretty in the mist, like an electrical storm. He wished it was not happening but it was and there was nothing he could do to stop it. He had no gun, and he had a bad leg. He was useless.

Then there was a new colour. Charlie remembered seeing the farmhouse in the hamlet on the day he was shot in the leg. He remembered the charred corpse in the back garden and the blackened wall around the French windows. He remembered how the curtains had fluttered in the wind. And now here he was watching it in motion: a dragon breath of orange fire burning up and out in the silver mist.

III

Miriam's mother locked the door of their campervan and they climbed on to the bed. All of the fixings in the little shell of space were bolted securely down and the only protection they could fashion was a wall along the side of the bed made of blankets and pillows.

'Edward liked making forts like this,' said Miriam.

Mary was crying softly and covering her ears. The gunfire was everywhere. The sound of breaking glass, punctured metal, screaming, shouting made a malicious symphony.

Miriam was fully aware of how absurd it was to be plumping up pillows and folding up blankets but she did it anyway, if only to have an outlet for all the excess energy. As she worked her mind fell back in time to the afternoon that Edward was born. From her hospital bed she had looked out through the only window and watched a fluffy white cloud cross a clean blue sky as she held the baby in her arms. She remembered how the sweat cooled on her face, and how she had looked at the tiny body of her son, at his little nose and his closed eyes and his thin, delicate lips, and how she had been struck by a crunching happiness. She turned to Mary and placed a pillow on the ramparts of the fort and tried to smile.

III

David ran blindly through the mist, down a narrow corridor between two lines of caravans. The man who had been with him at the sandbags was behind him. He said nothing but David was glad for his presence. They came to the end of the metal corridor and out into the open. David's feet slid on a patch of mud and he skidded.

A bullet flashed past him and slammed into a car. He was being shot at.

Quickly, he threw himself down and turned his body to face the source of the attack. From the mist the outline of his assailant emerged. The proboscis of his gas mask was pointed at the sky, slung back off his face.

The marauder fired again but this time not at David.

Somebody grunted and the man who had been behind him splashed into the mud.

Without thinking, David pulled the trigger. The stock of the rifle flew back into his shoulder and sharp pain flashed across the top of his chest and up one side of his neck. David winced with it and watched the man he had shot spin round. He didn't fall. David fired again, and then again. The man in the gas mask fell back and David fell still. He had done it. He had killed him.

He checked his nameless friend. His eyes had stayed open in death. David blocked out any feelings. He took the man's rifle and threw it over his shoulder and pocketed the spare ammunition. Then he went to the man he had shot and stood over him. He was wearing a bulletproof vest. David stepped quickly back but the man didn't move. Crouching over him, he saw his neck was covered in blood. It was a lucky shot.

The chemicals in his body made him shake. He should be dead. He would be dead if he hadn't been lucky. If the mist hadn't been there he'd have been picked off without a second chance. He puffed out his cheeks and blocked out the thought. He took the man's gun.

It wasn't like his rifle. It was one of the short, stubby guns he had seen the police carry at airports. He aimed it at a car. He wanted to make sure he knew how to use it.

He pulled the trigger and one bullet was fired. He pulled it again. Another bullet. Satisfied, he ran, crouched, into the mist.

|||

The gunfire came in short, sharp exchanges. So far nobody had come to the lighthouse. Charlie had returned to Emily's bedside. By this time there were only three people in the ward with the Sadness in them. One of them had been brought in yesterday. The others were in their third and final day. Each of the victims had one person keeping a bedside vigil and each of those was a woman of fifty years or older.

When Dr Balad came into the room he went straight to Charlie. He was carrying a large filing box.

'Will you help me, Charlie?' The lines in his face had deepened.

'What do you want me to do?'

'It is nearly time for me to go and I need you to make sure of something.'

'What are you talking about?'

'You know what I am talking about.'

'Let me do it. Let me drive the van.'

Dr Balad smiled weakly. 'Would that it be so simple. You are a good lad, Charlie – a good man. Here.'

He extended his arms and offered the box to him.

'These are the notes I have made, for what they are worth. I want you to make sure they are preserved. Should we survive perhaps they will be of some use one day, if not as a scientific study then as a historical document.'

'Dr Balad, I'm the wrong person to give this to. I'm leaving the camp. If we get through this then I'm going.'

The doctor regarded him with disappointment.

'Give them to George. He's the best person to look after these. He can be trusted.'

'My dear boy,' Dr Balad said softly. 'Have you not heard? George and Andrew are dead. They were killed. I am sorry to say it, but they are gone.'

'What do you mean?'

The doctor said nothing to this.

'Charlie, please, take my papers.'

'I'm not the person you think I am. I can't look after them. My head, it's . . . I can't be trusted with them.'

'You must. There is nobody else here. The lighthouse is empty.'

'Give it to one of the women.'

'Charlie.'

'Then let me drive the van and you look after the notes. These people need you much more than they need me.'

'You can't drive the van. I have to do it.'

Charlie was hardly listening. How could George be dead? He was the thing that bound the camp together. If he was dead there could be no replacement. The last time he had seen McAvennie they had argued. Charlie assumed he could apologize later because that was the template: argue, apologize later.

Dr Balad gave him the box and Charlie took it. Without even a shake of the hand, the doctor turned and walked out of the ward. Charlie placed the box of papers on the chair next to Emily's bed. He looked at her body. It was too much. The descent was too fast.

|||

He ran into the main foyer of the building. He didn't care about the pain in his leg. In the dark, disused toilet he found the plastic bin filled with tools and grabbed a shovel. He leaned it up against the small reception desk in the foyer and went back into the ward. He rolled Emily's body towards him and knelt below her. Dragging her into the cradle of his arms he rose up. Pain tore both ways along his thigh. He stumbled back but found his footing and moved slowly into the night.

The air was freezing. The silver mist condensed into droplets on his face and hair. His clothes became heavy with it.

He carried Emily across the grass, her head lolled backwards over his arms. On the other side of the low white wall that looked out over the sea, he picked out a nice patch of grass and laid Emily down on the wall, clambered over and lifted her again. He set her down gently on the ground.

He went back to the lighthouse to collect the shovel. The sounds of guns and people shouting could only reach the periphery of his mind. He found his way back to Emily and thrust the blade of the shovel into the grass and pushed it into the soil using his right foot as a weight. The spade slid easily into the wet earth. He levered the handle back and forth. He dug the shovel in again and this time slid the blade underneath the soil at an angle. The roots of the grass ripped easily. Charlie readjusted himself. The base of his back ached and his bad leg throbbed.

As the square of soil came out of the ground he could sense the roots and fibrous joins in the mud tear apart and sever. He dropped the chunk of soil down behind him and started the process again.

He checked his memory. Emily's face was still clear. That would be enough to take with him. The memories could go into a box and be taken out later, when it was time.

The shovel struck a rock. Charlie went on to one knee and used his fingers to dig it out. The mud was thick and damp. His hands scraped it away and he felt his fingernails pull gently away from his fingertips as the mud slid beneath them. The rock was large and heavy. Charlie lifted it to his chest and dropped it down away from the grave before lifting the shovel again. He took a deep breath and began the process again.

He looked at the dark outline of Emily's body. The ambient mist drizzled on to it like magical powder and he wished then that she would come back to life, sit up, smile, say hello.

He dug for over an hour and all the while there was no sight or sound of anybody coming to the lighthouse. The screaming had largely died down but the exchanges of gunfire had not. The hole he had excavated came up to his knees. His body was exhausted. The fibres in his muscles and cartilage bristled and his bones felt as though they no longer fitted together.

Setting the shovel down against the low white wall he knelt at Emily's side and scooped his arms underneath her back. Her face was silver and, even without the lens of sentimentality, peaceful. Her grace was still there.

Lifting her up, Charlie stepped down into the grave and lowered her as softly as he could into the soil. He arranged her arms and legs, straightened her nightdress and brushed her hair behind her ears. He caught a flash of future, of him sitting in a room reading a book ten years from now, and Emily not being there, and he had to close his eyes for a second.

Next, he stepped up on to the grass and fetched the large rock he had dug out of the ground. He placed it on the grass above her head. It would make a nice headstone. Fetching the shovel from the wall he scooped some of the dark soil up and dropped it into the pit. It smattered on to Emily's nightdress with a light pitter-patter, dappling the white cotton with dark specks.

||||

The fighting seemed to have been going on for a long time. The panic had been so dense that Edward had felt heavy and fallen asleep. He didn't know what time it was but it felt like the middle of the night. There were no gloomy lines of light around the boarded-up window any more. The cellar was silent, the other kids asleep. He lifted his head up and rubbed the sleep from his eyes. His father had once told him that sleep in the eyes was sand sprinkled by the ghost who comes to people's beds to make their dreams. He wondered what his dad was doing now and felt happy for a moment because when he pictured his father's smiling face it reminded him of what safety felt like.

It was time to make a move. Edward found Michael and John sitting next to the dusty old sofa against the wall.

'We're getting out of here,' he whispered to them. The two boys sat up. 'Follow me.'

His eyesight felt sharp, even in the dark. He knew this cellar so well. He had been taught to find his way to every corner of it without the need for light. The boys went to the far shelf. At the bottom of each shelf was a fixed plinth. Edward knelt down and with his fingertips found the loose part of the plinth that he had discovered once whilst playing, and pulled it away. Reaching in he felt the barrel of the shotgun he had hidden there so that he wouldn't have to ask his mother for the keys to the gun cabinet should danger ever arise. He reached inside again to collect the satchel of shotgun shells. He had practised loading the cartridges in the dark many, many times. It was easy. With a refreshing familiarity he cocked the barrel and slid two of the cartridges in before snapping it shut.

'Fucking hell,' said Michael, when Edward showed him the gun. 'Do you know what you're doing?'

'Yup.'

Saul had fallen asleep beneath the window. Edward stirred him awake.

'Come on, Saul. Move out of the way. We're going.' He turned to the room of boys. 'Wake up,' he hissed.

The boys who had been sleeping moaned. The others sat up straight.

'We're going,' said Edward. 'Who's coming?'

The boys mumbled quietly in confusion. Michael and John gently prodded some of the sleeping bodies near them.

'What's going on?' said one of them.

'We've got a gun.'

The boy leaned forward. 'Are you crazy?'

'If we don't go now we'll never go.'

'Don't,' said the boy. He jumped to his feet and his skeletal body appeared as a black shadow in the dark. 'You'll get us all killed.' His voice was pleading, filled with fear.

'Look,' said Edward. 'I know it seems scary, but dying isn't as scary as that.' An old memory came to him like an old friend. He had drawn on it many times over the past year, since everything he had known had been taken away, and each time he thought of it, it made him feel better. 'When you die you're just returning a favour to the world. That's all life is – a favour from the world. And when it's over you go back to where you came from. It's not scary.'

The dark shape of the boy standing in front of him did not move, but neither did he answer.

Edward remembered how his granddad used to speak to him; the way he always sounded so kind and how that kindness had made him feel.

'You've heard the guns down there,' he said. 'Most of the men aren't even in the house. We've got to go or we'll be stuck in here for ever and I don't want to do that. And you lot don't either. Now come on, get up.'

The boys started talking all at once in a low murmur. He went to the sofa and John helped him drag it over to the area underneath the boarded-up window. Edward looked at the wooden board. He hoped that John would be able to get through it.

'OK, now get out of the way. I'm going to blow that board away and you lot need to climb out, right? Go down the cliff path and when you get near the camp make sure you start shouting so they know you're kids and don't try and shoot you or something.'

From the dark he felt the eyes of the other boys on him.

'What are you going to do?' one of them said.

'I'm going to follow you. But I'll stay here to stop them coming down the stairs.' He lifted the gun. 'This makes a lot of noise.'

More of the boys stood up and got themselves ready. The ones who were too scared to go said nothing. Edward thought he could hear a gentle sobbing coming from somewhere near the back wall.

'Is anybody else coming?'

The dim outlines did not move.

Edward raised the rifle. There was nothing more he could do. His hands were steady. He felt calm. He made sure that after he fired the two shots he could get his hand easily into the satchel strapped over his shoulder to reload.

Pushing the stock firmly back into his shoulder and taking a solid stance with planted legs just like he had been taught, he closed one eye, took aim with the other, held his breath and fired.

The sound rang in his ears. Before he could see the damage he fired off another shot to make sure. The gun shook in his hands but he kept his footing.

The board had split in half but not shattered. Without any hesitation John jumped on to the sofa and used his weight to rip the remainder of the board down. Michael climbed out first. None of the boys spoke.

Edward turned quickly and crouched down underneath the stairs and reloaded. He could hear footsteps running towards the door. The cartridges slid perfectly into their chambers and Edward closed the gun.

'Go on,' he whispered to the boys who were still sitting on the floor. 'You can do it.'

But the boys didn't move. There was more light in the room now. They looked like big rocks sitting on a beach at night.

Through the gap between two of the wooden steps, Edward poked the barrel of the gun. When the single man came through the door to investigate, he couldn't even see the boy taking aim at him.

|||

The marauders made their way through the camp in small advances. They went from van to van and cleared their way. Before them was life. Behind them was death. The only way to escape was to break through their line and run out into the fields behind. Getting through the line was not the difficult part. The marauders were not organized, and they were not in large numbers. But they had men hidden in the field, concealed by the mist, who would pick off the few people who made it into the open.

There was another explosion. Its shockwave shuddered the ground beneath them. David turned to the man next to him. 'This is ridiculous.'

'We shouldn't have killed their man.'

He stood shakily and rubbed his eyes.

'Are you OK?'

David nodded. 'Yeah. I'm fine.'

They were at the car park wall. Dark shapes ran past them but they could not see who they were. The two men stayed still and hoped that nobody saw them. It was all so amateurish. The men of the camp who had been guarding the fences had scattered into disorganized groups. David had already seen many dead bodies lying in the mud. It was a massacre. Fires glared here and there as orange fog reaching up in the night sky.

David didn't want to move from this spot. His spirit was flaking away to nothing. Whenever he crossed a patch of open land it was with his gun pointed down and his eyes closed. Desensitization to the conditions had to be instant. Nature left you with no choice. Hesitation would cost you your life.

But despite his better instincts he scrambled to his feet.

'Come on,' he said to the man. 'We'd better keep moving. Just remember to aim for the arms and the legs.'

The man nodded his understanding.

They kept close to the wall, moving downhill, until at last they came to the long, wide path with the line of lightbulbs hanging on the wire alongside it. Through the veil of mist the lights looked like alien orbs hovering in the air.

Across the way two black outlines were kneeling down behind one of the tents. They had not seen David. Neither of the figures showed the muzzle of a gas mask protruding from their faces. It meant nothing, though, because many of the marauders had abandoned their costumes to the mist. David had already made up his mind. He was going to call to them. All he was waiting for was the courage to do it. He knew the only way to win this fight now was in numbers. They had to organize. Any other way would seal their fate. It was a risk he had to take.

'Hey.' The men turned their heads and David waved to them. A recklessness came into him. 'Empathy, compassion, trust,' he called clearly. It was the only thing he could think of.

The shoulders of the two men visibly relaxed.

'There's a group of them up the hill,' shouted one.

As he said it David saw something move in the darkness behind them.

He tried to shout a warning but it was too late.

The figures were suddenly silhouettes against a river of flames, their clothes catching like tinder, their screams cutting a gash out of the darkness. They ran out into the muddy path and rolled in agony, trying to extinguish the flames on their bodies.

David tried to lift his gun. In wide-eyed horror he saw the shape come quickly at him, out of the mist. He fired a shot but missed. And then the man next to him was on fire, all up his arms and chest, and then he was engulfed. He screamed in the pain of it and David could smell the burning flesh. He turned his face away from the scorching heat but it was everywhere. He threw himself down and fired again and again, but the man with the flamethrower was gone. His arm was on fire. He looked at it surreally. There was no pain. He calmly rolled it in the mud and the flames died before they could reach his skin. He looked at the three men around him, lying motionless in the mud, fire striking out of their backs. There was a realization. They couldn't win this. The marauders were too strong.

Something flashed by quickly: a man. He ran faster than a normal person; he was infected. He disappeared wraith-like into the silvery air. A riderless horse thundered past after him.

|||

He smoothed the soil on the grave and thought, that is that. Emily was buried and there on the cold cliff top beneath the shadow of the lighthouse was where she would stay. His hands were filthy with mud. His clothes were covered in it. Making his way over the low, white wall and back to the lighthouse he became aware, as he had before, of something dangerous nearby. The new sense was firing in him. The tall, gloomy tower of the lighthouse reached up into the mist where it ended in an indistinct haze. Dr Balad's van was still parked outside.

The sensors in his ears became keen. His breathing lightened. He went into the lighthouse through the foyer and into the main ward where his new sense was immediately vindicated by the sight of bright red blood on the floor. It had accumulated in small, circular puddles. The beds in which the victims had been lying were similarly stained red. The thin white nets had darkened, the sheets were soaked through and, jutting out from behind the beds, on the floor, were the protruding arms and legs of the recently dead.

Charlie scanned the room for signs of movement. If it had been one of the sick people then they might be hiding. He recalled Dr Balad telling him that most of the sufferers, even the most violent, maintained a level of cogency.

Cautiously he stepped weaponless into the ward and counted out with cool method the bodies of six people: three who had been ill and three family members. He made a conscious effort to consider his situation rationally. A marauder must be in here.

'Dr Balad,' he called loudly.

His voice echoed off the walls. He didn't care about making himself known. A reckless wind steered him now, blowing in from the new roads. He went to the far end of the long room and put his hand on the cold metal handle. The darkness that he had for so long railed against had now settled utterly over him. Formless ideas became solid, insecurities became pools of strength, and the new roads were now the only roads down which he could travel.

Charlie pulled open the door. The circular room was dark. An oblong of white light from the open doorway in which he stood splashed on to the stone floor, at the centre of which was his own long shadow and there, right in the corner, a hand that had drawn itself into a weak claw. The wrist led to a white sleeve and then into darkness.

Charlie pulled the hand into the centre of the white light. He already knew what had happened but he had to make sure. He owed the old doctor that much.

The doctor's jacket had red circles of blood around the neat tears in the material. Actually they weren't quite circles. They looked more like the shape of carnations: circular with jagged edges. He glimpsed a glowing green light beneath the sleeve of Dr Balad's white lab coat. He rolled the waxy cloth away. It was a chunky diver's watch with a digital face. Large black numbers ticked away the seconds.

Above, the sound of footsteps not moving quickly, not moving slowly, came down the spiralling stone staircase. Up there was where the violent people were kept.

Charlie unclipped Dr Balad's watch. It was ticking backwards to zero. With the watch fastened to his own wrist, and the responsibility of the doctor's final task now passed to him, Charlie turned to run.

When the voice called to him, his breathing slowed. He turned back and looked at the man who had killed the doctor and the helpless victims in Emily's ward.

'All the time I've been here,' said the man, 'nobody really knew what I could and couldn't do. They didn't see my true nature, or at least a demonstration of it, and so they always hoped there was something good in me they could bring out. And I was allowed to stay. But look what I've done.'

Mims stepped into the white rectangle of light and held up two blood-soaked palms. A large knife was balanced precariously between the fore and middle finger of his left hand. A cold and repugnant smile split his face.

'People thought that when the doctors cut me open they extracted my humanity, that the way I was was in some way to be blamed on their demented sciences. But it was never true. I was bad before. All the doctors did was allow me to become the person I always was. And it doesn't even matter. With no *reason*, nothing matters. Nothing ever did.'

|||

Down the hill David saw a woman with two children sliding across the mud, in plain sight. He ran out to her without thinking.

'Hey,' he called. 'Come on, follow me. You can't be out in the open like this.'

Another explosion, this one close by, boomed around them. David fell into the mud and quickly lifted himself up. He took the mother and children to the wall of the car park. Focusing his attention on getting the young family to something like safety, he led them along the wall to the beach. Maybe they could get out that way. The mother clutched the youngest child, a boy, to her chest. The little girl held on to her coat tails, just a silhouette in the mist.

It seemed like the whole camp was on fire. He couldn't tell where the mist ended and the smoke began. There was screaming all around him. Just keep going, he told himself. Just keep going.

|||

Hours had passed. A few times the guns had been so loud they shook the flimsy steel frame of their refuge. At other times the noise had lulled and Miriam thought that maybe the fighting was over and a new chapter was about to begin. But it always started up again. When it did Mary would snap awake. Her little head would shoot up off the mattress and she would look around in confusion. Neither Miriam nor her mother slept, not with the knowledge that Edward was out there.

The air was so cold that her breath condensed on it. Outside the window the ethereal silver mist was swirling against the glass. It was no longer still. When the door handle finally moved, Miriam and her mother both reacted with an involuntary intake of breath. There was somebody outside. At last their time had come.

Joseph had always told her this day would arrive, that one day the bad men would gain power and that she needed to be ready for it. But here she was now, unarmed and unguarded. She was defenceless.

The person on the other side of the door threw themselves bodily into it. The whole campervan rocked backwards under the force. Even in the gloom Miriam could see the dent in the door.

Mary woke with a start. Miriam's mother went to her and held her in her arms. There was another massive bang and the dent in the door bulged further. Miriam knew what was happening. The person on the other side of the door was ill.

'Leave us alone.'

Her voice was shrill and weak. The large windows in the van didn't open and there was nothing to smash them with. They were trapped.

The banging stopped. Miriam held her breath and tried to listen for movement.

A shattering explosion of air cracked loud. The lock was blown off in a metallic clang and something lodged itself in the wall behind them. They had a gun. Miriam fell back on the bed.

In he came. He stopped in the doorway and seemed to sniff the air. And then his black, shadowed head turned to Miriam.

'Found you,' he said.

She knew the voice. It was slower and deeper but it definitely belonged to the same man she had helped all those months ago; the man Joseph said he had killed but whom he had spared.

'Paul?'

'Stop calling me that.' His voice was a scream. All cadence rushed out of it.

Miriam froze with shock.

And then his voice became slow and heavy again.

'It's not my real name. I told you that.'

Miriam dared not move from her position on the bed. What little light there was glinted off the silver plating of the small handgun he was holding.

'So,' he said. 'Here we are. I've been looking for you for hours.'

His body seemed taller than before but his frame was still emaciated. Miriam didn't know if she should talk to him or not. She said nothing.

'Remember that day when your husband threw me out? I told him to kill me. I told him I would just come back, but you know what he did? He gave me a sleeping bag and water.'

The inside of her mouth became moist.

'Do you think I should have been grateful for that?'

'Please let us go.'

'Why should I have been? He had already beaten me to within an inch of my life, humiliated me, and then he thought he could make it all better by letting me go at the end. But you know what? I've always been the sort of person who can't let go of things. I keep the most terrible grudges. And that's why I had to find you.'

There was a burst of gunfire outside the van. With the door wide open the sound was ear-shattering. But it did not affect Crowder.

'I can't forgive your husband for what he did, nor can I forgive the pitiful way you looked at me.'

Miriam felt sick now.

'Why do you pity me? Hmm? You are no better than me. And yet you really do think you are. But let me tell you: you were only in that big house whilst I was on the roads because of chance. I'm a better survivor than you. You could not last out there like I have. It is me who should pity you and your ridiculous compassion. I will die. I can feel it inside me. All I want to do is make sure I take you with me.'

Suddenly and quickly Crowder jumped backwards. He hopped deftly down the steps of the campervan and pulled something up.

He had somebody with him. It was a woman. Miriam saw her long hair through the mist. She was tied and gagged. Crowder cut her bonds and forced her into the campervan. He roughly yanked off her gag and threw her on to the bed.

Mary screamed and Miriam's mother rubbed her back to soothe her.

The woman sat up on the bed. She moved easily and with grace.

'Please, you don't have to do this,' she said quietly. Her voice was warm and exotic.

Miriam watched her place her hair behind her ears.

'Now,' said Crowder. 'Line up against the wall.'

III

This is just another test but this time I feel prepared. I am ready for this, he thought. A cold hatred, built up over the months, was reaching its pinnacle. The part of him that had denied it, ignored it, fought against it, had gone.

'I told you this place would collapse,' said Mims. Droplets of blood dappled his face.

'You killed them,' Charlie said.

'I can't help myself. It's just an urge I have now.'

They were standing far enough away from each other that were Mims to strike Charlie would have time to prepare.

'I told you I was going to kill you.'

Mims stepped quickly to his right. Charlie did the same to keep the distance between them.

'Don't you feel betrayed by the way this place has fallen? It all happened as I said it would. You ripped yourselves apart.'

He moved right again. Charlie followed. They were making their way around the edges of an invisible circle with Dr Balad at its centre.

'You don't know what I'm talking about, do you?'

They moved again. Charlie could see the open door behind which Mims had been kept. He couldn't have escaped himself. Dr Balad must have let him go. The old man had trusted Mims.

'All of this needn't have happened. You had one of their people, Charlie. One of the men in black clothes. The good doctor was kind enough to keep me informed. He thought that by telling me these things I might change, I might become a *good* person. And the people of the camp beat the poor man to death,' Mims said with a relishing smack of his lips. 'Don't you see? If the people of this camp had been able to show just a little restraint' – he hissed the 's' in the middle – 'then this attack would not have happened. If these people that you and all the others like you trust so dearly had not shown themselves for what they truly are, then you and I would not be standing here, the doctor would still be alive and all would be well with the world. All I do is reflect what other people truly are. I'm just a mirror. This camp was always going to fail. Add people to any system and watch it fall.'

He moved again.

Charlie's back was now to the base of the staircase leading up into the tower.

'You're not a mirror,' said Charlie. 'You're just a prick.'

Mims lunged. He flew over the doctor's body. Charlie put his arm up to block. A white pain seared across it. Mims had slashed him with the knife. He felt the skin on either side of the blade's path slip away and warm blood flow.

He fell back under Mims's weight. When they hit the floor Charlie used the momentum to roll over. He brought his knee up and crow-barred his body from Mims. With enough space between them he used the soles of his feet to push him off.

Mims fell away but recovered quickly. He lunged again for Charlie. Charlie rolled away from him and managed to get to his feet. His leg bolted with pain. He reached his arm out and caught Mims's knife hand with his wrist, just knocking it off course. The blade whooshed ferociously past his ear. There was an intense, alien strength in his assailant. His energy was alive and wild.

But Charlie felt the same thing inside him now. This was easy. With his free hand Charlie grabbed the back of Mims's head. The blood from his arm dropped on to Mims's face and Charlie fell backwards, slamming the top of Mims's head into the stone steps.

He got to his feet. Mims was still breathing. He had rolled back down to the stone floor, near the edge of the rectangle of white light. He clambered on hands and knees and made a strange, low noise like a donkey braying.

Shaking now, Charlie began to ascend the steps of the lighthouse. They were very steep. Intermittently he came to a thin, wooden door, behind which lay the infected people who would become violent. He didn't know why he climbed, he just climbed.

The steps went on and on into the interminable sky. Already he could hear Mims chasing him. His leg hurt badly and the sleeve of his bloody arm was soaked through and heavy. He came at last to the final bend in the narrow staircase. Ahead of him a low light threw uncertain shadows on the steps until he reached the summit of his climb and he came to a heavy, wood-framed door with glass panels. Past it were three giant lamps encircled by a grated metal gantry. Thick black wires curled over the metal railings near the lamps, leading into sturdy power boxes. He was at the top of the lighthouse.

Tall glass windows, taller than Charlie himself, wrapped themselves around the giant lamps and gantry. Beyond them the silver mist felt its way along the glass, looking for weaknesses; a way in.

Charlie climbed up to the gantry and walked slowly round it. He ran his hand along the smooth metal railing. On the far side he came to a glass door. It was open and he passed silently through it into the night.

He was standing on a narrow balcony. The floor was made of the familiar whitewashed blocks. The round, salt-pocked railings that skirted the platform were cold and rusting. The mist was so thick he couldn't even see the ground below. If he fell it was possible he would fall for ever.

He turned back and watched Mims come. His dark shadow appeared in the doorway and moved silently round the gantry inside towards the glass door. Down in the valley the sound of human screams came from the dark.

Charlie could see the mist clearly against the glass. Within it were many patterns and eddies, each one seemingly independent of the next, each cutting its own path. But beyond that, beyond the individual patterns, he saw something else. It was moving generally as one. All the little swirls were following one route. Upwards. The mist was rising.

Mims came to the glass door and looked through it. His face was daubed with blood from Charlie's arm. Charlie smiled to him and waved and Mims nodded. He surveyed Charlie from head to toe and then, without ceremony, stepped outside.

|||

'Whoever you are, whatever your name is, please let us go.'

She didn't know why she was pleading. She knew she was no longer speaking to a human being. The barrier between him and chaos had been obliterated.

'You,' he said, addressing Miriam's mother. 'Give the child to your daughter.'

It was all happening too quickly. Crowder had something in mind but he was not taking time to savour it. The air was distressed and distended with panic.

'Don't.' Miriam thought she might pass out.

All four of them were sitting with their backs against the far wall. The pathetic fort of pillows and blankets stood between them and the looming edifice that was Crowder. His outstretched arm held the gun steady and still.

Mary was passed from Miriam's mother, across the lady Crowder had brought, and into Miriam's arms. Her little body was heavy and she had wet herself. But she did not cry. She was so still. Had her eyes not been open Miriam would have thought she was sleeping.

'Miriam,' he said. When he spoke her name her skin contracted over her bones. 'Choose. In three seconds I will shoot both of them, unless you choose one of them. One.'

She closed her eyes and wished the world would swirl open in a vortex and suck her in. She wanted to choose by inaction, say nothing, but she could not do that. The thing at the end of the bed was just a machine and it would carry out its threat. Her thoughts were blocked and she could not process properly.

'Two.'

Time changed. Rather than seeing a nebulous idea of the future, her whole being became detached from the line on which she had travelled her whole life and she could only comprehend the idea of the present. Her mother was going to die in the present. The other woman was still and said nothing.

'Th—'

Miriam couldn't breathe.

'The other woman.'

The air came out. Her mouth, her tongue, her lips had formed around it, squeezing and moulding the air into those three words.

The woman sitting next to her gagged for air. She put her hand to the hole in the centre of her chest to hold the blood in. Her mouth spasmed and spluttered. The sound of the shot rang out in Miriam's head followed immediately by a mushrooming, stridulous tinnitus. The other woman, the one she did not know, beat out the final machinations of her heart and then her body went flat and she was dead.

Crowder stood over them, emotionless.

'Now. Choose again. Your mother or your daughter.'

|||

The young mother of the two children was terrified. David could see it in the quick, jerky movements her head made whenever there was a noise. Her little boy clung tightly to her chest and the girl kept close behind her. David went behind them with his gun poised to fire if he saw any danger.

They came to the stone pillars of the car park and the sound of human chattering came into the air.

The heavy silver mist looked as though it might be dissipating. He could see further now than before. They ran into the car park and passed the stone utility block.

A large group of people were near the entrance to the beach. They were trying to get out. A narrow bottleneck had formed. David scanned the area for the marauders but there were none. He checked that the woman and her two children were OK to go and approached the crowd.

They clutched possessions to their chests, dragged bags behind them, told their children to keep close.

'Hey,' he called out. He had spotted a guard standing in the grass-covered dunes away to the left, above the bottleneck. David pushed through the crowd to get to him. 'Where are we going?'

The guard waved him on. 'Anywhere. Just get away.'

'But the beach just leads to the house – where they are,' he shouted above the noise of the people.

'Stay here then.'

David looked around him. This was insane. Streams of people were flowing into the car park now. It was every man for himself.

As quick as he could he fought his way back through the herd of bodies and found the family he was protecting. He tugged at the mother's arm. Her face was ashen. Her mouth was a small, circular, black hole and her eyes looked at him as if pleading for a way out of this hell; not just their immediate predicament, but a way out of this new, cold, dangerous world that nobody understood – a return to the old ways.

'Are you OK?'

He couldn't even tell if she was hearing him. They pushed forwards in the crowd towards the bottleneck. David saw one of the mother's hands reach down and take hold of the daughter's collar. The crowd was swelling behind them. It was becoming a crush. David looked as far as he could over the heads of the people in front. There was still a way to go yet.

But he didn't know where he was going anyway. Where would this path lead? After the camp there would be nothing. Everything they had worked towards, all their tents, supplies, clothes would be left behind. This was craziness.

Despite that, there was no choice now. Even if they wanted to, they could not get back. They were being carried forward in great heaves, as if the path to the beach was a great, inhaling gullet sucking people through it in giant breaths. The human tide was too strong to push against.

Somebody clattered into his back and he was shunted forward into the little girl. She fell to the ground. It was so tight that David couldn't even look down to find her. Claustrophobic panic was conducted through the bodies and they were sucked forward again. David couldn't stop. Groans of discomfort muffled the air. The little girl's body was behind him. The mother tried to turn.

'Jenny,' she called. 'Jennifer.' Her voice was discordant.

David was trying to stop the surge but the sheer weight of people around him was too great.

'Stop,' he yelled.

Nobody listened. Nobody could stop.

'There's a little girl back there.'

Somebody behind him heard him. 'What did you say, mate?'

'Back there, there's a girl.' He nodded backwards.

The man to whom he was speaking was tall and large-framed. He was able to shift his body round.

'Oh God, please get her back,' the girl's mother cried.

The small cluster of people in that tiny human cell heard the call and tried to look down.

David felt like his ribs were going to cave in. His gun pressed painfully into his chest. It was difficult to breathe. And then there was a release. A quirk of the surge freed some tiny space in front of him. He swivelled round and gulped precious oxygen. He could see behind him and a strong emotion ran through him. The little girl was being passed over the heads of the crowd. It was hard to believe how far back she was. He must have moved forward fifteen yards.

'Over here.' He thrust a hand into the air.

Other stifled reaches went into the air, passing the body along them.

David pushed the back in front of him and the girl was dropped into the space, where he held her in his arms so she couldn't get hurt.

Then there were screams coming from somewhere near the back of the crowd. He closed his eyes and concentrated on taking short, shallow breaths through his nose. Wherever the current told him to go he went, knowing it would inevitably feed him on to the beach. The mother kissed her daughter's head and face with desperate intensity.

The ground shuddered beneath the force of some unseen explosion and in the back of his mind he wondered how many of the marauders they had managed to kill. He hoped that in exchange for the camp they would have extracted a good pound of flesh.

Breathing was becoming even more difficult now. His chest was in a lot of pain. The shallow breaths were not enough and his lungs gagged for air. He was being asphyxiated where he stood. He tried to move forward but the ocean of people moved at its own pace. There was too much blood in his brain.

'Christ,' he whispered.

The screaming at the back of the crowd grew louder in his skull. They were being slaughtered.

'Come on,' a voice called.

David opened his eyes. Two men were standing on top of a corridor of sandbags, ushering the herd. There was a sudden rush, like being pulled into a black hole, a whistling in his ears, the return of oxygen, and then he was through.

He ran out into the sand. He needed to get away from the crowd and recover a sense of space. He found the mother and set her daughter down next to her.

'Go,' called one of the guards from the sandbags. 'Don't hang around.'

The woman looked at David. 'Where do we go?'

The screaming was so loud now. The poor people behind him were in agony.

'Anywhere. Just run.'

He started moving. The camp had to be let go of. It was over.

|||

It was enough for her. She cried openly and squeezed her arms around her daughter. This was the final demonstration that the atrocities of the last year would never, ever be cleaned. The filth was too thick and dense to be forgotten.

'One.'

'Kill me,' Miriam heard her mother say. 'I beg you.'

'That is not how it works. Only Miriam can choose. Two.'

'You're just going to kill us all anyway,' Miriam screamed. 'What's the point in this?'

She opened her eyes, and there was a moment of recognition as the future opened up again before her in an explosion of whiteness. Her mind tripped into place and her lungs ceased their inhalation mid-breath. There was no time. She spoke.

'Just shoot,' she said.

A massive pulse of shock and sound boomed inside the hollow chamber and Crowder fell violently forwards. Smoke rose from his back and Edward lowered the gun.

'Oh God,' she cried.

'Eddie?' Mary said quietly.

The boy looked tiny with the long, metal weapon held outwards in his arms. He hadn't hesitated.

Miriam put Mary down, crawled over the bed, over the body of the dead man and to Edward. She snatched the gun from him, threw it down and pulled him to her, taking his head in her hands and pulling his face into her shoulder.

III

The ledge on which they were standing was so narrow. The three rungs of the metal railings, the only thing between them and the precipitous fall, seemed too fragile. There was something inviting about the drop. It called you in.

Mims and Charlie stood there looking at each other. Neither of them said anything. The mist rose behind Mims. Away to Charlie's left the air was clearing. The distance into which he could see deepened with each passing second.

They ran for each other and collided hard. The railing bent outwards under their weight with a groan. Mims pushed Charlie back. His centre of gravity moved up him and he spilled backwards. Mims manoeuvred his body to the side, between Charlie and the windows. He was trying to force him through the gap between the lowest rung of the railings and the bricks.

Charlie gripped the rung with his injured arm. With gritted teeth he forced the back of his head into Mims's face.

Rolling away, Charlie stood. Mims rushed him. His wild chaos was too powerful for such a small space. It was out of control. Charlie ducked and Mims threw his arms over Charlie's back. With a thrust of his legs, Charlie forced himself up and

Mims was thrown clear of him and over the top of the railings.

Instinctively Charlie pushed out a hand from between the second and third rungs. It caught Mims before he fell. Charlie's body was dragged out and it hammered into the railings. They shuddered under the weight but held.

Charlie looked down into the face of the man who had tried to kill him. Mims's snake tongue flailed outside his mouth in a silent scream. He tried to loop his legs up on to the brick ledge but Charlie knocked them back.

'If you pull me up I'll kill you. That's a promise.'

'So you want me to drop you?'

Mims stopped kicking. 'You won't drop me.'

Mims's weight was pulling Charlie down over the railing but as long as the metal held, he could hold on. The arm that kept Mims up was the one that had been slashed with the knife. But Charlie could hold on.

'It's in your nature to save me. You're compassionate in a dispassionate world. It's the reason people will never think like you, or McAvennie, or anybody else like you. You know I'm right – just look at what's happening down there. They're running for their lives.'

The mist was thinning so fast that Charlie could see the blackness of the night behind it.

'You're in the minority. You'll never win. People are selfish and spiteful and just want to look out for themselves. You and your society, you can't just overwrite billions of years of life. That's your problem. You could never kill another person. You're on the wrong side of that line. That's why you won't let me go.'

In his mind, Charlie saw the man in the hamlet falling lifeless from the rooftop.

'But you forgot something,' Charlie said.

Mims said nothing in reply.

'People like you, people who think they know everything?' The blood from his arm dribbled on to Mims. 'Usually don't.'

He let go of the wrist. Charlie could see the bottom of the lighthouse now. The mist was almost gone. Mims made no sound as he fell. Just before he struck the ground his arms opened, wing-like. His face stared up at Charlie and Charlie drew his head in from the ledge, turned his body round so he was lying on his back, and looked out at the sea, at the clear moon cutting a silver line over its calm surface.

And that was his test, he thought. He had let a helpless man fall to his death when he could have been saved. And it wasn't just because of self-preservation. He had enjoyed it. Regret rushed into him.

The people in the camp, his neighbours and friends, were still down there. And he was not helping. He sat up and let the gentle wind cool his face. Thoughts tumbled fast through his mind. With his eyes closed he saw Emily again on the lawn beneath a sunny sky, there was warmth in his bones, she was making her daisy chain and he leaned in to her to speak his first words. He was sensing the river of good that flowed through the favourite people in his life: his family, his old friends, Emily, Miriam, George McAvennie. He thought of them all and remembered how Dr Balad had described them: people who had something in them that made other people love them. Charlie opened his eyes. The night was so dark, so black.

'It's just the absence of light,' he said aloud.

That was what George had said. He would never say what he was feeling inside to anybody else. It would sound ridiculous and sentimental, but it was real. He couldn't, and didn't want to, deny it. His body started to tingle. His chest swelled. McAvennie wasn't lying, he wasn't wrong. It really was true. Mims was not going to define him. His *reaction* to Mims's death was his definition. Charlie sat up and looked at the watch on his wrist.

III

The mist had almost gone. David could see the sea. The tide was as full as it would become. The sound of the surf doused the screams.

He ran as fast as he could but he was malnourished and his legs were weak. He could see the shapes of other people all around him running blindly into the darkness.

He thought of his parents, of what might have happened to

them. This was the same: dread of the unknown, fear of the future, panicked confusion. Over a small series of moments he began to lose hope. He had lost the young family he was supposed to be protecting just as he had lost his own family.

He listened to the sounds around him. There was the hiss of the ocean and dull footfalls of those running away and the quick wheeze of his breathing.

'Just keep running,' somebody up ahead shouted.

The hard, sharp fact that the camp really had collapsed hit him like a brick in the ribs. This was the end now. His head swayed from side to side and he wondered if the people around him were thinking the same thing. Why were they even running?

He ran for ten more seconds and then the change came. The motion in his legs slowed, slowed, and he stopped. He held his hand out in front of him and could hear the sound of his pulse in his ears. The hand blazed bright pink in the white light. This was impossible, he thought. Night can't just end. Above him, the sky was still black.

The yellow of the beach glowed brilliantly before him and all the people burned to full technicolour life. And they had all stopped running.

The moon sat in the sky as it always had, no lighter and no darker than it had ever been. But this light was different. Bathed in it, David felt suddenly unafraid. The people in front of him turned in unison. They pointed back up the beach and David watched as they looked at one another with confusion.

This was so familiar. Being there on the beach, surrounded by his neighbours, it was like those nights when they had bonfires and McAvennie would promise that everything would be OK if they would just stick together.

He looked up at the cliffs and had to cover his eyes because the light was so bright. It was the lighthouse. Somebody had switched the light on.

|||

The beach looked like a slice of lemon, the green of the grass like molten emeralds, the blue of the sea like pure sapphires. But the most beautiful part of it were all the people. When the light hit their backs it stopped them in their tracks. It held them in a trance. Charlie felt what they felt. Across the space his heart beat to the same rhythm as theirs. The light turned them round and now they were facing him. They looked like tiny, multicoloured plasticene models on the set of a children's television show. Stationary, arms at their sides, they looked up at the light. He waved to them but they couldn't see him.

Charlie checked the watch on his wrist. There were just five and a half minutes left on it. He looked over the edge of the railings and saw the large white truck parked below.

|||

They looked up the beach, expecting to see a black wave of killers coming towards them along the crisp, yellow sand, but that was not what happened. The light that lit up the beach in such a vivid expression of colour showed the people that nobody was chasing them. The marauders had not followed.

David stood there in the light and watched the perspiration rise from his shoulders. He closed his eyes and the light was so bright that he could see the insides of his pink eyelids, the red veins swimming across them like the bare winter treetops.

He still had his gun. All around him were other men, most of them armed. They looked at each other and sense clicked into place. They could not leave the camp. If they lost the camp they would all die. What McAvennie had always said drifted silently through them. With all the light in the air, it was hard to be so afraid of the dark.

Without saying a word, speaking in silence, everybody began walking back to the camp.

|||

The body of Mims lay as a tangled mess of limbs behind the van.

In a way, Charlie wished he had landed on the roof of the van. It would have been fitting that the two of them should ride together on the road to oblivion. He left him on the concrete, his body obliterated and cold.

The keys were in the truck. He started it up and found the headlights and two beams of light flowed out before him, just catching the final remnants of the mist in their streams.

The road from the lighthouse down to the camp was clear. He wound down his window and felt the air on his face. There were two and a half minutes left. He was ready for this. He didn't feel any fear. He pictured driving headlong into the low wall at the front of the house. The van would probably get through the wall and maybe even into the house itself. There would be no pain. It would all happen quickly.

He got through the stone pillars of the car park and the road narrowed. A large crowd were near the entrance to the beach, the light from the lighthouse throwing them into stark relief. The men had formed a defensive line around the people and sandbags were being passed over the heads to make a wall. Some of the men were making their way cautiously back into the camp. There was no sign of the marauders.

When the men saw the van approach they turned their guns towards it. Charlie leaned out of the window and waved to them. If it had been dark they would not have seen his face and he would already be dead, but now the men held fire. A few of them recognized Charlie because they were McAvennie's men.

'Let him through,' they shouted.

The guns were lowered and Charlie swept past. The men knew what the van was. They knew the plan.

He pulled through the deserted car park. Bodies lay at the side of the road. Some wore gas masks. Most didn't.

There was a sudden, loud bang at the back of the truck. Charlie's heart leaped. He checked the watch. One and a half minutes. There was nobody in his mirrors. He couldn't see where the attack had come from. Placing his foot firmly on the accelerator he sped between the caravans and cars. Then there was another bang and then another. He looked over his shoulder, out of the window, but couldn't see anybody.

He checked the watch again and there was one minute left. He had to keep going. He closed his eyes for a second and took a deep, cleansing breath. He wasn't going to stop.

Now he was on the road heading up the hill to the house. He turned off the headlights. The light from the lighthouse was just enough to see the graded difference between the black grass and the blacker road.

His foot was hard down on the pedal but the gradient of the hill stopped him getting up any speed. It was dark but they could surely see him coming. Machinegun fire rattled from somewhere up on the hill. Charlie held his hands firm on the wheel.

The windscreen made a series of thumping sounds and spider webs cracked across it. Charlie ducked. The bullets thudded into the seat behind him. He threw the switch on the headlights in an attempt to blind his attackers but the bullets kept coming. The van veered wildly across the road. He tried to check the watch but his arm wouldn't turn properly.

He thought he had been shot again but then his body slid into the door and there was a screeching sound. The van was up on its side and Charlie became sickeningly aware that he would never get the truck to the house. The horizon flipped and the passenger side of the cab was crushed in as it struck the ground. The twisting steel came towards him. He watched it approach and shunted as far away from it as he could before his body became weightless again and the truck flipped once more. In the mirror he saw the back door fly open and sheer clean off and violently pirouette off into the darkness. The truck landed flush on its side. Charlie's back was against the driver's side window. The glass cracked and cut into his skin. Involuntarily his arms pulled him away and the truck came to a halt on the grass.

Stillness. He was trapped. The passenger side was crushed. The driver's window was against the ground. His body was twisted round so his face was against the broken windscreen. His chest was crushed against the steering wheel.

The headlights shone across the grass. The house was just ten yards away. The marauders were there, looking at the shattered carcass of the van. There were so many of them. Down on the camp he had seen hope on the faces of those men who were trying to fight back.

But there was no hope against this. Mims was right. The watch in his wrist ticked quickly to zero and Charlie closed his eyes.

He waited and wondered if this was what finally happens. Maybe that last moment of life was able to stretch itself. The watch beeped quietly. The bomb hadn't gone off. Charlie opened his eyes again.

Five marauders came out on to the grass and into the two beams of the headlights, their dark bodies like shadows against the brilliant green of the illuminated grass.

From the back of the van something started screaming. There was somebody in there. The marauders closed in around the truck. A huge, black horse moved behind them. Charlie watched as one of the men stopped and quickly lifted his gas mask off his face. There was more banging inside the truck, this time like footsteps. And then the marauders stepped back. And then they fired their guns.

Bodies streamed out from the back of the truck. They ran so fast. A few fell under the rain of gunfire but even they struggled to their feet. They threw themselves on to the armed men, two on one.

'I don't believe it,' Charlie whispered.

The infected men and women flowed past the fallen bodies of the gunmen and into the little garden and then into the house. Charlie watched the relentless advance into the building, and the sight of men being thrown clean through the upstairs windows to the ground below. Muffled gunfire came from inside the house and Charlie smiled. This was going to work.

|||

There were people moving around outside. Miriam grabbed her children and pulled them away from the door. She could hear men talking amongst themselves and she thought she could sense a jovial note in their sounds. She looked at her mother.

There were two dead bodies in the small, cramped space and the air was acrid with the smell of heat and blood.

When the figure appeared at the door she watched it calmly. Her finger was against the trigger of the shotgun but she didn't fire. Death was already too close.

'Are you OK in there?'

The voice was clear. There was a jangle of excitement in it.

'Who are you?'

'It's OK,' said the man. 'We're the good guys. Come on. The beach is safe. We're taking everyone down there. Let's get you out of there.'

|||

He had to turn his body around in the tiny capsule of space as if it was a spinning globe. The folded metal where the passenger side of the cab had collapsed was sharp. Jagged limbs of steel dug into his flesh as he manoeuvred his way to the opposite of his original position. He needed to get out of the cab before the infected people in the house finished their massacre.

He pushed against the shattered windscreen with his feet. The glass gave easily and fell away as one satisfying mass. Charlie crawled backwards out of the cab. His arm brushed against his face and he felt the stickiness of half-congealed blood from the knife wound.

The air was wonderfully cold when he fell on his belly on to the cool grass. He rested there for a moment and felt the soothing waxiness of each individual blade on his cheek before the time came to struggle upright. He swayed on the spot with dizziness and then placed one uneven foot in front of the other. Pausing briefly he listened to the dying screams of the men in the house and laughed at how diabolically clever Dr Balad's plan had been. One of the dead men was just feet away from him. Charlie stole his gun and looked at the heavenly light shining on the bright beach making it look like a giant sliver of moon. The green-blue of the sea, white and foamy at the fringes, looked, with the black night sky behind it, like the beach from some paradise in another galaxy.

Charlie went as quickly as he could down the hill, where the fighting perpetuated itself in the drilling sound of quick gunfire bursts. Most of the marauders had returned to the house on top of the hill and he found it hard to believe there could be many more down there.

As he came to within a hundred yards of the camp, the large, dark form of what looked like an army personnel carrier rumbled out from between the entrance gates.

Charlie hopped clear of the road and lay down in the grass. In the light of the lighthouse he saw a solitary man running up behind the truck.

Coolly, Charlie aimed the short, stubby rifle he had stolen at the windscreen. He fired without even thinking about it. The gun cranked one bullet from its magazine clip. It pinged into the windscreen and ricocheted off into space. Charlie was surprised by his accuracy. He fired again with the same result and so he aimed at the front tyres and pulled the trigger, firing rounds in quick succession. He didn't stop firing until the truck lurched downwards. One of the tyres had been shredded. The effect was less dramatic than he had hoped for. The thick tarpaulin at the back of the truck was thrown aside and his gunfire was returned.

They couldn't see him. He was too far away. Their fire was aimless, scattering over the grass like seeds on barren land. Charlie aimed again and fired calmly back at them as if he was doing nothing more than playing a video game.

Behind the slowing van the man who had been chasing had still not been spotted. He threw something, stopped and ran off into the grass, throwing himself dramatically to the ground with his arms over his head. A pregnant moment of expectation held time still. There was loud shouting from the truck. And the truck exploded outwards.

Charlie watched the explosion mushroom in a self-sustaining fireball that kept going and going. It went out in all directions. At the base of the truck a circle of fire flowed out along the ground. From some heated epicentres fingers of yellow flame spat like the tails of meteorites into the sky.

The shockwave reached Charlie and his body felt like it was being dragged backwards by an invisible force. Shards of shrapnel whistled on the air and landed all around him and he laughed with a sense of uncontrolled freedom.

He looked at the skeleton of the truck. The square metal bands that had been the steel structure of the truck's back end had been snapped open and were now facing up into the sky like the cracked-open ribs of a giant insect-like monster.

He went down to the remains. Nobody moved within. He couldn't even see any bodies. They must have been vaporized. He liked that idea – there was a sense of completion to it.

Through the flames he saw the man who had thrown the grenade. He was coming round the fire towards him.

'Did you see that?' His voice had the enthusiasm of a small child. 'Did you see what I just did?'

He was a man of around fifty years, but the pride lifted his body and made him seem a lot younger.

'It was pretty good.' Charlie beamed.

'Was it you who was shooting at them?'

'Yup.'

'Nice one. Good teamwork, eh?' He placed his hands on his hips and shook his head. 'They were trying to steal our petrol.' He laughed. 'I bet they wish they hadn't now. Did you see the size of that explosion?'

Charlie looked at him as they shared the satisfaction of their small victory. He was remembering something. The orange glow on the man's face reminded him of something.

'Oh my God,' he said, with sudden recognition.

He flung out the back of his hand and tapped the man in the chest. Blood from his arm inadvertently splashed on to the man's sweater.

They both looked at the stain.

The man brushed it off. 'Forget it,' he said. 'My mother-in-law gave it to me.'

Charlie looked at him. 'You can't remember me, can you?'

The man shook his head.

'I met you on the first night I came here. On the beach. Remember?'

'Sorry.'

'You gave me and my girlfriend a baked potato.'

The light of recognition came into his eyes, if not of Charlie himself then of his action.

'Oh yeah, I remember,' he said.

The two of them shook hands and started laughing as the recklessness of their actions caught up with them.

The man's smile beamed out and the orange light in his little dark eyes looked like it came from within the eyeballs themselves. He used his free hand to pat Charlie warmly on the shoulder.

'What a coincidence.' He laughed. 'So how's it going?'

|||

He looked at his little sister's face through the dark. They went down the hill, led by the men, and her body wobbled on the uneven ground. She turned her face to him and almost tripped. Edward reached out for her and pulled her up.

'You OK?'

'Yeah.'

He lowered his voice and leaned in to her ear. 'Robin Red Breast, where are you?' he said.

She looked at him again, and half a smile was on her lips.

'In the clouds,' she said quietly.

Edward nodded seriously and they walked on.

There were a lot of fires in the campsite. Men were calling to each other somewhere off in the distance, but Edward felt safe. He was with his family again. That was all he cared about.

'Ed,' he heard her call.

He looked down and Mary was holding something up to him.

'Look,' she said.

He took something soft from her hands and held it up to the light.

'It worked!' he said loudly. The grey fur of the rabbit foot glistened orange at its edges. One of the surges he felt for her rushed through him. 'You'd better hold on to this.'

He handed it back to her and she awkwardly shoved the foot back into her jacket pocket. Edward turned and smiled at his mum and grandmother behind him, and then turned back towards the bright light of the beach.

'Everything is sun,' he whispered under his breath.

III

As they went downhill, along the low wall of the car park towards the beach, Miriam put her hands together and found herself unable to say anything.

Ahead of them a milky cone of light scythed its path through the night as a finger of hope but she felt little from it. She should be so happy. Edward had come back and everybody was still alive. They had made it. And yet she could still feel the dead weight of the woman pressed against the side of her body. The other woman.

Across the wall, in the car park, she saw the man with the thin blond hair and glasses whose son had been killed. She watched unblinking at the act he and the four men he was with were about to carry out. They had captured a man she knew. They had left his flamethrower strapped to his back in some bizarre symbol of indignity. His hands were bound in front of him.

The five men were unaware of the family passing behind them. They raised their rifles in unison and gunned down their victim. The man slumped to his knees and that was how he stayed, without enough gravity at his tilting side to pull him to the ground.

Miriam stopped. The others didn't hear her and kept on going down the hill. She thought she had heard something. It had sounded like a faint mewing. There it was again. It was coming from the other side of the wall, up the hill, away from the beach.

Leaning over the wall she saw, slumped against it in the shadows, a bundle of black blankets. Something was wriggling inside them. Checking to make sure nobody could see her, Miriam rolled her body over the wall to the other side, all the while trying to protect her baby from being crushed under her weight.

There was a nagging thought at the back of her mind: she should not be doing this. But the thought could not hold sway over the infinitely stronger compulsion to reach the dark bundle of blankets. The air drained of noise and the blankets moved in such a way that the face of a young infant came out of their darkness to peer at her through two tiny black eyes. The child looked strange. It was too small for the stage of its development, like it was just a tiny version of the human form without being actually human. Its jaw was sharp and jutting. It looked as if it had no flesh or skin.

Two minute white fists appeared from the folds of black cloth, balled up so tight they looked like little marble rocks. The child opened its mouth and closed it again, up and down, up and down, soundlessly.

Miriam went to it and crouched down and looked into the black eyes. Tiny flecks of colour were in them, swimming like tadpoles. The colours of the rainbow, she thought haphazardly.

'Oh,' she said, suddenly surprised.

The child had disappeared. The blankets were gone. She was looking at an empty patch of ground. And then she was standing up again. She was at the perimeter fence. There was a crack in it and she was staring through it at the black line of trees across the moonlit field. Something like a sludge oozed invisibly over her skin and she stepped through the crack in the fence. A desperation fell over her as if somebody had cut open her belly and everything had come sloshing out and she entered into a state of bleakness that she had never even known could be possible. This was it. She was crying; a deep, desolate sadness was right through her, to her very core, and it was time to go.

PART FOUR

MIRIAM

Walking across the tilled soil was difficult. Her feet sank into the mud but she kept going, one foot in front of the other in front of the other. The field was long, the air was cold and the blackness of the night made her feel as if she was the last person left on Earth. She came to a low wooden fence and climbed over it. She was standing beneath the eaves of the first trees of the forest and there she paused, turned and looked at the beam of light coming from the lighthouse.

Her pupils contracted just a fraction and she stood there in her mud-caked shoes and saw nothing beyond the photons of luminescence; no deeper meaning, no affection for the people caught in its streams, no sorrow for those who had died beneath the spiralling columns of grey smoke before it. Pinpricks of pain stabbed her temples. They were all of them fighting and struggling, and to what end? They would come to their deaths and grieve over the things they had never done, their regrets, their all-too-short lives and think, was this really all it was? And the world would turn away from them and say, it really was.

Miriam walked into the forest. The trees were tall. Their trunks were branchless until they reached the high crowns, their bark glowed an eerie silver, and she put one foot in front of the other in front of the other. Any animals that may have been watching were silent and still.

She walked without rest for three hours into the night. Sometimes the trees would break and return to fields and she would walk across them and the half-light of the moon would cast a vague shadow before her. Sometimes she would cross a dark country lane between two tall hedges. Sometimes she would come to a dead end, unable to pass a thicket or some brambles, and when this happened she would turn back and try another pass because no matter what lay before her she was compelled to keep moving.

She became aware as she walked of nebulous things happening inside her, of her body turning into a hollow shell. Before, she had been aware of her skeleton and muscles and organs and ligaments, but now it was just a void. Into the void, from a spring that had opened at her centre, poured a dense, viscous fluid. The spring was the same spring that had sometimes poured the syrupy golden liquid into her, but this new dark matter was not like that. Her body filled slowly with it, starting at her feet. *Drip, drip, drip.* When it reached halfway up her thighs it became too heavy for her and she fell on to all fours and started to crawl. Her knees hurt and she cut the palms of her hands on sharp rocks.

Through the trees the light of dawn danced above her head and she felt as if the forest was leading her somewhere. As she crawled her hands sank into the grime and her knees slopped against it. The mud spat up and speckled her arms. The hem of her skirt dangled in it and became heavy.

A sudden sense of grief beat across her chest like a heavy weight. It punched through hard, seeking out the quiet corners of her soul, filling them with its endlessness. She remembered her father and the loss since his death, which she had filled with happy memories of him, and which had dissipated in the streams of time, came back to her tenfold. It had festered for so long beneath those coping mechanisms that it had grown unseen, like a virus amplifying in damp lungs. The grief, the untouchable desperation of it, fell on to her body like a heavy blanket pressing her down.

This was it, she knew. That was what happened. What everybody else had been through was going to happen to her. This was what happened when her hope died. That was what the baby with the colours in its eyes had been.

She clamped her teeth together. Whatever dam had been in place to hold the grief in its safe reservoir had been breached. It gushed through in dark, oily torrents, and she knew that the flow would not end yet because Henry's grief had not arrived.

She could feel it rearing up as an immense wave. It dragged the sand of her hope into its midst and used it to perpetuate its own growth. As the wave crashed down she fell on to her side. The mud washed into her hair, into her ears, over the collar of her shirt and on to her skin. Henry. Tendrils of emptiness lashed within her ribs. They found their way to every corner of her, searching out the happiness in her with blind, slapping thrusts. Miriam's body became taut in muscular spasm as the tentacles invaded. They broke through the membrane of her womb and slithered around the face of her unborn child, lifting up its neck and threading their ends into the child's ears, its nostrils, its mouth, its tear ducts, until the child was incorporated into it in a hermetic symbiosis.

Miriam screamed. The noise of her scream seemed to part the branches of the trees overhead and continue on and up, into the sky, over the forest. She screamed until the lining of her throat became dry and tender, until the point when her voice being drawn along it was like a metal file scraping against the gullet.

The faces of the dead swam before her and Miriam was forced to look at them. She could not turn away because the thing that tempered grief, that broke it down into bearable chunks her soul could endure, was gone. She placed her left palm on her face and tried to dry her tears but her hand was slick with mud. She could smell it: damp and earthy.

She opened her eyes. It was light. The sky beyond the dead trees was iron grey, pregnant with water. It started to rain and the rain was freezing. It congealed with the mud and then, after she had lain there for an unknown period, it started to cleanse her face and hair.

She became aware of something else inside her body, a white candle with a delicate yellow flame hovering above the wick. It was a counterpoint to the dark fluid. They both occupied the same space inside her, but also not. She only had one body yet it was somehow both light and dark at the same time, as if there was some filtering barrier separating the two states. On one side of the filter was the dark fluid, but if she followed the vision round she would cross the line, the image would flip and she would be with the candle. The flame flickered and spluttered like a sickly child battling against colic, but it was alive.

She had crawled into a hollow and was surrounded by a ring of the silver-barked trees. As she looked at the trees she thought she could see the bark changing. It was as if an invisible brush was painting a line of colour on each trunk, each brushstroke a different colour: orange, red, yellow, violet. An ancient and instant recognition of the colours of the rainbow hit her and the weight of the grief that had been dumped in her began to lift. The difference was hardly perceptible but it was there and from that minute difference she drew a deep and cleansing breath. She looked again at each swipe of colour but the rain was falling heavier, the mist was sinking, the trees were clear and the colour was gone. The weight of the grief came instantly back to her and she trembled beneath it.

She knew she had to move. If she stayed there she would soon be dead. Despite everything, a base urge that was separate from the darkness, something animal and primitive, would not allow her to willingly surrender her life. The level of suffering that lay before her was inconsequential to the urge; the toughness of life itself dictated that she would have to face it, regardless of the pain it would cause.

She rolled on to her side, the sound of falling rain all around her, and tried to stand. She crawled out of the shallow hollow until she came to a muddy ridge that ran through the forest like the spine of some long-dead, crooked monster. She moved slowly along the ridge and looked down on either side. The rain of centuries had carved scoops out of the land. In some places the drop from the ridge was precipitous. Sharp black rocks jutted from the soil where it had been stripped away by the small gulches that cut zigzagging routes into the forest.

She followed the ridge until what she guessed was late afternoon. It wound its way for interminable miles, so deep into nature that the long absence of human presence was tangible. Nature itself had maintained its old power here.

The rain fell long and hard. Miriam's hair slapped against her face like rat's tails. The ridge terminated at the base of an ancient tree. Its trunk was gnarled and deeply striated with vertical lines that had been prised open over the years to create dark, gaping slits. Great leathery wings of fungus had infected it all the way up.

A rushing sound filled her head. She looked around her but there was no source. The sound was so loud she could feel the membrane of her eardrum stretching, its seams approaching failing point. She covered her ears with her hands but the sound was inside her head. The rush changed frequency and morphed into both a high-pitched scream and a deep, base-end rumble. It filled the space between her brain and her skull and prised the two apart. She closed her eyes and opened her mouth in a silent scream.

And then everything became still. She was watching a past memory of herself. She was with Henry, sitting in a rowing boat. Edward was asleep in her arms and Henry was saying something but the vision was without sound. The memory made her feel happy. It was the day she had told him she was pregnant with Mary. That had been a good time in their lives. Their family was in its vibrant infancy and life had been filled with infinite possibilities. She often thought back on that time, when the present was difficult. Happy memories suffused her being and calmed her when things were tough.

She saw more memories, all good, all the memories she thought back on often and which made her feel still. The feeling of the dense fluid filling her body lessened and Miriam started to breathe. She could feel her body fighting against the thing that had infected her and as she watched the good memories they gave her strength.

She was in a new memory now. She could see Joseph. He was sitting in the back garden of their old house, in a chair in the shade of a tall brick wall. It was a sunny day not long after the wedding. She had forgotten that day. The memory of it had sat unused inside the glass pane of her memory files. Joseph and Henry had argued over something but Henry had refused to say what. But she had known. Joseph didn't like her. She had come into Henry's life and stolen him away from his brother. That afternoon had been the first time Joseph had told Henry this.

Then she was sitting on the bed in their bedroom, on her own. She was crying. That memory too had nestled unobserved since the time of its formation. She had cried because of the rift that had opened between Henry and his brother. Joseph had told him he was too young to start a family. It had angered and upset Henry, and when he told her, Miriam had felt an enormous guilt that she had engendered such resentment in her brother-in-law. She had not meant to do it, but it had happened nonetheless.

As the bad memories were revealed to her, dusted off and taken from the secret compartments of her mind, Miriam swirled around a vague realization. There were more bad memories than good; life had been hard, a series of struggles from one thing to the next like a great snowfield punctuated rarely by the pinnacles of genuine happiness. Her mind had shown her only those peaks but Miriam now realized that the memories of her old life had been viewed through a strange lens. Something inside her had warped the truth of her past to allow her to forget the reality of how things had really been. But that filter was gone now. The memories showed her, over and over, the buffeting experiences to which she had been subjected for most of her life.

The death of her father had been a terrible, life-shattering experience, and yet she had always looked back on that time and persuaded herself it had made her strong, had made her truly appreciate the love her parents held for her. But as she replayed the full truth of those months she remembered the cruelty of death, the absolute absence and non-returnable nature of loss. She remembered how people had tried to comfort her by peddling ideas of his living on through her, and how they had meant nothing, sounded stupid, and did nothing to fill the human-shaped imprint her father had left.

Her past was not one long, beautiful journey at all; it had been an arduous, painful crossing through time that was pointless, filled with false meaning and directionless.

The memories cascaded for what seemed like hours and with each new vision she felt the petrifaction of her heart as it grew harder and harder and harder until only the very centre of it was still made of fleshy, organic matter.

And then her mind was in the cellar again and Joseph was raping her, telling her that what he was doing was going to destroy her, and she knew what the dark fluid in her was.

Her soul seemed to scream with unbearable agony as the despair smeared itself over its surface. An unnatural osmosis was taking place. The pores of her soul spluttered open and the despair sludged in through the gates. It fused with her essence until it became part of her, and instead of looking out on it she was looking in.

She forced herself back to the forest and when she did she thought she was looking at three figures in front of her: her mother and her two children. She went to speak to them but her lips would not part. They were looking at her as if she was doing something unspeakable. She stepped forward and saw that their faces were melting. Their noses and mouths were merging, the sclera in their eyes was bubbling and their cheeks were slumping. Miriam went to scream but still her lips would not part. The faces of her family slipped downwards off their skulls. In their place were cream-coloured ovals, flat and featureless; the faces of automatons. As Miriam looked at the three simulacra of her family she felt no emotion. She did not care that they had fallen away from her because, she now knew, they were not, and never had been, a part of her. Her family, her friends, everybody she had ever met – who were they? They didn't really care about her, just as she had never cared about them. The life that had been hers for the last eleven years she had given to her children, purely because of some primitive urge to protect her young. But not any more. She wanted her life back. The seemingly unbreakable, undying love she had felt for her children had vanished in those scant few moments and when it was gone she could not comprehend where it had come from in the first place, or how she could possibly have felt it.

The rushing sound came back into her head and her family were gone and she was back at the ridge in the woods. It was night. Beyond the trees she could see the stars and she lay there for a moment, considering what it was that had just happened. It couldn't have been a dream because dreams did not feel like that. She tried to cry but nothing came. She was exhausted and needed to sleep and so she crawled in between two buttresses of the old, gnarly tree, laid her head against the soft padding of the fungus and fell asleep, expecting to dream again of the burning beach and her husband being dragged into the water. It was a dream that didn't come. She didn't dream of anything. Her sleep was shallow, her mind always aware of the wild world existing just beyond the lids of her eyes.

When she awoke it was day again. More clouds hung saturnine

and smothering in the sky. Miriam sat there, in the folds of the old tree, and looked at the forest around her for three hours. With slow, deliberate motions she fanned her hands through the dead leaves beside her, brushing them clear of the soil.

When the rain started again it was merciless. It fell in heavy, driving streams and struck the ground in tiny craters along the ridge. The tree sheltered her from the water but the compulsion to move was with her again and so she crawled out from her shallow cave and on to the ridge. She had to return to the forest floor but the ridge was high up here. The rain was so heavy it had saturated the soil and so she crawled back along the ridge, the way she had come, to find a place to descend.

As she crawled she thought of God and why He would do this to her; why, after all she had given Him, He would do this to her. Although, really, she knew. She came at last to one of the rain-formed gulches. The water was so powerful that a chunk of the ridge had fallen away, like the gap between two vertebrae over which she would have to clamber.

She remembered the dark innards of the campervan and saw again the black face and the silver handgun. She felt the weight of the woman she had condemned against her and she paused at the edge of the gulch.

'I'm so sorry,' she said.

The rain thundered all around her. There was water everywhere. She placed one of her hands into the gap in the ridge. It sank deep into the mud. She put her other hand in, this one further along, and then she brought her knee in and moved her hands further across, and then her other knee, and all of her weight was in the freezing stream and she felt the ground slump beneath her as she sank down into the saturated loaminess that failed and spilled her body over into the fast-running waters of the gulch. She snatched for purchase but there was none to be had and down she tumbled, through the mud and the water, the weight of her baby pulling her body into a roll so that her face was pushed down into the running stream and she couldn't breathe. She turned her head and gulped down air but the air was thick with guilt and it lined her throat like oil. She had killed that woman. That was why God was doing this. She had failed His test and this was the retribution for her choice. That really was the truth of the Sadness: it was a punishment. Everybody who had suffered its violation was paying a price for something they had done to displease God. He had looked down on Earth and in His divine right judged each of His creations and selected those who deserved damnation to be infiltrated by the dark fluid of despair.

'Please stop this,' she screamed, as she fell through the turgid, broiling waters. The water filled her mouth and she swallowed it to try and please Him, to show Him she was sorry, that she understood the terrible thing she had done. She screamed. Her throat was tender and raw and her voice raked at it like the backwards stroke of fish scales. 'Please,' she screamed, 'I'm so sorry.'

Her body rolled to the bottom of the gulch and came to a rest in a wide, cold puddle. She lay in it and cried and felt the outer layers of her body beginning to freeze. It was all she could do to straighten her arms and crawl on her knees to the edge of the puddle, where she flopped down in the soaking mulch of the long-dead leaves. They reeked of tangy bacterial processes and made her retch. She closed her eyes and when she opened them again she saw a ghostly white figure floating towards her through a mist that had flowed into the valley. The figure was not solid but rather an indistinct sketching of the human form. It raised a wispy arm and pointed accusingly at her through the mist.

'I know,' she said slowly. 'I know what I've done.'

The figure halted its approach and she looked at it. Was this really it? Was this the thing she had loved so much since her father died? It radiated warmth. It was benign and passive and yet, she thought, if it was like this, then why would it subject her to this torment? But that thought faded swiftly as the white figure flickered in and out of the mist, sometimes strong, sometimes weak. When its signal was strong she could nearly see the features on its face.

'What comes after this?' she said.

But the figure said nothing. It hovered silently in front of her and tilted its head to one side, as if confused by what it was looking at.

Miriam looked down on herself. She was still wet and cold from the rain but her clothes and skin glowed vividly from the millions of light sources that infused the mist. The figure lifted its hand up to the level of its head and turned its palm towards Miriam. Its long, slender fingers waved like fronds of grass in the wind. They were not solid things: as they moved they came apart, floated like a wake, then rejoined to become a hand once more. A cherry red vapour emerged from the palm and the figure pushed it towards Miriam until it floated right up to her in a hazy line and into her chest.

When it entered her she felt it push against the pool of despair and she looked up into the face of the white figure. Its ears rose up and she thought she could make out a grey hole where the mouth would be. It was smiling. She felt its benevolence and munificence flowing through her as the cherry red haze floated around the little candle in her chest, feeding its fire, bringing up the light, clearing the shadows.

'What are you?' she said.

The figure curled its fingers one after the other into its palm and the stream of red haze was cut off. The remainder of it drifted into her chest and swirled around the candle in gentle, steady orbits.

The indistinct figure then began to be blown away into the mist as if the particles from which it was made were not together. Its head was carried away on the breeze like the peak of a desert sand dune being lifted from its bed in hyperbolic curves. As it faded the red haze faded with it and when it went Miriam could sense the despair coming back. She fell to her knees and lifted her arms out to the dissolving figure.

'Don't go,' she said quietly. 'Don't leave me on my own like this.'

But the figure let the wind scatter it to nothing. As it dissolved she felt the version of it that had lived inside her dissolve with it. The promises of it, the comfort it brought, the way it had ushered her through life – it was all gone. It had never been there at all. All of it had been a lie, a veil she had pulled between her and the world to make living more bearable. There was no such thing as God and its infinite absence was like the creation of a singularity in her. The black hole swirled into being, the red haze was drawn into it, and then it closed in on itself and all was dark once more.

She was in the forest again and the mist had disappeared. The realization of her place in the universe shunted into her. She had thought that humans were closer to angels than animals, that there was some divine purpose to existence, but now she saw the whole world before her. Everything could be touched, seen, heard, smelled, tasted, and nothing more than that. There was nothing mysterious beyond it. This planet was what happened when hydrogen and helium had an eternity to create it. She was skin, bones, DNA, genes, cartilage, ligament, muscle, and no more than the sum of her parts. Billions of years from now the universe would expand to the point where everything that had ever been would be so far away from the next particle that the whole thing would be nothing more than a frozen, desolate void and all she had known would be forgotten, never to be recorded or remembered, all her actions and memory just dead bytes of information drifting into entropy. Everything would return, as it had come, to nothing. The universe and every living thing in it would die and there would be nobody waiting at the other end, no everlasting, no happiness beyond the puny happiness of life that was so fleeting it could hardly be experienced at all. There was no reason.

The rain had eased its ferocity and fell now in silent curtains. A new, machine-like energy was in Miriam that came from her physical body alone. She crawled to the nearest tree trunk and placed her hands against the slippery bark of it and pulled herself steadily to her feet. Wrapping her arms around the slender trunk she ratcheted upright. Her legs were shaky. If she let go of the trunk she would fall but she felt some base need to stand upright, to feel the length of her spine, the muscles in her legs, the straightness of her neck.

She hugged the tree and stared blankly at the forest in the way a small child holds on to the leg of a parent. She made her mouth into an 'o' shape and then stretched it as wide as she could sideways, then retracted to an 'o' again. She savoured the shifting muscles in her face. She had started crying again and could not stop, despite the fact she could no longer remember why she was crying.

At last she felt as if her body had adjusted enough to her upright position to attempt a step. She placed her left leg out in front of her, toppled the ball bearing of her balance forward, and her body advanced. She stuck out her leg to stop herself from falling and it held. She toppled forwards again, shakily this time, but her right leg moved into its position and she did not fall. She walked out into the centre of the wide forest path and stopped. Swaying where she stood she cleared the tears so that she could see.

She was in a long, flat-bedded valley. It was an ancient place. Along the valley sides there jutted severe outcrops of wet grey rock. In some places the rock was a sheer cliff face from which, in one place, there tumbled a fresh spring.

Used to the new weight in her legs she clambered up to the spring and drank the water in greedy, thirsty draughts. It was cold and fresh. When she had taken her fill Miriam returned to the valley floor and trudged solemnly along it, one foot in front of the other in front of the other.

The pool of despair inside her was now lapping against what would have been the bottom of her ribs. It wouldn't be long now before it reached the flame of the candle.

At dusk she found the carcass of a bird. The distant calling of hunger forced her to bring it to her mouth and she bit into its plump breast. Cold blood flowed over her chin and the meat tasted rank. In the corner of her eyes she saw the yellow pennant that was the bird's beak and, closer, its dead, beady eye. She spat the meat to the ground and wiped her mouth against her muddy sleeve and moved on.

Just as the light of day faded she found the first signs of human presence she had seen in two days. Plastic beakers and spoons had been discarded. They made the land dirty. It seemed disrespectful. In the centre of the valley floor was an abandoned hut. The roof had long since disappeared and the walls were crumbling. A small, thin tree grew inside it, its base hidden in the gloomy shadows of the coming night. Large rocks encircled the hut and as Miriam looked at it there came a movement from inside it: black against black, a disturbance of the darkness.

A dog emerged from the hut. It had belonged to Joseph. She had loved this creature once but looking at it now she could not remember why.

She was tired again and so she crawled into the small space of the hut and lay down. The animal followed and lay next to her.

She could feel the warmth from its body against her back and she thought she was about to fall asleep but that slip of the mind into unconsciousness eluded her. Whenever she was just about to fall something would pull her back, like an elasticated length of rope tethered to the conscious world.

She lay in the darkness and curled her neck round so she could see out of the crumbling entrance of the hut. She watched the night fall imperceptibly between the trees like a sooty snow that stole light from the air and left in its place messy blotches of murk until at last there was no light at all and she was returned to the completeness of dark.

Sleepless, an image started to resolve in her. She was sitting in the back garden of the house on top of the hill. Edward and Mary were running along the gravel paths between tall rows of fertile plants. Her mother knelt down and harvested some of the vegetables into a wicker basket. A small bundle of cotton blankets was in Miriam's arms and within them lay a fleshy, wriggling, pink baby with tiny, curious fingers and large, alert eyes.

The garden faded and she was in a house. The walls were freshly painted, the smell of it faint in the air. At the far end was a huge window beyond which lay the clear skyline of some unknown city. She turned and Mary was standing in the doorway but this Mary was a young woman, tall and confident as she smiled and asked her mother if she liked the house. Edward came up the stairs behind her, carrying an enormous wooden packaging box that teetered precariously in his arms. He was every inch his father's son: those large, boyish eyes, the strong jaw, the thick, healthy hair.

Then she was in a warm living room in an old Victorian house with vaulted ceilings, parquet flooring and solid wooden furniture. She was sitting next to a real wood fire and looking down on her grandchildren playing with their new toys. A Christmas tree stood in front of the large bay windows beneath which a fat, scruffy cat had curled up into a ball and fallen lazily asleep.

She knew what she was looking at, just as she knew that in a few moments the Sadness would snatch them away again because none of them would come true, not in the new world.

But the image of a true future did not come. She looked out from the hut into the tenebrous dark and nothing happened.

Slowly, she fell into a second shallow, fractured sleep. As she slept she became aware of her own death, nothing more than a ticking clock running down its mechanism to nothing; when the monster in its cave had taken all that it wanted, she would be so changed that her body would be unable to continue. It was so close now. The dark fluid had almost reached the flame.

In the morning she was woken by the sound of rustling outside the hut. The black dog was lying next to her but its head was up and alert. Miriam looked out through the entrance but the rustling was coming from the side of the hut. Something small was scurrying in the leaves. She waited for a moment and then a large starling hopped into view. It paused, as if it was aware of the eyes on it, and twisted its head in short, jerky movements. When it saw Miriam watching it from the hut it hopped round to face her. Its spangled plumage glimmered in the grey morning light. It ducked its head down quickly and lifted a leaf into its beak and then it shook it violently from side to side before dropping it back to the ground and fluttering off into the lowest branches of a nearby tree. Miriam watched the bird with a blank passivity.

She crawled out of the hut and used the front wall to hoist herself up to her feet before continuing her journey. The dog followed. It tried to remain out of sight but whenever she turned round there it would be, further back down the path with its mouth hanging open and its fat pink tongue lolling over its lower lip.

The wooded valley did not seem so ancient here. She picked her way along it all morning. The going was very slow and she was forced to rest often. But every time she stopped the urge to carry on became too great to quell and she would stand and move on. Her body was shaky; the sugar in her blood had fizzled away almost to nothing. She was wandering aimlessly and alone through the final stretches of her life.

She could feel herself drowning. The despair was almost at the flame of the candle and, as it rose, Miriam found herself trying to stretch her neck as high as it would go, as if she was in the waterlogged cabin of a sinking ship.

She tried to run and fell. The huge lump in her stomach bore the weight of the fall and the great mass of it spread beneath her abdomen. If only the baby wasn't there. It was draining her of her own energy, siphoning off reserves to which it had no claim. It was a malignant and vile thing from the most terrible moment of her life; a parasite. She no longer wanted it in her body, taking what was hers, slowing her down.

She crawled to the edge of the valley floor and found a long, thin stick. She sat with her back against a rock. The creature kicked against the side of its womb as if it knew what fate was about to befall it. Unthinking, Miriam snapped the stick in half. Where it broke there was now a sharp, juicy point that she tapped with the tip of her finger. It would do. She closed her eyes and inhaled a deep, full breath. The creature had come in on a raft of violence and it was fitting that it should leave by the same mode.

But then something happened. She opened her eyes and the world had fallen into a vacuum, as if it had held its breath in anticipation of some massive catastrophe. A huge sonic boom shook the sky. Dark ripples splashed across it. The shockwaves hit her and pushed her back. She dropped the stick and the reservoir of tears that had been building breached their defences. The pool of density had snuffed out the candle.

Streams of her essence flooded out of her body in great torrents. Everything she had been was emptying. As it gushed past it picked up the baby and dislodged it. An immense pain bolted up through her in a spastic convulsion. The child was coming. The death of the candle had initiated a natural abortion.

She closed her eyes with the agony and the pain slipped away. Up the wooded valley, in the direction from which she had come, she saw a cave she had passed by unseeingly. It was large and black. An old tree grew on a sloping ledge above its entrance. A low, groaning sound rumbled from within the cave and then, from the dark, a huge talon appeared. The greedy monster thief had come at last.

Its head slid from the cavern and turned to watch her through lidless, obsidian eyes. The head was shaped like that of a snake. Two calciferous horns grew from its brow, tapering to electric sharp points. Its scales hung from its jowls in rotting lines and when it opened its mouth bubbles of saliva oozed from between lines of thin, sharp teeth. It brought its body from the cave and stood up on two reptilian hind legs, baring its fleshy underbelly flecked with brown melanomas and scored by scars.

Miriam turned away from it and ran. Her body was heavy but the primitive urge to survive pushed her onwards. The Sadness could not touch that because it was in the animal part of her. Another contraction pulsed through her. Her legs buckled in the crippling pain but she did not allow herself to fall. As the pain subsided she heard the monster scream out behind her. Its footfalls shook the earth.

She knew it could not hurt her, that it was not real. It was just an approximation of death, the means by which her mind would make the final transition. She thought of the monster's bounty in its cave and what it would save of her for its collection. Every memory, every sense, every feeling was evacuating her as her life ran down its final processes.

Another convulsion racked along her body, this one so powerful that it knocked her from her feet and sent her reeling across the damp leaves of the valley floor. She screamed. The baby was moving downwards through her. Her body was shifting states in an attempt to numb the pain. Her mouth opened wide, her lips stretching and cracking under the flash-boiled pain. As the baby eased through her she felt it against her and it reached out its hand and pressed her. A white flash thrashed to life at the connection. The pain was so full she could no longer tell where it ended and she began. It infused her so utterly that everything else was blanked; reset to zero. It drew her along its gauntlet and peeled off her layers of skin. The baby was coming. Her head swayed slowly on her neck, her face turned upwards to the sky. She screamed with the pain but the pain was so complete it was as if she had never been without it. A low, dull pain forced her hips outwards; there was an elongated, fleshy pain in her centre; a needle-sharp pain attacked her skull and a frantic, stretching pain cracked up her spine. Sweat coursed out of her and her hands became claws that dug into the soft ground.

The baby was crying now, somewhere at the edge of the world, and Miriam sat there with her head turned away, her legs open, exhausted. The monster was gone and in shattering flashes things began to come back. She felt something ancient rumble to life in a place so deeply buried that the Sadness had not known it was there. As it blazed up in her she felt like she was being passed along the notes of the world's symphony. Held in its rapture the despair trembled at an impossible frequency until its inner skeleton became brittle and frail and then it shattered, a whirlpool formed in her centre swirling slow, then fast, then wide, and the despair was being sucked out of her, its level dropping below the wick of the candle, which burned at once to life in an incandescent ball that threw the despair's whirling, broiling surfaces into a graphic iridescence as it dropped away from her through some deep sinkhole.

Millions of images flickered before her so fast that before she could comprehend them they were gone, like a series of changing pictures on a hummingbird's wing, as her memories restored themselves to their correct spaces. The idea of her death folded backwards and she saw once again all the hopes and dreams that had kept her strong. As these things happened, as all the processes and machinations cranked and turned within, she lifted her baby from the forest floor and held it in her arms. It was slick with blood and slime and it wailed in cold discomfort but it was alive and it was hers. She looked around the forest, sobbing, and its beauty seemed to glow from within it. The way the trees climbed up to the sky for the light of survival and down through the ground for the food of sustenance, the way they fed themselves in their own autumnal shedding, the way the water had carved the valley floor on which she was now sitting, the way all the world's processes clicked together to form the life that blossomed on, flourished in and returned to its depths became starkly and movingly apparent.

As she looked up into the sky, at the swaying, leafless branches of the trees, she felt her body tingle as the golden, honey-like fluid flooded into the centre of her. She touched the top of her baby's head. It fitted easily inside her palm and she thought of her children and how she needed to get them back.

She was nearly at the end of the wooded valley. The sides of it levelled off further ahead and there was the raised grey line of a road. She gathered her breath, made the baby as comfortable as she could in her muddy clothes, rose to her feet and started walking.

III

The thin road was long but she was glad for the consistency of the concrete under foot. The sound of the baby crying was the only noise. A nascent calm had emerged in her. She was still alive.

The lane joined another, wider, lane. Her legs ached and she was running on the combustion fumes of the last drops of blood sugar but there was no option other than finding her way back to the house. Pele waddled steadily beside her, as reliable as ever. His coat was matted with mud but he seemed healthy.

The winter birds called across the fields, past the hedgerows and thickets, and when they did the baby in her arms stopped crying. Miriam looked at its scrumpled face, eyes pinched shut, lips parting and suckling on air, new hands opening and closing with first-time wonderment as it conducted an experiment in bone and muscle movement. She thought that maybe she would call her Emily.

The sound of a car in the distance hummed unseen. She didn't feel any danger when she heard the noise. Danger seemed like something very trivial to her, a facade behind which lay little substance. The sound grew in the air. She was standing at a section of lane where the road had dipped into the lowest point of a hollow. The car trundled around the bend. Two round heads, their faces grey circles through the windscreen, turned towards her and then there were pointing arms of excitement and the car was slowing to a stop. The window descended and a cheery face hung from it.

'There you are,' he said, though she didn't recognize him. 'Everyone's been looking for you.'

He had grey hair and soft, friendly features. His eyes shifted downwards to the wriggling pinkness in her arms and his mouth gaped open, his eyebrows rising up like two doffed hats and then an upturn at the edges of his lips.

Miriam lifted the baby up a fraction.

'It's a girl,' she said.

|||

It was so warm inside the car. The very idea of warmth had been something that had been forgotten over the course of the past few days.

The man who was driving the car was not as animated as the man sitting next to him, who kept turning back to her and smiling enthusiastically.

'Where have you been?'

Miriam clutched her baby to her and looked into the man's eyes and said, 'I don't know.'

He accepted this answer.

'Have you heard the news then?' he asked. Miriam said nothing. 'It's over,' he said. 'It's all over.'

|||

The news, the man told her, had come from two places at once. He spoke quickly in a way that made him sound younger than he looked. As she focused on his face the trees that flashed past behind the windows became a tawny blur.

With everything that had happened on the camp nobody had noticed at first. It was only that morning that the idea had come to one of the women. She had asked her friends, and then her acquaintances, and then, as hope bubbled up inside her, strangers, and all of them agreed with her that, no, they hadn't heard of anybody falling ill.

Old radios had been dusted off and the old frequencies tuned in to. And there they were: the tentative, nervous, hopeful reports, as if there had been a mass awakening right across the globe. It seemed, the man said, that it really was over.

Miriam listened to him and as he spoke she was unable to process the information to any depth. It squalled in the shallows. She turned away from him and placed her muddy forehead against the cool glass of the window.

The hedgerow was broken here and there by a wide, metal

cattle gate and she could see the fields beyond, overgrown and wild.

|||

The front door of the house was closed. She looked from the car window at the broken coils of barbed wire that had been pulled from their brackets and hung now half on, half over the old brick wall. The windows at the front of the house were smashed and there, on the brickwork next to the door, was a wide splatter of dark red blood.

The man opened the car door for her and she stepped out into the cold. She looked down the slope to the camp. Halfway down the hill, pushed clear of the road, were the charred carcasses of two vehicles, one that had belonged to McAvennie, the other a larger vehicle that looked as if its end had been equally violent. As she absorbed all the devastation she thought the despair in her should start anew but it did not.

She entered the house by the conservatory, Pele panting behind her. The kitchen was empty and ransacked. She picked her way through the mess and went down the hallway into the living room. A man she knew was sitting in the old chair by the window. He didn't seem to mind the cold wind blowing through the broken glass on to his face. When he saw her he stood up, and looked at the baby.

'You're back.'

Miriam said nothing.

'I'm David,' he said awkwardly.

'I know,' she answered. 'I remember you.'

There was a box at his feet.

'Here.' He held out a letter to her. 'It's from Charlie.'

Miriam stepped into the room. 'Is he . . .'

David shook his head. 'No. He left the camp.'

Miriam nodded.

'He said he couldn't stay.'

She took the letter from him and looked at the envelope with large, round handwriting on it.

'He left you this as well.'

David lifted the cardboard box and set it down on the chair.

'What is it?'

'They're the papers the old doctor made. Charlie wanted to make sure they were safe and said to give them to you.'

'What happened to the doctor?'

'He was killed.'

'You should look after them. They'd be safer down there.'

David answered, with a shake of the head, 'He said to give them to you.'

She caught a glimpse of herself in the mirror above the fireplace. Her face was smeared with dried mud and her hair was thick with it. Her eyes were red and tired and yet she had never felt quite as alive as she did now. It was not a joyous, overwhelming flood of emotions, but a cool, precise, solid feeling that ran deep in her river.

She looked at the box, nodded to David and turned away to face the staircase down which sang the voices of her children.

'Wait,' he said.

She paused but did not turn back to him.

'They said you had it, that you were ill.'

She took her hand from the banister and lowered her head.

'Is it true?'

Miriam said nothing in reply.

'How are you here?'

'I don't know.'

'Was it the baby?'

She remembered the child's touch as a white flash but it wasn't that. She felt it keenly. Whatever had cleared her and brought her back was different from that. But it didn't matter.

'I don't know.'

She went up the stairs, slowly, with the sleeping baby light and easy in her arms. Mary and Edward were in their bedroom at the back of the house, sitting side by side on the bed, their backs to her as they looked out of the window at the silver sky. They were singing one of the songs from school. She stood just outside the room, on the soft carpet of the landing, and watched and listened. Edward had his arm around Mary and Mary had her head on Edward's shoulder.

A great upwelling commenced at the very core of her. A hand touched her neck and she turned. Her mother's eyes were on the baby and for a moment there was a pause into which was poured a realization in both parties that Miriam, somehow, really was alive, that she had come back, and she had brought in her arms the guarantee of a future.

'Kids,' she said.

The children turned their heads.

Acknowledgements

I would like to thank my parents for their continuing support because without their help, simply, I would not have been able to write this book. Huge thanks to my good friends Ian Worgan and Chyrelle Rayman-Bacchus for reading early drafts of a very long book and offering excellent advice that I badly needed. I would also like to express my thanks to Mair and Mike Cockell who were kind enough to let me use their caravan, where I edited the book in the middle of nowhere, with no distractions; and thank you to Rafe for making the arrangements. Thanks to Shaun Petty for reading very early drafts. Thanks also to my friend Rhodri Thomas for helping me find time to write the novel when I needed it. And to OTR, in whose drunken company many of the ideas in this book were crystallized. Thanks, as always, to Margaret Pearce.

At Transworld I owe huge thanks to Jane Lawson, who really got behind the book at a difficult time and who fed me Lebanese food. Also at Transworld, Manpreet Grewal, Kate Samano, Kate Tolley and Polly Andrews have helped enormously. Thanks to Matt Johnson for his incredible covers and Mari Roberts for her painstaking copyedits. And thank you to Laura Morris, my literary agent; for a more supportive and kind person I could never have asked. Finally, I really need to thank Rochelle Venables, for editing this book, guiding me through, reigning in the stranger parts, and pouring far more into it than she needed to. My debt of gratitude for what she did is infinite.

Rhys Thomas is the author of *The Suicide Club*. He is thirty-two and lives in Pontyclun, Wales.